The Destroyermen Series

Into the Storm
Crusade
Maelstrom
Distant Thunders
Rising Tides
Firestorm
Iron Gray Sea
Storm Surge
Deadly Shores
Straits of Hell

DESTROYERMEN

BLOOD IN THE WATER

TAYLOR ANDERSON

ACE
New York

ACE
Published by Berkley
An imprint of Penguin Random House LLC
375 Hudson Street, New York, New York 10014

Copyright © 2016 by Taylor Anderson
Penguin Random House supports copyright. Copyright fuels creativity, encourages
diverse voices, promotes free speech, and creates a vibrant culture. Thank you for buying
an authorized edition of this book and for complying with copyright laws by not
reproducing, scanning, or distributing any part of it in any form without permission.
You are supporting writers and allowing Penguin Random House to continue to
publish books for every reader.

ACE is a registered trademark and the A colophon
is a trademark of Penguin Random House LLC.

ISBN: 9780451470645

Roc hardcover edition / June 2016
Ace mass market edition / May 2017

Printed in the United States of America
1   3   5   7   9   10   8   6   4   2

Cover art by 3DI Studio

For: The "Snipes."

Indeed, anyone who ever served belowdecks aboard a ship in combat, whether in the engineering spaces, the ammunition handling rooms, the magazines—it doesn't matter where. To paraphrase what Isak said when he . . . did what he did in *Deadly Shores*, this one's for all the ones you never see, who did what *they* did in the hot, dark places belowdecks. Without them staying focused and performing their duties just like it was any other day when their ship steamed into battle, the ship couldn't fight. It couldn't even move. It might've been easier for some, never seeing the bomb, the salvo of shells, or the torpedo coming at them, knowing it was about to hit. For most, I imagine, it had to be a hell of a lot harder.

ACKNOWLEDGMENTS

As always, thanks to my agent, Russell Galen, and my editor, Anne Sowards. The more I get to know and work with Anne, the more I appreciate her! I'm sure she must be the best wild, wandering prose tamer in the business.

Thanks to all my great pals who continue to provide, um, "character inspirations." I've named most of them so often that I'm going to quit before they get too puffed up. They know who they are. I still appreciate all the great (and really smart) folks who I jabber with on my Web site. Their input and their (mostly) sound arguments have kept me from veering off down some really stupid trails from time to time. I *can't* name all of them here, but special thanks (in no particular order) to Bill, Charles, Clifton, Alexander, Joe, David, Matthieu, Alexey, Justin. . . . I'll get to more of them next time! If you check out the Web site and scroll the posts, you'll very quickly figure out who I mean. Extra special thanks to Captain Pat Moloney. And Jim, of course, for being particularly "inspirational"—in odd and amusing ways.

Finally, my greatest thanks go to my wife and family, the most important people in the whole wide world.

CAST OF CHARACTERS

(For those new to the series, don't be alarmed by the number of names listed here. They don't *all* appear in any one volume. Many not currently active in the narrative *do* remain active on the sidelines, however, and may turn up again. The list is updated with each volume as a courtesy to those who have followed the series from the start—so they'll always know who is where.)

See index for details of ships and equipment specifications.

Note:

(L)—*"Lemurians," or "Mi-Anakka" (People) are bipedal, somewhat felinoid folk with large eyes, fur, and expressive but nonprehensile tails. They are highly intelligent, social, and dexterous. It has been proposed that they are descended from the giant lemurs of Madagascar.*
(G)—*"Grik," or "Ghaarrichk'k," are bipedal "reptilians" reminiscent of various Mesozoic Dromaeosaurids. Covered with fine downy fur, males develop bristly crests and tail plumage, and retain formidable teeth and claws. Grik society consists of two distinct classes, the ruling or industrious "Hij," and the worker-warrior "Uul." The basic "Grik-like" form is ubiquitous, and serves as a foundation for numerous unassociated races and species.*

At "Grik City" Madagascar

USS *Walker* (DD-163)

    Lt. Cmdr. Matthew Patrick Reddy, USNR—Commanding. CINCAF—(Supreme Commander of All Allied Forces).

    Cmdr. Brad "Spanky" McFarlane—Exec. Minister of Naval Engineering.

    Cmdr. Bernard Sandison—Torpedo Officer and Minister of Experimental Ordnance.

    Lt. Tab-At, "Tabby" (L)—Engineering Officer.

    Lt. Sonny Campeti—Gunnery Officer.

    Lt. Ed Palmer—Signals.

    Surgeon Lieutenant Pam Cross

    Ensign Laar-Baa-Ra (L)—PB-1B "Nancy" pilot.

    Chief Quartermaster Patrick "Paddy" Rosen—Acting First Officer.

    Chief Bosun's Mate Jeek (L)—Former Crew Chief, "Special Air Division."

    Chief Engineer Isak Reuben—One of the "original" Mice.

    Gunner's Mate Pak-Ras-Ar, "Pack Rat" (L)

    Earl Lanier—Cook.

    Juan Marcos—Officer's Steward.

    Wallace Fairchild—Sonarman, Anti–Mountain Fish Countermeasures—(AMF-DIC).

    Min-Sakir, "Minnie" (L)—Bridge Talker.

    Leftenant Doocy Meek—British sailor and former POW (WWI). Now liaison for the Republic of Real People.

    Corporal Neely—Imperial Marine Bugler.

***Salissa* Battle Group**

USNR *Salissa*, "Big Sal" (CV-1)

    Admiral Keje-Fris-Ar (L)

Atlaan-Fas (L)—Commanding.
Lt. Sandy Newman—Exec.

1st Naval Air Wing

Captain Jis-Tikkar, "Tikker" (L)—"COFO"
(Commander of Flight Operations); 1st, 2nd,
and 3rd Bomb Squadrons, and 1st and 2nd
Pursuit Squadrons aboard *Salissa* (CV-1).
Lt. Cmdr. Mark Leedom—COFO at Grik City.
Lt. Araa-Faan (L)—Leedom's Aryaalan Exec.

USS *Santa Catalina* (CAP-1)

Lt. Cmdr. Russ Chappelle—Commanding.
Lt. Michael "Mikey" Monk—Exec.
Lt. (jg) Dean Laney—Engineering Officer.
Surgeon Cmdr. Kathy McCoy
Stanley "Dobbin" Dobson—Chief Bosun's
Mate.

Frigates (DDs) attached: (Des-Ron 6)

USS *Tassat*** (Badly damaged at the Comoros
Islands)
Captain Jarrik-Fas (L)—Commanding.
Lt. Stanly Raj—"Impie" Exec.
USS *Scott****
Cmdr. Muraak-Saanga (L)—Commanding.
(Former *Donaghey* Exec. and sailing
master.)
USS *Nakja-Mur**
Lt. Naala-Araan (L)

Arracca Battle Group

USNRS *Arracca* (CV-3)

Tassanna-Ay-Arracca (L)—High Chief,
commanding.

5th Naval Air Wing

Frigates (DDs) attached: (Des-Ron 9)
> USS *Kas-Ra-Ar***
>> **Captain Mescus-Ricum (L)**—Commanding.
> USS *Ramic-Sa-Ar**
> USS *Felts***
> USS *Naga****
> **MTB-Ron-1 (Motor Torpedo Boat Squadron #1)**—5xMTBs (#s 4, 7, 13, 15, 16)

AEF-M
(Allied Expeditionary Force—Madagascar)

II Corps
> **General Queen Safir Maraan (L)**—Commanding.

3rd Division
> **General Mersaak (L)**—Commanding.
> "The 600" (B'mbaado Regiment composed of "Silver" and "Black" battalions), 3rd Baalkpan, 3rd, 10th B'mbaado, 5th Sular, 1st Battalion, 2nd Marines, 1st Sular

6th Division
> **General Grisa**—Commanding.
> 5th, 6th B'mbaado, 1st, 2nd, 9th Aryaal, 3rd Sular

1st Allied Raider Brigade ("Chack's Raiders," or "Chack's Brigade")
> **Major Risa Sab-At (L)**—(Chack's Sister)—In temporary command.

21st (Combined) Allied Regiment
> **Major Alistair Jindal**—Commanding. Imperial Marine, and Chack's (currently Risa's) nominal exec.

1st and 2nd battalions of the 9th Maa-ni-laa,
2nd Battalion of the 1st Respite.

7th (Combined) Allied Regiment

Captain Enrico Galay (former corporal in the Philippine Scouts)—Commanding.

2nd and 3rd battalions of the 19th Baalkpan, 1st Battalion of the 11th Imperial Marines

1st Cavalry Brigade

Lt. Colonel Saachic (L)—Commanding.

3rd and 6th Maa-ni-laa Cavalry

Hij Geerki—Rolak's "pet" Grik, captured at Rangoon, and now "mayor" of Grik prisoners at Grik City.

SMS *Amerika*

Kapitan Adler Von Melhausen—Commanding.

Kapitan Leutnant Becker Lange—Von Melhausen's Exec.

Adar (L)—COTGA (Chairman of the Grand Alliance), and High Chief and Sky Priest of Baalkpan.

Surgeon Commander Sandra Tucker Reddy—Minister of Medicine, and wife of Captain Reddy.

Diania—Steward's Assistant and Sandra's friend and bodyguard.

Gunnery Sergeant Arnold Horn (USMC)—formerly of the 4th Marines (US).

Lieutenant Toryu Miyata—formerly of *Amagi*.

Mission to Meet "Ancestral" Lemurians

Ensign Nathaniel Hardee—Commanding PT-7.

Lt. Col. Chack-Sab-At (L)—Commanding the expedition.

Courtney Bradford—Australian naturalist and engineer. Minister of Science for the Grand Alliance and Plenipotentiary at Large.

Chief Gunner's Mate Dennis Silva

Lawrence, "Larry the Lizard"—orange and brown tiger-striped Grik-like ex-Tagranesi (Sa'aaran).

Corporal Ian Miles—Formerly in 2nd of the 4th Marines.

The Republic of Real People

Caesar (Kaiser) Nig-Taak

General Marcus Kim—Military High Command.

Inquisitor Kon-Choon—Director of Spies for the Republic of Real People.

TFG-2 (Task Force Garrett-2)

Long-Range Reconnaissance and Exploration

USS *Donaghey* (DD-2)

Cmdr. Greg Garrett—Commanding.

Lt. Saama-Kera, "Sammy" (L)—Exec.

Lt. (jg) Wendel "Smitty" Smith—Gunnery Officer.

Captain Bekiaa-Sab-At—Commanding Marines.

Chief Bosun's Mate Jenaar-Laan

In Indiaa

Allied Expeditionary Force (North)

General of the Army and Marines Pete Alden—Commanding. Former sergeant in USS *Houston* Marine contingent.

I Corps

    General Lord Muln-Rolak (L)—
        Commanding.

1st (Galla) Division

    General Taa-leen (L)—Commanding.
    1st Marines, 5th, 6th, 7th, 10th Baalkpan

2nd Division

    General Rin-Taaka-Ar (L)—Commanding.
    Major Simon "Simy" Gutfeld (3rd Marines)—
        Exec.
    1st, 2nd Maa-ni-laa, 4th, 6th, 7th Aryaal

III Corps

    General Faan-Ma-Mar (L)—Commanding.
    9th and 11th Divisions composed of the 2nd,
        3rd Maa-ni-laa, 8th Baalkpan, 7th and 8th
        Maa-ni-la, 10th Aryaal.

VI Corps

    General Linnaa-Fas-Ra—Commanding.
    Colonel Enaak (L)—5th Maa-ni-laa Cavalry.
    The Czech Legion
    A near-division-level "cavalry" force of aging
        Czechs and Slovaks, and their continental
        Lemurian allies. They are militarily, if not
        politically, bound to the Grand Alliance.
    Colonel Dalibor Svec—Commanding.

Flynn Field

    Primary Army/Navy air base in Indiaa, on the
        north shore of Lake Flynn, West of Madras.
    Colonel Ben Mallory—Commanding.
    4th, 5th, 7th, 8th Bomb Squadrons (PB-1B
        Nancys) and 3rd, 4th, 5th, 6th Pursuit

Squadrons (P-1C Mosquito Hawks "Fleashooters"). The 3rd Pursuit Squadron is composed of eight operational Army Air Corps P-40Es

Lt. Walt "Jumbo" Fisher—Commanding Pat-Squad 22.

Lt. (jg) Suaak-Pas-Ra, "Soupy" (L)

Lt. Conrad Diebel

2nd Lt. Niaa-Saa, "Shirley" (L)

S. Sergeant Cecil Dixon

At Madras (Indiaa)

First Fleet (North)

Baalkpan Bay Battle Group

USS *Baalkpan Bay* (CV-5)
Commodore Kek-Taal (L)—Commanding.
5th Naval Air Wing—14th and 17th Pursuit Squadrons, 20th Bomb Squadron.

Frigates (DDs) Attached: (Des-Ron 10)
USS *Bowles****
USS *Saak-Fas****
USS *Clark***

"New" DDs
USS *James Ellis* (DD-21)
Cmdr. Perry Brister—Commanding.
Lt. Rolando "Ronson" Rodriguez—Exec.
Lt. (jg) Jeff Brooks—Sonarman, Anti–Mountain Fish Countermeasures (AMF-DIC).
Lt. (jg) Paul Stites—Gunnery Officer.
Lt. (jg) Johnny Parks—Engineering Officer.

Chief Bosun's Mate Carl Bashear

Taarba-Kaar, "Tabasco" (L)—Cook

USS *Geran-Eras* (DD-23)

Cmdr. Cablaas-Rag-Laan (L)—Commanding.

*Repairs to USS *Mahan* (DD-102) have been suspended until a floating dry dock can be spared for her.

At Baalkpan

Cmdr. Alan Letts—Chief of Staff, Minister of Industry and the Division of Strategic Logistics. Acting "Chairman" of the Grand Alliance.

Cmdr. Steve "Sparks" Riggs—Minister of Communications and Electrical Contrivances.

Lord Bolton Forester—Imperial Ambassador.

Lt. Bachman—Forester's aide.

Surgeon Cmdr. Karen Theimer Letts—Assistant Minister of Medicine.

"Pepper" (L)—Black-and-white Lemurian keeper of the "Castaway Cook" (Busted Screw).

Leading Seaman Henry Stokes, HMAS *Perth*—Director of Office of Strategic Intelligence (OSI).

Among the Khonashi (North Borno)

"King" Tony Scott

Brevet Major I'joorka—Respected warrior and Scott's friend, commanding the 1st North Borno Regiment.

Lieutenant (jg) Abel Cook—Liaison Officer.

Imperial Midshipman Stuart Brassey

Sergeant Moe the Hunter

Pokey—"Pet" Grik brass-picker.

Eastern Sea Campaign
>   **High Admiral Harvey Jenks (CINCEAST)**

Enchanted Isles
>   **Sir Thomas Humphries**—Imperial Governor at Albermarl.
>
>   **Colonel Alexander**—Garrison Commander.

Second Fleet

USS *Maakka-Kakja* (CV-4)
>   **Admiral Lelaa-Tal-Cleraan (L)**—Commanding.
>
>   **Lieutenant Tex Sheider (Sparks)**—Exec.
>
>   **Gilbert Yeager**—Engineer, one of the "original" Mice.

3rd Naval Air Wing

(9th, 11th, 12th Bomb Squadrons, and 7th, 10th Pursuit Squadrons)
>   The wing is normally composed of upward of eighty aircraft, but is currently badly understrength.
>
>   **2nd Lt. Orrin Reddy**—COFO.
>
>   **Sgt. Kuaar-Ran-Taak, "Seepy" (L)**—Reddy's "backseater."

Line of Battle
>   **Imperial Admiral E. B. Hibbs**—Commander.

9 Imperial Ships of the Line Including:
>   **USS *Destroyer* (Former *Dom Deoses Destructor*)**
>>   **Cmdr. Ruik-Sor-Raa (L)**—One-armed former commander of USS *Simms*, commanding.

Lt. Parr—Former commander of HIMS *Icarus*. XO.

HIMSs *Mars,* Centurion,* Mithra*

Attached DDs:

HIMS *Ulysses, Euripides, Tacitus*

HIMS *Achilles* (DD)

Lt. Grimsley—Commanding.

USS *Pinaa-Tubo* (Ammunition Ship)

Lt. Radaa-Nin (L)—Commanding.

USS *Pecos*—Fleet Oiler

USS *Pucot*—Fleet Oiler

2nd Fleet Expeditionary Force (X Corps)

"Army of the Sisters"

General Tomatsu Shinya—Commanding.

Colonel James Blair—Exec.

Governor-Empress Rebecca Anne McDonald

Governor-Empress Saan-Kakja (L)—High Chief of Ma-ni-laa and all the Filpin Lands.

Lt. Ezekial Krish—Aide-de-Camp to Governor-Empress Saan-Kakja

Sister Audry—Benedictine nun.

Colonel Arano Garcia—Commanding El Vengadores de Dios, a regiment raised from penitent Dominion POWs on New Ireland.

Combined Force—4 regiments Lemurian Army and Marines, 2 regiments "Frontier" troops, 5 regiments Imperial Marines—(3 Divisions) w/artillery train.

General Ansik-Talaa (L)—Former Commander of Saan-Kakja's Filpin Scouts; is organizing XI Corps from reinforcements nearly equal in numbers to those that constitute X Corps.

Major Dao Iverson—Commanding 6th Imperial Marines.

Nurse Cmdr. Selass-Fris-Ar, "Doc'selass" (L)—Daughter of Keje-Fris-Ar.

Capt. Blas-Ma-Ar, "Blossom" (L)—Commanding 2nd Battalion, 2nd Marines.

Spon-Ar-Aak, "Spook" (L)—Gunner's Mate, and 1st Sgt. of "A" Company, 2nd Battalion, 2nd Marines.

Lt. Anaar-Taar (L)—"C" Company, 2nd Battalion, 8th Maa-ni-laa (Finny's replacement).

Lt. Faal-Pel, "Stumpy" (L)—"A" Company, 1st Battalion, 8th Maa-ni-la. Former ordnance striker.

Lt. (jg) Fred Reynolds—Formerly Special Air Division, USS *Walker*.

Ensign Kari-Faask (L)—Reynolds's friend and "backseater."

Enemies

General of the Sea Hisashi Kurokawa—Formerly of Japanese Imperial Navy battle cruiser *Amagi*. Self-proclaimed "Regent" and "Sire" of all India, but currently confined to Zanzibar.

General Orochi Niwa—Friend and advisor to General Halik.

General of the Sky Hideki Muriname

Lieutenant of the Sky Iguri—Muriname's Exec.

Signal Lt. Fukui

Cmdr. Riku—Ordnance.

Grik (Ghaarrichk'k)

Celestial Mother—Absolute, godlike ruler of all the Grik, regardless of the relationships among the various Regencies.

The Chooser—Highest member of his "order" at the Court of the Celestial Mother. Prior to current policy, "choosers" selected those destined for life—or the cook pots—as well as those eligible for "elevation" to "Hij" status.

General Esshk—First General of all the Grik, and acting Champion Consort to the new Celestial Mother.

General Ign—Commander of Esshk's "new" warriors.

General Halik—Elevated Uul sport fighter.

General Ugla, General Shlook—"Promising" Grik leaders under Halik's command.

Holy Dominion

His Supreme Holiness, Messiah of Mexico, and by the Grace of God, Emperor of the World—"Dom Pope" and absolute ruler.

Don Hernan DeDivino Dicha—"Blood Cardinal" and commander of the "Army of God."

League of Tripoli

Representatives at Zanzibar:

(French) **Capitaine de Fregate Victor Gravois**
Aspirant Gilles Babin
(Spanish) **Commandante Fidel Morrillo**
(Italian) **Maggiore Antonio Rizzo**
Teniente Francisco de Luca
(German) **Oberleutnant Walbert Fiedler**

Aboard *Savoie*:
Contre Amiral Rauol Laborde
Capitaine Dupont
Lieutenant Jean Morrisette

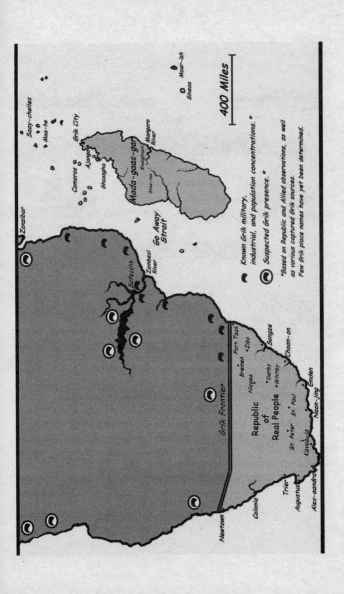

400 Miles

● Known Grik military,
   industrial, and population concentrations.*

◉ Suspected Grik presence.*

*Based on Republic and Allied observations, as well
as various captured Grik sources.
Few Grik place names have yet been determined.

Maar-iah

Simeoa

Scay-chellas

Maa-he

Grik City

Camoras

Ajanga

Mada-gaas-gar

Ghasseha

Mangoro
River

Endaigh

Shire River

Go Away
Strait

Zanzibar

Sofesshk

Zambezi
River

Fort Taak

Zöo

Songze

Chaan-an

Grik Frontier

Breman

Nicgaa

Darby

Whitby

Emiden

Republic
of
Real People

St. Peter   St. Paul

Kavaadia

Naan-jing

Colonia

Trier

Augustus

Alex-aandra

Newtown

Recognition Silhouettes of Allied Vessels

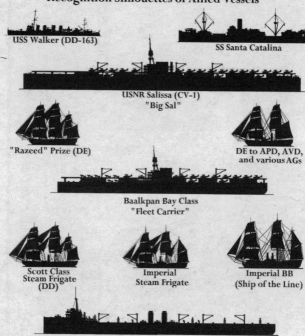

USS Walker (DD-163)

SS Santa Catalina

USNR Salissa (CV-1)
"Big Sal"

"Razeed" Prize (DE)

DE to APD, AVD,
and various AGs

Baalkpan Bay Class
"Fleet Carrier"

Scott Class
Steam Frigate
(DD)

Imperial
Steam Frigate

Imperial BB
(Ship of the Line)

USS Tarakaan Island
Self Propelled Drydock (SPD)

USS Andamaan

Recognition Silhouettes of Enemy Vessels

Grik BB
(identification of alterations is pending)

Grik "Indiaman"

(Funnels off-set to starboard side)
Grik CV

Grik CA

Tatsuta

"Improved"
Grik CA

The "Holy Dominion"

"Dom" BB
(Ship of the Line)

"Dom" DD (Frigate)

The "League of Tripoli"

Leopardo (DD)

Savoie (BB)

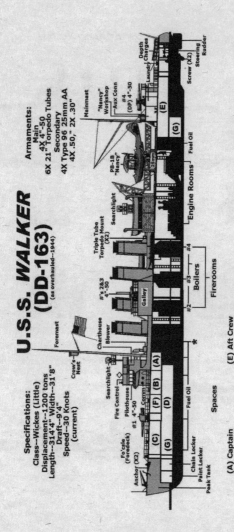

U.S.S. WALKER
(DD-163)
(as overhauled—1944)

Specifications:
Class—Wickes (Little)
Displacement—1200 tons
Length—314'4" Width—31'8"
Draft—9'4"
Speed—30 Knots
(current)

Armaments:
Main
4X 4"-50
6X 21" Torpedo Tubes
Secondary
4X Type 96 25mm AA
4X .50," 2X .30"

Spaces

(A) Captain
(B) Officers
(C) Chiefs, Warrants, P.O.s
(D) Fore Crew

(E) Aft Crew
(F) Wardroom
(G) Storage/Magazine

∗ Temporary fuel bunkers fill the space for #1 boiler

Foremast
Crow's Nest
Searchlight
Fire Control
Pilothouse
#1 4"-50
Fo'c'sle (Foredeck)
Chain Locker
Paint Locker
Peak Tank
Anchor (X2)
Fuel Oil
Charthouse
Blower
#'s 2&3 4"-50
Galley
#2   #3   #4
Boilers
Firerooms
Searchlight
Triple Tube Torpedo Mount (X2)
25mm
PS-1B "Nancy"
Engine Rooms
Fuel Oil
Mainmast
"Nancy" Workshop
#4 (DP) 4"-50
"Aux Conn"
Laundry
Depth Charges
Screw (X2)
Steering
Rudder

I've never been such a slave to the "proper" definitions of words that I'm afraid to tweak them slightly to fit my own purposes from time to time, at least in my own mind. Perhaps that's a common peculiarity among thoughtful but absentminded persons, or perhaps it's a sign of laziness. Either way, I've never carried a dictionary all about, and at least I don't constantly distort or entirely invent new words—and their definitions—on the fly, as that most interesting being Dennis Silva was always so fond of doing. But correct or not, my definition of the word "theory" is, essentially, that it is an assumption that has been tortured to death.

Unlike many, I don't then consider the resulting theory to be a true, incontrovertible fact; it merely remains a very good, thoroughly examined assumption, more likely to be true than not. Sadly, however, in real life, divorced from the benign chrysalis of the laboratory, one rarely has the opportunity to clearly differentiate between an assumption and a theory, and neither has much of a chance to be properly determined "fact" before one must quickly apply it and simply forge ahead—for good or ill. Even so, one would imagine that reasonably intelligent beings would have a better than even chance of having their "assumptive theories" proven right. Unfortunately, I'm always amazed by how stunningly often that is not the case, at least on this magnificent, malevolent world.

It happens to me more often than most, I'm sure, and I hope I manage to display a sufficient measure of contrition when it does. I blame it on my exuberance, my near-instinctive predisposition to spring upon the closest, most convenient conclusion and grasp it with both hands. How often has this trait led me far astray, with embarrassing, even calamitous results? I can't begin to guess. I won't even try to count the times, for example, that while fishing the waters off Western Australia as a lad, I was utterly positive I'd hooked one particular species of fish, only to discover it was something else entirely. My belief was based on where I was, the time of year, what type of bait I'd used, and other fish already caught.

Sometimes I fancied I had the experience to judge by the way it struck and fought the hook, or the glimpses it revealed when it thrashed the surface. All surely sufficient information to transform an assumption into a theory, at least, I should think. More often than not, however, despite my conviction, I was mistaken.

As an engineer in later life I was often called upon to sort out some problem or other that, based upon the information at hand, should've been quite simple to resolve—only to find that it ran much deeper, or was caused by some other obscure, never-considered factor that required a wholly different solution than I'd envisioned. And even after we came to this world, an occurrence that should've cured me of relying on mere assumptions ever again, my predisposition went completely rampant and I immediately began spewing assumptions as theories, taken as facts, about all manner of things. This may possibly be forgivable when one considers the fantastic circumstances we found ourselves in, but we were most emphatically not in any laboratory, and the consequences of false assumptive theories were often far more catastrophic than I first imagined possible because the stakes were so much more profound. Lives, cultures, entire species were at risk, not just the meager reputation of the author of a flawed treatise.

And tragically, on occasion, I was not the only one to assume far too much, and the cost in blood remains enough to make me weep even now. The sorry fact of the matter was that regardless how sound our reasoning, how firmly rooted in evidence, experience, or common sense, it seemed there was always a better than even chance that any theory constructed about the nature of this world—or our enemies across it—would be wildly, horrifically wrong. I'm again compelled to roughly quote (to the best of my memory) a comment once made, quite offhand, by the enigmatic Dennis Silva: "'Ass-ume' is just a big word for 'ass.' There's way too many 'ass-umes' runnin' around this joint, an' they all smell like shit."

Courtney Bradford, *The Worlds I've Wondered*
University of New Glasgow Press, 1956

***Christmas Island
South of Java***

Contre Amiral Rauol Laborde paced the bridge of his elderly battleship, *Savoie*, scratching absently at his thin mustache. It was a nervous habit, he knew, and he tried to control it, but the dead-calm heat in Flying Fish Cove, where his ship was anchored, was almost unbearable, and the mustache always itched. *What a relief it would be to simply shave it off! But that won't do,* he decided. *The men are used to it.* More important, it was part of the persona he endeavored to affect: the figure of the confident, dashing commander. And that image was particularly vital now, after his powerful ship had been forced from its station at the southern African port of Alex-aandra, the capital city of the Republic of Real People. The Republic was a nation composed of an odd mix of vaguely catlike creatures calling themselves Mi-Anakka and of various human cultures apparently collected across the ages.

His assignment had been to intimidate the Republic into, essentially, inactivity, and prevent it from joining a faction of Americans and other catlike folk in a wider war against the vicious reptilian creatures to the north. He still didn't fully understand why that might be. *Why* not *let the barbarians of this twisted world exterminate one another?*

He supposed there must be a reason, but he wasn't sufficiently well connected to—or possibly trusted by—the leadership at Tripoli to be privy to their grand strategy. He snorted, looking out the bridge windows, past the two gunhouses forward on his ship's fo'c'sle, at the lush island embracing his *Savoie*. He was a holdover, one of the few remaining flag officers of the old regime retained by the "new" France that had joined Italy and Spain to form the fascist Concert of Versailles, or, more specifically, the Confédération des États Souverains. He'd survived the purge only by pretending to embrace the new order. One of the reasons he'd been given his isolated and ambiguous assignment in the first place was that enough of the other officers with the invasion fleet originally sent to conquer British Egypt—but who had instead wound up on this . . . other Earth—had probably voiced their suspicions to that effect, he reflected resentfully. Still, it had gotten him and his ship away from Tripoli and all the bitter intrigues that racked the leadership of the Triumvirate, composed of the highest-ranking officers from the three most important powers involved in that "old world" invasion. France had supplied the most ships, though the Italian vessels were generally newer and more capable. All had supplied armor and some aircraft crated in transports, but Spain had sent the most troops. Ultimately, each had a claim that theirs was the strongest member of the current alliance, or "League of Tripoli," that they'd established after arriving in this world. The "Third Triumvirate," some ironically called it, with the expectation that it would eventually go the way of the first two triumvirates of ancient Rome. The French general Faure was currently "first among equals" owing to the support of the German contingent, which didn't rate full representation and had already changed several times over the past six years. *And the Germans are fickle,* Laborde mused. *Throw their support behind whoever benefits them most.* They had the smallest contingent of all but were disconcertingly capable and therefore disproportionately influential. *Sooner or later, one faction or other will emerge as the unquestioned leader of the League as the rest are pushed aside, and whoever that is will likely owe a heavy debt to the damn Boche.*

Laborde was disgusted with the politics and really couldn't care less who wound up on top in the end as long as he and his crew could remain French. And as ridiculous as he considered the League, he didn't want it to disintegrate into open warfare with itself. The League was far from perfect, but it represented the closest thing to modern civilization he'd seen on this distorted world—with the possible exception of the Republic. But the Republic of Real People was largely composed of, well, *animals*, after all.

What disgusted him and his crew most at present, however, was that their old but still mighty ship had been chased away from Alex-aandra by a meager *wooden frigate* armed with *muzzle-loading cannon*, a few primitive ironclad monitors, and a handful of shore batteries of unknown capability. He still didn't know whether it had been a bluff, but even though the League had been subverting the American-led alliance for some time, he remained under strict orders not to provoke overt hostilities. When the leader of the Republic—*They call him Kaiser!* he thought, and snorted again—presented his ultimatum, Laborde had had no choice but to depart. He'd wanted nothing more than to test the primitives; let *them* fire the first shots so he could atomize the puny American-Lemurian ship and devastate the city with *Savoie*'s eight 340-mm guns. But Alex-aandra, with its comfortable villas and impressive harbor, would make a fine addition to the League someday, when it had the resources and manpower to expand across the globe. He understood and supported that much of the "Grand Strategy." The Triumvirate wanted Alex-aandra intact and planned to get it through guile—and perhaps a more irresistible show of force when the time was right. That still didn't make Laborde feel any better.

He glanced around the bridge, past the sailors, who recognized his desire for quiet contemplation. Emplaced around him were four bronze plaques, each engraved with a single word: *"Honneur," "Patrie," "Valour,"* and *"Discipline."* All were interrelated, but there was no *patrie*, no "homeland," anymore. That left him most compelled by *honneur*—of the sort, in his mind, that one earned only through *valour*. But his had been savaged by ignominious retreat in the face of what he considered a pathetically meager threat, and if his honor had been stained, how could he expect to maintain *discipline* among his crew without the *patrie* to sustain him? It was a terrible equation, and he had to do something. Yet there he was, *hiding* at the League's most far-flung, secret outpost, on Christmas Island, south of Java, where they'd been observing the American-Lemurian-Imperial alliance for nearly three years, quite literally in its own backyard.

Even this can't last much longer, he fumed. *They will find this place eventually.* There'd been small chance of that while what little Allied shipping willing to venture beyond the Malay Barrier crept close along the coast to avoid the terrible monsters of the Indian, or "Western," Ocean. But things had changed, and the Allies had developed countermeasures to repel the great ship-eating beasts. Laborde imagined it was a type of sonar, such as his own people used to the same effect. In any event, the Allies now ran entire convoys through the Sunda Strait to Diego Garcia, and ultimately to Madagascar. Christmas Island lay south of that route, but the Allies had already established a way station in the Cocos Islands. It was just a matter of time before they chose to do the same there. They'd immediately recognize the purpose of this outpost and might finally even suspect what had happened to some of their missing people and ships. Discovery would be catastrophic from an intelligence-gathering perspective, and Laborde couldn't imagine that the Allies would appreciate the League's continued presence. It might even precipitate the open hostilities they'd been avoiding. He contemplated that while glancing around the harbor. The facilities there were not extravagant, little more than a fueling and listening station, after all. There were camouflaged fuel tanks and a radio shack on a shore entirely infested with large (and, he had to admit, frightening) crustaceans of a sort he'd never seen before. Some were large enough to trip or even hamstring a man with their claws. And if they ever got a man down, other crustaceans would swarm in and tear him apart before he could be saved. Laborde hadn't seen this—the Italians who operated the base had spread the tales—and he wondered darkly whether they were true or merely told to keep his men from going ashore. But if they *were* discovered, he wondered, would he be ordered to retreat yet again or would he be allowed to fight? Nothing he knew of that the Allies had could possibly compete with his lone ship. They had a pair of old destroyers, at least one of which was supposed to be damaged beyond repair. They'd armed an even older cargo ship of some kind that they'd found not far from there on the Java coast, but it was small and weak. Otherwise, all they had were steam frigates with large but short-ranged guns. They'd be no threat at all. None of the known Allied carriers was anywhere close, but their airpower might still pose a menace, primitive as it was, because the island was within extreme range of a base they'd established at Tjilatjap. But *Savoie* was well equipped for air defense, and they'd lose a great many aircraft overwhelming her. And *Savoie* wasn't alone.

A Spanish oiler armed with machine guns shared the little bay, anchored near an Italian destroyer, an "exploratori" of the *Leone* Class named *Leopardo*. By the standards of the Great War, she was practically a light cruiser. Well armed and fast, she alone was more than a match for anything the Allies could send to boot them out. He understood there was even a pair of submarines that provisioned there. One hadn't been seen for some time and was presumed lost, but the other, a German boat, had visited and departed just before he arrived. All in all, he felt secure. The question was, what would the Triumvirate instruct if it came down to it? He *couldn't* flee again if he wanted to maintain discipline and the respect of his crew!

"Amiral," said Capitaine Dupont, standing beside him, breaking his reverie. Laborde hadn't even noticed the wiry, light-haired man's approach.

"Yes, Capitaine?"

"Sir, our . . . 'observers' have reported that the big steamer *Amerika*, which the Republic calls their 'War Palace'"—he managed not to snicker—"has sailed from Diego Garcia, bound for the Sunda Strait." He shook his head. "Our adversaries are so naive! They have tightened their wireless communications and changed their codes, but still talk quite freely over their high-frequency transmitters, their 'TBS,' trusting to its short range. And thankfully, they still do not suspect that we have learned their, ah, 'Lemurian' language from captives we have taken."

"Most naive," Laborde agreed, then shrugged. "So? She will pass near us. Nothing we did not already know."

"She would make a fine prize," Dupont urged with a small, predatory grin.

"Indeed. But I need not remind you that we are restrained from any overt acts." He grimaced. "The Third Triumvirate would not approve." Dupont was of the "old school" as well, and Laborde felt free to use the skeptical term in his presence.

"They might if they knew who was aboard her," Dupont replied.

Laborde raised his eyebrows in question. "I thought she was carrying wounded troops from their campaign against the principal Grik city on Madagascar, back to their capital of 'Baalkpan,' on Borneo?"

"She is," Dupont confirmed, "but she also carries other, more important passengers. Passengers that, in terms of intelligence and . . . leverage, might mean more than make up for our loss of this place if we are forced to abandon it."

So. Dupont can read my mind, Laborde thought. *How many more aboard can do that?* "But . . . our orders stand. We cannot act."

"Untrue. We are allowed to use whatever force we must to prevent our discovery, including whatever *discreet* 'overt acts' that may require."

Laborde scratched his mustache. "No," he decided. "We cannot. If we attempt to capture *Amerika*, she will send a distress signal. All would know what we have done."

Dupont's predatory grin grew. "She would not . . . probably. She retains the short-range high-frequency voice transmitter. No doubt the Americans gave it to her. But her long-range communications gear seems to have suffered a casualty."

"Indeed? The timing is most interesting. Do you suppose one of our operatives might be responsible?"

Dupont looked thoughtful. "Under the circumstances, it would be amazingly coincidental if that were not the case. Which also leads me to wonder if it might not be the *desire* of someone in authority that we should . . . do something about her?"

Laborde was torn between a quickening elation and despair. "They might repair their transmitter," he said, brooding.

Dupont released a frustrated breath. "And what if they do? Yes, *Amerika* might manage a distress signal, but we could interfere with it. And they constantly use their TBS, thinking no one can hear because none of them are ever close enough. If *we* get close enough to warn them not to send wireless messages, they would have to comply. Their ship is full of wounded, after all." Laborde frowned in distaste, but Dupont continued. "And if they sent a message anyway? Yes, people would know, but what could they do?"

"Despite your speculation, our explicit orders—"

"Were to *flee* Alex-aandra without a shot," Dupont said—almost snarled—"and 'linger in the vicinity of Christmas Island' until further instructed. The Sunda Strait is in the vicinity," he stressed. "If we happened to be there and *Amerika* suddenly appeared on the horizon, we would have no choice but to act. Would we not?"

Laborde scratched his lip more vigorously, but looked at Dupont with new respect. "We would be risking a great deal. *Amerika* is large and fast and would make a fine addition to our fleet, but she is old and somewhat dilapidated by all accounts. Her capture alone might not be enough to save us from the wrath of the Triumvirate even if we were not revealed. The quality of these important passengers would have to be great indeed."

Capitaine Dupont smiled and began to list the names gleaned from unguarded transmissions. When the significance of some of them began to dawn on Contre Amiral Laborde, he smiled as well.

CHAPTER

1

East of Diego Garcia (La-laanti)
September 25, 1944

I t had been a day of squalls, very much like the day
they were swept to this world—and war. But the
squalls, like the world, were also profoundly different. The irony, Sandra Tucker Reddy thought as she
leaned on the boat deck rail of SMS *Amerika*, just aft of
the starboard bridgewing, was that even though the world
was wildly goofed up, the war even more savage than the
one she remembered, and the very ship she traveled on
not . . . exactly right, the squalls marching across the horizon were entirely normal in every respect. They were
dark blotches on an otherwise bright, blue day, some dense
enough to make them completely opaque. Others were
more ephemeral, mere dangling wisps that barely touched
the sea. But none had that . . . malevolent, pulsing, singu-
larly greenish hue that had been the most visual feature
of the squall that somehow brought the old US Asiatic
Fleet destroyer USS *Walker*, her, and who knew who or
what all else, to this very different world.

Again, Sandra idly wondered what her reaction would
be if she ever saw another such phenomenon. Would she
try to reach it, hoping it might transport her back to the
world she came from? Or would she flee in terror? After
all, there was significant evidence now that the . . . well,

"bridge," for lack of a better term, wouldn't necessarily take her back *exactly* where she came from, judging by the various historical inconsistencies among other groups that had arrived here over time. So the implication was that even if they traveled "back" through one of the mysterious squalls, they'd likely wind up somewhere else just as weird. Courtney Bradford's theories about that still confused her. *They probably confuse him too,* she thought fondly. *But it seems to make a kind of sense to Matt, even if he doesn't pretend to understand why or how. Of course, as Supreme Commander of all the Allied powers, he has more pressing day-to-day concerns. Let him focus on winning the war—and surviving,* she prayed. *Courtney's imagination can run rampant on other things.*

Absently, she touched her belly, feeling for the child beneath the barely perceptible bump. *No,* she thought. *Even if I knew the bridge would take me back, the time to wish for that is past.* Her husband, Matt, was here, as was his surviving crew, and all the people that comprised this new Union they'd built. As "Minister of Medicine," she was needed by the Alliance and, more specifically at present, by the shipload of human and Lemurian wounded SMS *Amerika* was transporting to Baalkpan. *And ultimately,* she realized, *this world is home now. This is where I belong.*

She shook her head to clear the unbound sandy brown hair from her eyes and leaned more heavily against the rail. Down below, the purple sea creamed to white along the fragile, age-thinning sides of the old liner-turned-commerce raider–turned . . . hospital ship, Sandra supposed. *Amerika* had given them their first notion that different pasts were represented on this world. Where she came from, she'd been fitted out as an auxiliary cruiser by the Imperial German Navy during the Great War. After a fairly successful spree against mostly British merchant ships, whose crews she'd taken aboard and treated virtually as guests in the finest traditions of the Hamburg-America Line, she tangled with a British auxiliary cruiser" named *Mauritania*. After what had to have been one of the strangest naval battles of the war—two great, stately, completely unarmored ocean liners slugging it out with light guns at high speed in mounting seas—both ships had been heavily damaged and at least partially disabled. Sometime during the night, tossed by a terrible storm that threatened to finish what *Mauritania* began, *Amerika* wound up . . . here. In much the same situation as USS *Walker* after her passage through her squall—shot up, and in need of friends—*Amerika* found a haven near where Cape Town, South Africa, should have been, but was now "Alex-aandra," the capital of a diverse nation called the Republic of Real People, composed of both Lemurians and humans who'd arrived at various times throughout history. *Amerika*'s crew and prisoners had joined the Republic, and *Amerika*, with her spacious and luxurious accommodations, and most especially her meager but modern armaments, had become the "War Palace" of the father of the current "Caesar," or "kai-saar," of the Republic, named Nig-Taak.

Some of the interesting things about the situation from Matt's historical and Courtney's scientific perspectives were that many of the human cultures that blended into or influenced the Republic over time had been out of time or place themselves, and the clincher had been that not only did *Amerika* and *Mauritania* never fight a duel in the history they knew, but *Amerika* had been seized to become an American troopship during the Great War. As far as Matt knew, she still served that purpose under a different name. Regardless of that, she was here, representing the Republic of Real People, the newest member of the Grand Alliance against the voracious, reptilian Grik, whom the Allies had finally pushed all the way back to Persia and Africa, the place of their supposed ancestral origins. A Grik army under General Halik still survived— under observation—in the rough mountains west of the Indus River, but Halik was . . . different. No one really expected him to stay out of the war if another army joined him to reconquer India, and certainly nothing like an alliance had been contemplated, but left to his own devices it was believed he'd focus foremost on the survival of his army.

The Republic had also morally, if not literally, joined the war against the evil "Holy Dominion," a nation of twisted human zealots infesting much of Central and South America. Just as Matt had delivered yet another stunning if costly defeat on the Grik at Madagascar, Lord High Admiral Harvey Jenks of the Empire of the New Britain Isles had won a naval victory over the Dominion Fleet near the isle of Malpelo and General Tomatsu Shinya had smashed a Dom army north of Guayak. It seemed to Sandra that, despite the numberless Grik reserves on the African mainland, and the fact that Shinya still had a mountainous jungle continent to fight across before he could threaten the Dom capital of New Granada, the tide of war might have turned at last. But still, she worried.

Matt's forces on Madagascar were so few, and even with reinforcements on the way, he might be hard-pressed to hold what he'd gained, much less take the fight to the Grik. The Republic was planning an offensive against the Grik in the south, while Matt kept their attention on Grik City, on the northern tip of Madagascar, but the Republic offensive had been delayed by the intimidating presence of representatives of yet another power called the League of Tripoli that no one knew a great deal about. They knew the League was powerful, though, and in addition to having an old French battleship they could afford to park indefinitely in the harbor at Alex-aandra until it was finally bluffed away, they'd actually attacked Matt's First Fleet (South) with a submarine. The sub was destroyed, but not before it did a great deal of damage and sank the only vessel that could perform serious repairs to *Walker* and the other ships in Matt's little fleet. In spite of this, the League had still assured the Republic that it meant no harm, but it was clear that they had an agenda of their own and remained a veiled menace to the Alliance.

In the East, Shinya was on the march, pushing the Doms, but his force was relatively weak as well. And in the aftermath of the Battle of Malpelo, an already difficult supply problem could soon become a crisis. If Shinya stalled and the Doms had time to gather enough troops to put in his way . . . Sandra shook her head again. She could worry about those things, and about her husband, Matt, but she couldn't do anything about them. Her priority was to get the wounded aboard *Amerika* back to Baalkpan, where they could get the real rest they needed to properly heal. Arguably, the early Iron Age Lemurians they'd met on this world, industrialized, and taught to fight had better "medicine" than she, a mere Navy nurse, had brought with her. Their curative "polta paste" was but one example. But she'd brought *trauma* medicine, *military* medicine, of a kind the generally peaceful Lemurians had never much needed, along with the teaching and organizational skills required to treat the victims of an increasingly worldwide war. Matt had been right all along. They had plenty of medics, "corps-'Cats," and even good surgeons in the field these days. It was time for her to quit following the fleet and get back to her real job at last.

"Good afternoon, Lady Saandra . . . Reddy," came Adar's familiar voice beside her. Adar was the High Sky Priest and High Chief of Baalkpan, chairman of the Grand Alliance, and a very dear friend. "Forgive me," he said, his eyes blinking amused confusion, "but I may never get used to this hu-maan changing of names when they mate!" Sandra knew better. Adar probably understood humans better than any Lemurian alive. She also knew he enjoyed throwing the "lady"—bestowed on her by their Imperial allies—at her because it never failed to fluster her. She turned to him with a scolding smile. He was dressed, as always, in what some referred to as his "Sky Priest suit," a purple hooded cape with embroidered stars flecked across the shoulders. Beneath that was only a simple red kilt, like those worn by Lemurian wing runners. His large silver eyes regarded her from a gray, furry face, and his tail swished slowly behind him, causing the cape to shift. His face was as outwardly expressionless as many humans considered any Lemurian's to be. They used body language, ear and tail motions, and complex blinking to reveal things that humans relied on eyebrows and very different facial muscles to achieve. A grin was a grin, and 'Cats could even manage a kind of frown, but to most humans, that was it. Sandra knew 'Cats well enough by now to recognize other, subtle expressions, however, and she got the impression that, in spite of his playfulness, Adar was troubled. "I hope I am not intruding," he added.

Sandra straightened, feeling somewhat guilty. There was nothing pressing at the moment. All the wounded who'd come aboard *Amerika* had either passed beyond her aid and been buried or burned when the ship touched at Laa-laanti, or were as well on their way to recovery as she and her staff could help them along under the circumstances. Still, she *had* come out here for a brief respite from the moans of the suffering. Even worse than the sounds of pain, though, were those who remained cheerful and appreciative despite their disfiguring or crippling wounds.

"Not at all, Mr. Chairman," she lied.

"Excellent," Adar said. "Would you care to walk with me? I do feel inexplicably restless."

"Of course."

They strode aft, beginning to pass the more ambulatory wounded, who took their ease on actual deck chairs that the ship's original German, and now very mixed, crew had never discarded.

"Having left the 'tip of the spear,' as Cap-i-taan Reddy has been known to refer to the point of contact with the enemy, I do find myself anxious to resume my duties at Baalkpan," Adar confessed quietly, nodding at those who watched them pass. "But I also find myself unsure how to proceed."

"Just be yourself," Sandra answered a little shortly. "You're a good leader, Mr. Chairman."

"Adar, please. As always. But as to how good a leader I might be . . . I know that many doubt. Myself, not least among them."

"I see," Sandra answered, and she did. Adar *was* a good leader, but he'd also proven both impetuous and indecisive. She'd once ranted at him for a moment of indecisiveness herself when *Walker*'s fate was in the balance—on the heels of his impetuosity. "Very well, Adar," Sandra agreed and considered. "But why are you talking to me about this? You've got a whole staff to advise you."

"True, but none of them speak with Cap-i-taan Reddy's voice. I have come to rely on his counsel more heavily than any other."

"I can't do that either," Sandra objected.

"But you know the man and his thoughts well enough to stand in his stead in this instance, I think. I would like to know your opinion of the 'Union' Alan Letts has arranged. You've read the particulars?"

Sandra shifted uncomfortably. Matt had very specifically *not* advised Adar too strongly on this subject. Just as he'd practically insisted—finally—that Adar leave the war to him, he'd bent over backward to stay out of the politics of the Alliance.

"Of course I have. Everybody has," Sandra hedged. She knew most of them by heart. The Articles of Union were very similar to the Constitution of the United States, after all, with a few notable exceptions. Provisions had been made for only one legislative body, for example, but its numbers would be determined by the populations of the states, or "Homes" they represented. Some interesting, possibly temporary concessions had been made to the seagoing Homes and other smaller population centers, most of which would eventually join larger Homes as semi-independent jurisdictions, their High Chiefs becoming like mayors or county commissioners. Factionalism was inevitable; it already existed. But with members free to leave one state or Home to join another that they agreed with more strongly, and leaders still subject to popular vote, or acclamation—and removal by the same means—it seemed workable. It would be chaotic; democracies always were. But she certainly couldn't think of a better way to get so many disparate groups to work together.

She took a breath. "I guess I like it. It'll be a mess, but maybe not as bad as we've already been dealing with."

"Cap-i-taan Reddy feels that way?"

Sandra nodded. "He does."

Adar smiled and blinked his gratitude. "Then it will be as Mr. Letts has formed it. I had already decided that, I suppose, but I wanted Cap-i-taan Reddy's opinion."

"You know why he couldn't tell you straight up, right?" Sandra asked.

"I do. And I honor him for his restraint. But he has helped form us in so many ways, Alan Letts in particular, how could we not share his opinions to some degree?" He glanced forward. "What remains then is a name. And a flag. Not all Homes will submit to the Banner of the Trees to represent them. They have symbols of their own." He sighed. "It would be ironic if the Union were to fail over mere symbols."

"Symbols are more important than you know, Mr. Chairman," Sandra said.

"Perhaps. Ahd-mi-raal Keje-Fris-Ar believes so as well. The first time he saw your Amer-i-caan flag flying above a captured Grik ship, he had an epiphany that resulted in the Banner of the Trees! It is a . . . powerful symbol, and even I am not unaffected by it." He sighed again. "We shall see," he said.

Sandra saw a small form approaching beyond Adar's cape. "If you'll excuse me? Come here, Diania," she said softly, extending her hand for the tablet the woman bore.

"By all means," Adar agreed. "The status of our wounded is far more important than our little chat."

"The list," the dark-skinned beauty offered, carefully enunciating her words. The version of English she'd once spoken was almost incoherent. Sandra looked at her. Diania was an "expat Impie gal" she found in Maa-ni-la, there to escape the system of virtual female slavery that had prevailed in the Empire of the New Britain Isles at the time. Sandra immediately swept her into the Navy for a variety of reasons, but mostly because she liked her and because if female Lemurians could serve on *Walker*, and ultimately all Allied ships, then female humans should be allowed to as well. Matt had not been pleased at the time, but the notion and the necessity grew on him. Things in the Empire had changed dramatically since the rise of Rebecca Anne McDonald to the position of Governor-Empress, and a few women even served on Imperial ships now. But Diania stayed with Sandra, essentially as her steward and bodyguard. In the latter, she'd been taught by and ultimately fallen in love with a man three times her age: Chief Bosun of the Navy Fitzhugh Gray. After his loss at the first Battle of Grik City, the light that had animated the young woman's face had dwindled to a cinder and Sandra worried a great deal about her.

She displayed the tablet to Adar. "The list of those deemed fit to return to light duty," she explained. "Not that there is a lot for them to do aboard here, but each one is a victory."

"Indeed. Thank you for all you have done." He glanced at the tablet. "So many! And this list is tabulated how often?"

"Every day."

Adar closed his eyes. "I have been right all along. The Heavens *did* guide you to us!" Sandra's face reddened, and Adar smiled. "I will leave you now." He paused. "If you should think of a name for our new nation, please do not hesitate to inform me! Enough of our people owe you their lives, I suspect you could call it anything you liked and it would be accepted by acclamation!" With that, Adar turned to stride forward, leaving Sandra and Diania to stare after him.

"What *do* ye want tae call it?" Diania asked hesitantly. Sandra smiled at her, glad to hear real interest in her tone. "I'd call it 'Virginia,' but nobody would understand why."

"*I* would, um, Miz Minister," came a deep male voice.

Sandra and Diania both stared at two deck chairs occupied by an extremely unlikely pair.

"I suppose you would at that, Gunny Horn," Sandra said with a smile.

Gunnery Sergeant Arnold Horn was a black-haired and -bearded version of Dennis Silva, who was the pride—and terror—of the Amer-i-caan Navy on this world. He was not quite as powerfully built, and not nearly as reluctant to let people know how smart he was, but he and Silva had a history of some sort that dated back to their days in China together. Ever since Arnie's arrival here on the ill-fated *Mizuki Maru*, they'd been thick as thieves. Again. Both had been wounded in the assault on the Celestial Palace at Grik City, but Horn's injuries were more severe. Seeing him here wasn't unusual; he often basked on deck, allowing the cooling breeze to wash over him. Sandra was surprised by his choice of companions, however. Reclining on a chair beside him was the diminutive, by comparison, form of Lieutenant Toryu Miyata. Miyata had defected from the Grik—and the Japanese maniac Hisashi Kurokawa—when he'd been sent to deliver an ultimatum to the Republic. Instead, he warned the people there, came east with *Amerika*, and ultimately joined the attack against the Celestial Mother. He'd been the most badly wounded member of the assault force to survive, having had his leg nearly torn off by some kind of huge, terrible beast unleashed to guard the lower levels of the palace. He hadn't lost the leg—quite—but he'd never be an athlete.

It was the sight of the two of them, an Imperial Japanese sailor and a "China" Marine, sitting companionably together, that gave Sandra a start. Of course they'd shared a tough mission; a nightmare none of them expected to survive. But that didn't erase the war they'd come from. If *they* could get along . . . Gathering herself, Sandra waved the tablet at Horn. "You're on this list, Gunny."

"I know. Ain't it grand?" He lifted his T-shirt to expose a jagged purple scar halfway between his right hip and lower ribs, the result of a wickedly barbed Grik spear. Diania suddenly gasped and turned away. Sandra looked at her, concerned, doubting she was compelled by modesty. She'd been accustomed to running around practically nude in her former life, and had seen plenty of wounds and scars much worse than Gunny Horn's. More likely the wound reminded her too graphically and unexpectedly of when Horn got it—in the same battle that killed Chief Gray.

"Oh, I'm sorry, Miss Diania," Horn said, flustered, misunderstanding. "My manners aren't much to speak of."

The kind words probably too much for her to bear, Diania blurted, "Excuse me, I beg," and briskly strode off forward. Sandra watched her go, then turned to Arnie.

"It's not you," she said, and Horn frowned comprehension, pulling his shirt back down. "Maybe," he agreed, "but I wouldn't have . . . not for the world."

Sandra nodded, realizing for the first time that Horn might actually be sweet on Diania. There was no reason he shouldn't be. She was beautiful, and now—however tragically—unattached. But Fitzhugh Gray's ghost still loomed large in Diania's life. He'd always been the perfect gentleman toward her and never openly acknowledged his feelings until the very end—and then only to Matt—but he'd been the center of Diania's world. Sandra hoped Horn, or someone with similar apparent integrity, might eventually heal Diania's broken soul, but there was no telling how long that might take.

Still watching the direction the woman had gone, Miyata sat up on his chair. "It looks like we will be steaming through one of those squalls. Gunnery Sergeant Horn, would you mind helping me up? Perhaps we should go inside."

Horn stood. "Sure," he said, helping the Japanese officer to his feet. "Say, Miz Minister, how much longer can we expect to enjoy this little pleasure cruise? It's not like I'm ungrateful for the rest, but I feel fine. Probably didn't need to come," he prodded—again. "And I'd kind of like to get back in the game. Who knows what trouble that idiot Silva will stir up without me to yank his chain."

Sandra laughed, tempted again to ask directly exactly what kind of "history" the two men had that made them so . . . compatible. Some shared adventure in China, she assumed. She shook her head. Later. "Kapitan Von Melhausen remains . . . indisposed, as you know. He's an old man and I'm sad to say his mind isn't always what it was. Kapitan Leutnant Becher Lange has effective command. Have you met him?"

"I've seen him. Had a few words. We're not exactly pals, but he seems to know what's up."

"He does," Sandra assured, "and he told me that we're three days away from the Sunda Strait at this speed. Another two, at most, to Baalkpan." She smiled. "So in less than a week you'll be free to begin lobbying Alan Letts for a new assignment. Even after Adar's return, Alan will probably be the best person to pester for something like that."

"And I'm cleared for duty?"

"*Limited* duty," Sandra stressed.

"Good enough." He smirked. "Not that there's much to do around here." A gust of wind ahead of the squall whipped against them. "C'mon, Miyata. Let's get you inside." Horn glanced back at Sandra. "Thanks. And . . . please tell Miss Diania I apologize for startling her so."

"Of course, Gunny Horn. And you're welcome."

Zanzibar
Sovereign Nest of "Jaaph" Hunters
September 25, 1944

"So, General of the Sea Kurokawa, what, in your opinion, will the reptile leader, their, ah, 'General Esshk,' do now?" Capitaine de Fregate Victor Gravois asked politely. He was seated on a chair in the open air opposite Kurokawa, who was nattily dressed, as usual, in his French naval uniform, round hat with patent leather brim, silk scarf, and highly polished boots. Kurokawa wore a "uniform" as well, though his was based only loosely on the one prescribed by the Japanese Imperial Navy. It was festooned with all sorts of imaginative ribbons and medals, likely of his own design. In contrast, Gravois's tunic was unadorned, with the exception of the "badge of devotion" to the fascist party that united the various members of the League of Tripoli. The badge resembled the emblem of the PPF at a glance, but the outer border embraced not only the yoke and arrows of fascist Spain, but the Italian fasces as well. He'd earned other decorations in his career, of course, many he was quite proud of. But his business was clandestine action, after all, and he disliked revealing more about himself than was absolutely necessary. Waiting for Kurokawa to reply, he dabbed his thin mustache with a napkin and managed an engaging smile in spite of the vile grain wine that had just polluted his lips. This was the first time he'd met "socially"—and practically alone—with Kurokawa since he and his delegation arrived weeks before, and he'd managed, somehow, to keep from spraying the foul fermentation at his host. Kurokawa was a madman, Gravois had no doubt, but he was also an amazingly capable, cunning, and *dangerous* madman. Insulting him, and the revolting wine he seemed so childishly proud of, after Gravois had worked so hard to arrange this informal meeting between them was perhaps not the most diplomatic—or survivable— thing Gravois might do.

The two were not entirely alone beneath the bright canvas awning overlooking the . . . odd-looking warships in the bay. Kurokawa's most intimate staff members and the other members of Gravois's delegation from the League of Tripoli were all absent, though Gravois's companions were well aware of the meeting. Kurokawa's were not. The only others present, besides guards stationed out of earshot, were Gravois's aide, Aspirant Gilles Babin, and a young Japanese officer named Iguri whom Gravois recognized as "General of the Sky" Hideki Muriname's executive officer. They were seated opposite one another a short distance away, silently staring at the admittedly impressive fleet that Kurokawa had amassed on the southwest coast of Zanzibar. The fleet was composed largely of Grik dreadnaughts and cruisers he'd "appropriated" and improved and altered over time, as well as their largely Grik crews, who'd grown as slavishly loyal to him as they'd once been to their Celestial Mother. Gravois suspected that Kurokawa actually imagined himself to be the equivalent of that creature to them in his mind. He suppressed a shiver.

"Technically, he is not their 'leader,'" Kurokawa said, smug in his greater knowledge of the Grik. "Esshk and his 'Chooser'"—Kurokawa frowned—"a despicable but useful creature, have arranged the elevation of a new 'Celestial Mother.' I am told the ceremony is . . . noteworthy," he said, brows rising slightly. "She reigns now, in name. But you are correct that Esshk is essentially in charge." His eyes narrowed. "And likely to remain so. I suspect, having tasted the power of 'regent champion,' he will never fully relinquish it, and 'Celestial Mother' will increasingly become a ceremonial title."

"Indeed?" Gravois said with genuine interest. He waved a hand. "I bow to your superior understanding of the reptile folk. But again, what do you believe he will *do*? His latest attack against your enemy was quite decisively destroyed, after all."

Kurokawa gazed at him, his expression pregnant with a hidden secret, as well as great satisfaction that, for once, he knew something that Gravois, with all his elaborate means of gathering information, did not. "Captain Gravois," he said at last, "I actually know *exactly* what First General Esshk means to do. *Is* doing now, as a matter of fact!"

Gravois feigned surprise. "Bravo! I had assumed you were in contact with him." He hadn't "assumed," he'd known. The "secret" envoys hadn't been as secret as Kurokawa obviously thought. But learning what those contacts entailed had grown increasingly urgent to him—and his superiors.

"I have," Kurokawa admitted, still smug. He'd clearly been bursting with the need to gloat over his arrogant visitors, but Muriname had always been present during previous discussions and had somehow wordlessly restrained him. But Muriname wasn't here today. He was flying with Gravois's German pilot, Walbert Fiedler, in the Ju-52 that brought the delegation from the League of Tripoli to this place, observing as Muriname's primitive, by the League's standards, air force made practice attacks against one of Kurokawa's large ships underway. "We are 'allies,' after all," Kurokawa practically chortled.

"You convinced him that you remain loyal, even after your . . . past differences?"

"Little convincing was required. I merely told the truth about the formidable nature of the forces that defeated ours in India—a nature he has now seen for himself—and the disloyalty and treacherous incompetence of his protégé, General Halik, of course." Gravois already knew that if anyone in India had been incompetent or treacherous toward First General Esshk, it had been Kurokawa himself, but he said nothing. "I did make a few judicious omissions," Kurokawa added with a self-satisfied smile.

"And Esshk needs me far more than I need him at present. He was glad to accept my explanation—and award me the regency of India and Ceylon in perpetuity! Once they are recovered, of course."

"Confirming the declaration you had already made yourself, and incidentally, what you told your loyal Grik here to get them to support you! Ha!" Gravois barked in genuine admiration. "What had been something of a fiction is now a fact and you need not be concerned that certain inconsistencies might arise to cause you difficulties!"

Kurokawa's face reddened. "I *was* regent of India and Ceylon," he snapped, "before Halik allowed the defeat of his army and the Americans and their ape-man lackeys drove me out! I will rule there again, as well as over all the lands that border the Indian Ocean. With or without your help!" He stopped, eyes smoldering in his round face. "Aid me now as a friend and earn my appreciation, or deny me and earn my enmity!"

Gravois was always surprised by how quickly Kurokawa's moods could shift, and he raised a placating hand. "I and the League of Tripoli would like nothing more than your conquest of this entire region. It is inconveniently distant from us to properly monitor the beings who rule here, and we have no interest in it for ourselves. Much better that it be ruled by a friend and partner we admire and trust."

Kurokawa settled back in his chair, somewhat mollified, and sipped his wine. "Then you will acquire the other things I requested? General of the Sky Muriname grows weary of Maggiore Rizzo's condescending glances at the aircraft he has labored so to create, for example, and if my enemy retains a single advantage over me, it is his few modern warplanes." He leaned forward. "Do not disappoint me in this, Captain Gravois."

Gravois winced. He'd procured a promise from the Triumvirate to supply Kurokawa with several modern planes and pilots—it wasn't as if the League had unlimited numbers of them, or the means to make more!—but he'd been admonished to ensure that Kurokawa was reliable enough to use them wisely and discreetly. The League still wanted to avoid open conflict with the Grand Alliance for a few more years, at least, if at all possible. But if

Kurokawa could rid them of the nuisance the Alliance was sure to become with a minimum of resources . . .

"You will not be disappointed, General of the Sea," he said softly. "But I do beg you to share your insights regarding the plans of the Grik." He paused long enough to take a cigarette from its case, light it, and then, somewhat hesitantly, offer one to Kurokawa. Kurokawa was stunned. He hadn't tasted a real cigarette in two years. He greedily accepted the offering. "And," Gravois continued lightly, "whether or not you have told Esshk anything about the League of Tripoli."

Kurokawa paused again, absorbing the bitter-rich Turkish tobacco smoke into his lungs, finally wondering if he'd revealed too much. Deciding it really didn't matter, he chose an unusual course of action, for him, when it came to dealing with these strangers from the League. He decided to tell the truth. They had so many sources of information, they'd probably find out for themselves in any event. "I have renewed my association with First General Esshk for a variety of reasons that I explained to him as well as you. I have not necessarily stressed the *same* reasons to either of you," he allowed with a sly look. "But all Esshk knows of the League is that it exists as 'another ally' against our common enemy. I told him nothing about where you come from or what you might offer to our association." His face clouded. "Simple enough, since you still hold those particulars very closely." All Kurokawa had been told was that the League controlled the Mediterranean and most adjacent shores. He'd surmised a bit more, and other members of Gravois's delegation had let things slip from time to time. The German pilot Fiedler, for example, had revealed the most detail. But of the League's resources, all he knew was that they were "considerable." He believed that based on what he'd seen, and the information they'd provided him about his enemy.

"As for Esshk's plan, much is already in place and has been since before the last attack on the Celestial City." He chuckled. "It seems that he used a certain rival regent and a great many obsolescent troops and ships to serve the joint purpose of weakening the enemy while at the same time consolidating his power. Quite ingenious, actually. All the while, he has been massing his better troops—troops that *my* discoveries concerning Grik mentality helped create!" He glanced at his glass and took another long pull from the cigarette. Gravois couldn't tell if his expression was triumphant . . . or envious. "He prepares them for an overwhelming invasion of Madagascar," Kurokawa continued after a moment, "aboard a new fleet of ships he conceals in a great lake up the Zambezi River, beyond the known reach of enemy reconnaissance." He spread his hands. "I do not know what his fleet consists of, and only assume it is composed of more of what I had here. Sound, but poorly executed designs," he defended. "He may have refined them further, as have I. Esshk is a great many despicable things, but no fool. I suspect this time he will want to protect his new army by some means instead of counting only on overwhelming numbers." He sucked more smoke and coughed slightly. "He also took a page from his rival's plan and has been quietly landing troops of his own on the southwest coast of Madagascar— the better troops his rival had disdained. To cover this, he continues to hold the enemy's attention by providing inconsequential targets in the strait that their ships cannot ignore, and by expending his dirigibles in constant attacks against their forces in the capital city to keep their airpower occupied. His entire plan is not dissimilar from the one his rival attempted, as a matter of fact," Kurokawa reflected thoughtfully, "but will fall with greater weight and better troops and equipment upon a weaker, more dispersed defense."

Gravois frowned. "To try the same thing a second time, even better equipped, strikes me as . . . risky, to say the least."

"Ah, but there is a significant element to this plan that was missing from the last: a final diversion that our enemies cannot possibly resist, that will leave his forces at the Celestial City utterly at Esshk's mercy." Kurokawa smiled as if anticipating the greatest possible pleasure. "Me," he said simply. "I will attack the southbound convoy that protects and transports the enemy's First and Third Corps, as you so kindly suggested to me when you cautioned me to allow the first convoy to pass unmolested! Captain Reddy, still at Madagascar by your report, will have no choice but to rush to the convoy's aid, and I will finally enjoy destroying him at last!" Kurokawa seemed to practically shiver with anticipation.

"I was wondering if Esshk meant to coordinate with you this time," Gravois said, forcing a dry tone. "That could make all the difference. But it will be risky," he stressed again. "Your enemy may finally know where to look for you, if you do not destroy him completely. Even then, distress signals may allow the enemy to guess, at least, that the attack was launched from here." He spread his hands as well. "And, alas, it appears he finally suspects he has long been observed and monitored, and not only does a heavier screen than usual off the entrance to Port Madras prevent direct surveillance"—Gravois wouldn't expand on what assets he had in place to directly observe the enemy—"but has begun changing his codes at apparent random." Gravois shook his head. "His codes have always been beyond our ability to decipher, but the changes betray suspicion. Finally, some elements of his fleet have started exercising much better communications discipline, particularly in regards to their short-range, high-frequency voice radio we have relied on for so much of our information. I fear I can no longer tell you exactly what will constitute your target convoy. All I know for certain is that it will be large, and is considered critical to the success of your enemy's plans. Obviously, they will protect it to the best of their ability. We have intercepted the occasional mention of 'new' ships, for example, and must assume they will be more capable than those you have seen in the past."

Kurokawa's face had been puffing up, his eyes pinching more tightly throughout Gravois's cautionary comments. Finally, he stood. "As *my* forces are more capable than any *they* have seen!" he thundered. "Time and again, Captain Reddy has thwarted me, wounded me, *marooned* me! But I have surpassed him at last! I have better, more powerful ships, and faster, deadlier aircraft! This time it is I who will have the advantage!" His outburst had driven Iguri and Babino to their feet in alarm, and Gravois stood as well, waving a reassuring hand at his aide. Iguri had to be accustomed to his master's fits by now. Kurokawa looked up at the awning above and closed his eyes, visibly calming himself. "Perhaps it is difficult for you to understand, Captain Gravois," he said, voice brittle, "but I have worked and suffered far too hard and long, delayed my vengeance, my *destiny*, too often. The time is near when I must balance the scales at last, come what may. I am confident of victory, for all the reasons I have given." He stopped and stared hard at Victor Gravois, his eyes burning with an inner light. "But even should I not achieve it, I believe I will settle for revenge this time."

Gravois smiled and nodded understandingly, but his mind recoiled from what he saw. *Kurokawa truly is insane.* He took a breath. *But does it really matter?* Gravois's duty, his *mission* here, was to covertly encourage whatever circumstance he could arrange that would ensure the destruction of every power in this part of the world that might one day rival the League. There were limits to how far he could go, of course, and he even regretted certain aspects of his mission. But ultimately, largely due to the madman with whom he'd shared some of the last cigarettes on earth and some truly loathsome wine, he didn't really have to do much at all to ensure a mutually catastrophic spasm of destruction that would one day leave this ocean—and the world—ripe for League domination.

"Then I will help you, as your ally and friend," Gravois said. He snorted softly. "And as that of your intriguing First General Esshk! As I assured you, *some* modern aircraft are already on their way, though it may take longer for them to arrive than you have to prepare for the closest approach of the enemy convoy." Kurokawa sat, but leaned forward eagerly. "We were able to confirm," Gravois told him, "that the convoy sails today or tomorrow, and does still mean to pass the Seychelles to augment the new Allied presence there in some way. That is only approximately eight hundred miles away. That will put it in extreme range, even of your aircraft here, if you can recover them at sea— or do not mind losing them," he probed, curious, "in . . . let me see . . . ten days, more or less?"

The drone of planes, more than a hundred, intruded on their conversation then. They were returning from an exercise in the strait between the island and the mainland. All four men resumed their seats and watched them approach and begin circling the three airfields surrounding the harbor as pair after pair broke off from each formation to land. They were noteworthy little planes, Gravois had to admit, particularly considering the conditions under which they'd been made. The same was true for all of Kurokawa's creations, and those of his enemies as well. Gravois frankly wondered if his own people could've done so much with so little in such a short time. The difference was, of course, they hadn't *had* to. He opened the leather case protecting his binoculars, took them out, and gazed skyward.

Kurokawa's planes were vaguely similar in appearance to the small fighter aircraft the Alliance had deployed, except they were slightly larger, green and gray instead of blue and white, and were reputed to be faster and better armed, if not as maneuverable. They were wood-and-fabric monoplanes with fixed landing gear, specially designed so that Grik with superior intellects could control them. He'd seen how they did that: by providing for the pilots to basically lie on their bellies, controlling the rudder pedals in the back of the cockpit with their feet, while using a stick in the front in a straightforward way. Most important, considering the mission Kurokawa had in store for them, they could each carry two fairly respectable bombs. If the Allies hadn't improved their antiaircraft defenses, the planes should be very dangerous indeed. He was less impressed with their Grik pilots and suspected the experienced Lemurians would be a handful for them if they were able to sortie in time to make a concerted defense, regardless of any deficiencies in their planes. Muriname, despite his confidence in his new pilots, meant to counter that with Japanese squadron leaders that he'd trained himself. Gravois wondered if the few human pilots would be enough to make a difference and anticipated a most interesting contest.

Around half of the "fighter bombers" landed on the jungle airfields proficiently enough, Gravois thought, followed by a handful of twin-engine aircraft he hadn't yet seen himself. Fiedler said they were dedicated light bombers. Most interesting of all, two squadrons, very carefully and with evident hesitation, landed on two of three large ships anchored in the harbor. Gravois understood they'd once been ordinary Grik battleships, but all their upper works and armaments had been removed. This resulted in a much higher freeboard supporting a huge, elevated flight deck. Four funnels were rigged out to the side, and an offset control tower and pilothouse was the only structure above the level of the flight deck. *These are Kurokawa's—and his enemy's—greatest achievements,* he thought, slightly enviously. *Even the League has nothing like them, powerful as it is in other respects. But until now, there's been no need. I will have to try to see what I can do about that.*

There was no arresting gear to catch the planes as they landed, but the flight deck was big enough—at least while motionless and in calm seas—that the pilots had little trouble stopping their planes with brakes. Only one managed to stand his aircraft on its nose, shattering the propeller and probably wrecking the engine. *But they have many engines,* Gravois mused. *I have seen the factory myself. All in all, it is this capability, along with the element of surprise, that makes me most confident that Kurokawa can prevail.* Finally, the only aircraft remaining aloft was the Ju-52. It too eventually swooped low, its three engines crackling as it flared out and disappeared behind the trees between them and the airfield.

"I must meet Muriname now," Kurokawa said, implying that their meeting was at an end, "to hear his evaluation of the exercise. I am particularly interested to learn his opinion of how our newest planes and pilots performed," he added with a triumphant gleam in his eye, obviously meaning the twin-engine bombers.

"Very well," agreed Gravois, standing and gesturing at the airfields and the ships. "A most impressive display. If the improvements to the rest of your fleet are anywhere near as successful as your aeronautical undertakings appear to be, you should have little difficulty in realizing your goals—and your revenge. My compliments."

Kurokawa stood as well. "Thank you, Capitaine de Fregate Gravois," he said. "We should meet like this again, away from other tiresome voices that cloud the issues and make perfect understanding so elusive."

"Indeed," Gravois agreed with a false smile.

The Go Away Strait
Near Grik City, Mada-gaas-gar
September 25, 1944

"I'm afraid she's finished, Skipper," Commander Brad "Spanky" McFarlane murmured somberly as they inspected the cold, shattered number three boiler in the sweltering heat of the fireroom. Number four still roared, burning fuel oil and making steam for the hungry turbines aft in the engine rooms, and the temperature must've been close to a hundred and twenty degrees. But number four was the last boiler they had online, having already secured number two before it failed as well. What Spanky didn't add, standing in his customary pose with hands on his skinny hips despite the single crutch still propping him up, was "I told you so." He didn't have to. Matt Reddy knew. And as Supreme Allied Commander of all the various forces united to defeat the dreaded Grik in the West and the evil Dominion in the East, what difference did it really make? What else could he have done? The old US Asiatic Fleet "four-stacker" destroyer USS *Walker* (DD-163) was his ship, and he loved her more than he could say, but she was only one ship now of many, fighting a war that stretched the length of a world they barely knew. He used her as hard as he had to in order to get the job done, though it tore his soul with every wound she suffered. He had no doubt he'd use her up entirely before all was said and done. Even rebuilt more than once over the course of this terrible war, *Walker* had endured far more than any had a right to expect, saving him, her crew, the woman he loved, and arguably an entire species from extermination time and again. And somehow, she'd just helped them deliver yet another victory in the face of near-impossible odds. USS *Walker* was his beloved ship, but she was also a deadly tool in his practiced hands, a tool he couldn't afford to leave idle. But how often could she do it? How much more could she take? Now part of the answer had been revealed.

As Spanky predicted, since they'd continued steaming without repairs to the condensers, the salted feedwater had corroded and eroded the boiler tubes to the point that one had finally failed. The water flashed to steam, snuffed the fires, blew up the already cracked and crumbling fire bricks, and turned all the other tubes in the boiler into something resembling a ball of blackened, shredded guts. After another grim look inside, Matt turned to Lieutenant Tab-At—Tabby—his Lemurian engineering officer, standing beside him. She was also peering within the ruined boiler. The musty smell of sweat-foamed gray fur beneath her grimy T-shirt was almost overpowering.

"How are your girls?" Matt asked.

Tabby blinked reassurance at him, tail swishing with relief. "They gonna be okay. They get steamed a little, but them Impie gals're tough." Matt noticed with surprise that Spanky nodded agreement. He'd once been engineering officer himself, and the loudest opponent of females of any kind, even Lemurians, in "his" firerooms. But that was a long time ago in more ways than one. 'Cats, like Tabby, and then the expat Imperial women who'd gravitated to the engineering spaces, had proven themselves over and over.

"Where's Isak?" Matt suddenly asked, looking around for one of the extremely squirrelly firemen called "Mice" who'd since advanced to chief engineer. Isak's half brother, Gilbert, the other "original" mouse, was acting engineering officer (under protest) in the carrier *Maaka-Kakja*, fighting the Doms in the East.

"I told him to knock off," Tabby said, shrugging. "He was about dead. Been at it since before the tubes blew." She had to think. "The night before yesterd'y?"

Matt looked at her and blinked amazement in the Lemurian way. "And he actually *did*? You didn't have to run him out?"

"I guess. Ain't seen him. We got enough guys on this."

"Well," Matt continued, shaking his head and waving at the boiler, "I'm sorry about this."

"I know, Skipper," Tabby said, and she did. But there hadn't been any help for it. Ever since the second Battle for Grik City, they'd been chasing and destroying Grik ships sneaking back and forth between the Comoros Islands and the African mainland, apparently intent on picking up the pieces and salvaging what they could after the recent disastrous assault on Grik City. There'd been apparent attempts to make salvage runs up the Seychelles as well, but one of the first things the Allies did after the latest battle was divert a replacement regiment of Austraal Marines and their combat engineers to Mahe, the largest island in the group, to start work on an airfield. It would take some doing, and right now there was a total of two Nancy floatplanes there to provide air support.

And the Grik salvage effort had used only the old "Indiaman"-style sailing ships, not much of a threat in themselves, but each could carry upward of five hundred warriors, and every one they finished off was one fewer the Grik would have to attack them with again. It was important work from a practical standpoint, but the necessity had left Matt a little . . . uneasy. Not only had the enemy attempt to rescue warriors and equipment from unsupportable positions been suspiciously uncharacteristic, leaving Matt wondering just exactly what was behind it, he'd had very few ships left to perform the task. The "protected cruiser" *Santa Catalina*, a freighter salvaged from a Tjilatjap swamp on the south coast of Java and armed and armored, was too slow and used too much fuel for the hunt. The steam frigates of Des-Ron 6 had been virtually wiped out. Nor had there been any aircraft to spare for the task. The near-nightly raids by massed Grik zeppelins had continued largely unabated, and they still didn't know where their bases were. Somewhere inland of the African coast, obviously, since they'd combed the coastline itself pretty thoroughly. Matt hoped for better recon soon, but for now they had to make do. That had left only *Walker* and a couple of steam frigates, or "DDs," from *Arracca*'s screen to do the job. Matt didn't know how many Grik ships had slipped through the ragged net, quite a few most likely, but they'd probably shattered enough to render the Grik return on their effort fairly futile before the targets started drying up. The DDs would stay out a while longer, but *Walker* was finally headed for the barn. Matt gestured again at the boiler.

"Can you fix it?"

Tabby sighed and swished her tail. "Not out here. An' I can't do much for number two. We outa spare tubes an' it'll do the same as this one, probl'y, the first time we try to fire it up again." She nodded at number four. "An' we *plugged* so many tubes in that one, I bet we only boilin' two-thirds the water we should. 'Least its condenser ain't leakin' an' there ain't no saltin'—but it's . . . tired, Skipper." She shrugged. "Maybe when the rest o' First Fleet gets its ass down here? They finally bringin' that big self-movin' dry dock down, an' it wouldn't hurt to stick *us* in it for a while," she added hopefully.

"We'll see," Matt replied doubtfully, not liking the idea of having his ship immobilized with Grik zeppelins dropping bombs on them. But maybe they could do it at one of the islands to the north?

"Then, with them two brand-new tin caans comin' down, there oughta be spares enough to fix our boilers right," Tabby pressed.

Matt nodded, encouraged and a little thrilled at the thought of finally seeing the two near carbon copies of *Walker* that had been building at Baalkpan for almost a year. The first was USS *James Ellis* (DD-21), named for *Walker*'s old exec who'd gone on to commands of his own but was killed at the second Battle of Madras. Perry Brister had her, having left *Mahan* to assume command. It would be good to see Perry, Ronson, Bashear, and a bunch of the other fellows again, Matt thought. The second new destroyer was USS *Geran-Eras* (DD-23), named for the

High Chief of the Home-turned-carrier *Humfra-Dar*, destroyed off Colombo. She'd been commissioned a few days after *James Ellis*, and the last *Scott* Class steam frigate had taken number 22. Cablaas-Rag-Laan had *Geran-Eras*.

Unless something broke down, it wouldn't take nearly as long for even more new four-stackers to join the fleet, and the first new cruiser—basically an upsized version of the destroyers—was more than three-quarters complete. For the first time since he came to this world, Matt had visions of a real, semimodern fleet dancing in his head. He frowned. *If we can just hold out.* He was pretty sure the Doms had shot their bolt at sea, at least in the Pacific, *but Kurokawa's still out there somewhere and the Grik have to be building a better fleet of their own . . . somewhere else, beyond the range of our scouts. And, of course, there's the League. Who knows what they're up to, or even what they have besides that sub we sank and the battlewagon that sat on Alex-aandra and* Donaghey *so long.*

Matt noticed Spanky was frowning too. "What?" he asked.

"You didn't get me, Skipper. When I said 'she's finished,' I meant the ship, not just the boiler. She needs a yard. How many holes has she had shot through her, just on this campaign? She leaks . . . everywhere. *All* the boilers need work, and her gun tubes need relining bad. The number one gun's as liable to hit the fo'c'sle as the target at max elevation." That was an exaggeration, but not by much. Their temporary use of copper projectiles had extended the lives of their already worn 4″-50 gun barrels a great deal, but the new shells, though far more effective, were actually harder on the bores than the shells they brought to this world. They still used copper driving bands, but the iron casings forward of there had quickly eroded the rifling. "Now we've got the liners, we ought to do it," Spanky persisted. "The condensers, pumps, even the bunkers leak. We're gettin' salt water in the fuel now." He held his hands out at his sides. "More than ever, anyway." There had been a little saltwater seepage into *Walker's* fuel bunkers ever since she was built. It had eased a lot after her last refit, but now it was getting out of hand. "Hell, you've seen the lists," Spanky snorted. "Even

Earl's damn Coke machine is on the fritz, not that he puts anything in it." He shook his head. "The old girl's wearing out."

Matt nodded. "Yeah, but like I've told you before, she's doing what she's for." He smiled sadly. "Besides, I don't know about you, but I think—I hope—we really hurt the Grik this last time. I expect, based on reports and what I saw myself, that what they sent against us was their second string and a lot bigger shoe is getting ready to drop. But with the rest of First Fleet and Generals Alden and Rolak on their way, we're going to have a helluva *boot* to drop on them." He rubbed his forehead. "I don't know," he repeated. "It's just a feeling I have, and I may be wrong. God knows that's happened before. But if I'm right, and the Grik really are finally trailing blood in the water, I'm damn sure not going to throw the old girl out of the war now. She deserves to be in at the finish," he added softly, then looked back at Tabby. "Do what you can. We're done out here in the strait anyway. You can at least finish patching up the condenser for number two, and plug as many tubes as you have to to get it back online when we get back to Grik City."

"Ay, ay, Cap-i-taan. I'll do what I can."

Matt nodded. "Thanks."

Passing the steam frigates *Scott* and *Nakja-Mur* on picket duty several miles outside the harbor, they opened the narrow entrance to Grik City Bay late that afternoon. Following the revised channel markers to the broader expanse of the bay, where the bulk of what remained of First Fleet (South) lay at anchor some distance offshore, USS *Walker* came to rest at last. There wasn't much of a fleet left. *Santa Catalina* was there, as were a couple of newly arrived fast transports and oilers made by stripping captured Grik Indiamen and putting engines in them. Away from the docks, it would be easier to get underway and maneuver if necessary when the now inevitable nightly air raid came. Only the most heavily damaged ships, like Jarrik-Fas's USS *Tassat*, were tied to the pier, helpless against air attack, but helpless in any case. *Tassat*, for one, could barely keep herself afloat. The two great seagoing

Homes-turned-carriers *Arracca* and *Salissa*, under Matt's friends Tassanna-Ay-Arracca and Ahd-mi-raal Keje-Fris-Ar, stayed at sea with *Arracca*'s DDs to screen them. At least the air raids weren't that much of a threat to mobile ships. The Grik had begun lashing their dirigibles together in order to maximize their mutual defense and concentrate their bombing. The results were mixed, but it was now impossible to scatter their formation and shoot them all down. They always had plenty of warning of their arrival, though, and their direction betrayed their probable targets. Most nights, the men and 'Cats on the ships in the bay just watched as bombs fell on the great mound of the Celestial Palace, or "Cowflop," as it had been irreverently dubbed. The enemy had initially avoided targeting the huge stone edifice rising three hundred feet above the now barren ground of what had once been the capital Grik city, but once they apparently realized the bombing didn't really hurt it, they bathed the structure with firebombs and seared it with bright flames every night. Matt suspected the raids were more symbolic than anything now, a reminder that the Grik weren't finished with them, and they'd taken to bombing the Celestial Palace simply because it was the easiest target.

Chief Jeek's bosun's pipe trilled on the fo'c'sle, calling the special sea and anchor detail and fueling detail as *Walker* sidled up alongside *Santa Catalina* and took in fuel lines suspended from her cargo booms. Soon fuel oil coursed into *Walker*'s bunkers, pumped directly from one of the small oilers on the other side of the protected cruiser. Matt was in the pilothouse and stepped out on the port bridgewing to look up at "Mikey" Monk, *Santa Catalina*'s exec, overseeing the transfer. The ship's captain, Russ Chappelle, appeared beside him and saluted Matt. Matt saluted back with a grin, then cupped his hands and shouted, "I'll be over directly!" Russ nodded and waved.

"Meetings. Ugh," Spanky said from the captain's chair bolted to the bulkhead when Matt reentered the pilothouse.

Matt grinned sheepishly. "Couldn't fight a war without 'em. There's a Nancy floatplane hoisted on *Santy Cat*'s deck, so I guess Keje's already been flown in. Better go, I guess."

"You'll have to run if you're going like that," Spanky warned, waving at Matt's soiled and sweaty uniform. "If Juan catches you, he'll hold you down and wipe your face with spit on a hanky!"

Matt joined the rest of the bridge watch in a laugh. Juan Marcos was a Filipino who'd lost a leg fighting Doms in the Empire of the New Britain Isles at his captain's side, but still took what he saw as his primary duty very seriously. He'd started as *Walker*'s officer's steward, but had appointed himself "Chief Steward to the Supreme Commander," and would throw a fit if Matt left the ship in such a state. "No, no, I'll change," he replied in mock alarm, convinced that Juan would already have laid out a set of Lemurian-made whites in anticipation of his departure. "You have the ship, Spanky, and keep a sharp lookout."

"Aye, aye, Skipper," Spanky answered with a tolerant grin. As if he needed a reminder for *that*.

Matt, Surgeon Lieutenant Pam Cross, and Commander Bernard Sandison were received aboard *Santa Catalina* by a side party and a proper bosun's pipe. Not all Lemurians could manage a pipe and most used whistles instead, but *Santy Cat*'s Chief Bosun was a gruff Bostonian named Stanley "Dobbin" Dobson. Smiling, Matt and his companions saluted the Stars and Stripes aft and the collection of humans and Lemurians there to meet them before shaking hands all around. Russ Chappelle was there, as was Kathy McCoy, the surgeon commander of all of First Fleet. Both were matching Matt's smile. There were other familiar faces, but most unexpected was that of Dean Laney, his large form uncomfortably stuffed into another Lemurian-made copy of Navy whites adorned by the shoulder boards of a lieutenant (jg).

Matt reflected that there'd been a lot of promotions, of necessity, among the survivors of his old crew and that of *Mahan* and S-19. Russ had been a torpedoman on *Mahan*, and Bernie Sandison had been *Walker*'s own torpedo officer. Now Russ commanded what was arguably the most powerful ship in the Alliance, and Bernie, while back at his old job at present, was also "minister of experimental ordnance." Kathy had been a nurse lieutenant but had helped Sandra build an amazingly effective medical corps.

It was the same everywhere; General of the Armies and Marines Pete Alden had been a sergeant in USS *Houston*'s Marine contingent, left at a hospital in Surabaya when his ship met her fate. Ben Mallory, chief of the Army and Naval Air Corps, had been "just" an Army pilot. And the list went on. Ordinary men and women had risen to the challenge of this terrible war and the bizarre situation they faced in various ways, but even the few who'd never advanced beyond their original ranks and occupations, who remained "mere" destroyermen on *Walker* or any number of other ships now, had provided a professional, steadying influence on the hundreds of Lemurian sailors they'd helped form over time.

Now Matt realized that of them all, Dean Laney had always struck him as the absolutely least likely *Walker* veteran to distinguish himself in any way and advance beyond Machinist's Mate 2nd Class. He'd been a troublemaker all his life and Dennis Silva's chief nemesis in the old world they'd left behind. His technical knowledge was impressive, probably second only to Spanky's when it came to engineering plants, and he'd bounced from job to job in the various Allied industries making real technical contributions—until no one could stand being around him anymore. Engineering officer on *Santy Cat* had been his last chance before . . . banishment, Matt supposed. And even now he remained, by all accounts, an asshole, but Russ had no complaints about his performance.

"Laney," Matt said, nodding.

"Cap'n Reddy," Laney replied stiffly, self-consciously.

"If you'll follow me, Skipper," Russ said, gesturing aft, "everyone else is waiting in the dining salon." No longer under Matt's direct gaze, Laney drifted away and Matt got the distinct impression he was anxious to be just about anywhere else. He shook his head. "The 'dining salon'?" he asked Russ with a smile. Russ managed a sheepish shrug. "Aye, sir." Despite major alterations to turn her into a warship, including bolted-on armor plate and rebuilding much of her superstructure as a casemate to protect six heavy guns—part of the Japanese battle cruiser *Amagi*'s secondary armament of 5.5-inch rifles, to be precise—*Santa Catalina* had once been equipped to carry a few passengers. In her off-and-on role as a naval auxiliary over the years, these had usually been naval officers, and in the prewar, pre-air-travel naval culture she'd accommodated, officers had been accustomed to traveling in a degree of style, and a tasteful, if not luxurious, dining salon had been provided. During her refit, it was envisioned that such a convenience might still have merit and the space was not only retained but somewhat embellished with ornate Lemurian woodwork and tapestries. The ostentation of the furnishings had embarrassed Russ Chappelle when he first took command, but he'd grown to accept the salon's facility as a conference center. It was even larger and more luxurious than similar accommodations aboard the great carriers such as *Salissa*, now that their Great Halls had been done away with, and he was actually rather proud of it now.

They moved aft, past the casemate, and entered a protected doorway into the salon. Ahd-mi-raal Keje-Fris-Ar stood, teeth showing in a grin from his white-streaked, rust-colored fur, his white tunic and blue kilt covering his bear-shaped frame. Captain Jis-Tikkar (Tikker) was beside him, dressed in a flight suit. Apparently, *Salissa*'s— or *"Big Sal,"* as she was affectionately known—COFO, or Commander of Flight Operations, had flown Keje over himself. Tikker had been the very first Lemurian aviator and still proudly wore a highly polished 7.7-mm cartridge thrust through a hole in his long, pointed ear as a memento of an early hair-raising flight with Ben Mallory in the long-gone PBY. Standing quickly to join Tikker was Lieutenant Araa-Faan, another Lemurian pilot who'd originally been slated to command Grik City's land-based air. Wounded in combat, she'd been superseded by the arrival of Lieutenant Commander Mark Leedom, who'd earned a reputation fighting Grik zeppelins in Indiaa. She'd become his executive officer when she recovered, but didn't seem to hold a grudge. Mark was busy getting ready for the night's expected attack, and she'd come in his stead.

The AEF-M (Allied Expeditionary Force—Mada-gaas-gar) was represented by its commander, General Queen Protector Safir Maraan, stunning as always in her silver-washed breastplate and black kilt and cape. Matt smiled at her, noting that she was attended by Imperial Major Alistair Jindal of the 21st Combined Regiment of the 1st Allied Raider ("Chack's") Brigade. He was XO to Lieutenant Colonel Chack-Sab-At's sister Risa, who commanded the brigade while Chack was away. The strangest figure in the room was an ancient "tame" Grik named Hij Geerki, whom Pete Alden and Muln Rolak had captured at Raan-goon at the beginning of the push that ultimately brought them to Grik City itself. He was currently serving, appointed by Safir Maraan, as High Chief over the several thousand "civilian" Grik prisoners they'd taken. Sequestered on an exposed spit of land before the recent battle, they hadn't surrendered, didn't even understand the concept, so long weeks passed while they hunkered in the mud, subsisting off one another—until Geerki arrived to talk them out. Now they were under shelter of a sort and fed in exchange for general labor that Geerki coordinated, and Matt suspected their lives weren't much different from how they'd been under Grik rule. They worked, they existed, *like ants*, Matt thought, and only time would tell if they'd ever go beyond that.

Geerki looks awful, Matt thought, with his wrinkled neck, thinning, downy fur, and broken yellow teeth. What remained of his claws had been removed after his capture. As a specimen of the fearsome Grik, he wasn't much, had in fact never even been a warrior. Those were generally larger than the "civilian" Grik such as Geerki himself. *But he still looks basically like an upright, furry alligator,* Matt supposed, with long arms and real hands perfectly capable of wielding just about any weapon a human or Lemurian could. Fortunately, he was a dedicated convert to the cause of defeating his own kind and actually considered himself Rolak's property—*just as Rolak probably still considers himself* my *property, for sparing his life after the Battle of Aryaal,* Matt reflected uncomfortably. But improbable as it must've seemed to Rolak when he captured him, Geerki had been a godsend in many ways: as a spy, an interpreter, and now an administrator, and the energy with which he performed his evolving duties belied his apparent frailty.

"Now that you are here, we can eat!" Keje pronounced

grandly. "And we may want to hurry, in case the Grik zeppelins are tempted by such targets as *Saanta-Caat-a-lina* and *Waa-kur* floating so helplessly in the bay," he added darkly.

With Adar gone, Matt was the senior official of the Alliance present once again and he supposed that was why they'd waited, but he waved everyone to the table impatiently. "You're right," he agreed. "Let's eat."

In contrast to the care otherwise taken to make the salon as comfortable as possible, the dining table was flanked only by a pair of rough wooden benches. This was a common expedient since humans and Lemurians could both sit on them—equally uncomfortably. *Should've just used stools,* Matt thought. 'Cat tails made sitting in any kind of chair extremely painful after a while, but in lieu of their preferred cushions, stools were acceptable. *Stools are better for humans too, if they're tall enough.* Matt brooded, resignedly hiking a leg over the bench at the head of the table, where Keje indicated he should sit. Matt noticed suddenly that Russ Chappelle's face was burning red.

"What is it, Captain Chappelle?"

"Um, well, Captain, some time ago, before Second Madras, somebody swiped all the chairs from the engineering spaces. A kind of prank, I guess, to, ah, 'annoy' a certain engineering officer. . . ."

Matt's eyebrows rose, and he blinked.

"Yes, sir. Anyway, on the voyage down here, right before that stormy fight off Grik City, somebody, ah, removed all the chairs and stools from everywhere—and I mean *everywhere* but the bridge."

"As in removed . . ."

"Apparently over the side, Skipper, 'cause we can't find a single one."

Matt suppressed a burst of laughter. "I presume it's occurred to you to suspect the culprit might've been the . . . 'certain engineering officer'?"

"Yes, sir, of course. But . . ." Russ's face grew livid. "He's got alibis! I mean, hell—excuse me, Skipper—but hell! The whole damn engineering division swears he had nothing to do with it! And we're talking about *Laney*! Who'd ever cover for his fat, sorry ass?" He glared at the offending benches. "Anyway, when you said you wanted to meet here, I had the carpenter knock these up. Sorry, sir."

Matt stifled another laugh, but then considered what Russ had said. Who indeed? Obviously, Laney had found his niche at last, if he could inspire that kind of loyalty. Then Matt had a darker thought. *Or was it fear?* He mentally shook his head. *No. Even if Laney's division were entirely human, somebody would buck him if that were the case. And cowing a whole division of 'Cats? No way.* "This is fine, Captain Chappelle. And we'll scour the fleet to see if we can come up with a couple of extra chairs and stools." He grinned. "You might want to make sure one finds its way to the engineering spaces, though."

In the Lemurian fashion, no business was discussed while they ate. That was usually a good thing, Matt believed, but despite the threat from the air, he was anxious to get on with the status reports. He knew roughly what was going on, but he'd been at sea for several days and couldn't have the whole picture. The new transceiver nestled deep inside the Cowflop was the most powerful in the theater, and with its aerial erected atop the massive, ancient "Wall of Trees" to the south, the Grik could bomb their Celestial Palace all they wanted without interfering with communications. He eyed Safir Maraan while they finished their plesiosaur steaks. She'd just come from there and would have the most comprehensive news.

Mess attendants removed plates and returned with a kind of fruity, crusted pudding, the ersatz coffee most Amer-i-caans required, and hot tea imported from the Empire of the New Britain Isles. 'Cats were fiends for iced tea but had begun to enjoy the hot variety as well, using it like Matt and his people used coffee. Matt considered that: "his" people. Technically, every member of the Navy and Marines, human or Lemurian, was part of the "Amer-i-caan Navy Clan" now, having taken the same enlistment oath as his old destroyermen. He'd insisted on that from the start to prevent factionalism and divided loyalties. He was High Chief of that sovereign clan and had always enjoyed the same status as other High Chiefs of the various Homes, even though the only actual territory his clan "owned" was the oil-rich island of Tarakan off the Borno coast, and a little chunk of California where San Diego ought to be. It didn't matter. Just as some clans were composed solely of single, massive seagoing Homes, his included every ship in the Amer-i-caan Navy with a "USS" prefix that flew the Stars and Stripes, regardless where it was built or where its crew came from.

The weird part was, according to the draft "Articles of Union" Alan Letts had prepared, that now meant his "clan" would enter the new union as, if not the most numerous, then certainly the most militarily powerful "state"—with him as *governor*! What's more, there'd been very little opposition to the scheme. He didn't know if that was a testimony to him personally, or the notion itself. The Navy had always remained as unbiased as possible and stayed out of domestic politics, beyond that which sometimes threatened support for those prosecuting the war. And he'd taken great pains to prove he had no desire to be anything but the leader of his "clan." *And I guess it makes a kind of sense,* he decided. *Not only would the professional military that his clan represented have a greater say in how it was used, but it's still dependent on all the other "states" for material support.* He could see how the arrangement might someday be abused, but with the right training and traditions of impartiality and service instilled in his clan—his state—from the start, it would be an interesting experiment.

He glanced around the table. Dessert dishes were being taken away and only cups or mugs remained. He cleared his throat. "Any news from *Amerika*?" he asked, voicing his own most personal concern.

"Nothing since she sailed from Diego and passed out of range of her TBS," Safir answered promptly, anticipating the question. "And except for the fire in her comm shack, there was no damage. I'm sure she—and all aboard her—are fine. She will pass other ships headed this way and they will report her progress and relay any messages she might send."

"That fire, so confined and easily extinguished, still strikes me as suspicious," Keje muttered darkly. Of them all, he still held the greatest reservations about their Republic allies. Matt was tempted to agree for purely personal reasons, but shook his head. "The ship's old, Keje. Even older than this one, and there's been no modernization at all. Particularly to her comm gear. She didn't even test it for years."

"Tubes, resisters, and capacitors go bad," Bernie supported. "Wires and connections corrode, particularly in salt air. Solder is lead; wire is copper. Dissimilar metals . . ." He glanced at Matt. "Anyway, there was probably a short. We get them pretty often ourselves and we maintain our equipment a lot better. We have to . . ." He trailed off again and Matt smiled. "I'm sure we'll hear from her periodically," Matt agreed with Safir. Then his attention turned to the one she was most concerned about. "What have we heard of Colonel Chack's and Mr. Bradford's expedition?"

Chack, Bradford, Chief Gunner's Mate Dennis Silva, and several others had gone on a mission to meet the reported remnants of indigenous Lemurians still inhabiting central and southern Madagascar. Courtney Bradford just wanted to meet them, but the main idea was to recruit them to the cause of defeating the Grik. Even with the populous Great South Isle, better known as Aus-traal, joining the Alliance at last, combat losses had created a growing man—and 'Cat—power crisis to the extent that they could barely crew all the new ships and planes the burgeoning industries in Baalkpan, Maa-ni-laa, and the Empire were turning out. *Two* new carriers were completing in Maa-ni-laa, for example, but their deployment east with Saan-Kakja and Governor-Empress Rebecca McDonald had been delayed while they worked up slowly arriving pilots and crews. Building entirely new infantry divisions was almost impossible, and most troops left the training depots as replacements for losses in existing units. That should change, in time, as the Aus-traal-ans fully mobilized, but time was a far greater ally of the Grik than it was to them.

The expedition south had traveled aboard one of the small motor torpedo boats built in Ma-nil-aa, the "Seven boat," commanded by a young ensign named Nathaniel Hardee. Their first encounter with intelligent natives of some sort—they still didn't know who or even what they'd been—had been discouraging to say the least, and one of their number had been brutally murdered. Safir tried to order them back, but Chack—her mate—flatly refused.

"They probe up the river," Safir said in exasperation. "That is all I know. Our communications with them are just as frustrating as those with *Amerika*, it would seem. The mountains . . ." She trailed off.

"Chack is a fine warrior and very smart," Keje assured her, then laughed. "And with that man-monster Dennis Silva along, I cannot imagine any danger sufficient to overwhelm them."

There was appreciative laughter. Dennis Silva was a maniac, but he was *Walker*'s maniac, utterly devoted to his ship, his crew, his captain—and the few beings he considered friends. Chack was one of those. Keje was right. Silva had accomplished amazing things, but Matt—and Pam Cross, who was helplessly, possibly even self-destructively, in love with the big jerk—both knew he wasn't immortal. He was probably still hurting from wounds he got helping to capture the Celestial Palace. If Silva was at his best, Matt would lay odds the man could walk the length of the artificially predator-rich island of Madagascar all by himself with just a compass and a pocketknife and still gain weight. But he wasn't at his best, was he? His little Griklike Sa'aaran friend Lawrence would be a big help, as usual, but Lawrence was hurting too. That was one of the reasons Matt had agreed to let them go, dammit! To let them heal. He should've known the expedition would get weird. Everything always did.

"In any event, their last transmission reported that all but the casualty were well, and the Seven boat would proceed upriver, investigating signs of habitation along the way," Safir concluded. "We will just have to wait and hope for a break in the mountains or favorable aat-mos-pherics before we learn more."

Her tone changed. "Otherwise, USS *Donaghey* finally sailed from Alex-aandra, bound for the place you call Carib-bean." One of the first three true warships the American destroyermen had helped the Lemurians make, *Donaghey* (DD-2) was a classic square rig sailing frigate of 1,200 tons, armed with twenty-four 18-pdr guns, a pair of "Y" guns, and depth charge racks. Like *Walker*, she'd seen a lot of action, and was the sole surviving dedicated sailing warship in the Alliance. Her mostly Lemurian crew of two hundred sailors and Marines were under Commander Greg Garrett, *Walker*'s former gunnery officer, and she'd been chosen for the long-range scout specifically because her range wasn't limited by fuel capacity. Her mission had been delayed by the French battleship *Savoie* while she attempted to prevent the Republic from joining the Allied war effort.

We don't know nearly enough about Savoie *and this weird "League" she represents,* Matt thought moodily. *From what Greg and others have picked up, it seems clear the League's greatest power and concern is centered in the Mediterranean—for now—and their primary interest here is to keep us—or the Grik—from growing strong enough to threaten them.* He closed his eyes. *Idiots! The last thing we want is* another *war! The one—two!—we've already got are plenty! Of course, that's probably the whole point, after all.* He wished he knew where *Savoie* had gone after leaving Alex-aandra, but everyone's best guess was that she'd steamed back north across the Atlantic. How could she sustain herself otherwise? But they'd somehow supported a sub in the Western Ocean for who knew how long, and Matt supposed they probably at least suspected *Walker* sank it when it attacked his force on its way to Madagascar. *So we're already at war, in a sense,* he mused. *And if their blockade and threat of force at Alex-aandra wasn't an act of war, despite their protestations, I don't know what is.* Still, as long as they weren't actively hunting and shooting at Allied ships or cities, he'd try to stay content to merely learn as much about them as he could for the time being.

Inquisitor Choon, the Republic's chief snoop, believed the League had been gathering a lot of intel from the Allies, but *his* snoops had made progress of their own since *Savoie* sailed away, quietly catching a surprising number of spies that had infiltrated into Alex-aandra over a period of years. A far more complete picture of what composed the "League," and what it was capable of, shouldn't be long in coming.

Matt caught Safir looking at him and smiled. "Sorry.

Still thinking about those creeps that sat on *Donaghey* so long. Please continue."

"Greg Gaar-ett reported that the Republic could not have been more appreciative or helpful, and his ship is in better shape and better provisioned now than since she was made." She paused. "He did leave one of his two Nancy floatplanes and its air and ground crew with the Republic. They have experimental aircraft of their own, but have not dedicated a great deal of effort to producing combat planes until now. The example of the Nancy should be invaluable to them." She paused. "In addition, and as you left to Greg's discretion, he allowed Cap-i-taan Bekiaa-Sab-At to remain in the Republic as a military liaison and advisor." She smiled. "I authorized her promotion to major, and I understand they have given her the rank of tribune."

Matt nodded. That was fine, and having Bekiaa on the ground there would be a big help. Not only would she be able to advise Choon and the Republic general staff on hard-won Grik fighting tactics, but her unvarnished reports regarding the readiness of the Republic to open a southern front against the Grik, transmitted to Safir and her staff at the Cowflop, would be invaluable. Greg would miss her, though; they were good friends and Bekiaa was a fine Marine. Matt hoped Greg wouldn't miss her too much—when he really needed her at some point.

"How long will we have contact with *Donaghey*?" Russ asked.

"She should be able to relay transmissions through Alex-aandra until she is perhaps a third of the distance across the unknown sea to the west, to the unexplored land beyond," Safir murmured, her concern obvious.

Matt was concerned too. *Donaghey* would be all alone and beyond any help if she needed it, but he suddenly remembered that Safir had never been to the Empire of the New Britain Isles and was now even farther from her home near where Surabaya, Java, ought to be than she'd ever been. That anyone she cared about might go even *farther* probably filled her with a measure of dread not easily suppressed. Virtually every Lemurian they'd met was fully aware the earth was round, but they also knew that gravity (whatever that was) pulled down. Therefore, if anyone ventured too far from the "top" of the world, possibly centered somewhere between their ancestral home on Madagascar in the West and the Filpin Lands in the East, they'd simply fall off into the void of the Heavens. All their notions of nature and even theology had been based on this. Rain fell to earth and eventually every last drop found its way to the sea. From there it ultimately fell off, back into the sky that surrounded the world, formed into clouds, and fell back upon them. People who fell off couldn't survive, but their souls would reside in the Heavens, joining the countless stars above. Lemurian dead had traditionally been cremated so the smoke could carry their souls to the Heavens as well, to join all who'd passed before them alongside the Maker of All Things. To some, like Adar, the Maker was unseen, incomprehensible, and watched them from the Heavens beyond the stars. Others, like Safir, believed the *sun* was the Maker and watched them from much closer. But amazingly, thankfully, this seemingly insurmountable dogmatic difference had never been the same source of ruthless contention that much more subtle differences in interpretation had proven to be in human history. 'Cats were more flexible. They had to be when science assailed all they'd ever believed.

Most still believed the spiritual side of things, though, and after a bumpy start were generally able to accept even the very different views many of the human destroyermen held into their malleable theology once they realized their notions of an afterlife with the Maker were not that dissimilar. Beyond that, there could be problems when one got down to details, but Sister Audry, and now even most of the spiritual leaders in the Empire, recognized they needed unity above all things in this time of crisis and their more specific Catholic and British church teachings were gently applied in their separate quests for converts. Adar himself probably said it best when he proclaimed that they should all be free to find the Maker in their own way, merely sailing different courses to the same destination.

But the arrival of USS *Walker* and the necessary industrialization and education that followed had delivered a fatal blow to the Lemurian's understanding of nature, physics, geography—and one's ability to stand upright on the bottom of the world.

"Greg Gaar-ett is the best we have," Keje assured Safir—and himself, it seemed.

"Uh, any news from Fred and Kari?" Tikker asked hesitantly, and Matt scowled.

"None," Safir replied, as Matt expected. He had little doubt that Lieutenant (jg) Fred Reynolds and Ensign Kari-Faask were irretrievably lost at last. Fred had been *Walker*'s youngest crewman when she came to this world and ultimately became a pilot of one of the PB-1B "Nancy" floatplanes they'd developed early on. Better planes were in the works, and they had a kind of small pursuit plane that was hell on Grik zeppelins, but Nancys were still the backbone of Allied air capability. Fred and his Lemurian friend and "backseater," Kari, had gone off on a suicidal lark to find some supposed "other Americans" descended from arrivals from around the time of the US-Mexican War, who, as best they could tell, *might* control part of the Gulf Coast of North America. This all from a single meeting with an enigmatic spy who aided subversive elements in the land of the Holy Dominion. Granted, "Captain Anson," as he called himself, had helped Fred and Kari escape the Doms after they'd been forced down by what amounted to flying Grik, but there'd been no contact with Anson or his people since. And now, on the tail of a major action near a bizarre sea passage through what should've been Costa Rica, and was supposed to encourage contact with naval elements of these "other Americans," Fred and Kari had flown off looking for them.

To make matters worse in Matt's eyes, his own cousin Orrin Reddy had let them go. Orrin had reached this world through a separate, more hellish route than Matt, and in spite of his experiences before and since had never seemed to take things as seriously. Maybe it was his youth? But, a former fighter pilot in the Philippines who'd been captured by the Japanese, Orrin was COFO of all air assets in the East. He ought to know better. Fred and Kari were kind of . . . special to Matt—to everyone—particularly after their captivity. Maybe Orrin's brutal captivity in the hands of the Japanese made him take such things more lightly than others, but Matt still meant to have words with him.

"Has General Shinya advanced beyond Chimborazo?" Matt asked, changing the subject. "The last reports we caught, he was still consolidating his forces there."

"He advances," Keje ventured. Even *Big Sal*'s comm gear was better than *Walker*'s balky replacement set. "But must scout heavily to acquaint himself with the terrain. The country is very rough—and high enough that even his aircraft have difficulty. I have confidence he will press the Doms as hard as he is able."

"There is also the matter of supply," Safir added darkly. "After the 'victory' at Maal-pelo, most of our warships in the area either harry the remnants of the Dom fleet near El Paaso Del Fuego, or undergo repairs at the En-chaanted Isles." Decisive as the desperate sea battle of Malpelo was, the victory had been pyrrhic indeed. Nearly every capital ship attached to Second Fleet, including the carrier *Maaka-Kakja*, had been crippled, and the fleet's frigates, or DDs, had been practically annihilated. "Other than a handful of DEs, and a very small remainder of AVDs, nothing remains to protect the supply convoys to Guayak or Puerto Viejo." AVDs were outmoded frigates equipped to carry and service Nancy seaplanes. Even a few merchant ships had been lightly armed and converted. Here in the West they used Grik Indiamen, cut down and with steam engines installed, for AVDs, fast transports, light oilers, or just about any kind of auxiliary they could imagine. They'd always had plenty of the surprisingly well-made hulls. But even those were scarce right now. . . . "And after the great battle at Fort Defiance, Gener-aal Shin-yaa has little ammunition on hand," Safir continued. "If he were to meet serious resistance during his pursuit of the Doms . . ."

Matt shook his head. "All the more reason why the convoys have to go, protection or not. Shinya has to get off the dime and *chase* that slippery bastard Don Hernan before he has a chance to gather another army!"

"But only warships have the so-naar to discourage mountain fish!" Keje protested.

"And mountain fish in the Pacific, beyond the Empire

of the New Britain Isles, are only interested in getting to the Pass of Fire and Sea of Bones to breed. They leave ships alone," Matt countered. Keje had never been that far either. "Usually," Matt added. "At least that's the theory. Either way, it's a risk we have to take."

"Very well," Safir reluctantly agreed. "I will traans-mit the order."

Matt looked at his watch, surprised as always that the scratched and battered thing still worked after all it had endured. They had other watches now, big, bulky ones made in the Empire of the New Britain Isles, but he'd hate it when the Hamilton finally quit. "It'll be dark soon, and I'd like to get back aboard my ship. What's left?"

Keje blinked surprise. "Only what *our* next move should be," he said, heavily mimicking human sarcasm.

Matt shrugged irritably. "Our next move isn't really up to us until others get the lead out. We're stuck on the defensive until the rest of the fleet and our reinforcements arrive, and until the Republic is ready to move."

"And when might that be?" Keje asked Safir. "What is the latest on that?"

"All of First Fleet, including First and Third Corps, already embarked, have been waiting only for the final loading of Ben Mallory's Pee-Forties aboard *Baalkpan Bay*." She blinked mild accusation at Matt. "The modifications to the ship that were necessary before that could occur were what caused the delay."

Matt took a breath and laid his hands on the table. "Ben's been bugging me without stop," he confessed. "But it's more than that. He's the most experienced pilot with the most capable aircraft we have, and he's been on the shelf too long. He needs back in the war, and God help us, we need him and his P-Forties to wrap it up. They were decisive at Madras, and we sure could've used them here a few weeks ago. It's time to roll his precious hangar queens out in the sunlight and use 'em." He turned to Lieutenant Araa-Faan. "The airstrip's ready for something heavier than your Mosquito Hawks?"

"Finally. Especially the new, heavier Fleashooters, the C models, which are supposed to be on their way," Araa-Faan added hopefully. Silva had dubbed the P-1 Mosquito

Hawks "Fleashooters" the first time he saw them because of their resemblance to the larger P-26 "Peashooters" on their old world. Like so many of his irreverent nicknames, it stuck.

"They are coming," Tikker confirmed, then grinned. "But the *first* ones go to *Salissa*!"

"The first ones will go where they're needed most," Matt warned, "but the field will handle Ben's heavier planes?" he asked specifically.

"Commaander Leedom supervised the crush an' roll himself," Araa said. "It is as hard and smooth as we can make it. It'll be dusty, but it'll hold up—until the Griks knock holes in it."

"In that case, I'll leave it up to you." He glanced back and forth between Araa-Faan and Tikker. "Be sure to pass the word to Mr. Leedom. Whoever stops these damn raids gets the new planes—that's the deal. You've got the Clipper," he added to Araa. "Find where the Grik are marshaling their zeps and burn 'em out." He looked at Tikker. "And you have the P-Forty floatplane—and the same chance I gave the land-based air. None of the new planes, and especially not Ben's, are coming ashore until the Grik air raids stop. I won't lose them to anything so . . . stupid."

Safir smiled. "In any event, Cap-i-taan Reddy, to completely answer my brother Keje's question at last, the remainder of First Fleet should sail with the dawn." She blinked unease. "I fear I do not have such a definitive answer regarding when the Republic will be ready to move. Cap-i-taan—I mean, Major—Bekiaa has not yet had time to evaluate its army. She promised a preliminary report within the week."

Matt nodded, then smiled himself. "You know, it's kind of funny. Thinking of Bekiaa, the consummate combat Marine, trying to watch her Ps and Qs around a bunch of foreign officers and blowhard bureaucrats, brought Alan Letts to mind for some reason. Not that he's in Bekiaa's class as a line officer," he hastened to add, "but we're always here at the pointy end, so that's the perspective we carry around. Things can seem pretty overwhelming at times. But then I wonder what Alan thinks about it all from Baalkpan. It's got to drive him nuts. He sees an even bigger picture than we do, but has to deal with all the tiny details too, not to mention keeping all our 'friends' on the same page."

"Indeed," Keje agreed. "Not only has he somehow managed to sort out all the necessary logistics of a two-front war—our current shortages notwithstanding. He cannot foresee everything, after all, and success breeds as many difficulties as defeat. But more important, and at the same time, he has built a nation of highly individualistic creatures." He grinned. "He has herded whole clans of 'Cats into doing what few could really want to do for themselves, without the greater need that drives them. I did not think it could be done."

"Yeah," Matt agreed. "He's come a long way," he said, remembering when Alan had been merely an extremely unfocused supply officer. "I wouldn't trade jobs with him for the world," he added.

"He will, no doubt, be most glad to relinquish his acting duties as chairman of the Grand Alliance back to Adar when he returns to Baalkpan," Safir noted.

And I'll be glad when he gets there too, Matt told himself, *because it'll mean Sandra—and the baby—are safe in Baalkpan as well.* "No doubt," he chorused with the others, "and I guess his arrival there is all they're waiting for before all the representatives get together and ratify the Union"— he smiled—"and finally give it a name." He looked around. "Any idea which way they're leaning?" He assumed a mock expression of haughty dignity. "As Supreme Allied Commander, CINC-WEST, and High Chief of the American Navy Clan, I'm still pushing for 'New Texas' myself." Keje snorted, and Russ Chappelle had to hide his face. Pam Cross just stared at him, incredulous. That made Matt laugh. "I'm just kidding, I swear! Actually, just 'the Union' sounds okay to me." Keje and Safir were nodding and blinking amusement. Both knew that "Texas," wherever that was, was Matt's birthplace. But they were each heads of state in their own right. Keje was High Chief of USNRS *Salissa*, technically a "reserve" ship operating with the Amer-i-caan Navy. He'd already joined with Tasanna on *Arracca*, which enjoyed the same status, to become a bigger "state" of their own, and despite the age difference, there was talk of a more personal "joining" between them. Neither had a mate. Safir was queen of B'mbaado, but now also of her former enemy Aryaal as well—and the aged General Lord Muln Rolak was to be "protector" of both cities. Each had a say of their own, and all had proclaimed a preference for some variation of "Union."

"Well, we've all got a lot of work to do, here and back at Baalkpan," Matt said, standing. The rough-hewn benches groaned and squeaked as they were pushed back and the others stood as well. "Let's break this up. I hope Mr. Leedom tears 'em up tonight," he added, glancing upward, "and I'll see you all in the morning."

"One last thing, Captain Reddy, if you please," Russ Chappelle said hastily, moving to a cabinet nearby. He returned with a beautiful wooden case about ten by twelve inches and three inches deep. He hesitated a moment before presenting it to Matt. "We've been carrying this thing around a long time, and the 'right moment' to hand it over just never seems to come." He shrugged, with a glance at the others around the table, and passed the case. "This'll have to do," he said. Immediately, everyone began to clap and stamp their feet, so they'd all obviously known ahead of time.

Up close, in Matt's hands, the wood was even more stunning. It looked like a shiny swirl of dark chocolate and peanut butter, accented with fiery, shimmering flashes of purple and gold that seemed painted on with a feather but were actually in the grain of the wood. A polished plaque read: WITH UTMOST GRATITUDE TO CAPTAIN MATTHEW REDDY, and it was from, simply, ALL HIS PEOPLE. Eyes beginning to burn, Matt lifted the lid. Inside was the Single-Action Army Colt that had been found rusting in the captain's cabin of this very ship, but it had been transformed into a gleaming, nickel-plated thing of beauty. Fine engraving covered the weapon from the muzzle to the backstrap, and the grips had been replaced with the same exotic wood the case was made of. And in the grips, deeply engraved, was USS *WALKER* (DD-163). Fifty .44-40 cartridges stood in rows in a wooden insert flanked by decorative cleaning tools and screwdrivers.

They'd never adopted .44-40, so someone must've made *these* cartridges by hand.

At first, Matt didn't know what to say. He knew the Baalkpan Arsenal had toyed with copying the SAA for a while, but the 1911 Colt design had proven easier to produce, and it was a far better combat pistol in any event. But it was beautiful, and he loved it on sight.

"I'm told it was the first thing they ever nickel- or silver-plated on this world," Russ said quietly, "but that can't be so." He nodded at Safir Maraan's breastplate. "Maybe it was the first thing ever *electroplated*. Good practice, though."

Matt could only nod until he finally found his voice. "Thanks," he said. "Thank you all. And I accept the gift," he added with a wry smile. "Hard not to, with my name on it." Then, reluctantly, he closed the lid and handed the case back to Russ. "But you'll continue to take care of it for me, Captain Chappelle, here aboard *Santa Catalina*, where we found it. That seems only right. God forbid you ever need to *use* it," he continued lightly, amid chuckles, "but if you do, you have my permission." He hesitated, then went on more seriously. "And if that's ever the case, that you're down to nothing but fifty custom rounds in my fancy, shiny Colt, rest assured that I'll be coming as fast as I can—before you use up all the bullets." There were more appreciative chuckles, but everyone also knew that Matt meant exactly what he said.

CHAPTER
4

Baalkpan
Borno
September 25, 1944

I t was a beautiful, temperate, unusually dry afternoon at the Baalkpan Advanced Training Center (BATC). The haze from the factories surrounding the city was blowing east, away from the bay that separated Baalkpan proper from the installation where Major I'joorka's 1st North Borno Regiment was undergoing its final evaluation maneuvers before deployment east to join the fight against the Holy Dominion. The green regimental flag with a stylized—and very broken—Japanese destroyer and the words 1ST REGT NORTH BORNO INF hand-painted on it flapped in the early-afternoon breeze in the center of the Khonashi troops. About half of them were disconcertingly Grik-like in appearance except for what little coloration was visible beneath the tie-dyed frocks they wore. Clearly the same species as Grik, they were an entirely different race: tiger-striped rust and black instead of the typical brown and dun of the enemy. The other half of the new regiment were humans of ancient Malay descent. All were armed with Baalkpan Arsenal rifled muskets and arrayed in an open but precise skirmish order two ranks deep that extended roughly three hundred yards to either side of the flag, facing the dense jungle to the west.

Commander Alan Letts was there with a small staff to observe these final evolutions—and a little test that had been prepared. He'd come a long way from the admittedly lazy supply officer he'd once been aboard USS *Walker*, and his blooming organizational skills had earned him the duties of Captain Reddy's chief of staff, then Adar's, and finally his current extended stint as acting chairman of the Grand Alliance. His fair skin had always been highly sensitive to the sun, but his responsibilities had aged him more than the climate ever could.

Standing with him was a young lieutenant (jg), little more than a teenager, named Abel Cook. Cook retained the upper-class British accent he'd brought to this world aboard the old S-19, but his blond hair was sun-bleached nearly white, his face tanned, and his blue eyes had seen a lot for his few years. Beside him was his close friend Midshipman Stuart Brassey, on extended loan from the navy of the Empire of the New Britain Isles. His dark hair contrasted with Abel's, but they could've been brothers otherwise. Dominating both boys with his greater height and . . . intimidatingly lethal appearance was Major I'joorka himself, looking almost exactly like a Grik, complete with a full array of teeth, claws, and dark adult crest and tail plumage. Like half his troops, the only visible difference was his coloration—and the calm he projected in the face of a thunderous sound emanating from the jungle beyond the parade ground.

"Please excuse me, Mr. Acting Chairman, but what is that . . . amazingly loud noise?" Abel Cook asked, peering into the jungle and unable to contain himself any longer.

"Not 'acting chairman' much longer, thank God," Commander Letts replied with a tight grin, small new lines showing around his eyes and mouth. He pretended not to hear Abel's question as he also stared at the trees. "Adar's finally on his way back home, where he belongs,"

Slightly frustrated, Abel looked at Stuart, who arched his eyebrows and shrugged, glancing at Major I'joorka. There was another roar in the jungle, closer now, and the 1st North Borno shifted uneasily but held its ground.

"You've done a great job, Major I'joorka. Mr. Cook, Mr. Brassey," Alan said, still ignoring Abel's question. He scratched the back of his left hand absently, rolling up dead skin with his fingernails. "Your troops are outstanding. You've trained them well."

"Thank you, sir," I'joorka said. His English was much improved, but like Lawrence, he still tried to avoid words that required lips. He'd actually spoken a variety of English when Abel and Stuart first met him, being "War Captain" of all of "King" Tony Scott's Khonashi warriors. How Tony Scott, *Walker*'s old coxswain, had been named "king" of a band of combined Grik-like people and humans, hundreds of miles north of Baalkpan through impenetrable, trackless jungle, was a long, weird story in itself. But the result had been new, albeit stranger than usual allies with significant combat experience. All they'd needed was time to learn the standard tactics employed by all Allied armies before they could be plugged in anywhere, ready to fight. "I do . . . hoph the North 'Orno can still get the new 'reechloaders—the Allin-Sil'as—sooner than it gets sent to kill the ene'y," I'joorka urged again.

Alan glanced at Abel, who'd been bugging him mercilessly about that. "I'm doing my best, Major. There're only so many to go around."

"Other regiments and replacements training from the Great South Isle, uh, 'Austraal,' get Allin-Silvas," Abel pointed out.

Alan frowned. "Yeah, but I've told you. They're all going west, to fight the Grik. We make 'em and send 'em off as quick as we can—and there're a lot—but our industry's supposed to be focused only on that theater now. That's partly a matter of distance and logistics, as you know. Maa-ni-la's part of the Union, but sends most of what it produces to the Dom front. And the Empire's making Allin-Silvas now as well. They're supposed to be arming all the troops sent to fight the Doms." He snorted. "You're caught in the middle of a kind of turf war, I guess. We're building a republic here, and that's one of the problems you run into, it seems." He shrugged uncomfortably and sighed, knocking a readyrolled "PIG-cig" out of a thick card box and lighting it with a Zippo. "PIG" was the highly appropriate acronym for the Pepper, Isak, and Gilbert Smoking Tobacco Co. Alan took a drag, coughed, and looked at the offending tube amid a reeking cloud of smoke. "Damn things're gonna kill me," he wheezed. "Some folks say I should *decorate* those idiots for figuring out how to strip that waxy gunk off the local tobacco so it can be smoked." He grimaced. "Others want the little turds up on charges. Especially after we finally found out how they did it." He looked rueful. "That's classified, by the way. No sense causing an uproar when people will keep smoking them anyway, even after they find out." He held his up as proof. "There's still more people chewing tobacco in the fleet and in the army, but I guess half the populations of Baalkpan and Maa-ni-la are hooked on these now, humans and 'Cats both. The 'secret' will get out eventually, but maybe the war will be over by then and Pepper and those damn Mice can just run off and hide."

"What did they cut the wax with?" Abel asked. "I won't tell."

Alan arched an eyebrow at him. "Okay." He paused, then rolled his eyes. "Brontosarry piss." Brontosarries were domesticated sauropods about the size of Asian elephants, used to pull heavily laden carts, primarily. They were notable for their strength and stupidity—and the paint-stripper-like qualities of their urine. "They soak the green leaves with piss to break up the wax and then rinse 'em off with water and dry 'em in a smokehouse." Alan chuckled. "There's nearly as much security around the joint as we've got down at the shipyard. It's too humid to dry them the old-fashioned way, and I guess the smoke helps with the piss smell too . . . a little. Anyway, that's the story, and the whole big secret behind their 'scientific breakthrough.'"

"You're joking," Abel protested. Alan waved his smoldering cigarette under Abel's nose and nodded solemnly. "Oh my God. I can smell it!" Abel exclaimed.

"Returning to the problem at hand"—Brassey nodded at I'joorka—"can't Captain Reddy, as CINC of all Allied Forces, merely command that the First North Borno receive the weapons it needs?"

"Not the way it's set up now," Alan replied. "He can *request* it. He can tell I'joorka what to do with them when he gets them. He can even call the First North Borno to join him in the West—and we'd have to issue modern weapons then. But the representatives of the Republic have voted on the way we're allocating stuff and there's nothing I can do. I hope the rules get more realistic over time, more streamlined, so we can avoid things like this in the future, but the rules are the rules, and the last thing we need to do is break them just to suit us when the ink on the 'Articles' isn't even dry."

"Republics, by their nature, breed factionalism and, uh, 'turf wars' within the greater union," Stuart remarked darkly. "Our empire is much more efficient."

"Maybe now, with Governor-Empress McDonald in charge," Abel jabbed back, forced to take a side. The Empire was a staunch ally but hadn't joined the Union. "It was even worse there before, though, with the squabbling in the courts of directors and proprietors, the so-called Honorable New Britain Company. Open treason and rebellion, collusion with the Doms . . ."

"And too many members of our new Union still believe the Doms are the *Empire's* enemy, not ours," Alan groused. "I expect—I *hope*—things will get sorted out eventually, but right now we've already got large forces, naval, air, and land, fighting the Doms. Forces that a lot of folks think ought to be in the West with Captain Reddy. With all the losses we've had in both theaters, that does cause resentment," he confessed, taking another puff. "We've crammed all these people together from all over the place. People who didn't even know one another *existed* just a few years ago." He shook his head. "They're really trying to get used to that," he added a little wistfully, glancing across the bay where the once quaint city lay—a beautiful city of massive trees and high wooden pagoda-like structures with a good and distinct culture of . . . innocent peacefulness. A city that the vicissitudes of war had turned into a sprawling, ethnically and racially jumbled industrial complex. He wondered whether Adar would even recognize it after the months he'd been away. That thought deeply saddened him. "And they're getting a feel for each other and what it's like to work together," he continued. "I guess it's only natural they'd be a little, well, selfish, for a while." He looked thoughtfully at I'joorka. "You've got former enemies, other . . . tribes, like the Akashi, who you've fought forever, joining with you now. There's got to be some strain?"

"Yes," I'joorka confessed. "It is hard to end old hatreds so quickly." He considered. "It eases the 'strain' that King Scott, who led us to 'ictory against the Akashi, asked they to join us. The Akashi . . . reskect he, honor he—and his . . . asking honors they."

"But *we're* going east," Abel persisted. "The Union won't even arm its own people?" Alan didn't want to point out that to most members of the new Union, I'joorka's people, though already members themselves, were still strangers. Particularly disquieting strangers, given that many of them bore such a striking resemblance to the Grik. Lawrence had been embraced in Baalkpan as the hero he was, regardless of what he looked like, but he'd also been kind of a novelty. And Baalkpan now teemed with soldiers, sailors, factory workers, support personnel, and frankly, opportunists from all over the Alliance who'd never seen Lawrence—or any other Grik-like being— before. The human Khonashis with their dark skin and hair didn't look much different from Imperials of Dom descent, but the others looked like Grik. Period. Alan was concerned to see racial prejudice among increasing numbers of Lemurians for the very first time.

"The First North Borno is going east," Alan agreed, "and will be armed with modern weapons *in* the East. Look, fellas, I'm just running herd on this circus until Adar gets back. I can't wave a magic wand and make things happen like in the old days anymore. I wish I could." He nodded at the troops arrayed beyond. "In the meantime, those may be muzzle-loaders your guys have, but they're rifles. The best we have, of the type. They shoot slower, but they're just as accurate as the new weapons—and maybe more important, they look and feel just like them as well. The first new ones were conversions of those, after all. At least there won't be much of a transition when they do get Allin-Silvas."

The roar in the trees was continuous now, surging and bellowing, echoing yet muted.

Abel turned back to watch. "And the noise?" he asked again, just as a tall, narrow tree quivered and fell forward, finally revealing a squat, ugly shape surrounded by a swirl of blue smoke. It roared louder and crawled over the shattered tree, bounced, then thundered toward the line of infantry. Some of the Khonashi took a step back, but an apparently ancient Lemurian sergeant named Moe bellowed at them to hold the line as he paced behind them. Chasing him was a small "real" Grik called Poky, who carried nothing but a haversack and a notepad of stiff paper. Not many of the Khonashi so much as twitched, however, and wouldn't have even in the face of a "super lizard." This monster should've been even more terrifying since it wasn't a "real" monster they knew how to kill.

"My God," Abel breathed. "It's a tank!"

Alan grinned. "Yeah, I guess. Look it over when it gets here." He chuckled. "It'll take a few minutes. It's not very fast." He looked at I'joorka. "Congratulations, Major. The last regiment we did that to, from Austraal, ran all the way back to the bay and nearly jumped in the water! Your troops are steady enough for just about anything they'll run into."

"Yes, they are," I'joorka agreed, fascinated by the tracked . . . thing, still roaring and clanking toward them. "Sergeant," he called to Moe. "Clear a lane so that . . . tank can get through." Moe sketched a salute.

"It's certainly loud enough," Stuart said doubtfully. "But what is it for, besides breaking small trees and frightening troops in training?"

"What it's *for* is to protect the crews of the two machine guns inside while it advances into enemy fire," Alan explained. "It's only lightly armored, but it'll stop small arms, and even small roundshot from Grik or Dom field guns beyond a couple hundred yards. With tractor treads, it can go just about anywhere—as you've seen. It's loud because it has an unmuffled engine, just like those straight sixes we put in the PTs." The thing rumbled closer, looking like a faceted, riveted turtle shell about sixteen feet long and ten feet wide on caterpillar tracks. The muzzles of two machine guns protruded from sponsons near the front of the shell and a 'Cat stood, half-exposed, from a hatch on top. He wore a leather helmet with ear holes on the sides near the top and a big grin on his face. Alan shook his head. "Whether they'll do any good depends on whether we can solve all the problems with them—and build enough to make a difference. You're looking at a quarter of the operational tanks in the whole Alliance right now, and I'm not sure there'll be any more for quite a while."

"Why?" Abel asked, advancing to look at the machine as it finally churned through the line of troops and rocked to a halt a short distance away. Motionless now, the engine roar was still loud but bearable. Blue smoke wafted away from the rear. The 'Cat on top climbed the rest of the way out of his hatch and saluted. The gathered officers saluted back. "Why?" Abel asked again.

"In case you haven't noticed, there's a war on," Alan replied wryly. "And while that may make a fine argument for building hundreds of these things, there's still a metal shortage. Good steel, in particular. What's left of *Amagi* is just about gone, and we save that for really important stuff. We're getting more and more out of Indiaa now; the Grik foundries and mills we captured had started making some scary decent stuff, and we've improved it even more. We're getting billets of iron and steel for airplane engines, guns, projectiles, bombs, you name it. And we're getting good plate steel from the rolling mills the Grik built to make plate armor for their battlewagons. The trouble is, practically each and every plate our people ship back here is allocated before it even goes to sea. Right now, modern ships have priority. They howled like boiling monkeys when I diverted enough just for the four prototype tanks we built!"

Abel already knew the advantages that armored vehicles might deliver to their ground troops, "might" being the operative word. The thing was big and heavy, and he wasn't sure they'd fought many battles in places the thing could even go, much less contribute to the outcome. Stuart and I'joorka were quick to catch on to the advantages.

"Such a machine, impervious to wounds, could tear right through Grik—or Dom—positions," Stuart said.

"Allowing in'antry to attack through the holes it creates," I'joorka enthused.

"Ah, yeah, that's the idea," Alan agreed. "It's the whole point behind them. But my planners tell me the country we're fighting in right now, and we're liable to be fighting in when we jump across to Africa from Madagascar, is no good for tanks and we're better off focusing on other stuff," he added, confirming Abel's concerns. He looked at Stuart. "And squirreling enough steel away to make enough of them to send against the Doms just isn't going to happen, for the reasons I already mentioned."

"The Ardennes were not considered good tank country either, Mr. Chairman," Abel said, suddenly remembering. "Yet the Germans passed through them to get around the fixed defenses in France. With tanks."

Alan nodded. "Yeah. They had roads, but yeah. And we have to assume the Grik have roads. We know the Doms do. I didn't say I completely *agreed* with my planners. We wouldn't have any tanks at all if I did. But their assessments are considered by the representatives who vote allocations, and they want a whole fleet of *Walker* Class DDs, and the upsize cruisers based on them! Can't say I blame them either, to be honest." He was silent a moment. "Never forget, just like us old destroyermen, Lemurians are first and foremost people of the sea. So are Imperials," he said, looking at Stuart. "They'll always equate control of the sea—and now the air, thank God—with safety for their homes and people. And as this war moves farther and farther from their homes, they're starting to lose some of the urgency *we* think they should feel to eliminate the threat once and for all." He shrugged. "They feel safer now, and that's part of our problem. Even Captain Reddy and the war in the West are far enough away that people here can hardly imagine it. They're still *close* to that war because they're reminded of it every day. They work to support it; their loved ones are fighting—and dying—in it. And the Grik are the 'Ancient Enemy,' so they're still all in." He looked at Stuart. "But the war against the Doms is on the bottom of the world, as far as these folks think. It's understandable if they have a hard time staying 'all in' for that one."

"Understandable, perhaps," Abel almost snapped, looking at I'joorka and the Khonashis he'd fought beside to destroy *Hidoiame*. Whatever their shape, they'd cast their lot with the Union and the Alliance when they, of all people, could've hidden from the wars and watched them pass, regardless who won, with the least inconvenience to themselves and their prior way of life. "But unforgivable that they would deny anything that might help win the war—either war—to whoever might need it."

Alan was silent for a long moment, puffing on his vile PIG-cig, looking thoughtful. Finally, he tossed it away. "Congratulations, Major I'joorka," he finally said. "Your regiment has completed every requirement necessary at the Baalkpan ATC to be declared fully operational, and is now prepared for deployment in all respects. This little display today wasn't really part of the curriculum. It was as much for your benefit as anybody else's, so you'd really know what you've got. Please extend my warmest admiration to your regiment. You have some swell people. Graduation ceremonies will commence at oh nine hundred, the day after tomorrow. They'll be attended by your representatives and a lot of other folks from the city and across the Alliance. After that, you can start a liberty rotation as you see fit. Give 'em a break—but remember to warn your, uh, nonhuman troops to stay in groups." He shook his head. "Sorry I have to say that, and it isn't right, but like I said, folks have to have time to get used to each other." He shifted his gaze from I'joorka to the rest of the regiment, then back to the idling tank. "As we've discussed," he said, "your deployment will most likely be to join General Shinya's Tenth Corps." He smiled faintly. "His 'Army of the Sisters.' And *I* won't forget you when you're down on the bottom of the world, any of you, and I'll do my damnedest to make sure nobody else does either."

"Army of the Sisters"
September 26, 1944

A light, ragged volley of musket fire clattered from the trees bordering the brightly lit, rutted trail twelve miles south of the Dominion village of Kotopaxi, ninety miles north of Chimborazo. Most of the shots were wild, but one 'Cat in Captain Blas-Ma-Ar's Second of the 2nd (Lemurian-Amer-i-caan) Marines snapped a curse and clutched his arm. Blas made a loud *snick-snick* sound and pointed at the white gun smoke while the dark-haired, dark-skinned trooper riding beside her raised a hand, halting the column. Immediately, a squad of former Imperial lancers, now dragoons, led by Blas's First Sergeant Spon-Ar-Aak ("Spook"), unlimbered their carbines and spurred their horses directly at the ambush. Dingy, yellow-clad forms rose from their hiding places and bolted downslope, clearly hoping to lose their pursuers in the dense timber and deadfall. They didn't stand a chance. Spook's dragoons had amassed a lot of practice at this sort of thing over the last few days, and Blas would be surprised if any ambushers survived. "Corps-'Cat," she called, summoning aid for her wounded Marine as the woods below began echoing with shots.

"They try to nibble us to death," proposed Teniente Pacal, the swarthy man beside her, in charge of the company

of Sister Audry and Arano Garcia's "Vengadores" attached
to the sadly diminished "A" Company of the 2nd. Blas's
mission was to make contact with the bulk of what remained of the Dom Army and probe to discover its size
and disposition before the rest of the Allied forces arrived.
Shinya would then decide whether to attack immediately
or maneuver, possibly even attempting to simply cut the
Dom army off and starve it to death.

"They nibble with busted teeth," Blas replied contemptuously. The ambushes had been nearly constant since
they'd descended back below the timberline from the high,
cold mountain road above, and though they'd taken several
casualties, their attackers had been practically exterminated every time. Still, it was a nuisance, particularly after
the freezing, windy misery of their high passage. For three
days they'd traveled a rough, rocky trace, little more than
a game trail, which might've been difficult to follow if not
for all the abandoned military equipment strewn along the
path. At least for the first twenty miles or so. After that
there was less equipment, but a lot more bodies. Men and
animals, wounded in the battle for Fort Defiance, had been
left to die where they dropped, freezing hard as stone at
night and scavenged by carrion eaters during the day.
There were other bodies too: men apparently "sacrificed"
to appease the twisted God of Don Hernan de Devina
Dicha and the "Holy Dominion" he served after the defeat
of his "Army of God." Or perhaps they'd been examples?
Don Hernan was very fond of providing examples of what
befell those who didn't please him. Together, the trail of
accoutrements and corpses bore an eloquent if mute testimony to the precipitous retreat so recently effected. A
retreat that was increasingly looking like an escape.

"But they do slow us down," Blas added bitterly. "Makin'
us hesitate, even if we don't always deploy, in case the Doms
only run off to suck our dragoons to a trap." She blinked
at her companion as Pacal looked back at the Lemurian
female, a little nervously as usual. Sometimes still called
"Blossom" behind her back by her old Navy pals, Blas had
a reputation as one of the fiercest fighters in what General
Tomatsu Shinya increasingly referred to as "the Army of
the Sisters." And most of her reputation had been built

killing men like Pacal. The Vengadores were former soldiers of the Holy Dominion, captured after their defeat on New Ireland, who'd been converted to true Christianity—and the cause of destroying their former masters—by the tireless, gentle ministrations of their new spiritual and military leader, Sister Audry. She'd been a Benedictine nun, brought to this world aboard the old S-19, and constituted one of the three "sisters" that gave the army its unofficial new name. But Pacal knew Blas had a ferocious temper and it had been building for days as the ambushes nagged them—and they viewed the handiwork of his former countrymen.

"An' we can't just run off an' leave Spook to fend for himself if it *is* a trap." Blas snorted. "Which keeps us goin' at a crawl. So, gettin' many of us 'er not, they're still accomplishin' somethin'." She nodded forward. "But what?" Scouts sent ahead of the column, apparently too few to trip the ambushes, consistently reported nothing in their path. "You'd think the closer we got to Koto-paaxi, we'd finally run into a defense, some kinda hasty fort, or at least a bigger rearguard. There ain't no place for the Doms to go, past Koto-paaxi. The maps we captured show no roads between there an' Popayan," Blas said, referring to the next large village to the north, northwest, "and that evil baas-tard Don Hernaan has to know he can't escape by way of Quito, to the west. Our navy took a beatin' at Maalpelo, but his was practically rubbed out. He *can't* get away by sea." Her quiet rant, something she did fairly often in Pacal's experience, was interrupted by a growing flurry of shots deep in the woods that went on for several minutes. When it finally tapered off, there was a lot of indecipherable shouting (quite normal), then silence for a moment—until a crackly drone began to rise, echoing in the trees and off the distant mountains.

"About daamn time!" Blas exclaimed. "A plane! Finally! Lazy baas-tards."

Allied aircraft had been having a lot of trouble getting over the mountains from their bases on a couple of coastal lakes and Guayakwil Bay. The few Grikbirds that had remained with Don Hernan's army—large, flying creatures that looked like colorful Grik with wings—had apparently retreated with him, but in some cases, the mountains in the region jutted higher than Allied carburetors—or aircrews—could breath. And high altitude had been an increasingly evident problem for Lemurian aviators. Apparently, 'Cats required more oxygen than humans, and it had finally been determined that they risked hypoxia at anything much over eight thousand feet. Debilitating effects were more likely the higher they went and the longer they lingered there. That discovery explained a great deal, going all the way back to some of Tikker's high-altitude . . . antics . . . in the old PBY. But even the lower mountain passes were prohibitively dangerous, swirling with treacherous winds that could easily fling a plane out of control. And then, of course, there was the cold. Blas wore a peacoat over her tie-dyed combat frock and was *still* cold, even back down among the trees. How men like Pacal stood it without fur was beyond her. And flying even higher in an open cockpit must be pure hell. She looked up and shivered involuntarily.

"Course," she said, "until we find a lake 'er somethin' on the east side o' the mountains big enough to operate planes off of, for scoutin' or attackin', I guess I shouldn't gripe when one makes it across." She and Pacal and a number of troopers behind her scanned the sky for the aircraft heralded by the growing roar of its engine. They couldn't see it for the trees, but it should find the six-hundred-man-and-'Cat column easily enough.

"There!" several voices cried as a bright blue-and-white shape swooped by, north to south, low over the trees. It was a Nancy flying boat, with its distinctive fuselage, high wing, and pusher-mounted engine. It pulled up and banked to the east, coming around for another pass. When it flew over again, a bright wooden tube with a long streamer fluttered down near the head of the column. Then, with a waggle of its wings, the plane turned to the south.

"Must'a come up the Quito road from the sea," Blas said excitedly as a pair of Pacal's men dismounted to retrieve the message where it landed on the west side of the road a short distance into the trees. "They'll have flown right over the Doms at Koto-paaxi an' seen everything! They'll be headin' back to report to Shinya now."

A Vengadore approached with the message tube and

Blas took it, twisting out the plug. She pulled a fine piece of Imperial paper covered with a ragged scrawl from inside, briefly appalled by the waste. Paper was still "new" to her, and the stuff made in Baalkpan was rough and brittle. Of course, the Impies had been making paper for maybe two hundred years. She shrugged and tried to read the tortuously printed English on the page. Suddenly, with a snarl of rage, she shredded the sheet and hurled the fragments to flutter away on the light breeze.

"What is wrong, Capitan Blas? What has happened?" Pacal asked, alarmed.

Blas glared at him. "That slimy, creepy, murderin' *freak* is get away!" she hissed, her English slipping. "Iss annaar gikaa suk chik-aash . . . !" She stopped and took a deep breath, blinking apologetically. "Don Hernaan's got away *again*!"

"How?" Pacal asked, equally upset if not as furious.

"How should I know? Maybe he snatched the feet of his daamn flyin' Grikbirds an' flew the hell away!"

Pacal nodded at one of the fragments of paper lying nearby. "What did that say?"

Blas took another deep breath, blinking such a wide range of conflicting emotions that Pacal couldn't possibly decipher them. "Koto-paaxi is just like Chim-boraazo: burned out to the ground. They must'a done it three or four days ago, I bet, before we came 'round that last high turn in the road, or we'd have seen the fire at night or smoke in the day. We'd have come faster then, piss-aant ambushes or not," she added with a self-punishing tone.

"Was that all?"

Blas looked at Pacal. "It was the same as Chim-boraazo," she repeated. "There was no life, an' the same . . . 'decorations' was seen." She said the last with her lip raised over sharp canines. As far as they knew, every soul in or around Chimborazo had been murdered or herded away, and two hundred people, including Don Hernan's General Nerino, had been impaled and left for the Allies to discover. Lieutenant Pacal crossed himself as Sister Audry had taught his people, but quickly recovered. "We can still follow him."

"I'm not worried about *followin'* him. He's down in the trees now, an' he's got a daamn army. He'll leave a trail

like a land-walkin' mountain fish through a forest. But it'll
lead us right where he wants us too. Daamn! He must've
kept on nor' nor'east, roads or not." She blinked rapidly,
thinking. "With guides to show him the way, I bet. If Don
Hernaan let anybody at Chim-boraazo or Koto-paaxi live,
it was to be guides," she added, looking at Pacal almost
accusingly. "An' we got zip."

"My apologies, Capitan," Pacal ventured, "but all the
Vengadores are from the south, near Valparaiso, and never
even knew what lay fifty miles beyond our place of birth . . .
before we became *soldados*."

Blas snorted, then sighed. "I know. Not your fault. An'
even the Guayakaans don't know nothin' about the land
past these mountains. Same thing with them." She swore.
"So now he's on the loose, an' we're gonna need our own
guides to get around an' stop him before he gets to Popayan!
He makes it there, the road'll be open all the way back to
his daamn 'Temple City,' that 'New Gra-naada'! We'll never
catch his sorry ass then."

"Perhaps there will be survivors at Kotopaxi," Pacal encouraged. "Some may have escaped who can show us a way."

"I hope you're right, but I'm runnin' out of sunshiny
thoughts." Blas stirred impatiently, uncomfortably in her
saddle. She'd loved horses ever since the first time she rode
one in the New Britain Isles, but the saddles, though practical, were built for humans and made her tail hurt. "I want
after that baas-tard, an' even Gen'raal Shinya does too,
now. But we gotta know how to chase him!"

"Cap-i-taan Blas," called a Lemurian NCO, detailed
to picket the tree line Spook had entered with his dragoons. "First Sergeant Spook's comin' out."

Figures on horseback picked their way slowly through
the trees until they were in the clear, but to Blas's surprise
they stopped at the edge and turned back to face the woods.
Spook continued on, spurring his mount toward the front
of the column where Blas and Pacal were waiting.

"Report," Blas ordered, curious at his self-conscious
blinking. Spook was as brash as they came and uncertainty
wasn't one of his distinguishing personality traits. "Did
the Doms get away?" she asked.

"Not a one," he said, his blinking turning indignant, "but

we *did* get some surprised. Ran into some . . . other folks who'd already blocked the Doms' retreat. Served 'em up right handy for us too. Trouble is, we didn't know the difference between 'em at first an' shot 'em up a bit before they got it through to us that they *wasn't* Doms. . . ."

Blas was taken aback. "Other folks? What are they? Who?" she demanded. Spook shrugged and gestured back at the trees, where there was suddenly a great deal of movement within them as figures—hundreds of them—neared the cut. "You tell me," Spook said. "But they ain't Doms. Even after we aacci-dentay shot a few, they didn't shoot back."

The dragoons were backing their horses toward the column now, carbines at the ready, as people—humans—emerged into the sunlight. All were darker-skinned than the average Impie, just like Doms, so it was easy to see what caused Spook's confusion. But most wore ragged clothing or animal skins belted around their waists instead of any kind of uniform. A few were armed with muskets, but most carried bows and arrows or long spears. Nearly all had some kind of crude sword. At the cries of numerous surprised NCOs, the entire Allied column wheeled and presented their weapons.

"Hey!" Spook said.

"Hold fire!" Blas shouted in that carrying, Lemurian way. "Hold fire!" she repeated more softly, edging her mount to the right, closer to the approaching men.

"*Capitan!*" Pacal cautioned.

"I suspect it's all right, Lieut-en-aant Pacal," Blas said slowly, wonderingly. "They didn't attack the dragoons, an' I think it's likely they're the same people Gener-aal Shinya's been expectin' . . . for some time now. He's based a lot of his straa-ti-gee for this whole campaign on 'em, as a matter o' fact. Fred Reynolds an' Kari-Faask told him about 'em." She shook her head. "Honest, though, I didn't think to see 'em here—or so soon, I guess. If we ever even met 'em at all," she added, then looked at his uncomprehending face and grinned. "Come on. I'll prob'ly need you to talk to 'em."

More and more strangers emerged from the trees as Blas, Pacal, and Spook, along with several of Pacal's men, moved to meet them, joining the dragoons that still formed an increasingly insignificant barrier between them and the uneasy column. They raised no weapons and made no threatening moves, but their faces were hard and inscrutable. "How many *is* there?" Blas asked Spook.

"No idea, Cap-i-taan. There's already more than we seen in the woods. Hard to tell in there."

A group of about a dozen trotted through the middle of the gathering mass of men. *Not all men,* Blas suddenly realized, noticing a large number of women for the first time. Most of those didn't appear armed with anything more threatening than long knives, but they were just as lean and rough-looking as the males. Quite a few carried quiet, stoic infants in some kind of pack arrangement on their backs. The dozen kept jogging lithely toward her, eating ground in a long-legged lope she had to admire, oblivious to stones and fallen trees. Finally before her—not even breathing hard in the rarefied air after an exertion that would've left her gasping—about half the men stopped and bowed on one knee, staring at the ground at her horse's feet. They immediately began babbling something even she knew wasn't "Spaan-ish"—the "official" language of the Dominion—or even the language of the Guayakans. Half the men didn't bow, but stared respectfully up at her. These, she noted, invariably wore wood or bone crosses dangling from their necks. But they weren't the twisted, brutal-looking crosses of the Doms. They were just like the one Sister Audry wore—and those that were painted on the helmets of her Vengadores.

"Well, *say* something," Blas told Pacal through her teeth, clenched in a grin.

"Ah . . . *Hola*," Pacal said simply, utterly at a loss.

The column finally resumed its march toward Kotopaxi, moving quicker now that its forest flanks were suddenly, so unexpectedly secured by their new "friends," two of whom now rode at its head alongside Blas and Pacal. They hadn't been even slightly hesitant to mount the horses they'd been given, which suggested they had experience with the animals. One was an older man named Ximen, his hair and beard streaked with white, and he kept up an incessant, apparently happy dialogue with Teniente Pacal, occasionally touching the crude wooden cross bouncing against his bare, hairy chest with calloused fingers clearly accustomed to rough use. The other man, younger, named something that sounded like "Ixtli," continued to stare at Blas with a look of satisfaction as he too clutched a necklace charm from time to time. The difference was, his object was shaped in the likeness of what looked to Blas like one of the small feral cats she'd seen roaming loose in the Empire of the New Britain Isles, colored black.

She remained confused, and even apprehensive, considering how quickly they'd all just come together and proceeded onward as if the meeting had been planned in advance. But she had little concern that the "auxiliaries" her column had abruptly collected were other than what they appeared to be. There were quite enough of them to have badly mauled her force, at least, if they'd been enemies, and Spook eventually confessed to having actually been a bit unnerved by how savagely they'd fallen on the Doms in the woods. No, they were the "real deal," the very rebels Shinya had hoped they'd meet, but Blas supposed she'd been skeptical that they truly existed, and now to have them just . . . pitch in, so casually . . .

"Say, what's he keep lookin' at me like that for? And why'd he and the others"—slightly more than half of the hundreds of "wood people" had taken a knee when Ixtli turned to address them after Pacal and Ximen had spoken for a moment—"drop down an' stare at the ground?" she finally asked Pacal, but it was Spook who replied.

"Don't you remember nothin' about the people who . . . sorta helped Fred an' Kari when they an' that Anson fella escaped the Doms?" Spook shook his head and spat a stream of yellowish Aryaal tobacco juice, staining the white fur on his chin. "You're always so busy fightin' an' makin' my life miserable, you never pay attention to nothin' else," he complained, which elicited a bark of laughter from her, the first in a long while.

"I musta missed somethin'," she confessed. "I guess Gen-raal Shinya will sort it out." They'd sent a deputation of their new acquaintances back toward Chimborazo under guard, with a report of how they'd met.

"No need. I got the dope." Spook nodded at the older

man. "He's a . . . 'good' Chiss-chin, just like Sister Audry an' our friendly Doms. Or *mostly* like 'em, maybe. They been fightin' the 'bad' Doms for a long time. An' even though they don't believe alike, they've teamed up with Ixtli's pals, another bunch called 'Jagaar-istas,' er somethin', who been fightin' 'em too. But they think cats—which we look like—are, hell, I don't know, some kinda . . ." He paused, considering. "What's the backward o' 'demons'? Anyway, that's what they think we are. Thought Kari-Faask was."

"With great respect, we don't all think that, by any means," the younger man suddenly said in near-perfect English, almost knocking Blas out of her saddle in surprise.

"Hey! You speak Amer-i-caan!" she accused.

"Of course. My people always knew we would have to work with the Empire or"—Ixtli smiled—"others, in order to secure our freedom. You know Capitan Anson?" he asked by way of reply.

"Daamn! Why'd you . . ." Blas blinked. "We know *of* him," she deflected.

"Doubtless through communication with the Kari-Faask you mentioned," Ixtli surmised. "I am glad to hear that she escaped. Those who had her *do* believe as you say, but the tale of her and her human friend—and the opportunity they represented—spread far and wide. As for Capitan Anson, he and others of his kind taught me his speech for several years, when they visited our people."

"Guy gets around," Spook muttered.

"So it seems," Blas agreed. She looked at Ixtli. "We can talk about that later. So what *do* you believe?"

"In one true God," he answered promptly. "The same as our Christian friends. Only fringe elements of our faith have adhered to older . . . interpretations this last century or more. But we also believe God's son came to another world, the one we were all cast away from, as a man—thus our shape." He indicated himself. "On *this* world, the 'Christ' appeared in the form of the *ocelotl*—the jaguar." He shrugged. "And *left* this world for the one we came from." He rubbed his chin. "Which happened first, none can say, and it really has no bearing." He looked at her intently, gazing at her strongly feline face. "But you and your people are proof to *us* that he left his children here, his *ocelomeh*." He gestured back at the column. "His warriors."

"I've heard a lot of things . . . ," Spook began incredulously, but Blas shushed him. Pacal was looking at them, a small smile touching his lips.

"I don't suppose the particulars really are very important just now," Blas began.

"No, Capitan Blas," Pacal agreed. "The pertinent point at present is that we now have the 'growing' army General Shinya so desired." He waved at the trees. "Señor Ximen assures me that more of his people will come. Many more." He ventured a small smile. "And we now also have the guides and scouts—you so recently despaired of—that we require to bring the evil Don Hernan to heel!"

Blas nodded, but looked at Ixtli, still perplexed. "Then . . . if all your people, even the Jagaar-istas"—she glanced at Pacal—"an' even some of my troopers, are all the children of Christ . . : why'd you bow to me? I mean . . ." She stopped, still clearly flustered by that perhaps more than anything.

Ixtli smiled. "The Christians among us would join your alliance in the fight you make. Their Christ is a sweet spirit who taught love and forgiveness. Those who follow him fight just as hard as we, but it is more to restore that understanding of Him across the Dominion than for any other reason. My people have been persecuted far longer than theirs. We were the first to be sacrificed, enslaved, and fed to the monsters of the land and air who serve the evil Temple. Only in my lifetime did we join forces with the Christians to defy our common enemy." He paused as if trying to decide how to explain. "We bowed to you because we came to *you* and your *Saan-Kakja* in particular," he simply said at last, then smiled more broadly at her consternation. "*Of course* we have learned the name of your own highest official here. In a country that would slay us out of hand to feed its pets or placate a false God, it has long meant our lives to learn all we can. But the Jaguar Warriors would fight for you and Saan-Kakja specifically if we could. We remain more closely aligned with the *ocelotl* than the Christ because we think that you, like we, fight foremost to punish and destroy the Dominion, not so? We fight for revenge."

"Huh," Blas said. "Daamn." She sighed. "Well, just so long as we're on the same side. I can't speak for Gen'raal Shinya, an' we're not exac'ly pals just now," she confessed, reflecting a lingering bitterness over the way Shinya had used her battalion at Fort Defiance, "but one way or other, I'll work to get your people better sorted an' better armed. I'm sure Gen'raal Shinya'll get that straight with the fellas you sent to him. But if you're with us, you're with us all. You can't pick an' choose who you latch onto, see? We all gotta work together, an' that means you gotta learn the chain of command. My immediate superior's an Impie named Col-nol James Blair. Above him is Gen'raal Shinya. High Ahd-mi-raal Harvey Jenks is CINCEAST, but that don't hardly signify right now, since he's with a busted ship, an' Saan-Kakja an' Governor-Empress Rebecca McDonald are with the army. That's the way it is, though, an' we all gotta follow the orders they cook up whether we like 'em or not." She blinked questioningly at him, but when Ixtli made no response, she leaned back in her saddle, wrenching her tail to the side. "Now," she continued in a lower voice, "past all them, far as I'm concerned, is Cap-i-taan Reddy. Nobody's orders get between him an' me, if it comes down to it, an' you may have to make a choice with that in mind someday. But of all those I counted, I don't think you need to worry about any of 'em ever goin' soft on the Doms," she assured. "So, in the meantime, sure, you can work for me direct. Let's start by finishin' up clearin' the road to Koto-paaxi, then make sure what's left of the town is safe for our army to move up to. Then we'll work—together—to figure out how we're gonna catch Don Hernaan."

**The Caribbean
September 26, 1944**

"Heave, dammit!" gasped Lieutenant (jg) Fred Reynolds, pulling on a rope for all he was worth. He slipped in the loose white sand and wound up on his back, the fierce sun searing his already sun- and windburned face. He staggered back up with a curse and threw his weight back on the line.

"I *do*, daamn it!" snapped Ensign Kari-Faask in reply, blowing foamy sweat off her furry upper lip, her tail swishing indignantly as she strained on the same rope behind him. "Quit yellin' at me!" Slowly, the waterlogged PB-1B *Nancy* slid a little farther from the choppy water of the lagoon, up the beach, and toward the overhanging trees. The block and tackle secured to a mighty palmlike trunk squeaked petulantly, as if protesting the need to add its advantage to their efforts. "Plane wouldn't be so heavy if we'd did this yester'dy, like I wanted," she hissed. "Now the leakin', seepin' daamn thing's all fulla' water!"

"I'm not yelling at you," Fred huffed, "and it was as good as sunk half an hour after we set it down. What do you want me to do? Shoot more drain holes in it? We've got to hide it before another Dom ship comes nosing around. Lucky the first one didn't see it!"

"Which I said yester'dy," Kari reminded sourly, "before

we ever *seen* a Dom ship that might'a seen us, an' before the daamn plane weighed as much as that useless, rusty-ass ol' ship you hadda go gawk at!"

"Okay! Okay! Just pull, wilya? I had to look, and now we have to do this. C'mon, let's at least *try* to pull at the same time! One . . . two . . . *heave!*" The plane shifted several more feet, water gushing from several holes someone else had shot in the hull.

They'd been on the island—with no idea which one; it wasn't on any chart they'd brought—for three days, and the odyssey that brought them there across the trackless wilderness of the upper South American continent, the very heart of the "Holy Dominion," had been grueling and nerve-racking enough to rival many of their previous adventures. They'd spent their first day ashore dead asleep, wrapped in oilskins against the sun and bugs, their exhausted plane grounded on the shallow bottom of a small lagoon on the north side of the island. Fortunately, they'd cleared the hull of all supplies, weapons, and other equipment—including their precious wireless transmitter and emergency generator—before they dropped, and the Nancy sank only a foot and a half before it touched the sand. Gentle waves kept the plane shoved close to shore regardless of the tide. Fairly secure they wouldn't lose the plane, they'd employed the second day, against Kari's loud objections, exploring the jungle-shrouded, comma-shaped hump of land they'd reached, barely a hundred miles northeast of a major Dom seaport on the Atlantic coast.

The place had one particularly interesting feature protruding from the water off the southern tip of the "comma," that Fred had seen from the air and wanted to inspect immediately; specifically, the horribly rusted skeleton of a large, iron-hulled ship beached in the shallows. Any such discovery was always a source of amazement because as far as they knew, there was only one way a ship like that could be on this world; the same way they'd come—however that was. Fred was intensely curious about it. He was no expert, but it looked like an old collier to him. He wished he knew whose it had been and what had happened to its crew. When they finally picked their way as close as they could, armed with pistols, Blitzerbugs, and cutlasses in case they ran into anything that wanted to eat them, they found that even though the hulk rested close to shore, they couldn't reach it without a boat. And even if they had one, they probably wouldn't find anything of value. The ship had probably been there, disintegrating, for at least twenty or thirty years. Fred had been very disappointed.

Their next priority had been to find water, and discover if they shared the place with any people—or unpleasant creatures. The daylong search revealed no permanent habitation, though there was evidence that people came to visit from time to time. Judging by the junk on the beach, they probably came to strip wires and fittings, and tear hunks off the strange old ship. Nothing bigger than mosquitoes bothered them as they crept through the jungle, but small as it was, the island was still big enough to hide all sorts of monsters they might not discover at once. With their experience with such things, it was easy for them to stay alert. They didn't find any springs, and as low as the island sat, they doubted they would, but several unreliable-looking rain puddles turned up during their search. The water wasn't very appetizing, but it would do for now. Still, they began to suspect that any extended stay might prove unpleasant. On the plus side, the lagoon teemed with fish that were easily caught or trapped, so food shouldn't be a problem. At least in the short term. Fred resolved to rig something to catch rain and figure out how to explore the mystery ship further—if they decided to stay.

That was a choice already looming large in their minds. They had fuel for maybe another hundred, hundred and fifty miles, but the vast expanse of unknown ocean that had spread out, unbroken to the far horizon, had given Fred pause, and compelled him to set down and consider what they ought to do next. Their self-appointed mission was to contact "Los Diablos Del Norte," the "other Americans" apparently stranded on this world in the late 1840s, who existed beyond (and had apparently grown strong enough to pose a threat to) the Dominion. They'd been represented to them by a man who called himself "Captain Anson." He'd saved their lives and encouraged them to believe his people and theirs might join forces against the Dominion. He'd also told them that a major naval defeat inflicted on the Doms in the vicinity of the bizarre "pass of fire," a strange navigable strait through where Costa Rica ought to be, would signal his people to contact the Grand Alliance. Yet, in the aftermath of the Battle of Malpelo, probably the largest naval battle this world's Pacific Ocean ever hosted, that contact hadn't come, and Fred and Kari had taken it upon themselves to contact *them*.

The flight had been a nearly two-thousand-mile endurance test, half of which they'd flown all by themselves. Two other planes, carrying extra fuel to replace their own heavy load as they used it, had escorted them as far as they could, sending frequent observations back to Orrin Reddy by wireless. One of the reasons he'd finally let them go was their assurance that, even if they cracked up, they'd carry out the deepest scout of the inner Dominion to date. But they didn't see much to report through the dense jungle canopy once they left the high mountains behind, other than a few towns or small cities. The largest of these often surrounded roughly stacked pyramid shapes sometimes higher than the trees around them. Fred and Kari had both seen what kind of gruesome . . . activities were performed at places like that. But such towns, and the cropland surrounding them, were essentially just bare spots in the vast jungle. Doubtless there were roads beneath the trees, leading in significant directions, but they couldn't see them. The towns still might be important, though, as objectives for a march, or just to help update their understanding of the interior. Soon, however, they couldn't reliably report even that in real time. The farther they flew from Puerto Viejo, the worse their comm became. Sometimes, at night, they could bounce a clear signal over the mountains, with their best guess of their position. The other two planes set down with them on often dangerously small, claustrophobic lakes, to transfer supplies. And they'd camped on some very frightening shores, with spine-tingling . . . noises in the darkness around them. Sometimes they saw villages and people, and landed as far from them as they could, but they knew they'd been seen. All they could do was hope the locals couldn't round up any Dom troops to search for them before they lit out the following day. As far as they knew, the Doms had nothing like radio or even telegraphy, so they could outfly news of their sighting and no one should be looking for them the next time they set down.

Twice, their luck ran out. The first time was when they were attacked by a half dozen startled Grikbirds kiting over a particularly grubby-looking town for no apparent reason. The Grikbirds managed to tear up one plane before the others could shoot them down or chase them off. Fortunately for Fred and Kari, they'd already transferred all the supplies from the Nancy they lost, but it was probably small consolation for its crew. The plane went down in thick jungle and burned. The second time, the last time they set down in company with their escort, they overflew a village with a Dom garrison when they swept in to land on a very narrow lake that was probably better described as a fat place in a river. The garrison didn't come after them by land or boat, either of which might've caught them, but must've known they'd have to turn around and take off the way they came in. It was waiting the next morning, the fifth of their ordeal, firing volleys as they took to the air where the lake narrowed down near the village. Neither plane was seriously damaged, but both took a few holes. That was when their final escort waggled its wings and flew away to the southwest. Fred and Kari hoped they'd made it, but from that point on they were alone.

After that, they had no reason to land again. They had all the fuel they were going to get and they'd burn it in one long flight. They slowly climbed to ten thousand feet to muffle the sound of their engine as best they could. Kari got fuzzy after a while, but she wasn't flying. They turned due north and flew for several hours, Kari occasionally dropping a hose in a fuel can and pumping its contents up into the main tank in the wing. Finally, the tank was full one more time, but Kari had thrown the last of their cans out over the jungle. About then, the green sea of trees below turned blue and they'd crossed out over the Caribbean, becoming the first members of their alliance, their "nation," to ever see it on this world.

They traveled in a generally northwesterly direction, keeping the distant smear of Central America on the western horizon. Fred concentrated on flying and adjusting his course and Kari stared through her Impie telescope, looking for ships. They didn't see any for most of the day, not until it became clear that the far-off land was reaching back for them and it dawned on them that they must be getting close to some of the seaports that Anson had implied would be on this coast, near El Paso del Fuego. A few ships were seen then, and, judging they had to be Doms, Fred turned north once more.

The land abruptly reached for them again and Fred nearly overflew the biggest city they'd seen yet, complete with a pair of pyramid shapes and a bustling harbor. He turned east. By then their fuel was getting low and the plane was just as tired as they were. And there hadn't been the slightest trace of the people they'd set out to meet. Only then did Fred truly begin to realize how utterly idiotic their scheme had been. Orrin had tried to tell them; everybody had. Fred thought he had an edge over Kari when it came to geographical sophistication. She—all her people—still couldn't really grasp how big the world was. But she had that excuse. He should've known better. Setting out on a lark to find the mysterious "other Americans" had seemed like a good idea, and he'd actually expected to succeed. Kari trusted him because of his confidence. Now that they'd gone the distance, he finally knew how stupid he'd been.

It was in that state of mind that he'd spotted the island—and the wreck. Both were uncomfortably close to a large population of Doms, but by then his confidence that they'd find friends, or even another island, was utterly shot. He couldn't risk pushing on until they were forced down in the middle of the ocean for lack of fuel. And he wasn't afraid for himself. If something happened to him, those were the breaks. This whole stunt had been his idea and he was prepared to accept the consequences. He was afraid for Kari, though. She was his very best friend in the world and, convinced their "mission" was a bust, he wouldn't risk her life by pressing on into an even more hopeless situation. He couldn't.

So here they were, and finally, to top everything off, that morning they'd awoken to the sight of a distant sail that drew inexorably closer for several hours before finally, suddenly, hauling away to the east. They had no idea whose it was, but it almost had to be the Doms, and whatever they decided to do wouldn't matter at all if they didn't get the plane out of sight.

"One more hard pull, Kari," Fred wheezed. "We nearly got it!" The Nancy was under the trees now, with only its tail sticking out. But the tail was painted with bright white and red stripes, clearly visible from a long way off. If they could just get it a little farther, then cover it with a pile of palmlike fronds they'd cut that looked like giant whisk brooms, it should do well enough.

"Daamit!" Kari groaned after their final effort, pitching down in the sand. She lay there panting for a moment, then rolled over to look at him. Fred was lying beside her, up on one elbow and staring out to sea. "I near bust myself that time!" she groaned. The water pouring out of the plane pattered in the sand. "But you right. It'd be just as heavy if we done it yester'dy."

"Maybe," Fred said grimly, "but *you* were right. We should've done it anyway." He nodded out to sea, rising to his feet, and churned through the sand to the pile of fronds. A ship, perhaps the same they'd seen that morning, was approaching the lagoon from the east. Just a couple of miles away, they saw that it was a side-wheel steamer—like the Doms and Impies both used—but it was approaching under sail alone, its boiler cold. "Quick!" Fred said, tossing fronds to lean against the plane. "Maybe they haven't spotted us!" Kari jumped to help. In just a few minutes, they had the battered Nancy well hidden, and they scurried a short distance away where they'd piled all their gear, to watch.

"Uh-oh!" Fred murmured. "We forgot something!" Kari immediately knew what he meant. There was a damp, concave track leading from the water, across the beach, and directly to the hidden plane. She started to jump up, to race down and erase the track as well as possible, but Fred grabbed her arm. "Too late!" he snapped angrily. "They'd be bound to see us out there now, if they didn't already."

"They'll see the track!"

"Sure, but they'll think it was a boat, and maybe it's gone." He shook his head. "I'm such an idiot! Next time we land on a deserted island and you want to do something practical when I'm hot to go sightseeing, just punch me in the nose and take charge!"

"You bet."

Fred picked up his Blitzerbug SMG, blew sand out of it, and handed the other one to Kari. "They're not going to get us again," he said simply.

"Nope," Kari agreed, dragging an oilskin bag closer to her. Inside were six grenades. "It all goes in the pot, we make sure to blow the plane?"

Fred nodded. "The transceiver too. Or we can bury it now. One less thing to remember when the time comes—while making sure they don't get us either." Kari nodded, and they quickly wrapped the heavy wooden box containing their wireless gear and buried it in the sand. "Too bad we can't set it up an' send a last 'so long,'" she said as they finished.

"Yeah. Too bad." Fred shrugged. "Probably wouldn't hear us anyway." They settled back to watch the approaching ship. It didn't appear to be a Dom naval vessel, at least. The sails were plain, unadorned canvas, and there was only a small red flag with a crooked golden cross fluttering from the stern. The ship was armed, its sides pierced for half a dozen guns, but it only stood to reason that any ship on this world that could be armed, would be.

"Dom merchie," Fred definitively proclaimed at last. "Just like those troopships we busted off Scapa Flow."

"Which bust *us* too," Kari reminded. They'd been shot down by massed musket fire while throwing handheld bombs at the things. Fred winced at the memory. Not only had Kari been seriously wounded, but they'd both wound up in the *water.* Fortunately, the voracious fish hadn't had time to gather before *Walker* picked them up.

"Yeah. Hey, what's it doing?" The ship had reached the entrance to the lagoon, but there it suddenly dropped anchor and all its canvas began to vanish as its crew swarmed in the rigging. To their growing amazement, no boat was lowered, nor did it look like anyone on board was paying the slightest attention to the beach. Soon, to their even greater bewilderment, the ship's topmasts and upper yards were struck down to the deck. "Hey!" Fred suddenly blurted. "They're *hiding*!"

"Must be," Kari agreed. "But who is they hidin' from?"

"Beats me."

They watched the strange ship, practically radiating tension judging by the behavior of its crew, for more than an hour. In that time, the only things that seemed to notice them were biting insects and some strange purple crayfish-looking things that occasionally marched up, bold as scorpions, and spit tiny streams of stinging fluid at them. The stings weren't bad, but they left a rash, and Fred and Kari amused themselves by smashing the arrogant little crustaceans with sticks before they came within the roughly three-foot range of their weird little squirters. "Mr. Bradford would love these guys," Fred murmured, whacking another one. "He'd have already figured out everything about them, and named 'em too."

"They like little kinds o' those spiderlobsters that was seen on Talaud Island, before it blew its top," Kari said, scratching her arm under the fur. "I bet they squirt bugs an' small critters to stun 'em, then eat 'em. Maybe enough of 'em squirt us, we get stunned too."

"Say, you could be right. All the more reason to mash 'em." Fred looked thoughtful. "Let's call 'em 'scraypions'! We discovered 'em, and we've never gotten to name anything before."

"Why call 'em that?"

Fred was about to explain his play on words, when he noticed several things at once. First, there was a sudden increase of activity aboard the ship, which had grown still and watchful, and a puff of dark smoke gushed from the top of its tall funnel. After much apparent confusion aboard, a barge went over the side and was lowered to the sea. For the next fifteen minutes or so, men clambered down into the boat, some burdened with small trunks and other belongings. Finally, a small knot of what were obviously Dom soldiers—Blood Drinkers, by the red facings on their yellow tunics, Fred and Kari both realized in alarm—joined the other men in the boat and it began, very clumsily, pulling toward the beach.

"Well, that does it," Fred said grimly. "At the rate they're going, they'll be a while getting ashore. Let's get ready."

"Wait." Kari pointed. The smoke pouring from the funnel was thicker now, and the paddle wheels began to turn. The anchor cable grew slack, but then dropped into the water.

"They cut their cable!" Fred exclaimed. "Or just let it go. Why on earth . . ."

"Look there!" Kari pointed again. Another ship was slashing in from the east, all sails set and taut, a stream of gray smoke tearing downwind.

"Who the devil . . ."

"Somebody the Doms is scared of," Kari answered his unfinished question. "Somebody they hid from, an' is gonna *run* from . . ."

"And don't think they'll escape, so they sent somebody, maybe somebody important, ashore!" Fred finished for her. He grabbed Kari's telescope and focused it on the other ship. It *looked* a lot like one of the Allies' *Scott* Class steam frigates, or DDs, though maybe not as big. Its three masts and square rig were virtually identical, and there were no paddle boxes along its sides, so it had to have a screw propeller. At a distance, the main differences were that it had no white band painted between its gunports, making them impossible to count, and its flag was somewhat . . . different. He couldn't make out details. "It's them," he said wonderingly. "The Los Diablos! Anson's people. It has to be!" He grinned. "We found them after all!"

"Let's just hope we found 'em in time for 'em to save us from them guys," Kari said sarcastically, nodding at the approaching barge.

"I'm not worried about them. With nobody to back them up, I have a plan." The Dom steamer was slowly gaining way, her lower sails unfurling even as topmasts were sent back up. There was no way it could escape the sleek predator swooping down, however. Clearly, it was trying to distract the other ship from the men now going ashore. Fred didn't think it would work because the Dom probably wouldn't get very far before the chase ended. That other ship was *fast*, and he was sure it would come back to check if the Doms had done exactly what they had.

"C'mon," he suddenly said. "It looks like the boat's going to land a couple hundred yards down the beach. Let's go give them a welcome, shall we?"

"Fred, there's maybe sixteen men in that boat!" Kari objected.

"So? They're going to think there's a lot *more* of us."

They hadn't been in position for more than a couple of minutes, still panting from their sprint through the island jungle, when the heavily laden barge crunched onto the sand beneath the bright surf. A couple of men hopped out in ankle-deep water, holding lines, and stepped to the beach. "Now!" Fred hissed, and their two Blitzerbugs stuttered from the trees, spraying the water around the boat on full auto. Small geysers drenched the men as they hurled themselves down in the boat and on the shore.

"Don't move, assholes!" Fred roared, pitching his usually embarrassingly boyish voice as low as he could. "There's . . . a hundred muskets aimed at you right now, and if anybody understands English, he's got three seconds to tell everybody to throw their weapons in the water! One . . ."

The Blood Drinkers started to raise their muskets, and the Blitzers snarled, hitting them—and a couple of men around them. Shrieks tore the air over the swishing surf, and when a man shouted within the group, weapons started splashing in the water.

"All of them!" Fred bellowed. "We better not find so much as a toothpick on any of you or you all die! *Two!*"

"*Todo! Ahora! Obedeceme!*" the hidden voice shouted louder. Immediately, there were more splashes, large and small.

"Okay," Fred called. "Now, one at a time, jump out on shore, throw your coats and everything else you've got in a pile, and plant your faces in the sand, arms and hands spread. The last four men, drag out anybody who's dead or wounded, strip them, then do as the others!"

The voice—Fred now saw it belonged to a man with a large graying mustache and goatee, richly dressed in elaborately embroidered coat, breeches, and tricorn hat—went on for several moments and all the men did as he commanded. Two apparently dead men were dragged from the boat, but the four wounded managed to move themselves. Finally, all were lying on the beach under the blistering sun.

"You too, Mr. Fancy-pants," Fred called. "On your face!"

"I will not!" the man replied in English, his tone haughty, but also aggrieved. "It is not required!"

"*I* require it," Fred stated, a little confused, "so if you don't want some extra holes in your hide, you'll dump the duds and grab sand."

"You . . . speak strangely. Who are you?" the man demanded.

"You talk funny too. Now get down!"

Reluctantly, the man removed his fine coat and laid it gently aside, then sank to the sand and sprawled with as much dignity as he could manage. Fred stood and advanced from the trees. "Keep them covered! Shoot if they even twitch!" he called back. In spite of what he'd said, the haughty man raised his head to look at him as he approached.

"Who are you? Where is your commander? I will only surrender myself to him!" His eyes narrowed as he glared past Fred at the trees. "And where are your 'hundred' men?" he demanded, rising to his knees. "*Soy* . . . I am Don Emmanuel del Rio Negro, Envoy of His Supreme Holiness, the Messiah of Mexico, and Emperor of the World by the Grace of God! I will not be treated this way! There are rules that govern how we fight!"

"No rules between *us*, buster!" Fred snarled, pointing his pistol at Don Emmanuel. He'd left his Blitzer with Kari. "And you'll surrender to me or I'll blow your damn head off!"

"Then I ask again. Who are you?" His eyes swept across Fred's rumpled, sweat-stained flight suit. "What kind of uniform is that?"

"I'm Lieutenant Fred Reynolds, US Navy, and *I* command . . . a company of . . . I think you call them 'demon warriors.' Ensign Kari-Faask! Show yourself!" he called back at the trees. "Everybody else, stay down and keep these guys covered!" he added belatedly. Kari stood, her large eyes glaring, tail swishing rapidly. Don Emmanuel cringed in spite of himself. Obviously, he knew of Lemurians.

"I know who you are," the Dom practically spat. "I have heard your name! You are the Imperial *spy* who penetrated the Holy Temple, treading upon the sweet benevolence of His Supreme Holiness Himself!"

Fred was surprised to be so well-known. "I'm no Impie and I wasn't a spy. Kari and I were prisoners who escaped being *tortured* by your boss's main stooge, Don Hernan. But if you know me, and you know about Kari's people, then maybe you also know you better do what I say before I let my demon warriors eat you!"

"What? You mean we *not* gonna eat 'em?" Kari demanded in an exaggerated tone of disappointment.

With Fred still pretending to command hidden troops, Kari came out and securely tied each of Dom's hands behind his back—then tied them all together along a kind of picket line stretching from the trees to the boat. At some time during the process, it must've become apparent to Don Emmanuel and his men that Fred and Kari were alone after all, and they grew more sullen and less cooperative—until Kari fired a burst from her Blitzer into the sand at their feet. After that, they obeyed quite readily. They had no choice. Particularly when they realized that whether Kari really wanted to eat them or not, she'd far rather just shoot them than go to all the effort of tying them up.

Both ships had long since disappeared from view, hidden by the tall trees curving around on the west side of the lagoon, but about an hour later they heard a pair of dull reports, the thump of distant guns, carried back by the wind. Since there was no firing after that, they assumed they'd heard warning shots, and the Dom ship had quickly surrendered. Now, presumably, all they had to do was wait a while and they would have, miraculously, accomplished their impossible mission after all.

"So, how we gonna say hello to them other fellas when they come back?" Kari finally asked.

Fred looked at Don Emmanuel—who glared back with undisguised rage. "We're going to give them a present."

*   *   *

It was late afternoon by the time the strange warship—
and its prize—steamed back to the lagoon. The sails on
both ships were furled, and smoke streamed from their
funnels. Fred was surprised to see that, though the smoke
from the Dom was thick and black, it curled, wispy gray,
from the other. "Hey!" he observed. "They're burning oil!
Stands to reason, I guess, if they're from where we think
they are." They waited a while longer, sitting in the sand
while both ships hove to and the sound of splashing anchors reached them across the water, but he and Kari were
standing on the beach beside their prisoners when several
boats full of armed men dressed in blue or white round-
abouts pulled ashore. There were about fifty men, all told,
apparently Marines mixed with sailors. They hit the beach
and fanned out—efficiently, Fred thought—weapons at
port arms. The weapons were amazingly similar in appearance to the Baalkpan and Maa-ni-la Arsenal percus-
sion muskets still in wide use on the Allies' eastern front,
but these were painted black. Fred assumed that was to
protect them from the salt air. He grinned and waved. "Hi,
guys!" he called.

"Surrender your arms!" ordered a bearded officer. Unlike all the other men who wore blue "wheel" or tan straw
hats, he had a tall, narrow-topped shako on his head. Modest gold epaulettes adorned the shoulders of his dark blue
double-breasted frock coat, which had to be cooking him
in the tropical heat. A sword hung at his side from a white
leather belt. His sweat-glistening expression was more
stern than threatening, but his command had not seemed
to invite debate. Still . . .

"Hey!" Fred snapped. "We're the *good* guys! We
came *looking* for you, and caught these fellas trying to get
away!"

"They are monsters!" Don Emmanuel blurted. "Un-
civilized *beasts* who do not observe the rules of war!"

"What rules?" Fred demanded, turning to the Dom.
"The rules *you* use? Attacking civilians without warning?
Impaling innocent women and children? Slaughtering
whole villages? *Feeding people* to your flying lizards?" He

turned back to the strange officer and spoke rapidly. "You're fighting these bastards, obviously. You just captured one of their ships. That's swell; we're fighting them too, and we're kicking the hell out of them in the Pacific. We met one of your people before." Fred hesitated. "I *hope* he was one of yours," he added, "named Captain Anson. He said you were Americans who showed up in this world a hundred years ago." He gestured at Kari. "We're Americans too! We just got here . . . a little later."

The officer looked stunned by his outburst and Fred plowed on. "Ah, look, I know this is weird, but I think we're kind of on the same side, as I understand it, and we *did* come to meet you. Please! We'll hand over our weapons— if you promise to give them back—but we have to talk to somebody in charge! We've got news that'll help break the damn Doms for good, if that's what you really want."

"Americans," the officer murmured doubtfully, looking at Kari. He shook his head. "I can't know that, nor do I know a Captain Anson. Others may, and we shall see. But I thank you for capturing these men." He nodded at the Doms. "We were pursuing them quite specifically. As for you, I cannot on my authority promise to return your arms, but you will be treated as guests until your fate is decided." He paused, then straightened. "Please forgive me. I am Lieutenant Samuel Hudgens, executive officer of the New United States heavy frigate *Congress*. Who do I have the pleasure of addressing?"

Fred saluted, and Kari quickly followed his lead. "Lieutenant, Junior Grade, Fred Reynolds, late of the United States Navy destroyer USS *Walker*."

"Ensign Kari-Faask, also from *Walker*," Kari said.

"Ah . . . indeed," Lieutenant Hudgens replied, returning the salutes, eyes wide. "Other Americans indeed. *Both* of you?"

"Yes, sir," Fred and Kari chorused.

"But . . ." Hudgens shook his head. "We shall soon get to the bottom of that. But I must ask, if you did truly come looking for us from across a continent, how in blazes did you get here?"

Fred suddenly hesitated, eyes catching the warship's flag clearly for the first time. It was similar to the one

Walker—and all the American Navy on this world—flew, but not exactly the same; it had five red and white stripes instead of thirteen, and only five large stars in the blue field instead of forty-eight. But Anson had said "his" America wasn't quite as large as they might expect. So was it the size the flag implied that gave him pause, or the fact they'd been willing to change it? Captain Reddy had never permitted any change to *Walker*'s flag, except to allow their various actions to be embroidered on the one they flew in battle, and the unadorned version remained the official flag of his "American Navy Clan." To him, the Stars and Stripes they'd brought to this world now symbolized an ideal more important than any actual place. But these people had changed their flag. Did that mean "their" America might be different from the one he remembered in ways more important than size? He so wanted them all to be friends, but Anson had always been so cryptic—and why *hadn't* they tried harder to meet potential allies? Why had they avoided the Imperials so long? They knew they existed, and fought a common enemy. He took a breath. Whoever these people were, and whatever they stood for, they were about to have his and Kari's weapons to look at, obviously more advanced than what they carried, and they'd quickly find the plane. He couldn't hide what it was. But he suddenly wondered if he should dig up the transmitter. He assumed they had land telegraphy. The technology had been new in the 1840s, but they'd have had it, and he expected they still did. But if they didn't already have *wireless* communication capability, he'd be giving away a major strategic advantage. But then, if they were friends, they'd need the wireless set to coordinate with the Alliance, and that was why he and Kari had come in the first place, wasn't it? To facilitate that? He was just going to have to take the chance. Kari was looking at him questioningly.

"We came across the whole damn Pacific Ocean *and* a continent," he said absently, then looked at the officer. "You'll treat *both* of us as guests?" he demanded, significantly glancing at Kari again.

Hudgens looked surprised. "Yes, of course. We are fully aware of the, ah, 'unusual' nature of the world upon which we live." He nodded slightly at Kari. "I am not personally familiar with your people, Ensign, but your race is known to us. God knows we have encountered stranger folk! And you are, at least, an officer in a naval power allied to another with which we are not presently at war. You will be treated as such."

Fred was relieved—and intrigued by Hudgens's hint that his people knew Lemurians. Maybe they'd had contact with the Republic of Real People at some time? That made the most sense.

"Oh, so very polite, so very correct!" Don Emmanuel suddenly scoffed at the exchange, dropping his pretense of ill treatment. "Even to animals! That is why your nation remains a mere bump upon the road to our preordained conquest of all the world! Why you cannot possibly win against us!"

"Do be quiet, Señor," Hudgens reproached. He looked again at Fred. "You were about to tell me how you arrived at this place, I believe?"

Fred looked a little sheepish and puffed his cheeks. "Well, it's a long story, but"—he shrugged—"we flew."

CHAPTER 7

Ma-draas, Indiaa
September 26, 1944

"**G**oddamn maniacs," muttered Staff Sergeant Cecil Dixon, head of the 3rd Pursuit Squadron maintenance division. Colonel Ben Mallory agreed with Dixon's assessment but didn't respond as he watched the last of his precious P-40Es hoisted from the dock to the flight deck of USS *Baalkpan Bay*. Once there, it would be carefully secured for the long voyage south. At the moment, however, assailed by a stiff morning wind, the sleek warplane with the ferocious "flashy mouth" painted on the nose and a big cursive M just forward of the canopy looked more like a great fat spider twisting by a thread with its feet dangling down. Worse, it was trying to spin out of control as 'Cats on the dock and aboard the carrier—the namesake of her class—tried to hold it in check. The plane was much heavier than the crane operators were accustomed to, weighing around seven times as much as the first P-1 Mosquito Hawks, or "Fleashooters," and over six times as much as the upgraded C versions now cramming the carrier's hangar deck, and it rose in the air with a frustrating hesitancy that only prolonged the two men's anxiety. *Theirs too*, Ben realized, when he saw a cluster of his 3rd Pursuiters, pilots and ground crew, watching as nervously as he. The "old hands" included Lieutenant (jg) Suaak-Pas-Ra, who everyone called "Soupy," the Dutch Lieutenant Conrad Diebel, and the tiny—even for a Lemurian—Second Lieutenant Niaa-Saa, dubbed "Shirley" the day she showed up for training. All were veterans of the grueling antishipping raids and final attack that helped secure Madras for the Allies. Others had been lost, but more had joined them along with most of the remaining P-40s once stationed at Kaufman Field in Baalkpan. *The 3rd's grown tight,* he reflected. *Even Diebel, who was once an arrogant SOB who didn't much care for 'Cats, has found a place. He's the coldest fish in the barrel, by far, but he's grown as devoted to the squadron—and the cause—as anybody.*

Dixon flashed a glance at his boss and Ben tried to look unconcerned, but Dixon knew him well enough to catch the way his hands tensed behind his back. "That's *your* plane, Colonel," Dixon reminded him unnecessarily. "If they crack it up, I'll have their damn tails for parachute straps!" He looked in the direction of the admin shack down the dock. "Should've waited for a calm before loading them up," he muttered darkly.

"No choice, Cec," Ben replied. "We've been holding up the whole damn fleet. General Alden said we go today or he leaves us. That simple." He frowned. "And I'm not getting left behind again." He waved at the plane. "If they crack it up, it'll be an accident," he said mildly, but with a twitchy smile. "And you'll patch it up—just like always." He shook his head. "Nobody's fault. It's damn windy. They already got the other seven aboard." He turned to Dixon, deliberately ignoring the operation underway. "You did fine work, by the way, getting eight of our nine ships ready to go. God knows how you did it."

Dixon forced himself to quit staring at the plane and met his gaze. "Could've gotten the ninth bird ready, but spares are getting tight. Had to skimp someplace if we wanted enough to bring along." He grinned. "At least they've all got six fifties again. That took some scavenging, to round 'em back up!" Early on, they'd taken two or more guns from each plane and used them, along with a number of spares, to arm Nancys for antizeppelin or ground attack roles. Some even went to Second Fleet, but enough remained in theater to scrounge. They also had reliable ammo again, now that the Baalkpan Arsenal had finally perfected the brass drawing process. They were making good barrel steel now as well, though not for fifties—not yet. They were concentrating on copies of the Browning .30, in both air- and water-cooled varieties. The guns and ammunition both required less material to produce than fifties, were light enough for troops to lug around in the field, and they could put a pair of them in the wings of the new P-1Cs. Any pilot who'd lost a .50 from the nose of his or her Nancy was more than happy to trade for a .30. They could carry more ammo—and the weapons didn't try to shake their planes apart.

"Yeah." Ben grinned back. "If we're finally going to get to take our ships back to the pointy end, it only makes sense to make them as effective as possible. Give 'em all their teeth back!" He glanced back at his plane; he couldn't help it. To his vast relief, he saw it touch gently down on *Baalkpan Bay*'s towering flight deck at last. He breathed a satisfied sigh, just as Dixon stiffened slightly to a variety of attention and brought his hand up in salute. Ben turned.

"As you were, gentlemen," General of the Armies and Marines Pete Alden said over the noise of the wind and the bustle on the dock. He was accompanied by a small group of mostly old friends, including General Lord Muln Rolak, commander of I Corps, and the XO of his Second Division, Major Simon "Simy" Gutfeld, of the 3rd Marines. The captains of both of the newest destroyers in the Allied fleet—Commander Perry Brister of USS *James Ellis* (DD-21) and Commander Cablass-Rag-Laan of USS *Geran-Eras* (DD-23)—were with him as well. Tagging along was Lieutenant Rolando "Ronson" Rodriguez, Brister's Exec.

"Are you guys finally done?" Brister rasped. The young man's rough voice hadn't matched his boyish features ever since he'd damaged it through sheer overuse during the Battle of Baalkpan. He also hadn't made any secret of his frustration over being kept on a leash so long. He and his crew had been moving heaven and earth to get *Mahan* back in the fight, but she needed more attention than they could give her at Madras. To the extreme annoyance of the original crew that brought her out, Brister and his *Mahan*s had been given *James Ellis*—the first of a new class of near carbon copies of *Walker*. Some of her 'Cats had stayed with Brister. Others went to Cablass and *Geran-Eras*. Her skipper was given one of the captured Grik dreadnaughts they'd turned into something else entirely. Nobody was happy about it, not even Perry, but it made sense to put his experienced crew to use. He'd stated exactly once that it might be more reasonable to spread his crew out among *James Ellis*, *Geran-Eras*, and the other new DDs being built, but didn't repeat his suggestion when Admiral Keje— still his immediate superior—hadn't run with it. Besides, Cablass was an experienced, aggressive skipper, and most of his crew had served on *Walker* or *Mahan* at some time in the past. Scuttlebutt had it that politics—and Adar—had something to do with at least one of the new *Walker* Class DDs keeping an all-'Cat crew, but there wasn't any real evidence for that.

"That's the last of them," Mallory replied, nodding up at the huge wooden carrier, smoke hazing the tops of her four clustered funnels. "We're ready, General."

"Fine," Pete said, nodding. "I want to clear the harbor mouth just after nightfall." He grunted. "Too much weirdness at sea these days. There's always sea monsters, but now there's mystery subs and French Nazi battleships. . . ." He spat a stream of yellowish tobacco juice into the bay. "An' we've got a helluva lot of precious eggs in these baskets: yours"—he nodded at *Baalkpan Bay*—"and the others." He started to pace down the long dock to a point aft of the carrier where the rest of the anchorage was visible. The others hastened to catch up and joined him where he stood. Out on the water, surrounded by the busy industrial city that had changed hands so often, was an impressive force. The Home-size self-propelled floating dry dock, or "SPD," USS *Tarakaan Island*, was moored close in, currently loaded with half of III Corps, thousands of tons of supplies, field artillery, ammunition, spare parts, and a squadron of motor torpedo boats (MTBs). Beyond her were dozens of new-made oilers, transports, and other auxiliaries built from the same plans as the latest *Scott* Class DDs, or sailing steam frigates. When the Allies started building copies of *Walker*, they didn't stop making the other ships, they just repurposed them. Plenty of the older-style warships would still accompany the fleet, and the dozen DDs of Des-Ron 10, including the veterans *Bowles*, *Saak-Fas*, and *Clark*, guarded the harbor mouth. Just inside them, riding at anchor in the middle distance, were two very familiar shapes, and Ben kept catching himself looking at them like they couldn't be real.

Two years after every imaginable dimension was taken from *Walker*, during her rebuild after the Battle of Baalkpan, she'd finally spawned two daughters. *James Ellis* and *Geran-Eras* looked exactly like her from where Ben stood, down to the color of their paint and the flag they flew. He snorted to himself. *"Finally"? I ought to be thinking, "So soon?" Lemurians were testing the waters of their own iron age when Walker and the rest of us first showed up, but to go from that to this . . . to everything! Not just steel-hulled destroyers, but airplanes! Torpedoes! Machine guns! True, the Grik threat focused their industry and ingenuity a helluva lot, but the achievement those two ships represent is . . . stunning. Sure, they had a pattern,* he thought, *but we didn't even know how to make everything it took to build 'em. So many things have literally been reinvented. 'Cats love machines, and just knowing something's possible is always a leg up, but it takes . . . intuition to find that first rung of the ladder in the dark.* They'd originally thought 'Cats were too literal minded and not given enough to abstract thought to come up with much on their own, but they'd been wrong. They *were* literal minded, but also very artistic. Ben wondered about that combination.

"More precious eggs," Pete Alden growled, nodding at two massive former Grik dreadnaughts captured after Second Madras that were moored a little farther down the dock. Both had been heavily modified in different ways, for specific purposes. One was taking on an uninterrupted stream of troops.

"First Corps," Rolak said, eyes blinking pride. All his troops were dressed and armed alike, wearing tie-dyed smocks and kilts and carrying Baalkpan Arsenal Allin-Silva breech-loading rifles. Most were veterans of terrible, vicious combat, and they marched determinedly up the long gangway for what they hoped would be the final campaign.

"Going to battle against the Grik aboard one of their own former ships has a certain pleasant irony, does it not?" Rolak asked.

Maybe so, Ben thought, but no one had much liked the idea of converting one of the ironclad beasts into a troopship at first, considering the Grik had carried live "rations" chained below for their crews. The rations had been other Grik in this instance, but that wasn't always the case. Both prizes had been given transverse compartmentalization for safety and new, Lemurian-made engines for reliability. Oil-fired boilers replaced the coal-burning ones they'd been built with, and the dank, gloomy holds had been sweetened as much as possible and illuminated with electric lights. The huge guns had been removed, making the ships far more stable, but they weren't helpless. Each carried four of the new dual-purpose 4″-50s at the summit of their casemates fore and aft of the two remaining funnels (their four boiler rooms had been trunked into two stacks), and the DPs could engage targets on the surface and in the air. Four .30-caliber machine guns constituted their close-range antipersonnel and antiair capability. Everyone knew the Grik had to be working on new things—ships, certainly. But they might have come up with new aerial threats as well. Even if they hadn't, some defense against zeppelins and their "suicider" flying bombs was appropriate. The freeboard forward had been raised and their speed increased to keep up with *Baalkpan Bay*'s fifteen knots. Regardless of their new specializations, both still wore the sloped iron plates covering their heavy wooden casemates, and had even added more that extended slightly below their waterlines like abbreviated torpedo blisters. The waterlines of Grik dreadnaughts had always been their weakest point, even against heavy shells or bombs landing close aboard.

USS *Sular* was a troopship capable of transporting more than two-thirds of I Corps's ten thousand troops, and her sides were hidden behind sliding racks that could drop as many as a hundred stacked dories into the sea. USS *Andamaan* was . . . different, meant to be a kind of "protected seaplane tender." She carried troops and landing craft as well but had another primary purpose. Her casemate was no longer armored on each end but was equipped with great foldaway doors flanked by heavy cranes. The interior gun decks had been removed and the funnels further trunked to lie within the massive support beams. The result was a monstrous hangar spacious enough to accommodate twenty assembled PB-1B "Nancy" two-seat floatplanes, or six of the massive four-engine PB-5 "Clipper" seaplanes stowed diagonally. It was never envisioned that aircraft should land aboard her, but even the big Clippers, mounted on catapult trucks, could take off from the fo'c'sle or aft deck and be recovered by the cranes when they returned.

Andamaan carried the latest version of Clipper: the D model. They had the same large, deep fuselage of their predecessors but had done away with the aerodynamic protrusions on each side, intended to provide stability in the water. Those had been less than satisfactory. Instead, they'd returned to fixed wingtip floats, and their broad wings were more robustly braced to support the heavier new radials. These were essentially the same five-cylinder engines employed by the P-1s, but they'd been "stacked" to create ten offset cylinders. The result was an impressive boost in horsepower, and the same concept had been used to increase the performance of the P-1Cs. Another advantage afforded by additional bracing was that these Clippers could now carry four five-hundred-pound bombs or a single Baalkpan Naval Arsenal Mk-3 torpedo under each wing.

"Not 'pleasant,' but convenient after all, I guess," Pete said, replying to Rolak. "I didn't like the idea of cramming our guys in those fat targets any more than you did at first, but I confess Spanky's scribbles look a lot better now—after the yard apes interpreted 'em. And they ain't just targets. They're fairly fast, and they can fight." He nodded at *Andamaan*. "It was nearly as hard for me to let 'em cram my new Clippers in that one. You know how long it took to get 'em!" Rolak nodded and blinked commiseration. Pete and Ben had been pleading for more Clippers ever since the first Battle of Madras, for long-range reconnaissance primarily, but they wanted them armed as well. The problem was, there just weren't enough to go around. Not only had it taken quite a while to put them in large-scale production, but their initially envisioned role as rapid transport between the far-flung Allies had swallowed them up as quickly as they were made. Even now, one Clipper took the same time and resources to produce as nearly a dozen P-1s or Nancys—and nobody could get enough of those either.

"I *was* skeptical at first," Rolak agreed. "I had to see them for myself before I was convinced of the sense of Minister McFaar-lane's 'scribbles.'" He smiled. "I now most emphatically approve . . . of *Sular*, at any rate. And as I said, it is somewhat ironically satisfying to use Grik hulls against the enemy. I never questioned the merit of turning them into large transports of some sort, as long as their machinery was made more reliable. I just did not think it could be done so quickly. Indeed, with all the dangers, known and surmised, inherent in such a long voyage across a deadly sea into the heart of enemy waters, I am quite content to shield as many of our troops behind Grik armor as we can." He blinked, looking at *Andamaan*. "Shielding aircraft, whose business it is to quickly fly away from their ships at need, did strike me as something of an . . . awkward extravagance" He took a long breath. "But I find myself vaguely comforted that our Clippers will be protected as well."

"We could've just flown them down. They have the range, and Jumbo was willing to lead the flight," Ben said, reviving an old dispute. Walt "Jumbo" Fisher was one of Ben's guys, and now commanded the six-plane Patrol Squadron (Pat-Squad) Twenty-two. "We could've *stacked* that hangar with crated Nancys and Fleashooters."

"Indeed, Col-nol Maal-lory," Rolak said, smiling slightly, probably amused by his persistence. "But they only *barely* have the range, and Cap-i-taan Reddy wants us to use the Clippers along the way, to scout parallel to our course. And use them in our defense as well, if necessary."

Pete arched an eyebrow at Ben. "Still tryin' to slow us down? We *ain't* unloadin' an' reloadin' *Andamaan* now, and that's final." There were chuckles. "Still," he persisted thoughtfully. "A lot of eggs . . ." He turned to look at Perry Brister, and then nodded out past the former Grik dreadnaughts toward the DDs. "Speaking of eggs, Commander Brister, and fresh-laid ones at that, what do you think of our screen?"

"I've got no major complaints," Brister rasped. "The sailing steamers'll do their jobs just like always. Some steady crews there. And *James Ellis* and *Geran-Eras*"—he nodded at Cablass—"got worked up pretty well on their way out here." He grinned a bit ruefully. "They're not *perfect* copies of *Walker*, you know. I mean, everything . . . *kind* of works like you'd expect, and engineering and the gun and torpedo directors are pretty much exactly the same. But other stuff takes you by surprise. The plates're thicker, more like *Walker*'s and *Mahan*'s used to be, but that's not it." He shrugged. "I don't know. My *Mahans* haven't been aboard *James Ellis* long enough to discover all the differences, and who knows what we'll find, but so far . . ." His brow furrowed. "In some ways things are a little . . . cruder here and there, but in others, more . . . refined, almost *elegant*, if you know what I mean. And some stuff is bigger, clunkier, but seems to fit together better, see?"

Pete laughed. "I'm surprised the 'Cats didn't paint murals on the bulkheads and hang tapestries everywhere."

"You haven't seen the curtains to the officer's quarters and the wardroom," Brister deadpanned. Everyone laughed at that.

"What is wrong with murals and tapestries?" Cablaan asked innocently, fueling the laughter.

"But you have no reservations about your screening assignments?" Pete finally asked.

"None, sir," Perry replied. "We'll take good care of all our precious 'eggs.'"

"Good," Pete said, his voice now void of humor. He gestured out at the fleet. "Because this is it, friends. The last gasp. We're taking two corps to Grik City, but they aren't just any corps—they're First and Third—to join what's left of Safir Maraan's Second. We're the cream." He shook his head and Ben could tell he was trying to make it clear just how important this convoy was without casting too much gloom. It didn't matter. Everybody knew. "Once we get down there," Pete continued, "it's not like we won't get reinforcements. We will. We'll get more troops—and planes too. I'm even hoping we can get Sixth Corps sent down pretty soon, once we know Halik's gone from Indiaa for good." He paused. "Personally, I think he is. He gave his word to stay out after we ran him off, and God help me, I think he'll keep it. He was always different, but that Jap, that General Niwa he runs with, changed him even more." He shrugged. "I don't know exactly why, but I'm as sure as I am of anything else these days that he'll leave us be. Which means we'll get Sixth Corps at some point." He looked at Brister. "And we'll get more shiny new tin cans like yours. The next couple are already being built." There were satisfied nods. "But what we *won't* get is another First or Third Corps," Pete ground home. "Does anybody here think, no matter what else they send us, we can still win this war without 'em?"

There was silence.

Sighing, Pete shook his head. "Sorry, guys. Just layin' it out. This convoy *must* get through." He looked at Ben and managed a small smile. "We ain't getting any more P-Forties either, and for some reason Captain Reddy thinks they're important." The smile vanished. "Anyway, if we do get hit, your orders are to fly your planes the hell off *Baalkpan Bay* and get 'em back here or to Grik City, whichever is in reach. Keep 'em fueled and ready at all times, is that clear?"

"No, sir."

Pete raised both eyebrows. "Excuse me?"

"I mean, what if nothing's in reach? There *will* be a point where that's the case."

Pete considered. "Just have to jump that creek when we get to it. You'll have to either sit tight and hope you can ride out whatever it is, or get them off so *Baalkpan Bay* can get her own planes in the air. If it comes to that, things'll be pretty rough anyway, so I'd recommend you fly 'em and fight 'em. Try to recover as many as you can on *Baalkpan Bay* with those idiotic nets you rigged. Stupid Army!" He snorted in frustration. "Building planes without tail hooks, or the spine to take one!" He looked Ben in the eye. "Try whatever you like, but if that doesn't work?" He waved his hands helplessly. "Tell your guys to put 'em in the water as close as they can to something that can fish 'em out."

Ben felt a chill run down the small of his back, imagining himself in the terrible, predator-rich sea, trying to decide whether to jump in the water—or close his canopy and ride his plane to the bottom. "Yes, sir."

PT-7
Mangoro River
September 26, 1944

"Do you see them?" Lieutenant Colonel Chack-Sab-At asked just loud enough to be heard over the deep-throated burble of the twin engines pushing the Seven boat up the narrow, muddy red waters of the Mangoro River. He wore his tie-dyed Marine tunic under rhino pig armor, and his helmet sat tilted forward on his head to shield his large, sharp eyes. His tail, brindled like the rest of him, swished edgily beneath his kilt, and his ever-present Krag-Jorgensen rifle was slung loosely on his shoulder.

"Yep," replied Chief Gunner's Mate Dennis Silva, spitting a long yellowish stream over the raised coaming around the starboard side of the boat's conning station. Then he nodded imperceptibly. He also wore a helmet, like everyone on the boat, but there wasn't any leather armor big enough for him. Instead, he merely wore his ordinary "uniform" of black eye patch, T-shirt, dungarees, and an assortment of weaponry. He *was* protected, though, by the large ammunition box and the Lemurian-made copy of a water-cooled Browning machine gun he stood behind.

"Yep," the colorful tree-gliding lizard named Petey

croaked tentatively, clutching Silva's shoulder and peering over it at the landscape beyond the shore. He was just parroting what he'd heard, but the tension in the boat had clearly affected him. No one paid Petey any mind.

"How can you see them?" Chack demanded. "You haven't even looked!"

"More over here," Silva simply said.

"Oh. So they watch us from *both* sides now."

"Evidently. An' Larry's lookin' for me too, ain't ya, little buddy?"

Lawrence, or "Larry the Lizard," was a Sa'aaran, originally from the tsunami-swept island of Tagran. There remained some debate whether he was just another race of "Grik," or an entirely different, if related, species. He preferred to claim the latter. He was smaller than a Grik, and colored with orange and brown stripes. He was also very smart, understanding English and Lemurian, and fluently speaking both—as well as his lipless mouth would allow. Initially treated like an annoying pet by Silva, he'd become, along with Chack, Gunny Horn, and a very few others, one of Silva's rare true friends.

"I 'atch, 'ut stay hidden, like I told," Lawrence confirmed.

"An' you stay that way, hunkered down outa sight. Can't take the chance your ugly, Grikish mug'll provoke the locals." Silva snickered. "Not that *that* seems to matter much," he added.

"I can't see *any* of them," Ensign Nathaniel (Nat) Hardee said resentfully in his refined English accent, but he remained crouched low as well, gripping the brass wheel in front of him hard enough to turn his knuckles white while he peered over the coaming ahead, searching the water in front of the bow for shallows or snags.

"None of us can actually *see* 'em, Mr. Hardee," Silva said. "Not really. They're bein' mighty sneaky. But we can see where they are." And of course, every now and then a barbed, bone-tipped arrow arced out of the foliage along the shoreline and slammed into the boat, confirming that the swaying fern-like fronds concealed more of whatever manner of creature that took sufficient exception to their presence to murder one of their company in a most horrid fashion. Silva's first reaction had been to hose the area with the Browning, then go collect a specimen of whoever—or whatever—was shooting at them. Even Chack wavered, but Bradford forbade it. Chack might be in overall command, but Courtney Bradford was in charge of meeting the people here. Granted, he wasn't quite sure how he'd manage that yet; they didn't seem particularly friendly. But he demanded a little more time to sort it out. Meeting them after Silva had shot them to pieces didn't strike Courtney as the most diplomatic approach. In the meantime, they might meet friendlier folk as they moved upriver. Silva and Chack both doubted that, and even if they were wrong, they were liable to start a war between any possible "friendlies" and the hostiles, over the power of the magic boat that moved upriver, if nothing else. Silva and Lawrence had been on the trip that discovered the Khonashi in North Borno, and that worked out okay in the end, but he was pretty sure this was a waste of time.

"It's kinda like them Western pictures," he blurted gleefully. "Here we are, the peaceable wagon train, tramblelatin' cross the prairie! I'm the handsome scout, o'course, warnin' ever'body how stupid this is. Chack's the stick-up-his-ass Yankee cavalryman, bound to do his dooty. The rest of Mr. Hardee's crew 'Cats is all the extras in the picture, doomed to get killed an' scalped." He turned to glare at Lance Corporal Ian Miles, crouching in the corner behind him. "Miles is the one I can't figure. Is he the yellow traitor, just waitin' for his chance to skip, or does he only *seem* that way so nobody expects it when he finally does somethin' worthwhile?"

"The hell with you, Silva," Miles snapped, but his tone was resigned.

"An' Mr. Bradford's the plucky ol' foreign schoolmarm," Silva continued, as if Miles hadn't spoken. "Hell, let's say she's Australian, of all things." Courtney Bradford *was* Australian. "Ever'body thinks she's nuts, but nobody wants to hurt her feelin's—no offense, Mr. Bradford," Silva added loftily as Courtney climbed up the companionway from below, an Imperial telescope in his hand.

"None taken, Mr. Silva," Bradford replied, replacing his large sombrero with a helmet, momentarily revealing his balding, sweaty pate. "You've saved my life often enough to mock me to your heart's content," he added with good humor. Carefully, he crept up to the coaming and slid the telescope over the top. "Where did you think you saw the last one?"

"Back yonder." Silva pointed at their wake with his bearded chin.

"Bugger! Do tell me if you see another."

"Okay."

"I as well, Mr. Bradford," Chack assured. "But I have no idea what Silva is talking about."

"I don't either," Silva admitted. "But these sneakin' Apache 'Cats, or whatever they are, probably do." He paused. "There's another," he added conversationally.

"Where?" Courtney demanded eagerly, scanning the shore.

"A little back, under them trees. Damn! It's too dark to see if it's got a tail or not! *Look out!*" He shoved Courtney down as another arrow boomed into the plywood coaming, its shattered point protruding through, mere inches from Courtney's face.

"My word!" Courtney gasped.

Silva reflexively pointed his gun, then paused. "Look, Mr. Bradford, these jerks *ain't* gonna sit down an' drink mint jaloops with you while you talk philosophy. Let's kill some, see who they are, then get the hell out of here. We got a war to get back to." He was still smarting from some of his wounds, even wearing a row of unplucked stitches here and there, but he was smarting more at having missed the most recent battle at and around Grik City.

"You may be right," Courtney admitted dismally. "You still aren't to kill any of them, but I don't know how we can accomplish our mission if we daren't even go ashore! I'd hoped to find a settlement of some sort along the river, but so far there's been nothing at all!" He stopped, considering. "Just a bit farther. The attacks have grown more frequent. Perhaps they are defending something and we're getting closer to a village of some kind. Just another ten miles or so, Mr. Hardee," he instructed wistfully. "Then we shall turn around at last."

"Aye, aye. If we can make it that far. The river is narrowing." It also wasn't the rain-swollen torrent it had been, its volume diminishing rapidly. He understood they were on the "wet" side of the looming mountains, but didn't trust the river to keep enough water to float them. If they got stranded . . . He tried not to let the relief show on his face. In addition to the more hazardous navigation, he was starting to worry about fuel. They'd brought extra, of course, but the original plan had been for him to drop the landing party at the mouth of the Mangoro and await its return. Since then, they'd endured a rough storm and the interior of Madagascar, already known to be amazingly hostile and "stocked" with all manner of creatures even the Grik considered "worthy prey," was full of intelligent, murderous weapon users as well. The human "Maroons" in the north had been very helpful to Chack's Brigade when it fought its way through the jungle to attack Grik City from behind. They'd even joined the Alliance. But these southern . . . people were numerous and hostile enough that even Silva wasn't anxious to leave the boat anymore. That brought Hardee back to fuel; it had never been expected that he'd have to chauffeur the delegation halfway across Madagascar.

"What the hell?" Silva murmured suddenly.

"What the hell!" Petey screeched insistently.

"Somethin's movin' through the jungle yonder, pretty quick, an' comin' this way!" Birds—and lizardbirds—swept out of the trees in a growing, cawing tide, and there came a rumbling crackle of shattering limbs that sounded dully in the humid air. There were some really scary "boogers" on Madagascar, and some were extremely large. Possibly even big enough to wade the river. Excited yips came from the forest, and Silva wondered for a moment if their tormentors were herding something at them. He'd heard the Doms did that with some kind of "super lizards" at Fort Defiance. He doubted it in this case, though, because even if he still couldn't get a good look at the shadowy shapes on shore, they were flitting through the trees—and maybe up in them?—to get *away* from whatever was coming.

"All hands, man your battle stations!" Nat shouted over the exhaust of the engines. "Prepare for action starboard!" Suddenly, it didn't matter who was in charge of the mission;

the Seven boat was his to fight. Two 'Cats hopped the coaming, rifles slung, and crouched behind the starboard torpedo tube, still wary of arrows from shore even though their tormentors were suddenly quite preoccupied. "Stand by to reverse the shafts!" Nat called into a voice tube near the wheel. He could control the throttle with a lever by the wheel, but the engines couldn't actually be reversed. The boat would back up only if a reversing gear was engaged. That could take a moment, and he wanted the two 'Cats in the engine room expecting the command if he gave it.

"Larry, old buddy," Dennis said conversationally, "run fetch me my Doom Stomper, wilya?"

Larry's eyes were wide and his crest was rising in alarm, but he nodded, very humanlike, and bounded down the companionway.

"I'd have gone," protested Miles. "I'm not doing anything."

Silva spared him a single glance with his good eye. "You should be. Grab a weapon. Besides, I don't want you even touchin' my be-loved Doom Stomper. An' if I sent you for it, you'd prob'ly wind up still doin' nothin'—belowdecks!"

Miles snarled something unintelligible, but took an Allin-Silva breechloader from the rack nearby and tentatively stood. Chack gazed at the former "China Marine," then back at his friend. Miles struck him as lazy, usually doing only what he was directly told to do, and he was the only expedition member, not part of the Seven boat's crew, who hadn't volunteered. Spanky sent him. Still, Chack didn't know why Silva disliked him so. Sometimes it even seemed like Silva was actually *goading* Miles into attacking him! Chack didn't like it and decided to make a point of finding out why. "Look!" he said instead, gesturing at the shore. Bradford stood now, spyglass glued to his eye. A Lemurian—clearly a Lemurian!—leaped from concealment in the trees and splashed in the water just as a four-legged brute the size of a Buick bounded in beside him. The thing looked like a horned toad with straight legs and a long, spiky neck. It completely ignored the floundering Lemurian as it churned, wide-eyed, toward the boat. Immediately, several more creatures just like it plowed into the water, disappearing for a moment before they began to swim. The 'Cat was still floundering, but others had appeared on shore, trying desperately to fish him out, but they were distracted by almost constant looks over their shoulders at the jungle beyond.

"They *are* 'Cats! Midget ones!" Silva roared triumphantly, racking the bolt on the Browning. "Sorry, Chackie," he added, knowing Chack had been afraid of this. No one liked the idea that Lemurians might be capable of genuine murder—and the kind of murder these had apparently committed in particular.

"You're still not to shoot them!" Courtney cried.

"I ain't! I'm gettin' ready to shoot those horny toad . . . llama things, if they get too close—an' whatever the hell's chasin' *them*!"

The sight on shore would've been almost comical if it weren't so desperate. Obviously, the 'Cat in the water couldn't swim, and his fellows were torn between helping him and running for their lives. They were naked and almost uniformly brown except for black-and-brown-striped tails much longer, proportionately, than Chack's. Their eyes were bigger too, and they wore manes, almost black, around dark faces. One continually menaced the Seven boat with a drawn bow as long as he was tall.

"Your cousins here are kinda cute, Chackie," Silva quipped—just as something monstrous exploded from the jungle. "Shit!" Silva snapped, forgetting the 'Cats on shore and the swimming creatures that seemed to be trying to veer around the boat. The monstrous . . . thing was just yet another type of "super lizard" in a sense: another huge, bipedal predator apparently designed primarily to carry a gigantic, horrifying mouthful of teeth around. But Dennis was always stunned by the variations that basic form could take. This one appeared to be covered in real fur—where there were gaps in the sharp spikes and bony plates it wore like medieval armor. The fur was lighter on the belly and striped and blotchy otherwise. The spikes and plates were a dark chocolate brown. The head was longer and narrower than other super lizards he'd seen, and it stood taller than those on Borno when it rose on its hind legs, a screeching 'Cat in its jaws.

"Shit!" squealed Petey, bolting from his perch and vanishing down the companionway in a streak of color.

"Not exclusively bipedal," Courtney exclaimed, reflecting Silva's less detached but no less appraising thoughts. The thing's front legs, or arms, were long and powerful, and it could obviously go as easily on four legs as on two. The 'Cats near the water gave it a ragged volley of arrows, puny pinpricks against something with a torso as big as the Seven boat. It didn't even seem to notice them until it gulped their comrade down, then it took a step in their direction. They were trapped on a narrow strip of ground, the same tangled brush and deadfall they'd been using for cover now preventing their escape. There was nothing they could do but leap into the water themselves, which they did with desolate cries.

"Protect them, Mr. Hardee!" Chack cried.

Silva looked at him. "Why? Them murderin' devils've been shootin' arrows at us all the way up from the coast!"

"We don't know if they're the same ones that killed Sergeant McGinnis or not!"

"They're the same ones that've been tryin' to kill *us*!"

"Mr. Hardee!" Chack shouted.

"Aye, aye! Action starboard! Commence firing at the . . . large reptile!"

Silva rolled his eye but quickly sighted down the barrel and depressed the trigger.

The machine gun stuttered loudly and two rounds blew mud in the air before the stream of bullets settled down and the rest started tearing bloody holes in the monster on shore. "I don't know how well this is gonna work," Silva roared over the racket of the gun and the engines. "Ought six is great for killin' Japs an' lizards, but big boogers like that? Well, I've had experience. Liable to just piss it off!" The monster emitted a high-pitched shriek that actually hurt their ears and spun to face them, its quarry floundering in the water now forgotten. "See?" Silva demanded, trying to redirect his fire at the thing's face, but, amazingly quickly for something so large, it sprinted into the water and came for them.

"Goddamn!" Silva yelled. "*There* you are, Larry! Trade me!"

Without a word, Lawrence handed Dennis an immense

rifle, a belt full of huge cartridges, and positioned himself behind the Browning. The *crack* of Chack's Krag and the heavy *boom* of Allin-Silvas in the hands of Miles and the two 'Cats to starboard briefly took up the slack while Silva slapped the breech of the huge weapon open. The Doom Stomper, like its muzzle-loading flintlock predecessor, the Doom Whomper, had been made out of one of *Amagi*'s damaged 25-mm antiaircraft guns specifically for killing super lizards. Dennis had used the Doom Whomper for other things as well, such as almost single-handedly ending—if not winning—the battle against Doms and rebels at New Dublin in the Empire of the New Britain Isles. To his sorrow, however, that weapon had been destroyed in action and Bernie Sandison had commissioned several breech-loading versions based on the Silva-inspired Allin-type "trapdoor" breechloaders that had become the standard infantry rifle in all the Allied armies. Instead of the robust and effective but manageable .50-80-caliber cartridges for the Allin-Silvas, though, the Doom Stomper was basically a four-bore rifle that fired a fifteen-hundred-grain hard lead bullet with a bronze penetrator on top of two hundred and fifty grains of powder. The even heavier loads Dennis once used in his old gun had been deemed detrimental to penetration, accuracy, and the health of the shooter. Three more Doom Stompers now existed in the Allied arsenal under another, official name, but no one else had yet been able to stay as focused on the target as they were on the recoil for the multiple shots required to sight one in. Silva pronounced all the failures "scum weenies" and considered the other weapons his personal "spares" in case he broke this one as well.

Now he slid one of the enormous cartridges in the breech, closed it, and cocked the hammer.

"Reverse shafts!" Nat Hardee shouted into his voice tube.

"What the hell?" Dennis said, then looked. The monster was almost upon them! Half wading, half swimming, it was churning right for the boat through a hail of bullets. "Oh," he said. "Say, even if I kill it, it's liable to flop right on us!"

"Exactly my concern!" Hardee screamed at him. A

hurried, tinny voice reported that the shafts were reversed, and Hardee slammed the throttles to their stops. The Seven boat roared even louder than the monster and bounded backward, Hardee looking over his shoulder and spinning the wheel from side to side with jerky motions. Smelly red water sprayed them from the flat transom, aft. The beast thundered frustration as the gap between them widened and Silva raised his big gun. He hesitated. "Hey, Chackie! I got a idea!"

Chack paused his own firing and blinked concern. Silva's ideas were often excellent—and insane.

"Let's *torpedo* the bastard!" Dennis gushed with a gleeful, gap-toothed grin. "Cap'n Blas shot a super lizard with a cannon at Fort Defiance, but I bet nobody's ever *torpedoed* one before!"

Chack blinked again; then, to Silva's surprise, he nodded. "As soon as we gain enough distance from that brute, you will torpedo it, Mr. Hardee."

Nat just stared at him.

"Is that understood?"

"Ah, aye, aye, Colonel. But the fish needs between fifty and seventy-five yards to arm." The torpedo pistols in the nose of the Baalkpan Naval Arsenal Mk-3 torpedoes worked very well, but their robust construction meant they weren't as sensitive or precise as the Mk-15s the destroyermen brought to this world. That wasn't usually a problem, since they didn't have the legs for a long-distance shot. Two thousand yards—or tails—was their maximum range, and five hundred was preferred. But as primitive, short-ranged, and anemic as they were—particularly by the standards of the Japanese weapons the destroyermen once faced—unlike the Mk-15s, they generally went where they were pointed and went off when they hit. If they had time to arm.

Silva slapped Lawrence on the back, disrupting his aim and causing a stream of curses from the Sa'aaran. "See?" Dennis said. "Chackie still knows how to have fun!"

"Really, Colonel Chack," Bradford said, taking the glass from his eye, "I must protest! The specimen might be utterly destroyed, and the Lemurians in the water could be injured as well!"

Chack nodded at Courtney. He didn't care about the

"specimen," but Bradford had a point. The 'Cats were beyond the beast, which, their fire slacking and likely enraged by its wounds, had redoubled its efforts to reach them. It had no chance unless they ran aground, and Nat's head was back to bobbing like a cobra's, trying to prevent that.

"I believe the natives are out of the water now, Mr. Bradford," Chack said. "But they still stand upon the shore. They watch," he added with satisfaction. "Let's give them something to see. Ease your throttle, Mr. Hardee. Keep this distance between us and the monster, about a hundred yards, but we mustn't miss. The torpedo would then impact the shore near the party gathered there."

"I, ah . . . okay." Hardee looked behind them as they neared a narrow part of the channel. "But I can't call the shot."

"Chief Silva will align the torpedo and give the command to fire," Chack said.

"With pleasure!" Silva practically giggled, lowering the hammer of the Doom Stomper. Shoving it back in Lawrence's arms, he hopped the coaming. After quickly checking to make sure the tube was ready, he nodded at Chack. "Starboard torpedo ready in all respects; depth is set at two feet," he reported officiously but with a huge grin still splitting his face. Chack nodded back, unsurprised. The 'Cats standing with Silva had maintained their weapons in ready condition no matter how unlikely it might seem that they'd need them. That was one reason Chack was willing to expend one of their two torpedoes now; what else was it good for on this mission?—and it might be *very* good for what he had in mind.

He took a last look at the monster. It was finally tiring, possibly growing bored with the chase. It was time. "All stop," he called to Nat.

"But . . . ," Courtney muttered, still not quite believing what they were doing.

"Fire when ready, Chief Silva, but don't miss!"

Silva squinted at the beast, as big as a bus. It had stopped, as if uncertain whether to continue its pursuit or return to shore. Maybe it could still catch the smaller morsels?

"*Can't* miss," Silva assured, and pulled the lanyard one of the 'Cats had handed him. The impulse charge detonated with a hollow *boom*, and the brass-bodied MK-3 fish splashed in the water amid a cloud of white smoke. A trail of bubbles surged to the surface in an accelerating line toward the indecisive monster. It noticed the trail as it drew near and watched with apparent curiosity for the last few seconds before the weapon slammed into its submerged flank.

Silva whooped when the monster blew apart within a great white cloud of smoke and a high geyser of dirty water. Bloody gobbets of flesh and shards of shattered bone splashed the river almost to the boat.

"Take that, you big, fat, boat-eatin' booger!" Silva shouted happily, his arms outstretched in exultation.

"I'm glad you enjoyed it, Chief Silva," Chack said, "but we didn't do it solely for your entertainment," he added, looking back at Bradford. "My primary intention was to awe the natives. Now let's see if it worked, shall we?"

Courtney nodded understanding, but looked at the blood spreading from the smoking, shattered carcass. "Such a shame, though. It does seem that every time I find something interesting to observe, someone blows it up."

"Don't 'orry, 'ister 'radthord," Lawrence consoled. "Us'll see another, I think."

Corporal Ian Miles shakily lowered his rifle and looked from Lawrence to Bradford, then from Chack to Silva.

"Crazy," he muttered to himself. "They're all crazy as shit."

The Indus River Valley
September 26, 1944

"My lord general!" gasped a warrior, crouching and bowing low to General Halik in the tall, lush grass at the top of the rounded knob rising in the center of the bustling tent city that Halik had established in the wilderness. The front and back of the warrior's leather armor were painted with three yellow bars and three white dots across the center bar, the emblem (influenced by Halik's friend "General" Orochi Niwa) of a commander of two hundreds, a *rikugun taii*, in Japanese, or "captain" in the "scientific tongue" of English. General Halik had long forbidden his officers to sprawl on their bellies and grovel in his presence as they'd been raised to do before senior officers all their lives. He and his staff had been working hard to foster the novel concepts of pride and dignity in his outcast army—again at Niwa's suggestion. His friend had argued that a respectful bow was sufficient to convey an officer's devotion to a higher rank, while reinforcing the notion that he remained "above" those he commanded. What's more, the *mutual* respect symbolized by allowing a simple bow as opposed to demanding abject prostration fostered a stirring of something akin to respect among even the lowliest Uul warriors toward their immediate superiors. There'd always been obedience through fear and conditioning, but it had never before occurred to any Grik army to follow commands because it trusted those who gave them to actually know what they were doing. The result, so far, had exceeded Halik's greatest expectations, and that simple reform had changed many of his junior officers into true commanders of the warriors they led instead of mere mouthpieces for the officers placed over them.

"Report, Captain," he said gruffly, glancing at his two companions, General Ugla and Orochi Niwa. Ugla was one of his most promising generals, and the first to recognize Halik's talent even though he'd been "elevated" to his exalted post from a mere sport fighter, and Ugla had been "born" a general. And Ugla, like Halik, disdained not only the trappings of his office, preferring to dress almost as simply as his warriors—with the exception of the elaborate helmet and cape of his rank—but he also preferred to actively command instead of merely designing battles and turning his warriors loose. That had been the role of Grik generals since the beginning of time: to stay aloof from what Halik had learned were the misidentified "joys" of battle, and never stoop to getting blood on one's own claws. That, Halik was convinced, was also why they were losing this war, and why First General Esshk—who could lead no other way himself—had instituted the policy of elevating Halik and others like him. His command and his army had been a grand experiment that would've worked, Halik was sure, given enough time. The fact that his army still existed after all it had endured was sufficient proof of that.

He looked again at the slight, dark-haired Japanese officer he considered his friend—another new concept: friendship! Orochi Niwa had come to this world aboard the Japanese Imperial Navy battle cruiser *Amagi* as a *rikusentai* lieutenant, a member of their Special Naval Landing Forces. Essentially, he was a Japanese Marine, as Halik imperfectly understood the concept, and therefore, ironically, from a similar background as Halik's greatest and, oddly, most respected nemesis: General Pete Alden. Niwa's counsel had influenced Halik's—and his army's—evolution more than any other single factor and

Halik suspected that if Esshk's experiment had not flourished elsewhere, it was because none of his other generals had Orochi Niwa at their side.

The trio had been discussing their long-delayed move to the west, across the regency of Persia, toward Arabia, and ultimately, south to join forces they hoped still remained loyal to First General Esshk. The trek they contemplated was a daunting one, across high mountains, through dense coastal forests and even a band of desert. Hopefully, they could secure ocean transport at some point, but with little knowledge of how the war progressed, they couldn't count on that. Ugla had been describing the difficulty of completing preparations to move their vast numbers of noncombatant "civilian" Hij they'd evacuated from India, including an astonishing number of brood females nested along the western coast of the lost province. Together, Halik's army and its dependent (and support) elements had swelled to over 115,000, but less than 40,000 were true warriors he could rely on, of the type that nearly destroyed the Allied armies in India and still managed a fighting withdrawal across half a continent. Another 20,000 warriors were of the "old style," unfit for much beyond what Niwa referred to as "cannon fodder," but their training progressed as quickly as their blooming intellects could accommodate it. Even many Hij artisans and support personnel were learning to use weapons—the first time any had ever been taught such things, as far as Halik knew. But at present, all he had for the vanguard of his force, to march across an inhospitable and perilous distance, was his core of veterans, warriors—*troops*—whose protection and survival had become his greatest mission. And the primary reason for him to go on.

So great was his devotion to what remained of his army and the . . . special thing it had become, he'd even toyed with abandoning the war entirely and settling in this bountiful land west of the Indus River. He had an . . . understanding with General Alden, and sufficient labor and females to establish a regency of his very own. Such things had been done before, but not by any general, and when it all boiled down to it, that's what he was. He couldn't see himself as a regent consort, or any other provincial leader within the Grik Empire, and where he was, otherwise inhabited or not, he remained within territory long claimed by the Grik. Niwa had said, essentially, "So what? Make it your own. You could become king of the Indus River Valley, independent of the Grik *or* the Alliance." He was tempted, but in the end, he just couldn't do it. As much as he loved—yes, *loved*—his army, his honor (another concept Niwa had taught him) demanded that his allegiance still belonged to his creator, First General Esshk.

He'd promised never to strike eastward again, into India, even if another Grik army should do so. That wouldn't keep him from rejoining the Empire, however, to fight the same enemy that threatened it elsewhere, and that's what he was currently preparing to do—if he had the time. His force *had* paused long enough to lick its wounds, lay in supplies, and even scrape up or make a supply of ammunition for the ten thousand matchlock muskets, crossbows, and forty-odd cannon he'd managed to bring with him. His Hij artisans were crucial for that, and they'd fashioned large numbers of firebomb throwers, catapults for "Grik fire," as the Allies called it, as well. He felt confident he had the means to move against any small force that chose to stand in the way of his reunification with General Esshk.

But this . . . delay hadn't gone unnoticed by Allied forces sent to watch what he did and, ultimately, shadow his march west. The force detailed to do so was a brigade of cavalry under the command of a talented young Lemurian colonel named Enaak, and an implacable Czech (whatever that was) colonel named Dalibor Svec. Enaak's 5th Maa-ni-la was a crack regular regiment armed with breech-loading carbines and mounted on fearsome, carnivorous me-naaks, creatures resembling long-legged crocodiles. Svec had three regiments of his "Czech Legion," or "Brotherhood of Volunteers," composed of a mixed force of humans and continental Lemurians no one had ever suspected existed until recently. His officers and NCOs were aging Czechs and Slovaks (whatever they were as well) from another world. The Czechs, as everyone called Svec's combined force, were equally well mounted on plant-eating beasts called kravaas, just as fearsome if not as swift as me-naaks, and armed with dangerous horns instead of jaws full of serrated teeth. The irregular Czechs carried older weapons, smoothbore muzzle-loading carbines for the most part, but had proven themselves worthy and savage foes. Still, the brigade of approximately four thousand watchers would represent little more than a symbolic token against Halik if not for their better weapons and mobility, two things he wanted no more part of, and he took great pains to avoid antagonizing them. Particularly Svec. That had grown increasingly difficult the longer he and his people tarried in the valley, and was yet another reason he was anxious to march.

"Lord General," the captain said, eyes downcast, "General Shlook begs to inform you that a detachment of the enemy seeks an audience. It has approached beneath a white flag, a symbol we have been instructed to recognize as an appeal for a peaceful meeting." Halik was again impressed, both by the report and the ease with which he understood it. *Proper speech is so often neglected as officers are formed,* he lamented. That was something else he was trying to change. He turned to the east, where such embassies usually originated. The river was quite distant now, a line of low hills separating it from where he'd established his base. He knew Enaak had crossed behind him and set up his own base camp beside the river itself.

"It must tempt you," Niwa said simply, and Halik was amazed again by how easily the Japanese officer could read his thoughts.

"It does," he confessed. "The rainy season has begun, and with the river at his back it would be a simple thing to crush our enemy against it." He hissed a sigh. "*If* he were infantry. As it is, I have no illusions that he would not discover our approach and merely flutter away." He then turned and regarded Niwa with large, reptilian eyes. "And, of course, I have given my word."

"Of course."

"We shall meet this delegation," he told the captain, striding east, down the slope they stood upon. "General Ugla, please assemble the staff. Our impatient enemies do not often ask to speak with us. When they do, it is usually to make threats or demands. I expect them to insist, again, that we push on at last."

"But . . . Lord General," the captain stammered. "The

delegation has approached from the *west*, yonder!" He pointed. Halik paused, turning.

"We know they scout around us," Niwa said. "And they know we know. Coming from the west, before they can return to their headquarters and confer, suggests the meeting they desire might concern an urgent matter." His thin lips formed a small ironic smile. "Perhaps this time they may not make threats or demands—or if they do, they may be of an entirely different sort."

Spurred by a strange inner urgency, Halik and his companions rushed to join his staff, which was assembling behind the gate through the western breastworks. He'd taken a page from his enemy and built defenses that encircled his entire camp. They encompassed a huge area and weren't particularly impressive at a glance, but they should slow an attack at any point of contact long enough for reinforcements to arrive from elsewhere around the perimeter. It had been a compromise to avoid friction with his watchers, something he couldn't have done with more formidable defenses that might look like he meant to remain indefinitely. He looked beyond the gate and saw a squadron of Czechs deployed into line atop their unnerving kravaas. They looked weather-beaten and worn, their mounts exhausted, like they'd been on the move for days, but they remained formidable, Halik knew. He'd long envied the Allies their domesticated beasts for the mobility they afforded them. He'd done a little "experimental domestication" of his own in the time they'd spent in the valley, having the awkward-looking food beasts called "neekis" that Niwa said resembled something that sounded like "i-guaan-a-don" trained to pull wheeled carts and artillery. They couldn't be ridden; they were too large, their backs too broad, and none had allowed the attempts they'd made in any case. But they served admirably as swift draft animals. He was anxious to put them to use.

In the center and slightly forward, Colonel Svec himself lounged in his saddle, one boot crossed before him, his wild hair and beard rustling in the freshening breeze. Beside him was a mounted trooper with a white streamer tied around the muzzle of his upraised carbine. The trooper's hair and beard were darker and not as wild as his commander's, but Niwa took notice.

"A slightly . . . Oriental version of the older man," he said quietly, almost to himself. "His, ah, hatchling, I suspect," he added louder, for Halik's benefit. He shook his head. "There is always something new," he said cryptically, "and of course the Czechs found women somewhere, at some time. But who were *they*?"

Halik looked at his friend questioningly, but Niwa just shook his head. Together, they and a small detachment, joined by General Shlook, moved through the gate. Ugla remained behind as ordered.

Dalibor Svec was a giant of a man, well suited to the kravaa that bore him, and he wore a perpetual scowl in Halik's experience. He also wore an impressive array of weaponry. A heavy saber dangled from a belt that also supported at least three flap holsters that could be seen. A bandolier of cartridges was slung over his shoulder, as was a long-barreled rifle Niwa had called a "Moisen Nagant," which he'd undoubtedly brought to this world. Another pair of swords, like Russian Sasquas, and a pair of Baalkpan Arsenal carbines were fixed to his mount. He regarded Halik, Niwa, and the others through weather-pinched eyes like they were snakes crawling toward him, their fangs bared. Halik knew Niwa actually liked Colonel Enaak and considered him a fine officer. He'd been a soldier even before the first destroyerman ever reached Maa-ni-la and brought his Home into the war. He could always be counted on to be rational and reasonable, Niwa said, whereas he wasn't always sure Svec was either of those things. But Svec and his people had been fighting an incredibly skillful guerrilla war against the Grik in India for decades. So skillful, the Grik hadn't even known it. They'd always thought the secluded outposts, supply trains, and food beast herders he and his people had massacred had been wiped out by local predators. They had been, Halik supposed. Just not by the kind they thought.

Svec urged his beast forward, his apparent son by his side. Halik forced himself to stand firm in the face of the close approach of the large, dangerous beast. It looked just as menacing as its rider. A few yards away, it stopped, and Svec leaned forward in the saddle. "You have company coming, *plazivy*," he snapped, using the term he always addressed Halik by. Niwa said he had no idea what it meant.

"What kind of company?" Niwa asked. Halik could understand English quite well, but could barely speak it. Niwa always translated whenever they met the enemy and often asked questions or said things he knew Halik would have even before he was told.

Svec looked at Niwa. "More of his stinking kind. *Your* kind. Another army of Grik approaches less than a week's march from here," he grumbled, then took a deep, frustrated breath. "We never expected they would just turn off the tap. That is why I counseled strongly that *your* force be destroyed before you were ever allowed to cross the Indus River."

"When you had the power to do it," Niwa interjected. Svec said nothing. It was no secret that a mere brigade of cavalry, regardless of its quality, couldn't destroy Halik's army by itself, and with the withdrawal of Alden and Rolak's I Corps, there was nothing left to back it up. III Corps still had a division of veteran troops scattered in detachments along the line of Halik's retreat across India, and General Linnaa-Fas-Ra was supposed to be rushing elements of his VI Corps forward to build forts and secure the river crossings. But Linnaa was a "political" general from Sular, known to be hesitant toward the creation of the new union. He'd been dawdling in the vicinity of the Rocky Gap hundreds of miles away for weeks while his green corps "completed training." No one really believed he'd be so craven as to not come at all, but he was certainly taking his time.

"Yes, Jap! Damn you!" Svec snarled. There was no use denying it.

"Then why did you come here to tell us this?"

"Only to see if you mean to honor your pledge, not to join such a force if it came," Svec said, directly to Halik. "I do not trust Grik 'honor'"—he almost spat the word—"but Colonel Enaak does, and I demand your answer before I report to him."

It suddenly dawned on Halik that Svec must trust his

honor to *some* degree, however grudgingly, or he would never have approached with this news. If Halik meant to join any approaching force, the first thing he should do was destroy Svec and his companions to prevent word from reaching Enaak. He wondered why that realization pleased him.

"I have sworn my intentions to you, Colonel Enaak, and Generals Alden and Rolak," Halik said slowly through Niwa. "It is my, and I believe my creator's, greatest wish that this army I command should survive to someday return to our sacred land. More is at stake than myself, or even the army itself, but I see the salvation of my very race in what this army has become, separated from the culture it sprang from." He sighed. "You know this, and may even still consider us an even greater long-term threat for that reason, but I prefer to hope that, even as we have remained in close proximity to you for some time without fighting, what this army has become might represent an opportunity for a more general peace between your people and mine."

"And you will forgive me if I remain skeptical." Svec snorted sarcastically. "But Enaak wants to believe," he added, "and I will take your assurances to him. The question remains, however: how will you *avoid* joining the army that approaches? I doubt its leader will share your ideals."

"I will insist that I retain full autonomy of action, as specified by the orders of First General Esshk himself," Halik said.

"And if that is not enough?" Svec demanded.

"I shall insist more forcefully," Halik simply said.

Svec grunted. "Then I'm sure all will be well," he said derisively. "But hear this: we could not effectively count the army that comes, but I estimate it numbers nearly two hundred thousand warriors. They come as a mob, so you have the advantage of discipline," he said grudgingly, "but they are armed with a similar mix as yours: muskets and cannon, combined with crossbows." He managed a rueful grin. "I hope you are prepared to 'insist' quite forcefully indeed, *plazivy*."

"What will you and Colonel Enaak do?" Niwa asked.

"We will not hinder you in whatever you plan to do—unless it appears you won't keep your word. We still have an armistice, do we not? But we will prepare to harass the enemy as best we can. We remain at war with . . . all other Grik, and must fight them whether you rejoin them or not. We cannot retreat back across the river, as you well know. Not now. But rest assured, we will be watching. And much of what we may do depends on what you decide—and whether your 'intentions' survive your meeting with those who come." With that, he barked something to his comrades and urged his mount away. The other riders, with long, grim glances back at Halik, peeled off to follow, clods of damp earth rising in the wake of the heavy animals they rode.

"General Shlook," Halik said mildly. "We have much to prepare and little time." He gazed westward, as if studying the passes through the mountains in his mind. "I must go meet whoever leads the oncoming force at once, to explain the situation. But the passes all lead here. That is why we chose this place to begin with."

"And if whoever leads the approaching army will not grant your right to refuse to join him?" Shlook asked.

"Then we may fight him here. Wars between regencies are common enough. Our people constitute no regency of their own as such, but I remain convinced they shall one day form the core of all regencies everywhere, and we must ensure their survival, come what may."

"What should I do, Lord General? Command me!"

"Call one of the Hij who has learned to control the neekis and have him prepare an animal and cart to carry myself"—he paused, considering—"and a ten of warriors under the command of Captain . . ." He paused again, looking at the captain who'd alerted them. "What are you called?"

"Sigg, Lord General."

"Captain Sigg," Halik continued. "We shall leave as soon as it is ready and move as quickly as we can to meet our visitors as far from here as possible. Other than that, you will begin immediately to strengthen our defenses." Halik coughed a laugh. "Our watchers can only be heartened to see that now, and I expect no complaints. But you and General Ugla must keep all our people ready to march at a moment's notice. Our goal is *not* to fight, after all. And if we do, there may be better places for it."

"I should go, and you should not," Niwa protested hotly. Halik coughed another laugh. "No, my friend. I *must* go, and you *cannot*." He gestured toward the mountains. "They may not even know of you and would likely eat you as soon as you appeared! No, I must go, and you must command here in my stead. Is that understood?" he demanded, glancing at Generals Ugla and Shlook. To Niwa's apparent surprise, both bowed their heads without complaint.

CHAPTER
10

PT-7
Mangoro River
September 26, 1944

"**B**uncha chickenshits all run off," Silva said buoyantly, still grinning, as they motored back toward the beach where they'd last seen the feral Lemurians. "Give 'em a show like that an' you'd think they'd show a little 'preciation!"

"Chickenshits!" Petey agreed, scrambling back to his perch on Silva's shoulder. "Eat?" he pleaded. Silva absently reached up and thumped him on the head.

Chack was staring at the little sandy strip and blinking disappointment. When he heard the locals were gone, Bradford had resumed looking at the place the giant monster sank. The water frothed and splashed with gathering predators of a sort no one had yet seen, and birds and flying reptiles swooped and snatched floating morsels. There weren't any flasher fish—tuna-size equivalents to piranha occupying most oceanic shallows—in the river. They didn't tolerate freshwater any better than sharks. But there were plenty of other things.

"'ait!" Lawrence hissed. "They return!"

They all strained their eyes to pierce the gloom beneath the trees, hastily taking up weapons once more. Chack's sharp eyes saw the movement next. "There's one," he said.

Sure enough, a single Lemurian stepped tentatively into view. It still held its bow at the ready, an arrow laid across it, but it wasn't drawn.

"Look!" Courtney said. "Look at him!"

"We *are*, Mr. Bradford," Dennis assured him.

The only way to tell it was one of the same 'Cats they'd seen before was that its fur was slick and wet.

"Go closer," Chack ordered.

"Aye, aye," Nat said, easing the wheel over, pointing the bow at shore. The 'Cat drew back, but then stood its ground.

"Prob'ly thinks we're gonna torpedo him too," Silva muttered to Lawrence, who nodded seriously. Chack took up a speaking tube. "We mean you no harm," he shouted in Lemurian, his voice carrying loudly. "As you must see, we have even saved some of your people!"

The feral 'Cat on shore responded with what sounded like high-pitched nervous gibberish to Dennis, though he'd grown fairly fluent in Lemurian. In his case, of course, "fluent" meant he could usually understand most of what he heard, as long as it was spoken slowly. And his own pronunciation was often slow and deliberately comical. But he hadn't understood anything the native said. "You get any of that?" he asked Chack.

Chack was blinking to convey uncertainty. "Some, I think. Perhaps one word in three."

"See?" Silva demanded. "No point in stayin' if we can't even talk to 'em."

"What do you think he said?" Courtney asked.

Chack looked at Silva. "That if we won't destroy him like we did the monster, a, ah, 'magician,' a speaker of ancient words, will come."

"Well, at least tell 'em to quit shootin' at us," Silva grumped.

Chack did so, and whether or not they understood, the arrows didn't resume. Eventually, the native on shore disappeared. "Did you get any notion of how long we'll have to wait to meet this 'magician'?" Courtney asked. Chack sighed and spread his hands. "None," he said. "I can barely understand him," he stressed again. "The magician may be nearby—or several days away. Mr. Hardee, you may as well anchor—and shut down the engines to conserve fuel."

There was no breeze on the water, and they waited in the oppressive heat. Fortunately, there wasn't much of a stink from the dead monster. The water predators and scavengers would probably feed on it for days or weeks, but it had sunk entirely out of sight. The place it disappeared remained obvious, however, the water churning and slapping.

"Well, this is a drag," Silva finally said, tilting his helmet back and taking a chew. He glanced at Chack. "Say, Mr. Bradford, whaddayou really think about them crossbreed human-Lemurians in the Republic? You an' Inquisitioner Choon gabbled on long enough about 'em, as I recall."

The "hybrid" Gentaa were reputedly very strange folk: a cross between ancient Lemurians and possibly castaway Chinese. By all accounts, they did kind of look like it. While sharing a number of similarities, they were generally taller than regular 'Cats but had shorter, less expressive tails. Their faces were less feline, and their coats tended to paler, shorter fur. Initially believed to be virtual slaves of the Republic, Garrett had reported that wasn't the case at all and the Gentaa had essentially claimed for themselves the distinction of the "labor class," particularly on the docks and in the heavy industry of the Republic. As such, they exercised very real political power in much the same ways as labor unions. But there'd been no Gentaa on *Amerika* and probably only Greg Garrett and *Donaghey* knew the real dope on them now.

Courtney might've been the only one on the boat who didn't realize Silva didn't give a hoot about the Gentaa, but only raised the subject of human-Lemurian hybrids out of boredom—to torment Chack. Silva and Chack's sister Risa had long engaged in an . . . ambiguous relationship that neither had been willing to define. Most figured they were just great friends and only pretended it was more, to get people's goats. A few, sometimes including Chack, suspected there had, at least at times, been more to it than that.

"Actually," Courtney replied absently, still glassing the turmoil around the carcass in the water, "I'm not convinced they're hybrids at all."

"What? Sure they are! Ask anybody."

Courtney chuckled. "Indeed. Ask Inquisitor Choon. Even he doesn't believe it."

"But . . ."

Courtney waved his hand. "Oh, he toes the official line, that the Gentaa came about as the result of some ancient union between the species. The Gentaa themselves ardently perpetuate that understanding, possibly in the complete knowledge that it isn't true."

"But why?" Chack asked with growing interest.

"In my view, the answer's simple. Consider: our society, the one we've so quickly created within the Alliance, has fully integrated its various species to a remarkable degree. Humans, Lemurians"—he nodded at Lawrence—"even creatures that cannot help but remind us of our greatest enemy. There's respect and friendship among us all, a friendship reinforced by shared suffering and strife. I can think of no better way to create the unity, imperfect as it remains, that we've achieved. Do you imagine we'd have all become such great friends so quickly if the Grik or Doms hadn't threatened our very existence?"

Chack looked thoughtful.

"Of course not," Courtney stated, answering his own question. "Had the Grik not been undergoing a period of expansion, to the extent of threatening Lemurian sea and land Homes as far as the Malay barrier at last, *Walker* wouldn't have had to save *Salissa* from them. We wouldn't have been forced to turn Baalkpan society on its head to repel an even greater Grik invasion, and we ultimately, most assuredly, wouldn't all be here together . . . *torpedoing* natural wonders in the rivers of the Lemurians' ancestral home! Our relationship with the Empire of the New Britain Isles progressed in much the same way: overwhelming need assisted by ability achieved through strife. That is, sadly, always the way of things, I fear." He looked at Silva. "*Walker* and her people would've survived, I expect, possibly arranging to shoot mountain fishes to death with her great guns and then tow them to a Home for rendering." He shrugged, blinking. "Who knows. But none of the facilities to repair her would exist and she'd have become increasingly difficult to operate and maintain without, frankly, a war."

He shook his head. "But I digress. My point is, the Republic had no such unifying force to bring its people together during its early formation. If anything, it was more difficult even than that since the various factions and species fought against each other from time to time! It took *centuries* to establish the harmony in which they live together today, as opposed to our few short years. And the Gentaa took advantage of that."

"How so? Why?" Nat asked with growing interest.

"To justify their unique and quite separate status within Republic society, of course! They took upon themselves the very real stigma of the result of, ah, let us say 'too close a cooperation' between humans and Lemurians. They became the 'sin eaters.'" He seemed to think about the analogy, then nodded. "Yes," he said. "And by forbidding further fraternizations between themselves and either of their 'related' species, they virtually eliminated further, um, intimate fraternization between humans and Lemurians as well, which had never been desirable to either group, truth be told." Only then did he eye Silva speculatively. The notion that Silva might have been "fraternizing" with Risa had scandalized all the humans in the Alliance, but hadn't really bothered the Lemurians—except for Risa's relatives, and Chack in particular. "Interesting," Courtney murmured. "But in any event, as the Gentaa grew to represent a past that neither humans nor Lemurians were proud of, they also became a unifying force, don't you see? They were an oppressed, outcast people whom both parents must succor, and they worked together to do it! Ha! And in the meantime, the Gentaa became an entire species of victims who could do virtually as they pleased. Choosing their current role was a brilliant stroke since, though remaining apart from either parent group, they've made themselves essential to them both!"

"Unless either one ever figures out the scam," Miles said, speaking for the first time, but making it clear he was interested.

"Oh, I think the 'scam' must be fairly well-known by now. But the system works, after all, and therefore remains the official story!"

"Huh," Silva grunted. "Well, if that's so, and they ain't crossbreeds, then what *are* the critters?"

Courtney shrugged. "Another distinct species, I expect. I honestly never believed that humans and Lemurians are similar enough to create offspring, but perhaps both—all three, counting the Gentaa—are descended from an ancestor common to us all? Or perhaps the Gentaa are truly the only species indigenous to the region?" He smiled happily. "Or maybe they came later, in much the same way the rest of us did. I do so love to speculate! But it hardly matters. I don't think they're hybrids."

"Huh," Silva said again, then "Huh," for a third time, before his one eye slid slyly toward Chack. "Well," he said with evident relief, "I guess this means that certain folks don't need to worry 'bout, well, you know, 'complications' no more."

Chack glared at him, his tail whipping. "'Certain people' *should* worry about what a certain healer named Paam Cross might think. Or do."

"She still don't own me," Silva warned, glaring back.

"She thinks she does, and perhaps more important, Cap-i-taan Reddy and his mate, the Lady Saandra, are now convinced of it as well. Paam is chief surgeon aboard USS *Walker* and prone to . . . fits of temper." Chack piously blinked extreme disapproval. "To inspire one of those fits might even constitute behavior detrimental to the war effort, in their view."

Silva just stared at his Lemurian friend . . . then guffawed. "My God, Chackie! You're gettin' good at this!"

"Silence!" Lawrence hissed, nodding his snout toward shore. "Excuse I, 'ut they are returned."

An old 'Cat, its face and mane bright with white fur, and dressed in a dingy robe cut somewhat like the one Adar always wore, slid down the embankment and halted, glaring at them. Probably the same 'Cat that was there before (it was impossible to tell) quickly joined him and stood at his side, half supporting him. Together, they just stood there, grimly waiting.

"Well," Courtney said. "Perhaps your unorthodox demonstration has served its purpose, Colonel Chack. Shall we go and meet them?"

Chack looked around. There could still be—probably were—hundreds of armed natives hiding out of sight. "We will approach," he stated. "But remain wary," he warned. "Lawrence will stay on the machine gun, and I want the mortar rigged and manned on the fo'c'sle." His eyes fastened on Miles. Reluctantly, the China Marine stepped over the coaming to join the 'Cats already moving to obey. "Chief Silva, please arm yourself with something more appropriate to the threat." Grumbling, Silva put his Doom Stomper in the rack and took his Thompson SMG. Quickly inspecting it, he inserted a magazine. "Okay, Chackie, let's go a'visitin'."

The Seven boat burbled closer to shore until the bow gently touched the bank. It looked as though the two natives wanted nothing more than to bolt, but they held their ground. One of the 'Cats on the fo'c'sle stood helplessly, with no one to throw his line to, and finally simply jumped across himself and secured the line to a fallen tree, casting nervous glances at their hosts. The feral 'Cats on shore just watched him finish his task and then clamber back aboard.

"You better go first, Chackie," Silva said, his tone serious for once. "Judgin' by what happened to McGinnis, they don't much like folks like me." Chack agreed. Unsaid was a fact they both recognized: Chack's comparative size might be intimidating enough, but Silva made two, perhaps three of the people on shore. "I'd stay on the boat an' palaver with 'em from the fo'c'sle, if I was you," Silva added as Chack stepped forward, his Krag slung over his shoulder. "But I'll cover you whatever you do," he assured. Chack had no doubt. He and his big friend had many superficial differences, but they'd die for each other without thinking. He heard Silva add, "You stay hunkered down outa sight, Larry. They might not hate humans a'tall. Might be *you* lookin' so Grikish that has 'em riled. But stay ready. If they try to hurt Chackie, we kill 'em all, clear?"

Chack was tempted to just hop down, as the crew-'Cat

had done, but the way the strangers regarded him gave him pause. They'd *known* the other 'Cat was of lower rank, and he was a far greater prize. For the moment he simply squatted by the jackstaff. "I am Lieuten-aant Col-nol Chack-Sab-At, of the First Raider Battalion. I command this expedition and represent all the Allied powers united beneath or beside the Banner of the Trees to destroy the Grik menace that has plagued your people and mine since the beginning of time. Whom have I the honor of addressing?"

The old 'Cat on shore seemed taken aback by the long title. Chack had hoped it would impress him. But the long-winded introduction had also given him a chance to study the strangers better. Yes, the cloak the old one wore was similar to Adar's, but the material was coarser and there was no embroidery. Other than that, neither he nor the warrior beside him wore any adornments other than strange necklaces of tiny bones almost woven together. He also noted clearly for the first time that they weren't alone. Other feral 'Cats lingered back in the brush and some were indeed in the trees overhead, creeping carefully closer. There were at least five or six that he could see so there were probably many more. *Silva's true "cat-monkeys" at last,* he suddenly realized. *And not behaving in the most trustworthy manner . . .*

The magician, or whatever he was, seemed to collect himself and took a step forward. "I am Heegar-Ep-Erok, High Shaman to the Erokighaani! You say you come peacefully, but"—his eyes narrowed—"you have tailless ones among you. They are bad. That you and they are together is bad. None of them have ever come to us without harm! No other tribes, even of those like us, have truly come in peace—and you expect me to believe you?"

To Chack's astonishment, he understood nearly every word the old shaman said. It was spoken in a very ancient, formal way, but the pronunciation was even vaguely familiar, much like the way old Naga used to talk. He'd never heard Adar talk that way, though, and wondered about that.

"Yes, I do," he simply said. "These tailless ones are our friends, and would be friends to you as well."

The shaman hacked derisively, but then made a show of considering the notion. He spoke. "It may be possible that, just because a thing has never happened, does not mean it can't. I beg you to forgive our discourteous welcome. I *must* still find it difficult to believe you mean us no harm, yet my eyes and ears both observed as you . . . slew the great geegaak." He peered intently, greedily, at Chack. "What magic did you use? From whence did it come? It is great magic indeed! Share it with us so we can defend ourselves from other monsters, and we will be your friends forever!"

Such a switch! From wary welcome to eternal friends— all based on the Seven boat's "magic." Chack didn't trust the old skuggik before him any farther than he could throw him, as Silva would say, and his gut told him that these people would never do.

"The, uh, 'magic' is our own, and we only have so much. We can bring more to our friends," he hastily added when he saw the shaman's eyes narrow, "but what we have we must preserve to use against the Grik."

"Grik? Grik?" The shaman looked at the warrior beside him. "I know no 'Grik.' The geegaak is the worst monster that haunts this river, in our land. Is it the same?" he added hopefully. "The Grik and the geegaak?"

"No," Chack replied, shaking his head. "The Grik are smaller, but there are . . ." He paused. Large numbers for things you couldn't see had always been a bit tricky for his people before the Americans came along. "There are hundreds of hundreds of Grik for each geegaak, and they build great ships, far larger than this, and swarm together without number when they attack."

The warrior spoke in the shaman's ear.

"Ah! You mean the . . ." He said something guttural that Chack didn't catch. Seeming to realize this, he added, "The lizard people."

"Yes, I expect so," Chack agreed.

"No one can fight the lizard people! They are too many!"

"We have and we do," Chack countered. "We've taken their great city to the north, ah, that way," he said, pointing. "They try to take it back and we need friends who are willing to help us stop them."

To Chack's amazement, the shaman dropped to his knees and threw twigs and dirt in the air. "There are no lizard people here! We do not *want* them here! And we will not go where they are! To do so would only bring them!"

"If they defeat us, they *will* come here," Chack warned, then realized he'd said the wrong thing when the shaman's tail flipping accelerated to a blur.

"Because of you! They will come because *you* came!"

"No," Chack objected. "They will come because that's what they do—but with help to defeat them, they will never come. Ever."

"There are no lizard people here. We cannot help you," the shaman said briskly, but paused and tried to hide a sly blink. "But the Shee-ree, beyond the great stony mountains, see lizard people all the time and have tried to get us to help them too. They send callers to all the river tribes, but none are foolish enough to go. The Shee-ree might help you, but you could never reach them."

"Why not?"

The old shaman laughed. "Because they dwell across the mountains in the great, wide land beyond. Do you have the magic to fly?"

"Not with us," Chack said. He couldn't help it. "But we have to push on to the Shee-ree, if they might help when no others will." Without another word, he turned to go.

"Wait!" called the shaman.

"What?"

"We are friends now, yes?"

"I hope so," Chack said.

"Good. If you continue up the river and harm no one, we will leave you in peace. Other tribes, closer to the mountains, will leave you in peace." His voice turned less friendly. "But when you turn back, as you must, they will want the magic you do not use against the lizard people. As will we."

Chack nodded curtly, then stepped back to his friends.

"I caught a little of that," Silva said. "Did it go like I think it did?"

"Oh dear," Bradford groaned. "I suppose I won't be going ashore to meet them after all."

"No, Mr. Bradford. Not if you expect to return. They would use you to get our 'magic' now, and still probably hold you until we brought them more. I expect the same from any other tribes they may have contact with on the river." Chack looked at Silva. "I doubt these are the same people who killed Sergeant McGinnis, but they're little different from them. Expecting a large population of friendly Lemurians itching to fight the Grik was probably unrealistic after all."

"Don't sweat it. The world can't be full of Khonashis and Maroons." The Khonashi, of course, were I'joorka's people, and Maroons were probably the great-great-grandchildren of the crew and passengers of a British East Indiaman who came here long ago. Two others from the same convoy had gone on to found the Empire of the New Britain Isles. But if the descendants from the one the Grik captured had reverted to primitivism, at least they, like the Khonashi, were friendly.

Chack nodded reluctantly, but continued. "But these 'Shee-ree,' if they exist, sound promising. So if you think 'the way it went' is that we must push upriver as far as it takes us, then leave the boat and continue on foot, you are right."

"Shit."

Chack looked at Nat. "Hopefully, we'll make contact with Cap-i-taan Reddy"—he hesitated—"and Gener-aal Queen Maraan at some point, but we will go on regardless. It will then be your task to carry word back for us." He looked at the shore. "You must be *very* careful! They very clearly want our 'magic,' as will anyone else we meet, no doubt. You will probably have to fight your way back, and they will be more prepared."

"I understand, Colonel, but I . . . I can't just leave you!"

Silva grinned. "That was your original order."

"No it wasn't! I was ordered to set you ashore and await your return! And we can't even do that now!"

"Don't worry, Mr. Hardee," Courtney said. "These tribes along the river may cooperate a bit, but they probably hate one another too much to combine against us. I doubt they'll even cross from one territory to another. Classic aboriginal behavior!" He shrugged. "And if the far side of the mountains is anything like it was on our world, which, according to that fellow on shore, it must be somewhat similar, at least"—his face turned grim—"I doubt enough warriors could survive beyond them to be of much threat to us at all."

"Us?" Chack asked, blinking at him curiously.

"Well, of course I shall accompany you!" Courtney grinned. "You haven't the authority to stop me if you wanted to! And the whole point of our coming is to meet new people, after all."

"What about them?" Miles demanded, pointing over the side. "We met *them*. We did our job, now let's get the hell out of here!"

Courtney looked at Miles, his expression neutral. "Indeed. Well, though I entirely agree with Colonel Chack's evaluation of the people here, we must press on and hope for better: people we can trust. And evaluating that is *my* job, actually. I've grown surprisingly good at it, you know."

SMS **Amerika**
The Sunda Strait
September 28, 1944

The afternoon squalls were even more prevalent that day as SMS *Amerika*, wet and steaming under the glaring sun from the periodic rain lashings she'd taken, neared the southern entrance to the Sunda Strait.

"The lookout reports a large ship in the strait, bearing *null*, *drei*, *null*, perhaps ten thousand meters," called a Lemurian near the cluster of speaking tubes on the aft bulkhead of the pilothouse. He spoke German, as did all the watch standers on *Amerika*'s bridge, but that was about the only place they did it anymore. Most of the crew spoke the polyglot version of Lemurian that had arisen in the Republic over the centuries, touched by everything from Chinese to Latin. But oddly, English had become the "official" language in the ship's engineering spaces. It was a bizarre tradition that had evolved over the last quarter century and, to some degree, reflected the fact that although she'd served the Imperial German Navy, *Amerika* had been built by Harland and Wolff in Belfast, Ireland. In addition, when she arrived on this world, full of English-speaking prisoners of war taken from merchant ships she'd caught as an auxiliary cruiser, there'd been more trained engineers among her captives than in her crew. As things normalized between the former enemies on this new world and they all became equal citizens of the Republic of Real People, the accents emanating from the voice tubes to the engineering spaces grew more diverse, with hints of Scotch, Welsh, Irish, even Indian, but they increasingly, stubbornly, spoke English. And so it had been for more than twenty years. Perhaps, though, the most compelling reason English endured only belowdecks was exactly because German was still enforced on the bridge. Now friends, the two factions enjoyed a rivalry of the sort that implied "You might tell us what to do, but we're in charge of whether we do it or not." Kapitan Leutnant Becher Lange, now in actual, if not official, command due to the growing infirmity of Kapitan Von Melhausen, found the tradition somewhat tiresome. Despite having commanded the ship when she captured them, Von Melhausen himself had always been amused and supportive of the ongoing jest, largely why he was so beloved by all the ship's crew, and had been retained in command far longer than was probably wise.

Becher Lange raised his binoculars and stared through the distortion of the wet bridge windows. "I see it," he said. "It is large, but another squall lies between us. It is ... indistinct." He stepped out on the bridgewing, where Chairman Adar, Minister Tucker, Diania, and several others had gone when the latest squall passed, to enjoy the breeze and the sight of the islands to the northeast. He smiled at them and nodded, looking though the binoculars again.

"What is it, Cap-i-taan Laange?" Adar asked.

Lange gestured. "A large ship in the strait, obscured by another squall. It is difficult to make out."

Adar squinted, his excellent vision nearly a match for the binoculars. "I see it, I believe. A dark smudge in the rain?"

Lange nodded. "It is raining harder now there. Is there any large vessel, a new aircraft carrier perhaps, due to join First Fleet South? I have not seen the new *Baalkpan Bay* Class of carrier, but the contact appears to be of similar size. Smaller than *Salissa*."

"Nothing I am aware of," Adar replied, blinking

uncertainty. "One was nearing completion at last report, before we lost communications, but even if that is her, I would expect her to still be undergoing trials and working up her air wing. She might be doing that en route," he allowed.

"Good afternoon, Lady Sandra. Gentlemen," came a soft, almost whispy voice behind them.

"Kapitan Von Melhausen! You should not be up!" Lange protested, moving as if to catch the old man. He looked like he might need it. He'd grown incredibly frail, and had weakened considerably just in the last few weeks. His carefully pressed blue coat almost swallowed him and his hat sat upon his balding head, down to his ears, as if it was several sizes too large. Sandra winced at the sight, regretting there was nothing she could do for him. His body was failing even more quickly than his mind now, and the only reminders of a once-imposing presence were his thick, white, carefully groomed mustache and a pair of sharp eyes that missed nothing—when his mind was behind them. This seemed to be one of those spells, and he gestured for Lange to hand him the binoculars.

"Why should I not be up? It is my watch, is it not? You will suffocate me with your sympathy if I let you," he added fondly. "I will not allow it! I will live as long as this ship!" he boasted, shakily raising the glasses and holding them to his eyes. "It *is* difficult to see," he confessed. "The rain begins to pass, but the land beyond now hides its shape."

"Kapitan!" came the voice of the talker from within the pilothouse. "Kapitan*s*," it quickly corrected. "The lookout says it is a *warship*! Huge! He has never seen anything like it!"

Sandra realized that she had, as the shape grew more defined—at least to her—and she was suddenly certain what it was. The general configuration wasn't all that different from *Amagi*'s, after all, and nobody friendly had anything remotely similar. "Oh my God," she murmured. "Turn the ship immediately!" she urged. "It's *Savoie*! It has to be!"

Adar and Lange both blinked astonishment in the Lemurian way. "How?" Lange demanded, his mind catching up with his disbelieving eyes and finally recognizing the class if not the ship itself, from across the gulf of a quarter century. It was clearly a *Bretagne*, a French "superdreadnaught." The very latest things in French naval power at the beginning of "his" old war, he'd familiarized himself with their silhouettes. There'd been only three at the time, under other names, but a fourth had been under construction. That one must have become *Savoie*. "How can she be *here*? And why? I do not believe she has come to join us!" he added sarcastically.

"Just get us away from her!" Sandra urged, almost shouting now. She didn't know how either. It was a long way from Alex-aandra, and where could the thing have fueled? But she thought she knew why, and the reason infuriated and terrified her.

"Left full rudder!" Lange roared in German. "Full steam ahead!" Almost as an afterthought, he added: "All hands to battle stations!" The last was a meaningless gesture. *Amerika* had two 10.5-cm guns, similar to *Walker*'s 4″-50s, capable of reaching *Savoie* at this distance. They might actually even dent her if they hit. The *Bretagne* Class had been armed with ten 340-mm/45 (roughly 13.5″) rifles in five twin turrets, although the word was that *Savoie*'s main battery had been reduced to eight guns in four turrets. But she still had a swarm of secondaries, all bigger than *Amerika*'s guns. And who knew how many machine guns *Savoie* might have. *Amerika* had quite a few Maxims at her disposal, old and new, but they'd make no difference. They simply couldn't fight, particularly with nearly three thousand wounded aboard, and Lange had a sinking feeling they probably couldn't run away either. "Send a distress call detailing our situation at once!"

"All we have is the TBS!" the talker reminded.

"Then we will hope that someone is close enough to hear. Perhaps a scouting flight out of Tjilatjap is nearby."

The Lemurian at the helm spun the big wooden wheel, and another rang up the engine order. The ringing reply from the engine room came without the customary delay, but it seemed to take a great long while before the big ship began to respond. SMS *Amerika* hadn't been in a real dry dock since 1914, and her hull had suffered, growing thin, leaky, and brittle over the years. A short stint lifted aboard the now-lost SPD USS *Respite Island* had helped, but the repairs completed then had never been envisioned as more than—literally—a stopgap. Despite all her years, however, and the impossibility of performing comprehensive repairs in the Republic, which had never been willing to appropriate the materials and labor to construct a dry dock large enough to accommodate her near-seven-hundred-foot length, and roughly twenty-five thousand tons, her engineering plant had been meticulously maintained. That meant she was still nearly as fast as she'd ever been, capable of almost eighteen knots. The trouble was, the rain-lashed apparition, finally emerging completely from the squall and glistening in the afternoon sun about six miles away, was probably just as fast.

Von Melhausen was still looking through the binoculars as *Amerika*'s human and Lemurian crew began racing for their battle stations, uncovering her guns. "They have added a heavy tripod mast, forward," he said, his voice oddly firmer than before. "And removed her central turret. Two fewer guns, at least. They have replaced it with an aircraft catapult larger than but similar to the one installed aboard *Walker*. I see no aircraft, though."

Spoiled by *Walker*'s comparative responsiveness, Sandra pounded the rail in frustration. "Can't this thing turn any faster?"

Von Melhausen cast a glance at her. "This 'thing' is a lady. An elderly one as well," he scolded gently. "You cannot expect her to dash about like a cheetah. She will show *that* 'thing' her heels soon enough, once she has completed her turn."

Sandra didn't think so. What was more, the range was falling rapidly as *Savoie* now charged toward them. *Amerika* was finally gathering speed, however, and her rudder was biting harder.

"Our call is not getting through!" cried the talker, his voice high. "Something . . . covers our signal! Wait! There is a message on the voice radio! It orders us to cease all transmissions and stop engines or—be fired upon!"

"They had to be expecting us," Adar said. "There is no other way they could be here now. No other reason for them to be." He blinked at Sandra. "Which means they are probably also aware of the nature of our voyage, the precious cargo we carry. I hesitate to endanger that cargo, but I believe we must oblige them to prove they are willing to go that far before we meekly submit. Judging by their behavior at Alex-aandra, it is reasonable to wager that they will show restraint. That they bluff."

"I hope you're right," Sandra said, but she agreed.

Diania looked at them, her dark eyes flashing. "Then theys also prob'ly know our *other* cargo!" she snapped, and Adar blinked at her questioningly. "You!" she said hotly, and turned to Sandra. "An' you!"

Sandra felt a chill. The wounded were her responsibility, her primary concern. She hadn't thought beyond that. But Diania might be right about *Savoie*'s objective here. The chairman of the Grand Alliance, and likely leader of the new Union they'd built, would be a great prize indeed, to any enemy. And she—it made her almost vomit to realize—would be a tempting source of leverage against the Supreme Commander of all Allied forces: Captain Matthew Reddy! Matt would never ransom her or Adar, or even a ship full of wounded soldiers, but she ached at the thought of the torment he'd suffer.

Lange's expression proved that he agreed with Diania's assessment, as well as Sandra's certainty that he and his ship could expect no concessions to save them if they were taken. "Keep calling for help. Try to get through. Tell those *inselaffen* in engineering to take all the boilers and engines can be made to give, as if the ship—and their lives—depend upon it, because they do!"

Amerika finally finished her turn and sprinted southwest, her dark coal smoke billowing high. It wasn't enough to spoil *Savoie*'s aim, but maybe it would be seen by friendly eyes. *Savoie* sent another demand that they halt transmissions and heave to, but *Amerika* surged onward. Fifteen minutes passed, then thirty. Finally, just as a sense of relief began to creep into many anxious hearts, the sun-dappled *Savoie*, her light gray paint nearly matching the clouds beyond her, suddenly flashed with fire and a roil of dirty brown smoke that gushed to leeward.

"The contact has opened fire!" the talker cried, just as

a pair of gigantic splashes arose several hundred yards ahead of *Amerika*.

"I saw," Lange muttered grimly, staring aft now at the charging battleship. The sea churned away from her bow and she seemed almost low by the head as she shouldered it aside. He knew that was an illusion. *Savoie* was designed to be a stable gun platform, and she didn't ride the waves as much as batter through them, keeping her deck—and guns—as level as possible. He sighed. She was also clearly gaining. Another warning came, then more shots, closer this time. Finally, an apparently very carefully aimed salvo landed close enough to shake the ship and drench the bridge with falling water. This was followed by a terse signal that there'd be no further warnings, and the next salvo would fall directly on the ship.

"What must I do?" Lange pleaded of Adar, who merely scratched his chin and stared for a moment, blinking.

"I will not order you what to do," he said at last, "but it is clear we cannot escape. Nor can we fight," he added, noting the way Sandra's eyes looked almost pleadingly at the ship's meager gun, aft. "If we fire at them, they will certainly destroy us. They have already proven they can." He spread his hands. "I see no alternative to obeying their command to stop. Perhaps we may at least continue to delay things long enough for friends to notice." Lange's eyes suddenly lit and he bolted inside the pilothouse. "All stop! Tell engineering to vent steam, at once! We make them think we are damaged!" He managed a desperate grin back at Adar and Sandra. "She is old, after all, and we have pushed her hard. If they want this ship, they will have to wait while we 'effect repairs,' which will take as long as we can delude them!"

"Damn," Gunnery Sergeant Arnold Horn muttered to Lieutenant Toryu Miyata. The two had arranged their deck chairs so they could "watch the show," with a lot of other wounded who'd walked or limped outside to see what was going on. But those last rounds had fallen awful close, soaking them both to the bone. Now the boat deck was packed with staring men and 'Cats, the engines had stopped, and steam and smoke roared skyward from the two garishly painted funnels amidships. "I think we broke something," he said.

"Or *they* broke it, with those near misses," Miyata speculated.

"Yeah. I bet you could knock a hole in this straw-bottom bitch's belly with a ball-peen hammer. League bastards. What can they be thinking? Scuttlebutt is they want to avoid a war, but can you imagine a quicker way to start one than by shooting up a hospital ship with Adar and Captain Reddy's wife aboard?"

"Who are they anyway, this 'League'? And what do they want? You were aboard *Walker* when she sank one of their submarines"—Miyata nodded at the gray steel monster steaming closer—"and that is apparently the same ship that interfered with the Republic's preparations to launch an offensive against the Grik. But frankly"—he waved at his foot—"I was preoccupied with other things and did not learn as much as I would have liked about them during my convalescence."

Horn shrugged. "Me too. Didn't really think about them. I sure never expected to see them here! They're some kind of French Nazis, I heard. But something else too. And they're supposed to be in a heavier weight class than us." He snorted. "I believe it, if they can spare that thing just to pester us!"

Miyata considered. "Well, they must have a plan. They could have sunk us. I wonder what they want."

His was obviously a universal sentiment, and as many of *Amerika*'s crew and passengers as could make it on deck slowly gathered to watch the powerful ship's relentless approach. Finally, when it lay just five hundred yards off, secondaries trained on the helpless old liner, Horn noticed a commotion forward around the lifeboat davit closest to the bridge where one of the *Amerika*'s motor launches was being lowered down even with the deck.

"Hey!" Horn said. "What the hell? Come on!"

Together, the two men pushed their way through the crowd, Horn half supporting Miyata, until they broke through beside the launch. Horn was stunned to see Adar and Kapitan Leutnant Becker Lange grimly stepping into the boat to join Sandra, Diania, and several sailors already seated. Lange looked nervous, and Adar . . . Horn never could figure out what 'Cats were thinking. Diania, just as expressionless as Adar, was holding a bag against her chest. He assumed it was packed with necessities for her and her boss. Sandra looked . . . deadly furious.

"Hey!" he said again, louder. "Where are you going?"

Sandra spared him a harried, bitter smile. "They've demanded our presence—specifically," she stressed, "aboard *Savoie*. We're hostages," she added with a curled lip. "They've assured us that *Amerika* and all aboard will be treated well as long as we go across, and we won't be harmed as long as *Amerika* behaves—and gets underway as soon as possible. She's a 'prize.'" She snorted. Then she glanced at Lange and lowered her voice. She probably wasn't worried anyone would blab, she just did it for general principles. "There's nothing wrong with the engines," she told Horn. "They're trying to buy time, hoping one of our ships or planes comes close enough to see what's going on and can get a message off, at least." She hesitated, darting an eye at Miyata. "You've . . . been a prisoner before, Gunny Horn. Endured things I can't imagine. I'm counting on you to take care of our people. Keep them organized; keep their hopes up. Keep them *soldiers*," she stressed.

"Lower away!" Lange snapped at the 'Cats beside the davits. The boat lurched downward. Horn stared at Sandra, then at Diania, his eyes wide. "No," he said simply, and stepped into the boat.

"Belay!" Lange shouted, glaring at him.

Sandra was glaring too. "I gave you an order!"

"Yes, ma'am, you did," Horn agreed. "You said, 'Keep them soldiers.'" He jerked his head back at the assembled wounded. "They don't need me for that, and there're plenty of officers to keep them organized. You need me to keep *your* hopes up . . . *because* I've been a prisoner—and I got away!"

"I've been a prisoner before as well," Sandra snapped, "and can take care of myself."

"Sure. But you had Silva with you then." He shrugged. "I may not be Silva—and don't ever tell him I said this— but I'm the next best thing. And besides"—he snorted angrily and held his hands out, palms up—"if he ever found out I didn't go, to look after you and Adar"—he nodded hesitantly at Diania—"and the rest, well, let's just say life wouldn't be worth living. If he let me live."

"I, for one, have never been a prisoner," Adar said wryly, "and would consider Gunny Horn's presence and . . . expertise a comfort."

Sandra tried to hide the hint of a sad smile by rubbing her eyes. "Oh, very well. Just don't do anything stupid."

"Never, ma'am." He grinned. "I told you, I'm not Silva. So long, Miyata!" he called to his friend. "I'll see you . . . wherever the hell they take us."

"Lower away," Lange barked again, staring speculatively at Gunny Horn.

Kapitan Adler Von Melhausen shuffled back and forth on his ship's quiet bridge, staring out the windows at the great dreadnaught off their starboard beam. He was filled with a fury he hadn't known since that terrible day thirty years before when he felt his ship shiver and buck with the impacts from *Mauretania*'s guns. The watch, human and Lemurian, all too young to remember that day—or the astonishing events that followed—had the feel of it, though. The sense of injury, violation. Helplessness. They were resentful, and occasionally glanced at him with sad, yearning looks. He didn't know what to do and vaguely, tortuously, remembered the last time he'd thought he did. He'd made a terrible mistake at the Battle of Grik City, and lives might have been lost because of it. He was unfit to command; his time had passed, and he'd even come to terms with that. But Becher was like a son to him. The ship would be in good hands when he was gone.

The motor launch came into view, cresting the light swells, laboring toward *Savoie*. He felt another stab of rage and his fitful old heart thundered in his chest. *The ship would* not *be in good hands! She was captured, and Becher was to be a hostage.* How had such a thing occurred? He stood straighter and clasped his hands behind his back. *Odd,* he thought. *Again I cannot feel my left hand! It is as if it is gone!* He kneaded it with his right, but felt nothing at all.

"Kapitan Von Melhausen!" the young helmsman murmured. "Are you all right?"

He blinked. "I am well," he said, and his voice sounded strangely slurred, even to his ears, but also stronger than it had been for . . . a long time? *Why would I think that? Have I been ill? Am I now?* He blinked again, and his eyes widened. *There is an enemy ship over there!* he suddenly realized anew, all thoughts of just a moment before, over the last quarter century in fact, suddenly swept away. *A French battleship! Oh, what a glorious accomplishment for a mere armed merchant ship, no matter what the cost! It is right there, and its guard is down! It is terribly powerful, but I too have a powerful weapon!* His left arm dangled uselessly at his side, and inexplicably, the vision in his left eye began to darken. Perhaps he should call the surgeon? It would wait until after he'd done one last thing.

"All ahead flank! Right full rudder!" he shouted, his voice sounding strong but far away. *It must be the wind blowing through the pilothouse. The cooling wind.*

"But, Kapitan!" came the shrill reply, and Von Melhausen stared.

My God! What is that . . . thing at the wheel? His mind demanded. *I . . . should know, I do know, but . . . No time!* With a burst of strength no one who saw him would ever suspect he might still summon, he slammed the horrified, blinking Lemurian aside with his shoulder and spun the wheel with his right hand. *Why won't the left one work? No matter.* "Full steam!" he roared, and even as he did, his left eye went entirely dark.

"No! Do not!" someone cried, but then Von Melhausen heard the bells ring up. He smiled. *Of course they did! I am still Kapitan of SMS* Amerika! *My crew will obey!*

"Oh . . . ah," Adar managed. He'd been staring back the way they came while everyone else gazed at the mountain of weapon-bristling steel they approached. He'd looked for a while himself, still amazed the thing could actually float any better than an angular slab of stone—which it resembled to him. But then something drew his gaze back to the sleeker, more pleasing lines of the old liner. The garish (even to him) paintwork applied by the Republic was now dulled by rust, but the long, coiling, serpent-like creature that adorned its side was still quite visible, and the hubris of the bold image, considering how vulnerable the great vessel truly was, suddenly struck him. Maybe it was simply fear that made him look back, reluctance to face the uncertainty ahead. He was terrified of what would become of him and his friends—all his people, for that matter. It was obvious the League meant to use them in some way that would not be helpful to his people's cause. But he had no choice. Balanced against the threat *Savoie* posed to so many helpless men and Lemurians who'd already sacrificed so much, whatever the League might do to him was insignificant. That didn't mean he didn't hate them, and maybe it was just the profound, bleak sadness within him that, no matter how well they were treated, the wounded aboard *Amerika* wouldn't soon be home in Baalkpan after all, that made him look back. For whatever reason, he noticed the dark smoke belch from her funnels before anyone else, and his keen eyes saw the water at her stern churn to life. Lange and Horn looked back when he spoke, and Lange suddenly shouted over the small, popping engine at the Lemurian holding the tiller: "Turn to starboard, for your life! We must get out from between them!"

"What?" Sandra said, turning around. "Oh no!" she practically shrieked, and Diania grabbed her when she tried to stand. The small gun on *Amerika*'s bow suddenly fired, quickly followed by the one positioned aft. The ships were close, but they still heard the shrill rip of the shells passing almost over them. Both impacted against the battleship—it was impossible to miss—but neither detonated. One crunched into the superstructure, leaving a visible hole. The other ricocheted off the hull armor and warbled off over the sea.

"No!" Sandra screamed again as *Amerika* gathered way, her length beginning to shorten as her rudder vectored the thrust of her screws. Her guns fired again and again, as shapes on her boat deck scrambled for cover, or possibly, some way to fight. Maxim guns stuttered down her length, throwing clouds of lead and copper dust among men aboard *Savoie*, as they too scattered for cover, or raced back to weapons they'd abandoned. In all, *Amerika* must have gotten off five or six unanswered salvos, only a couple bursting harmlessly against *Savoie*'s armored side. Doubtless they were the same rounds the old liner brought to this world and age had taken its toll on them as well. But in that time, the ship narrowed the gap to her captor enough that it was clear that Kapitan Von Melhausen—it had to be him; only he commanded the moral authority and devotion to inspire his crew to so rash an act— intended to smite *Savoie* with the only weapon he had that might actually hurt her: *Amerika* herself. That was when *Savoie*'s secondary armament, already roughly aimed, finally began coughing fire and smoke, and her great turrets with their massive guns started to turn.

Some of *Savoie*'s guns actually missed. They were panic firing in local control, and *Amerika* became a smaller target as she turned bows on, water creaming before her as she gathered speed. Most hit. Explosions racked the big ship as she came, hurling hull plates, deck splinters, and bodies high in the air. The blows came so quick that it grew hard to distinguish them. The foremast buckled and fell, then the aft funnel, likely struck by shells exiting the forward one, leaned and twisted until it toppled off the ship to port, crushing lifeboats and wounded troops as it slid over the boat deck. Smoke gushed and streamed away. Miraculously, the forward gun was still firing, as were a number of Maxims, peppering defiantly at the dread-naught, but *Amerika*'s bridge took a catastrophic hit and the entire structure was gouged away in a blizzard of shattered debris. Von Melhausen and all the blindly loyal men and 'Cats who'd opened this mad act had to have died then, torn apart like the ship they so revered, but the ship itself, as if intent on heeding their final commands regardless of the tragic cost, churned on, unerringly, directly for *Savoie*.

Diania and Horn were both holding Sandra now, as she wept in desolation at the carnage. Men and 'Cats she— and her dozens of medical friends, also dying—had toiled to save, *had* saved, in so many cases, were being senselessly slaughtered, and there was nothing she could do but watch. Adar was weeping too, the gray fur around his wide silvery eyes glistening and damp. Lange and his boat crew felt the same emotions, and others. Their home was dying. Their father was dead. Strangely, though, even as the bloodbath continued, the harm irreversibly done, another yearning built within every soul aboard the racing launch; a longing that, insane as it was, *Amerika*'s sacrifice not be in vain and that she somehow complete her final sprint to smash deep into the side of her murderer. Yet even that meager consolation was not to be.

The water aft of the fire- and smoke-spitting dread-naught spalled to life as her own screws started to bite, and her four massive turrets finally finished their stately traverse. With a stuttering, ear-shattering blast, all eight 13.5-inch rifles hurled half-ton shells at the ruined, smoke-streaming hulk from a range of less than three hundred yards. Also fired in local control, and with the target so close, half of them missed. If *Amerika* had been a little smaller, a little faster, or even just a little closer, all would've probably gone over. As it was, four of the massive shells slammed her in quick succession, gutting her like she'd been rammed in the nose by a freight train. Two exploded in her fo'c'sle, bulging her bow and blowing it out like a debris-spraying orchid opening to the sky. The entire foredeck, including the gun mounted there, simply vanished. At least one shell plowed deep, exploding in the forward boiler room. The detonation split the ship's side and the next bulkhead aft, rupturing more boilers that spewed a fog of scalding steam.

Amerika staggered, losing the near ten knots she'd achieved in the space of a breath. To the stunned eyes of those in the launch, she no longer even resembled a ship. The flash comparison that came to Gunny Horn was that she looked more like somebody had set fire to the Wool-worth Building, then picked it up and dropped it on its side in the Hudson River. "Son of a bitch," he murmured. Immediately, the smoldering wreckage began to settle under a massive, dark, steamy shroud.

"Turn us around!" Sandra commanded, her voice harsh and rough. "We have to save as many as we can!" As if shaken from a trance, Becher Lange barked at the 'Cat at the tiller to bring them about. Aboard *Amerika*, lifeboats were quickly dropping toward the water. Sandra was sure many of those aboard had begun to prepare for this just as soon as they realized what was happening. Some boats were full of wounded, further proof that someone had been thinking fast, but many went down empty, the more ambulatory sliding down the falls to fill them when they reached the sea. *Savoie* was still gathering way, but at least she'd stopped firing. Instead, she commenced a wide turn to starboard that would bring her back toward the destruction she'd wrought. *Amerika* was going down on a relatively even keel. Ironically, the extent of the destruction to her hull that would quickly sink her also momentarily prevented her from listing too far on her side, or assuming a downward angle too extreme to lower any boats at all.

"Quickly!" Lange urged the Lemurian at the throttle, but the 'Cat only blinked helplessly. The throttle was wide-open. And it became increasingly clear that *Savoie* would return long before the launch could reach the sinking ship—and that *Amerika* would be gone before they got there, in any event. Greedy water closed over the twisted wreckage of the fo'c'sle, and the angle finally increased with a booming cacophony of shifting machinery and sliding rubble. When the sea reached for the blown-out portholes beneath the promenade deck, only seconds remained. Surging upward amid a growing, moaning spume of venting air and screaming steam, the sea seemed to literally *gulp* the proud old liner into its depths. A few more lifeboats may have floated clear at the end, but it was difficult to tell amid the rushing white maelstrom of escaping air and swirling debris. The last they saw of SMS *Amerika* was her mainmast, aft, sliding swiftly down. For the first time, as it took its last hurried breath, Horn was struck by the coincidental similarity between the golden eagle-like creature on a white field flag of the Republic, and the flag of the Imperial German Navy. With a strange lump in his throat, he caught sight of *Savoie*, rushing to cut them off from the bobbing, spinning lifeboats and the countless wounded suddenly in the water. They didn't have much time at all. The voracious predators of this terrible sea would find them very quickly.

"No!" Sandra roared at the League battleship as it neared, its engines now churning the sea to slow it. "You can't leave them in the water!" Her voice cracked.

"He lived as long as his ship," Lange said woodenly, staring at the spot where *Amerika* disappeared. "Just as he said."

"He lived *too* long!" Sandra snarled, rounding on him, and Lange recoiled. "Long enough to kill God knows how many in his care!" She pointed at *Savoie*. "And for what?" The battleship showed little evidence that it had just been in a fight, and it soon loomed over them, rails once more lined with men. One had a speaking trumpet, and he called down in accented English.

"You will now please come aboard," he said. It wasn't a question, but his tone sounded almost . . . apologetic.

"Help those people in the water!" Sandra yelled back.

The man hesitated, but another leaned near and said something to him. "We will help them by leaving their comrades in the boats to save them—and not shooting the boats. *If* you come aboard at once," he called back. "Please," he added, almost pleading, "we cannot linger here, and will do what we must to leave as quickly as we can."

Sandra and Diania were the first to set foot on *Savoie*, followed by Horn, Adar, Lange, and the three Lemurian sailors who accompanied them. Sailors briskly and efficiently searched the men and 'Cats. Sandra and Diania weren't touched. Their first impression was that the ship was absolutely huge. In reality, it wasn't even as long as *Amerika* had been, but the contrast of open deck spaces with enormous guns, machinery, and fittings placed upon them was jarring. The robust-looking superstructure reared high in the sky and the great, gun-bristling turrets utterly dwarfed the men around them. Rust peeked from the occasional crack or blister in the paint—and there were a few places where *Amerika*'s guns had left their mark— but otherwise, the ship looked amazingly well maintained and practically new, despite its age. Another thing that jarred them was that the entire visible crew, and a fair percentage must've gathered to stare at them, were human males. Many were shirtless, dressed only in light gray trousers, but others wore white trousers and jumpers. The apparent officers were dressed all in white, with pith helmets on their heads. At Sandra's first glimpse of a man with a thin mustache and rank she knew equated to a rear admiral, she knew who was responsible for the atrocity she'd just witnessed. He flinched when he saw her expression and took half a step back. She raised a fist and started to advance, but Horn grabbed her arm. "Ma'am," he hissed urgently, drawing her attention back to the squad of men with rifles. Adar stepped in front of her, glaring at their captors.

"You have us," he said bitterly, "now put your boats in the water. Innocent lives are being lost with each instant you delay."

"Search them as well," instructed a wiry blond-haired officer beside the admiral. He spoke French, ignoring Adar and gestured at the two women.

"That will not be necessary," the admiral with the thin mustache said in English, avoiding eye contact with Sandra. "We have no women aboard to properly perform so . . . delicate a task. But if they bear weapons of any kind, they have this one opportunity to surrender them without consequences. If it is later discovered that they are armed . . . the conditions of their stay aboard *Savoie* will become less pleasant." He returned his full gaze to the relatively tall Lemurian in the star-flecked robe. "You are Chairman Adar?" he asked. Adar nodded. "And you must be *Amerika*'s commander," he said to Lange. "I am Contre Amiral Laborde. Welcome aboard *Savoie*. As long as you are my guests, you will be allowed every courtesy. But you are in no position to make demands, particularly after your attempt to damage my vessel."

"We had nothing to do with that!" Sandra snarled. "No one did, except the ship's former commander, Kapitan Von Melhausen! He was an old man, and your attack on us probably sent him over the edge! Now hundreds of wounded soldiers are dying as we speak!"

Laborde finally looked back at her. "Then Kapitan Von Melhausen was a very foolish old man. You must be 'Lady' Sandra Reddy, Minister of Medicine for your alliance, and wife of its chief military leader, Captain Reddy!" He allowed a slight, triumphant smile. "My apologies, madam, but that warship . . ."

"Warship?" Sandra interrupted incredulously.

"*Armed* warship," Laborde stressed, "fired at us, unprovoked, and without warning." Sandra struggled against Horn's grip.

"After you fired at us!" Lange insisted.

Laborde waved that away. "You had no communications. We merely fired to get your attention so we might avoid a collision in these persistent squalls, and peacefully converse. It is a time-honored tradition of the sea."

"So that's how it is?" Horn muttered, and Laborde's eyes bored into his.

"That is how it is," Laborde agreed stonily. "And you are?" He glanced back at Lange. "You were instructed to bring only yourself, Chairman Adar, Minister Reddy, and crew sufficient to operate your boat." He turned to Horn expectantly.

"Gunnery Sergeant Arnold Horn, USMC. That and my serial number is all you'll get from me."

"He is my personal advisor and bodyguard," Adar quickly interjected. "He will cause no trouble if you truly mean us no harm."

"And that one?" Laborde asked, looking at Diania.

"Lady Sandra's . . . servant," Adar said.

"Very well," Laborde agreed, apparently accepting Adar's explanation for the additions. "But the warship you were embarked upon fired on us, actually striking my ship not once but several times. I was forced to order defensive measures. Sadly, those measures caused some slight damage in return. I cannot be responsible if, in addition to her general, overall dilapidation, our measured response might have hastened her demise."

Through her fury, Sandra was sure the bastard was actually enjoying this.

"Regardless," he said, ostentatiously peering beyond them at the empty ocean to port, "and also in the tradition of all civilized seafaring nations, I have lingered in the vicinity long enough to rescue the occupants of the only lifeboat that I see. Sadly, *Savoie* can stay here no longer. Not only have we a rendezvous to make, but we are exposed to discovery by other, possibly hostile forces allied to the one we were so reluctantly forced to engage." He turned to an officer beside him. "Cast the barge adrift. Get the ship underway at once."

"Bastard," Sandra muttered. Laborde clearly knew all the other boats and dying swimmers were on *Savoie*'s starboard beam, and he was just toying with them now, perhaps rehearsing his excuses. Nothing she could say would sway him. Or would it?

"Von Melhausen wasn't stupid; he was old and sick. What's your excuse? You're a murderer and a coward. We know what this is all about. You think, with us in your hands, your stupid League can manipulate the Alliance and influence my husband's actions." She shrugged and managed a feral grin despite her inner turmoil. "You may even be right, but not the way you hope. The Alliance is devoted to Adar, but it'll survive without him in charge. It already has for quite a while. And you'll 'influence' Captain Reddy the same way the 'Honorable' New Britain Company did when it abducted people he cared about. It no longer exists. Yeah," she snapped, grinning more broadly, "you obviously don't have *any* idea what you've done. You'll 'influence' Matt the way your damn submarine that attacked us did, the sub he *sank* without pity, remorse, or even much effort." She took a long breath. "And sure, you'll 'influence' him to rescue us, but he'll damn sure destroy you, this ship"—she looked around at the silent faces—"and everybody on her, even if it costs our lives." She actually laughed at the expressions she saw. "You *still* don't get it, do you? You think, 'Oh, Captain Reddy came to this world with one little ship. It's old and worn-out. What can he do?'" She looked hard back at Laborde. "He built an alliance, an army and navy that's hammered all comers back on their heels. He made you *afraid enough* of him to pull a stunt like this!"

Laborde's face blanched, but then hardened. "Take Lady Sandra and her servant to the quarters we prepared for her. Chairman Adar, Sergeant Horn, and Kapitan Leutnant Lange can share the other. Since it is no longer possible to return the crew of their boat to *Amerika*, they must be detained as well. Take them to the brig."

"Sure, that'll keep you safe," Sandra called sarcastically

as she and Diania were led away. "But just remember this, all of you," she continued, her voice rising. "The only thing you've accomplished here is the murder of helpless people representing *every member* of our alliance! People the rest of us owe a debt of honor—and blood! Whether you admit it or not, you've started the war you've been avoiding, and your wild, idiotic explanation for what you did today won't save you." She laughed again as she was pushed down a companionway. It still sounded forced to everyone who heard it, but no one doubted she believed what she said.

"A moment, Chairman Adar," Laborde said, stopping the men escorting him, Horn, and Lange below. Somewhat apologetically at last, he gestured to starboard. "I really do regret what happened here today. It was not to be, and contrary to my wishes. But particularly now that it is done, I really cannot linger any longer."

Adar looked at him, blinking rapidly. "So few things ever go the way we would like them to," he said, remembering mistakes of his own. "But we must always face the consequences of what *is*, rather than our intentions."

For a long moment, Laborde didn't speak, but when he did, he licked his lips and prefaced his words with a glance toward the companionway. "Do you think she is right?"

"About me?" Adar asked, surprised by the question. "Almost certainly. My place has been ably taken during my long absence. I flatter myself that I will be missed by my friends, but I am by no means indispensable, or even necessary." He paused and blinked again, in a way Laborde could not understand. "Is she right about what Cap-i-taan Reddy will do? Oh yes. Absolutely."

"So, in honesty, I would be wiser to destroy the lifeboats in the water in order to delay reports of what has happened here as long as possible," Laborde probed more harshly.

Adar blinked disgust. "Perhaps that might be wiser, in the short term. But it would gain you only a few days. A week at most. Your ship is known. We had no idea you could be *here*, but you cannot keep it secret forever. Our ships and planes will soon discover the floating debris. They will study it and quickly come to the proper conclusion. Survivors will tell the truth, undistorted by your fiction, but the fact that you spared them may make some small difference one day. Helping rescue more of them might even lend credence to your claim that you did not want to sink *Amerika*." He paused, waiting for a reply. When there was none, he sighed. "Since I cannot sway you, I will add only this: if there are no survivors, I assure you most emphatically that the consequences Lady Sandra described will be visited tenfold upon you personally."

Laborde stiffened and motioned the guards to proceed. "You will join me for dinner, and we will discuss this at greater length," he said.

Laborde sat heavily in the chair in his quarters, a precious bottle of "old world" brandy standing on his desk, a full glass in his hand. There was a knock on the wooden doorway. "Enter," he said absently, staring at the dark liquor.

"Amiral, you sent for me?" asked Capitaine Dupont.

"Ah, yes." He motioned at the bottle, but Dupont shook his head. Laborde sighed. "That did not go . . . as we had hoped."

"No, Amiral," Dupont agreed, almost meekly.

"Instead of a ship full of wounded but otherwise unharmed troops with which to bargain, we have only a handful of individuals of dubious real value to balance the provocation we have made. Our explanation for the confrontation remains valid, but may not be enough to satisfy the Triumvirate." He gulped the glass of brandy. "Well, then there is nothing left to do. Allied ships and planes will soon be searching—and the current will carry the debris toward Christmas Island in any event. They will follow the trail, looking for boats that become separated from the others, and their discovery of our presence there will be swift."

"Yes, Amiral," Dupont agreed, still softly, but with a trace of accusation. Laborde looked sharply at him, realizing the very man who'd practically provoked him into pursuing *Amerika* in the first place had decided to play the "I was just following orders" gambit. Laborde would ensure it didn't work, if it was the last thing he ever did.

"Then, unless we are prepared to fight the entire

Alliance by ourselves, without support, the time has come to abandon our interests there. Determine a suitable rendezvous point and signal *Leopardo* and the Spanish oiler to evacuate the Italian garrison and join us at the designated coordinates. Ensure *Leopardo* knows to make every effort to inform the German submarine of our intentions as well. It may need to refuel before we proceed to our next destination. But *Savoie* will make no further transmissions after *Leopardo* acknowledges."

"And . . . what is our destination?" Dupont asked with rising concern. "Shall we round the Cape of Africa? Abandon this ocean entirely, without orders from the Triumvirate?"

Laborde glared at the man, even more furious at the implication of cowardice he thought he heard in his tone. "No. We will make for the one other place our people hold influence and we can expect a cordial welcome—and further orders." He stood and stepped to the chart pinned to the cork on the bulkhead and pointed at a small island just off the east coast of Africa. "Here," he said.

CHAPTER
12

**West of the Indus River Valley
September 28, 1944**

There was no improved road through the mountains, but the ancient trail worn by countless overland Grik caravans to and from India across the ages had made a path as plain and wide as any road Halik ever saw. Perhaps not as *smooth*, however, and he hid his unease, riding awkwardly on his feet in the deep box of a freight cart designed by Niwa and built by Hij artisans. The cart wasn't designed for the comfort of passengers, and Halik had bounced and swayed, ignominiously bunched in alongside the warriors he brought to protect him, for the better part of two days. They were all exhausted, and judging by their expressions and the queasy gulping of some, Halik's warriors were at least as uncomfortable as he. They were making good time, though. The Hij driver sat perched on a kind of bench at the front of the cart controlling the neekis as it trotted dutifully along, its long, powerful legs covering ground at an astonishing rate.

Hungry and sleepy, Halik caught himself watching the great beast's muscles bunch and ripple beneath the rough tan hide, its tail whipping back and forth like a metronome beneath the long twin shafts that secured it to the cart as it effortlessly, and apparently tirelessly, kept up the ground-eating pace. He realized with a start that he'd been almost mesmerized by the sight for a considerable time. He also realized that he'd felt a growing . . . admiration for the animal, and that surprised him. It was then, staring at the rear end of a grass-eating prey animal that regularly blapped out noxious emissions, that General Halik had a kind of unlikely epiphany that reinforced all the aberrant thoughts and notions that had brought him to this point. He'd grown used to neekis; they were ubiquitous on the plains of India and plentiful even here. Yet, until just recently, he'd considered them only a convenient source of food, easily herded and kept. What a terrible condemnation of the culture that created him that he, even as enlightened as he now imagined himself, would look at any life-form other than his own—and Niwa's—solely as a beast to be slaughtered and eaten, as if its life had no other possible purpose! Yet there he was, traveling at unheard-of speeds on a critical errand that only another life of a different form could make possible. He shook his head. He'd long ago learned to respect humans and Lemurians as enemies, and even feel vaguely uncomfortable with consuming them. And largely due to Niwa's influence, he hadn't thought of them as mere prey for quite some time. Of course, that attitude had been brutally reinforced when General Pete Alden rounded on his army and made *him* flee like prey. By that, and everything else the enemy had accomplished, they must certainly now be considered *worthy* prey at least, even by the most skeptical regents and generals. The Celestial Mother had probably, finally, come to that conclusion herself—right before they destroyed her. But what was "worthy prey"? It was *worth* something, besides food! Until now, that value had always been calculated by how difficult the prey might be to overcome, but he now appreciated a broader definition, including how worthy he and his race might be to survive a vengeful prey.

Others of his race, without his experience, would no doubt consider him insane, but he suddenly recognized that this wild notion of worthy *life* had been maturing, unnoticed, for some time. He'd long seen and appreciated the utility of the enemy's cavalry mounts, even wished he had such things. His ability to recognize that desire was what resulted in the comparatively simple, he imagined, taming of the neekis in the first place. And now . . . With a flash of insight, he abruptly doubted his encounter with the commander of the force they raced to meet would have a happy outcome. Whoever it was would still be steeped in the fundamental truth that their race existed to conquer and feed upon all others, across the world. Even other races who joined the Great Hunt were allowed to do so only until their value as a hunting partner was exhausted.

Uncertainty reemerged, and he looked at the backside of the running neekis. *But is that not what I have done, only more . . . imaginatively? If that creature is injured and can no longer serve its new purpose, it will become food once more. The same is true among the humans and Lemurians, no doubt. But if one of them was injured without hope of recovery, would the other turn against them?* He blinked. *Never,* he knew. *Just as I did not abandon General Niwa when he was gravely injured, and he did not abandon me—and our army—when we were defeated. But Humans and Lemurians are true friends, race to race!* He finally understood the vast difference between him—and a growing percentage of his army—and all others of his race: his discovery of friendship, as well as that indistinct notion called "honor" that Niwa was so intent upon. Honor was important to his enemies as well. Generals Alden, Rolak, Colonel Enaak, and even Colonel Svec appeared to prize it, and even expect it of him to a degree, ever since he'd ordered that Allied prisoners no longer be eaten. And why was that? Because even though he remained unclear about what the term "honor" might encompass, he'd learned that all else was built upon a foundation of respect, not only for one's enemies but, perhaps more important, for oneself. If one behaves with respect toward others, even enemies, one might earn their respect in return. *Now I know why my enemy is so implacable. Niwa even told me as much, but I did not understand till now. How can one respect . . . honor . . . any enemy that sees you only as food? We are more contemptible to them than they ever were to us.* With that ultimate realization, he had another: *Am I and my army even truly Ghaarrichk'k anymore? How can I find common ground and understanding with any creature such as I once was?* He felt a chill despite the warm, muggy air. *And dare I consider it . . . with even such as First General Esshk? In all honesty, is Esshk himself more likely to embrace all that I and my army have become, or, horrified, command our destruction?* The uncertainty that surged within him then was almost enough to make him order the driver to turn around.

"Ahead! Warriors, Lord General," the driver almost squeaked, and Halik shook off all concerns. He couldn't afford to let them show, and it was too late to act upon them. He stretched his neck upward as far as he could and peered forward, past the driver. A clump of warriors, perhaps two tens, was trudging down the slope ahead, the path bordered by tall trees reminiscent of those choking the coastal plain beyond the Rocky Gap far to the southeast. *Advance guards,* Halik thought contemptuously. *They may be better armed than the "old army" I remember, but they appear little better trained. With pickets such as those, General Alden would . . .* He stopped. *I might . . . ,* he realized, and was amazed by how little that distressed him.

"Stop the cart," he commanded. "They will attack our animal—and us—if we do not show ourselves."

Halik and his guards cleared the cart and deployed barely in time to check the surge of hungry warriors that saw nothing but an apparently suicidal food beast that did nothing but stand and stare at them as they approached.

"Stop!" Halik roared. Most did, instantly, at the sound of such a practiced and confident tone. "Stop this instant or destroy yourselves!" he thundered at the rest, and that got their attention. "I am General Halik, commander of all forces east of here, and this is my animal! You will not touch it!"

Finally recognizing the battle-worn helmet and cape that could only be worn by a general, all twenty Grik warriors hurled themselves at Halik's feet, where they twisted and squirmed on their bellies. It had been so long since he'd allowed his own troops to do such a thing that Halik was momentarily surprised, then repulsed. "Where is your serg—your leader of two tens?" he demanded.

"Is I," came a bubbly voice from a snout thrust in the leafy soil of the path.

"You will escort me and my party to your commander at once!"

"Yesss, Lord!"

Halik caught motion to the side and realized that every member of his party—all still standing—had turned to look at him, their expressions and posture confident and . . . worshipful? *Respect,* he reflected with certainty as he nodded gravely at his guards. *Self-respect is the key, not this mindless obedience bred of fear alone. Respect is the main advantage our enemies have always held over us, and it is truly the root from which all things might grow. Even honor.*

Back aboard the cart, they proceeded slowly through increasing numbers of Grik warriors clogging the path and overflowing into the woods on either side. Thousands of Grik, armed as Svec had told him, gazed at them with blank, hungry stares even as they gained a larger escort to protect their animal the farther they went. The warriors looked disconcertingly fresh, at first, until Halik realized how slowly they were advancing. *We may* still *have a week to prepare, even after I return to my army,* he thought. But prepare for what? He'd know soon enough. The horde thinned slightly at the top of a steep rise where the forest retreated from the path to border a wide mountain meadow flanked by distant peaks. Near the center of the meadow, about a mile away, an enormous pavilion dominated the scene and dwarfed the warriors shambling wide around it. It was dark red, almost black, and long streamers like those used on ships fluttered fitfully. Smoke rose from several flaps at the peak of the structure, evidence of fires inside, built to warm the space against the mountain chill that Halik had begun to notice.

"De regent an' his gen-rals is der," the sergeant Halik had appropriated announced grandly, pointing with both hands.

"How long have they been in this place, and how long will they remain?" Halik asked. The pavilion looked like it had been erected permanently.

"Dey is stay here since dis place found, Lord, an dat palace is made. Dey move when anudder good place is found an' de palace is made again."

Halik could hardly imagine going on campaign like that, but then, Hisashi Kurokawa had enjoyed his comforts as well. Either way, it was interesting. He already knew all the other places such a massive structure could be erected between here and his army, and there weren't very many. A group of officers arrived then, led by a general with a golden helmet and armor and gold trim on his red cape. He was staring at the neekis and the cart behind it with something like incredulity. Halik unconsciously fingered his own tattered, battle-worn garment and imagined the impression he'd make. Whatever it was, it was time to do it.

"General," he said, climbing up to stand beside the driver on his bench. "I am General Halik, chosen by First General Esshk himself at the personal direction of our Giver of Life to lead all the armies in India and Ceylon! I greet you, and beg an audience with the leader of your expedition."

Already astonished by the docile food beast in the middle of an army of predators, Halik's battered but powerful form appearing at the top of the cart beside a terrified-looking Hij and announcing what he had apparently overwhelmed the Grik general into speechlessness. For a long moment he merely opened and closed his jaws as if chewing a piece of gristle.

"You cannot be Halik," he growled at last. "He and his armies were ended by the prey we march to destroy!"

"Nevertheless, I am Halik and my armies still guard these frontiers," he said, speaking the literal if not practical truth. "Whoever informed you and your master of my destruction has . . . exaggerated. Please take me to your master now so I may greet him and report."

"Very well," the general replied, tail plumage spreading in indignation as he likely wrestled with the possibility that anyone might lie about such a thing. Apparently deciding that was not possible, he took a step forward. "But please . . . General Halik, do step down from that thing and away from that unnatural beast. The sight of them will inflame my master against you." He lowered his voice. "Lord Regent Consort Shighat, Sire of all Persia himself, reposes in the field palace. He does not look with favor upon"—he glanced back at the neekis—"such . . . deviant innovations. He considers them the root of all our difficulties with the prey we now face. Perhaps he has not yet noticed."

Regent Consort Shighat did not lounge in "repose" when Halik and Captain Sigg were ushered into his presence. Instead, he paced and apparently brooded restlessly before a line of what were probably his ranking generals and advisors. He had plenty of space for that, since the elaborately appointed interior of the "field palace" was just as vast as Halik had presumed, complete with four massive braziers that kept the space almost oppressively warm. Perhaps Halik had been outdoors too long. . . . Shighat paused when Halik was announced, and glared at him with ruby red eyes that malevolently reflected the flickering flames of the braziers. His slender frame and apparent age immediately reminded Halik of Tsalka, the former "Sire" of all India and Ceylon he'd once been presented to. Tsalka had been in his forties before he was destroyed and was the oldest Hij that Halik ever saw besides the strange little interpreter, Hij Geerki, that General Lord Rolak had somehow acquired. Shighat looked just as ancient as Geerki, possibly over fifty, but not nearly as ravaged by his years. He had all his teeth and claws, for example, perfectly manicured and filed razor sharp. His high, flowing crest had been darkened and carefully coiffed as well. And his black-red robes were richly decorated with thick fringes of what looked like tiny golden bones. His demeanor, however, was quite different from Tsalka's. Whereas Tsalka had radiated a kind of distracted benevolence when he and Halik met, Lord Shighat seemed at pains to contain some inner affronted fury.

"What are you doing here? You are supposed to be dead," he snapped, not even waiting for Halik to approach. That was probably just as well since Halik had no intention of prostrating himself, as required, particularly not in front of Captain Sigg, and that might have set things off in an unpleasant direction at the start.

"My apologies, Lord Regent Shighat," Halik replied in a respectful but very dry tone. "I have tried my very best to be dead on numerous occasions, but thus far have failed to accomplish it. I expect to be successful soon enough."

Shighat whirled to one of his generals. "Baseless rumors, as I suspected all along! Find any of the tale bearers still with the army that brought us news of disaster in the east and have them destroyed at once! Have them *flayed*!" He spun back to Halik. "I have marched half my levy across two-thirds of my regency, into its most inhospitable, uncomfortable reaches based on rumors that your armies in India and Ceylon were destroyed. *And all for nothing!* I must confess, I was perhaps too quick to credit those tales," he added, his eyes narrowing. "The forces that landed in the south and crossed my realm to join you were so"—he shuddered—"unconventional. Useless creatures, I knew at once, marching along in ridiculous lines, carrying strange weapons . . ." He shook his head. "I knew they would be of no use to you at all, and feared disaster when I saw them." He blinked and stared hard at Halik. "I am relieved that you prevailed against the prey in spite of them."

Despite Shighat's words, Halik became even more wary, if anything. The regent's scrutiny was unnerving. And he realized the "forces" Shighat referred to must be the "hatchling host," warriors trained from birth to do more than mindlessly attack. Warriors that now formed the backbone of what Halik had built and without which he certainly would've been destroyed. "They were quite useful, as it turned out," he commented carefully.

"As rations, no doubt," Shighat barked. "Not born proper warriors and raised to be such, what other use could they be?"

Halik attempted to change the subject. "Then, Lord, if you would, enlighten me regarding the content of these rumors? And their source?"

Shighat waved it away, his tone moderating with apparent relief. "All this tedious inconvenience for nothing," he said, rolling his eyes. "March, march, march, for weeks on end! And it is *cold* here!" He shook his head. "Lowly Hij, fleeing the remorseless swarm of the enemy prey, brought the news. I will certainly enjoy destroying *them*! They blabbered that Madras was lost in a terrible sea battle that actually *defeated* the great General of the Sea Kurokawa and his indestructible fleet!" Perhaps Shighat wasn't as opposed to "innovation" when it came to matters at sea, which he clearly didn't understand, any more than he understood what made good troops anymore. No fleet was indestructible, as Halik knew well, and Hisashi Kurokawa was anything but great. He wondered if Shighat even knew Kurokawa wasn't Ghaarrichk'k.

"Then they said that you had been pushed back to the interior of India, where your remaining armies were crushed!" Shighat continued. "Obviously, since you live, that was not the case." He paused, his eyes narrowing once again. "I never would have credited such nonsense had there not been so many reports from so *many* Hij," he said slowly, his tone turning sarcastic. "Yet here you are, a little the worse for wear, it appears, but alive. So I must conclude that you prevailed; a general chosen by the illustrious First General Esshk, and elevated to stand before the Celestial Mother herself. How could it be otherwise? But then, the very first question I asked you does arise again," Shighat said, his voice turning deceptively mild. "Why are you here, instead of driving the prey beyond Madras, and across the deadly sea? And since you are here, instead of where you belong, *why are you not dead*?"

It dawned on Halik then that Shighat had been toying with him. Of *course* he knew. Refugees had fled before Halik's retreating force in the *thousands*. Comparatively few had remained under his "protection."

Halik hacked to clear his throat, knowing that the next few moments were crucial. "Before I continue and make my report, can you tell me what you know of the progress of the war against the, ah, 'prey'?"

Shigat stepped back and regarded him. Then he looked at the generals, who had said nothing thus far. He blinked again and cocked his head. "Not that I can see how it could possibly matter to you, but there has been no word in a great while. No ships have touched our ports since the passage of the unnatural hatchling warriors that marched to join you." He snorted. "This is not unusual. The sea eats ships," he said simply, "and there is a war."

"No word for months, even with a war, must surely strike you strangely?"

Shighat didn't reply, and Halik nodded. "Then I shall give you word of a war you cannot possibly imagine: a war of machines and fire and noise and blood so deep it cannot be waded through. *Bones!*" he said harshly, "protruding from the gouged and mangled earth as thickly as grass stubble after the passage of a herd of food beasts because the bodies of neither side could be recovered, even to be eaten, because the fighting raged so long without pause upon *that same tortured ground*!" He shifted his gaze to the line of generals, gawking openmouthed. "My army was *not* destroyed, though it was only through the most amazing circumstances that I can make that claim. Yes," he continued, "Kurokawa *was* defeated, his 'indestructible' fleet annihilated by means I did not see but can certainly imagine, based on the terrible weapons and ferocious tactics the enemy you still call 'prey' inflicted on my force! Yes, I was driven back from Madras and harried all across India until I brought my army across the frontier into the regency of Persia. We guard its borders as we speak!" He looked back at Shighat. "And there is *more*. The enemy has crossed the terrible sea with the same mighty fleet that destroyed Kurokawa and brought the same destruction I described upon the Celestial City at Madagascar, the Celestial Palace erected there, and the Celestial Mother herself! Yes!" he snapped at Shighat, who recoiled from the words and his tone. "The Giver of Life is dead!"

"But . . . ," one of the generals managed. "That . . . cannot be!"

"It is the truth," Halik enunciated relentlessly. "General Esshk has retired—much as I was forced to do—across the Go Away Strait, to rally forces on the mainland. I suspect there has been more fighting by now, but know nothing beyond what I have said."

Shighat turned away, his robe rising to reveal the plumage that had lain flat against his tail in fear. For a very long moment, he merely stared into one of the braziers, the muscles in his wrinkled neck working beneath the skin. With great effort, he managed not to let his crest lay down upon his head. Finally, he turned to face Halik. "My brother Ragak, Regent Consort of Sofesshk, foresaw the calamity you detail," he said softly. "He warned General Esshk what would happen if he persisted with his unwholesome . . . experiments. I sent him word of what I saw when the hatchlings arrived, and pledged him my support. I pray only it is not too late and that Ragak has supplanted Esshk, to lead us until a new Celestial Mother can rise." His voice rose. "*We* did not rise to rule the world by changing what we are each time we met new prey! We devoured it in the swarms that made us what we are!" He faced his generals, his eyes blazing bright. "See? You see? It is just as I foretold! These . . . innovations have savaged us, and ultimately cost us everything we hold most sacred, even our Giver of Life!" His head whipped around to face Halik, but when he spoke, his voice was softer. "It is not your fault," he proclaimed, his tone a parody of sadness. "You are yet another of Esshk's broken tools. I know what you were, what you were born to be, and you cannot be held responsible for your failure. Tell me, how many warriors remain to you; pure, *proper* warriors, untainted by the malignancy of innovation that has ruined you just as surely as the helpless, marching wretches that joined you in the East?"

Halik took a deep breath, but cast his eyes downward. "Perhaps twenty thousands, Lord."

"Very well," Shighat said, his voice now infused with a similar benevolence to what Halik once heard in Tsalka's. Just as false? he now wondered.

"Then, General Halik, I require that you return to your army without delay and send that . . . untainted portion to meet me on the march. The rest—there cannot be many, I imagine—must be . . ." He paused, reconsidering his words. "May end their suffering at last. They *have* suffered, as have you; I heard it in your voice and saw it in your eyes. Relieve *yourself* of your suffering, General Halik," he said gently. "Let me avenge it for you and carry on from here." He spoke louder. "India and Ceylon have no regent," he said. "*I* must occupy that void, and drive the prey as we were meant to do!" He motioned to the general who'd escorted Halik and Sigg into the massive tent. "Go with them," he whispered, but Halik heard. "Make sure it is done. So great is their aberration, I fear . . . disobedience." He glanced meaningfully at Halik.

"What are you called?" Halik asked the general quietly, as though he were subdued by misery, as the three of them stepped through the shuffling horde, back toward the waiting cart and the—miraculously—still living neekis.

"I am General Yikkit," the creature said.

"You bring no guards?"

"No. You have guards, and I doubt more would fit—or be willing to ride—in your contrivance."

Halik stopped and looked at him. "But you will? Aren't you concerned that I might be disobedient?"

Yikkit regarded him carefully, his eyes furtively casting about. "I will. And I confess I am concerned about a great many things of late. Whether your possible disobedience is one of them or not is somewhat dependent upon how it might manifest itself, and toward whom. You are not the only admirer of General Esshk and his methods in this army. Tell me, did you speak the truth earlier? About everything?"

"Yes."

Yikkit appeared to consider that. "And *do* you intend to be disobedient? Will you actually destroy your army and yourself as Regent Consort Shighat commanded?"

"I believe his was more of a request," Halik replied lightly, but felt a rushing sensation in his chest.

"You know it was not."

Halik took another long breath and looked closely at Yikkit, his hand straying toward the sword at his side. "I think," he said slowly, "that I will probably not choose to do so."

"Then what will you do?"

Halik exhaled and watched the passing thousands for several moments. "I suppose that I and my army—which is far more capable than Lord Shighat can imagine—will have to defend our right to exist, from any army or regent that would dispute that," he answered, his hand grasping his sword hilt. It might be inconvenient if he had to kill Yikkit here, now, but sudden murderous quarrels between generals happened on occasion.

Yikkit nodded brusquely and stepped more quickly toward the cart. "That is what I thought," he said. "Good."

Halik was taken aback. "Why?" he asked simply, and General Yikkit stopped.

"Because I now see what you have seen, and such as Shighat can never recognize. Your eyes *do* reflect great suffering, but also vast experience." He jerked his head at Captain Sigg. "As do his." He was silent a moment, standing by the wheel of the cart. "I began as you," he confessed, barely audible. "A mere sport fighter, also elevated by First General Esshk himself. Unlike you, I was given no command of my own, but was sent here to reason with Regent Consort Shighat. I was not successful," he added bitterly. "I began to imagine I was alone with my deviant thoughts and strove to conceal them. How else could I remain so close to Shighat, let alone survive? But your eyes also reflect your thoughts, Lord General," he said, significantly acknowledging Halik as his superior for the first time. "Thoughts like mine. Most in your position would gladly destroy themselves as Shighat expects, to escape their embittered misery, which is all that Shighat observed. But perhaps I alone could see your mind when he gave you leave to do so. Your eyes no longer pretended to gaze at him with the deference due a regent consort of the Empire, beloved of the Giver of Life. They beheld him as their prey."

"Then climb aboard my deviant innovation, General Yikkit, and welcome," Halik said at last, releasing his sword hilt and grasping the rail above. "It seems we have a great deal to discuss, you and I."

Aboard the NUS Congress
The Caribbean
September 29, 1944

"And this device actually facilitates communication, without direct contact by wire, even beyond the horizon?" Captain Ezra Willis asked, amazed, gazing at the transceiver Fred Reynolds and Kari-Faask had removed from their plane. He, Hudgens, and several other men were gathered with the young aviators, standing around a long table in *Congress*'s gun room. Fred equated the term with "wardroom" in his navy. He was the only one seated at the table, but Kari was beside it, rigging out the tripod legs on the hand generator that she'd stand on while cranking the handles. Fred had opened the wooden case protecting the wireless set and was tinkering with it while their hosts gaped at the contraption in fascination. Captain Willis was a portly, hawk-beaked man, and he'd honored Lieutenant Hudgens's pledge to treat them well, much to Fred's relief. Not just for his and Kari's sakes, but for the sake of their mission to make friendly contact. Willis had also been very grateful for the Dom prisoners they'd given him, though he hadn't revealed exactly why they were so important.

The confined space was beneath a skylight, so there was plenty of illumination even without the gimbaled oil lamps, but the skylight was closed so they could speak in private, and the room was close with the cloying scent of burning fish oil, mildew, damp wood, and sweaty wool. So potent was the combined bouquet, Kari's own distinctive musty sweat odor went unremarked and apparently unnoticed. Of course, their hosts might've just been polite. Fred still didn't know what to think about that. In contrast to Captain Anson's relatively caustic personality, his apparent countrymen seemed to have surprisingly good manners. At least their officers did. The common sailors were just as earthy and profane as any sailors he'd known, but *Congress*'s officers, at least, seemed determined to impose a measure of civility aboard their ship—and perhaps the whole savage world around them. And it didn't strike Fred as a false affectation.

Around them, the ship creaked as it churned through a rising sea and the engine thumped the deck beneath their feet like a great iron heart. The sea coursed down the sides, hissing and bumping against the stout wooden hull in a relaxing, reassuring way that Fred had grown to associate with a well-found, healthy ship. The "New Americans" (what else was Fred going to call them?) immediately recognized the wireless set's detachable keyboard, but the rest was a mystery to them. Fred had been right: telegraphy was used by these people, as was a lot of the technology the destroyermen had introduced to the Lemurians. They were in fact on roughly the same technological level now—with a few big exceptions.

"Sure," Fred replied. "That's why we call it 'wireless.' It'll need a wire antennae rigged as high as we can get it for best results, but we don't need direct contact. The only questions then would be if there's anybody listening, and if it's working right. I don't think it's busted," he added worriedly. "It seems okay. But I just know how to operate it. I don't really know exactly how it works, and I can't make one." He nodded at Kari, who was winding the handles of the generator experimentally. "She's better at all that stuff than I am."

"Indeed?" Captain Willis inquired, studying Kari over his long nose. "Most interesting. I confess, I grow more pleased that we made your acquaintance with each passing day." This was the third day since they'd met, and *Congress* had lingered in the lagoon through the night of the first, making small repairs to the prize and carefully taking the hard-used Nancy floatplane aboard. Afraid they'd screw something up, Fred hadn't shown them how to disassemble the plane, or even told them it could be done. Consequently, loading it hadn't been easy, and they'd had to shift all the ship's boats and two of her guns. The guns were of great interest to the aviators. The ship mounted only twenty of them, but they were big, and they were *rifled*. Rifling its large-bore muzzle-loaders was something even the Alliance hadn't gotten around to. After that, Fred and Kari were fed—and gently questioned—in the Captain's great cabin, aft. Much to their relief, it had actually been a very pleasant and reassuring meal. Neither missed the significance of the fact that they were dining with the captain and his senior officers, while the Dom prisoners were locked away below.

They set sail the following day, in company with their prize, for a tactfully undisclosed destination. All the while, Fred and Kari continued to ask—and answer—questions. They described the war in the West (or East, depending on how one looked at it), between the Alliance on the one hand and the Grik and Doms on the other. They also related how *Walker* came to be on this world, as well as other events from the "old" world prior to that, which *Congress*'s crew found endlessly fascinating. In return, Willis, Hudgens, and the rest of *Congress*'s crew, growing more comfortable with their visitors, returned the favor and gave Fred and Kari a brief summary of the postarrival history of the New United States.

"How far will the signal carry? What is the, ah, range, I suppose?" Captain Willis asked.

"Pretty far," Fred allowed. "*Really* far, like thousands of miles, if the conditions are just right."

"What conditions?" Hudgens asked, disappointed. "You mean to attach conditions to the information you reveal?"

Fred blinked at him. "No! Nothing like that. *Weather* conditions, atmospherics, even time of day . . ." He paused, seeing how that would require more clarification. "No mystery, and no witchcraft, I promise. I'll try to explain. But let me ask a couple of things first," he said.

"Certainly," Willis agreed politely, sitting on a chair beside the table. "I will answer if I am able."

"You told us, finally. . . ." Fred grinned and sighed. "Frankly, the mystery's been eating me alive ever since we met Anson," he confessed, "that your 'new' US covers a little more territory than the states I remember as Texas, Oklahoma, Louisiana, Arkansas, and Alabama. It's got a president, a 'congress.'" He waved around him at the ship. "The works. We've even got a rough idea how things went for your, uh, 'founders,' back in 1847, though we're still unclear why the Doms call you 'Los Diablos del Norte,' and why you're still fighting them after all this time—besides them just being assholes who want to take over the world." He shrugged. "We were fighting guys like that where we came from, and maybe that's all it takes, but why do they hate you so bad?" He looked at Kari. "There's no reason not to tell us that, or pretty much anything. Apparently, we're the only ones in the whole hemisphere who *don't* know, and our people will eventually find out on their own. And if you don't want us to tell them, all you have to do is, well, keep us, I guess. Why not spill it?"

Kari blinked rapidly at him, thinking maybe he'd gone too far, especially with his suggestion about "keeping" them. But Captain Willis merely regarded him more seriously, steepling his hands in front of his face. "Lieutenant Hudgens, would you, please?"

Hudgens nodded. "Of course, Captain." He looked at Fred and Kari. "I do not know what 'Oklahoma' is. I assume you mean the territories north of the Red River? But they call us 'Los Diablos' because, weak as we were when we arrived aboard three small transports—one of them wrecked—with barely a brigade of infantry, a few batteries of light guns, and meager supplies, we—our grandfathers—conquered Dominion territory as far as the Valley of Mexico." He looked reflective. "Perhaps 'liberated' is a better term. We were not met as conquerors by the vast majority of people we encountered at first. The Dominion has changed little since that time, and you have seen the oppression its citizens endure."

Fred and Kari looked at him, wide-eyed.

Hudgens held up a hand and frowned. "We couldn't keep what we had taken, of course, once the Dominion mobilized against us. They'd apparently been focused westward, on the Empire of the New Britain Isles, we now believe, preparing to launch an attack across the sea. That is why we met so little initial resistance. When they turned their full might upon us, our roughly eighteen hundred men were faced by tens of thousands. We held the great city for a time, a city that may have no equal on this world, but ultimately had no choice but to withdraw to the north." He smiled. "But we didn't leave empty-handed. Like the Imperials in that regard at least, we did evacuate sufficient . . . 'brides' to ensure future generations, along with many thousands of civilians who sought our protection from the monsters in the wilderness . . . and a retribution we never expected."

He took a long, sad breath. "Tragically, at the time, our people had no idea what kind of *human* monsters truly infested the Dominion. They knew they weren't, well, 'at home' anymore, and that something extraordinary had happened to them; they were alone, and there were strange, deadly creatures at every hand, but the ordinary people seemed normal enough. Militarily, the Dom army was not dissimilar to the Mexican Army our forefathers had been sent to fight. But culturally, their leaders . . ." He looked at Fred and Kari in turn. "I believe you have some experience with that." He found a chair as well. "After we abandoned our gains, the Doms did so as well, scourging all the land between where we settled across the Rio Grande, to a point just north of the Pass of Fire you say our Captain Anson only recently revealed to you. All the land between, including the Valley of Mexico itself, and excepting only a few fortified coastal cities, was abandoned. Worse, the land was *exterminated* of human life, as if it and anyone living there had been contaminated by us. It remains a largely dead, uninhabited buffer between us to this day."

"Wow," Fred breathed. "But I guess that's consistent. They meant to wipe out everybody in the cities of Guayak and Puerto Viejo if they beat us there. They said so. And they did wipe out all the civilians in Chimborazo. At least those were the early reports we got before we flew off, looking for you." He looked at Hudgens. "But that doesn't explain why you didn't team up with the Imperials."

Hudgens shifted uncomfortably. "You should know, the Empire was expansionist even then. They had already established colonies on the California coast. We were few and militarily weak. And even as we grew in population and power, we continued to encounter new threats." He glanced at Willis. "Some we overcame. Others . . . linger. In any event, we considered it best to remain hidden from the Empire and observe. There were some rather extreme social differences between us as well. You may have noticed that the Empire treats its women . . . poorly. We treat them as the ladies, the mothers of our civilization that they are," he said somewhat proudly. He smiled. "And as you heard Don Emmanuel say, they do keep us 'polite.' In addition to that, however, the Imperials have grown ever closer to the Dominion in recent years, economically codependent in most unpleasant ways, using women as their basis of trade." He paused and raised an eyebrow. "Is it true what you said, that within a few years of our, ah, 'departure' from our old world, our nation was torn apart by a terrible civil war?"

Fred nodded. "Yeah. It was awful. North against South. Worst war we ever fought."

"I suppose the institution of slavery was a factor—the fuse at least, if not the only cause," Captain Willis grumbled, noting Fred's nod. He spread his hands on the table. "Our forefathers faced similar tensions in the early years, with factions desiring to enslave a percentage of the people under our protection. They and others we met over time. The majority wouldn't have it, whether they had originally hailed from northern or southern states, and the movement quickly faltered, thank God. But we saw varieties of slavery within the Imperial territories spreading across California. For that reason and others, we feared the Doms and Imperials would eventually unite against us. We were actually surprised to learn, through our observers in the Imperial colonies, that they were at war!"

"But . . . !" Fred sputtered, amazed. "That's all over!

The so-called Honorable New Britain Company that co-operated with the Doms is gone! The Empire has *freed* its women! It's complicated, but that's . . . kind of how the whole war started in the first place." Hudgens and Willis exchanged looks. "I mean," Fred continued, "didn't you know? Didn't Captain Anson tell *anybody* what was going on?" He gestured at Kari. "Our people, Lemurian and human . . . Americans, and the Impies, have thrashed fleet after fleet of Doms! We've secured the Enchanted Isles and invaded the damn Dominion itself! But we can only do so much, so fast, and we have another war, just as bad." He tilted his head in the general direction of the South American continent. "We're near the end of our rope out here. Anson said your people would lend a hand after we clobbered the Dom fleet they shifted through the Pass of Fire from the Atlantic to attack us. Well, we did! But now we're nearly bled out and need a hand! Anson was supposed to tell you all that and have you ready to jump on the opportunity when it came!"

"We didn't know any of that," Captain Willis said gently. He looked at Hudgens. "*We* certainly didn't, at least," he clarified. "I cannot say what our commanders and government might be aware of. Perhaps this Mr. Anson, whoever he was, never escaped the Dominion with the information you gave him, or the plan you made? All we knew was that the sea was less infested with enemy warships for the first time in many decades, thus our freedom to pursue our prize so close to enemy shores."

Fred and Kari digested that for a long moment. "So nobody over here knows that a combined Allied fleet just *destroyed* the greater part of what was left of the Dominion's sea power?" Fred asked bitterly.

"We did not," Captain Willis said. "And if our leaders truly didn't know, they soon will, when we take you to them."

"But . . . we need to act fast! The Doms are on the ropes! If we can hit them together, from everywhere, they're done!"

"I certainly hope you're right," Captain Willis agreed, nodding firmly. "And I'm inclined to believe that all you say is true, to your best understanding." He glanced meaningfully at Lieutenant Hudgens. "I am also suddenly quite infected with your sense of urgency. Your news, and the fact that we now have Don Emmanuel, may well be sufficient to convince my immediate superior, Commodore Semmes. His evaluation of the opportunity you describe will carry great weight indeed, and I am confident that if we convince him, our fleet *will* move against the Pass of Fire in force at last." His gentle smile returned, but it didn't touch his eyes. "Do believe me. Nothing would give me greater pleasure than to see the final end of the most *Un*holy Dominion, and all its abominable depravity, once and for all!"

Fred relaxed a bit, staring at the wireless set. "Swell," he said. "But what's that Dom got to do with any of this?"

"Don Emmanuel? Perhaps a great deal," Captain Willis said. "He serves his twisted pope as a form of 'foreign minister,' I suppose. Extremely well connected. He was once the primary Dom negotiator between our peoples, in point of fact." He frowned. "It is probably more accurate to say that he was the primary demander of concessions than negotiator, but there have been no meetings in recent years." He raised an eyebrow, looking at Fred. "Agents of our government, perhaps including your Mr. Anson, discovered that he had been dispatched eastward, to Africa, to secure an understanding with the reptile folk there."

"The Grik!" Fred gasped. "That's who else we're fighting! You know of them?"

Willis looked at Hudgens again. "Yes," he admitted. "A terrible enemy indeed. I honor your alliance even more now, and wish them all success. In any event, we and several other ships were sent to intercept him, but lost his trail on the voyage out. He was gone a great long time, and we suspected, frankly hoped, that the reptiles had killed him. Then one of our swiftest scouts sighted his ship again upon his return and the search was resumed. We just happened to stumble upon him, virtually at his own front door. We can only assume he made contact with the reptiles and made an agreement of some sort, to return from there alive after all this time."

Fred hesitated. "You know, he could've met with others. Besides the Grik."

"The League of Tripoli?" Willis probed, and Fred was stunned to silence. "Yes, we know of them as well. They are possibly the most powerful force on the globe, with all the arrogance of the Dominion, and far more powerful ships. It seems we have a *great* deal to talk about! But the League is yet another reason we have tried not to get deeply involved in foreign affairs. We do remain relatively weak, and they do not view us as a threat."

"This ship isn't weak," Fred pointed out.

"No, and we have a number of equally powerful ships in our fleet, as well as a fine—if modest—professional army. But our quality could never compete with the quantity of our enemies, or now especially the modern wonders possessed by the League." He looked speculatively at Fred. "Or so I have long thought. Like the League, I presume, your alliance has wireless communications and flying machines. Do you have ships that compare with theirs as well?"

"We're working on them," Fred hedged. "Kicking stuff around. Cooking stuff up. And we do have some ships and planes they'd hate to tangle with, but whatever threat the League might be—and they've made assholes of themselves a time or two—the Grik and Doms are our primary concern right now. Have to try not to worry about the League until we finish stomping a mud hole in *their* asses. No choice."

Willis laughed, the humor reaching his eyes at last. "Young man . . . Lieutenant, are you *sure* that you are an American naval officer? Though you make eminent sense, you do exhibit a certain . . . uninhibited turn of phrase."

Fred grinned back. "Sure I'm sure. Sorry about that. But maybe that's the best proof I can give that I *am* an American naval officer? Times, and the way people talk, I guess, change." He waved at Kari. "And you sound a little strange to us. More like Impies. A little." He shrugged and pointed at the wireless set. "So, you want me to try to get somebody on that? Sometimes, the 'conditions' I talked about are better at night, and it'll be dark soon. If we could at least tell our people we're okay . . ."

Willis sobered. "I would like nothing more, Lieutenant Reynolds, but until I can consult my superiors, I am afraid

I must forbid it. As much sense as you make, so does their caution—in the face of a great deal of uncorroborated information—make sense as well. However"—he held up a hand—"am I correct in assuming that you can receive transmissions and reports without your keyboard in the circuit?"

Fred nodded. "Sure."

Willis carefully picked the keyboard up and gazed at it a moment. "In that case, I will direct the ship's carpenters to assist you in rigging an . . . antenna, if the materials you require can be found aboard. Feel free to listen all you want, and I would appreciate hearing any information you learn that you feel comfortable sharing with me. But I will keep this with me for a time," he said, gesturing with the keyboard. "Perhaps not long. I do believe you, as I said, but involving us further in the . . . very wide war you describe is not my decision."

Fred licked his lips, his eyes following the keyboard. He could, of course, still transmit without it. Did Willis know that? He had to know that two wires tapping together would send a signal as readily with his set as with any telegraph equipment. Was this a test? He decided he'd just stick to listening for a while. Whether they could report back that they were alive or not wouldn't make any difference at all to the war effort. At least not until he could report that they'd have help or not. And it wasn't likely he'd hear anything from Shinya's forces anyway, although he might. Particularly if they'd crossed to this side of the mountains. He really wanted to pick up something from Greg Garrett and *Donaghey*, but that might take a while as well. It was a long voyage across the South Atlantic under sail alone, and who knew what winds they'd find on this world. Either way, it seemed he and Kari had fallen in with people who were at least sympathetic, and might even be convinced to help after all. He wouldn't do anything to screw that up. For now.

"Suit yourself, Captain," Fred said, stretching. He was still exhausted from his and Kari's long flight, and was beginning to believe that they might just be safe among friends. "And I'll tell you anything I hear that you might need to know, or that might help your superior officers make up their minds. But I have one other question. This is a fine ship and all—fast, tough, well-armed—but what do you fellas do about mountain fishes? You know, whatever you call them, those great, big-assed fishes that can eat a ship. I'd kind of like to know I'm not going to wake up inside one some night—or in the water." He frowned and rubbed his eyes. "I don't like being in the water."

The Indus River Valley
October 4, 1944

"Regent Shighat will establish his new 'field palace' here," Halik said, jabbing a claw at a clear spot in the nearly solid green-and-brown-painted fabric he called a "map." "Surveyors are already in place, preparing the site. And his army proceeds as expected, continuing its lurching advance down the old road, directly toward us here," he added somewhat disdainfully, jabbing again. "I have never seen, or even imagined, an army move so slowly. All of our preliminary preparations are complete, with time to spare."

General Yikkit was . . . impressed, to say the least, by what he'd seen of Halik's army, but there was no getting around the disparity in size between it and what he knew was approaching. He found Halik's confidence reassuring, but perhaps also unrealistic. "The image does not show the differences in elevation," Halik continued. "My artists are still not skilled at that. But the field palace will be considerably higher than we are here, as are the sides of the trail Shighat's army must follow. Trust me when I say that it is a most . . . advantageous place for us to meet him. You must greet his vanguard *here*, General Yikkit." Halik pointed once again, at a place the trail apparently widened out, at the foot of the mountains. "With the force that

Shighat expects to see. We will call it Sixth, ah, 'Division,' though it is somewhat over strength for that new designation. General Ugla, you will take the First Division, to the heights northeast of the road. General Shlook, the Second, on the heights to the southwest. I will join you with the Fourth and Fifth, on your left, but will stand ready to react to developments in the rear of the column, and assault Shighat's field palace directly. I do not know if he will personally come down to take possession of our"—he gurgled a chuckle—"'untainted' warriors, but we must be prepared for either eventuality. General Niwa? You will command the Third Division, supporting General Yikkit." Unsaid was the fact that Niwa would be in position to take over from Yikkit if he failed or hesitated.

Yikkit stared. He wasn't accustomed to maps and had only ever seen a few, on a much larger scale. Still, he could appreciate how this smaller one—if accurate—could help them plan. It was also obvious how the approach Halik indicated would funnel and confine an advancing force. He glanced uneasily at Niwa. The strange human didn't quite trust him, particularly with the role Halik had assigned him. And he found it equally difficult to trust General Orochi Niwa. His presence had come as a great surprise. He hadn't known First General Esshk had sent a Japh to accompany General Halik, definitely not that he'd given him such an exalted rank. But that was apparently the case, as was the fact that Halik and Niwa had grown uncommonly close during their time together. Then again, all those now present beneath Halik's command pavilion, erected upon the slight elevation surrounded by his unusually . . . purposeful army, seemed quite comfortable with one another. The ease and familiarity with which Generals Shlook, Ugla, Niwa, and even senior members of their respective staffs spoke to General Halik stood in stark contrast to the nervous anticipation and outright fear that Yikkit had grown accustomed to during any session with Regent Consort Shighat.

"How, may I ask, do you know exactly where Regent Consort Shighat will be—or indeed, any of his other dispositions so far in advance?" he asked uncomfortably. "I know you have scouts. Any General—except apparently

Shighat—would use them. But they cannot run fast enough to bring such observations so quickly . . . unless they actually ride upon the neekis!" He saw Halik glance at Niwa.

"No," Halik allowed, "we have trained some to pull carts and guns, as you have seen, but they will not accept us on their backs. We cannot ride them. We must rely on . . . other scouts with even swifter mounts for reports such as these."

Yikkit's mouth opened. "The *enemy* scouts for you? Without joining the hunt?" he demanded, mind reeling. At least he hadn't called the human/Lemurian cavalry force he'd learned was camped nearby "prey." Not more than once.

"We have come to . . . know each other," Halik stated dryly, "and in this one instance, our interests hunt together. I—all of us here—fight to preserve this army and what it has become. I first accomplished that by leaving India. Had I not, it would no longer exist. My former enemy, who has so" —his eyes narrowed in amusement—"graciously provided us with information regarding Shighat's movements, and . . . a few other small favors, wants *no* Grik in India. Not us, and certainly not Regent Consort Shighat. They scout for me—just now—so I might succeed in stopping Shighat. Our blood will achieve their aims." His eyes narrowed even more, and his crest rippled. "What an interesting irony! But their assistance aids our aims as well." He shook his head, his crest flaring wider in vague annoyance. "I explained this already."

"You told me how your army came to be here," Yikkit agreed, "but did not mention such active cooperation. I remain"—he took a long breath—"astounded, and still can hardly understand how you simply . . . stopped fighting them, without your whole army turning prey. It is further justification of First General Esshk's confidence in you, I suppose, but remains difficult to accept."

"Accept it, General Yikkit," said General Shlook. He and General Ugla, Halik's most trusted lieutenants after Niwa, remained skeptical of Yikkit as well, but all understood why his role in the coming battle was virtually essential. "And accept also that the active cooperation was equally surprising to us. If you better knew one of those who provide it, a particularly relentless foe named Svec, you would be even more amazed." Shlook grunted.

"He speaks the truth," Halik said. "The humans have a saying: 'The enemy of my enemy is my friend.' A most imaginative and flexible, if somewhat simplistic approach to such a serious matter. And I do not think it entirely applies us in this instance, though it is a close approximation. Perhaps 'the enemy'—us—of their greater 'enemy'— Shighat—is 'ever so slightly *less* their enemy just now' is a better fit under the circumstances." Even Niwa seemed amused, if Yikkit properly translated his strange face moving.

"In any event," Yikkit said, "I remain even more 'amazed' by what you have accomplished. Though the participation of generals in actual battles, instead of merely designing them, still gives me pause"—he flicked his own crest—"along with a certain . . . eager anticipation," he confessed. "It has been a long time since I wielded a sword," he added wistfully, then returned to his point. "Your army exhibits a stunning degree of willing cooperation between its parts, and its members show a level of devotion to you greater than any I have witnessed, short of that owed to the Giver of Life herself. It may even . . . exceed that," he proposed, now slightly nervous.

"Ah, you come to it at last," Niwa said, finally joining the conversation, and addressing all of them, not just Yikkit. "You see, General Halik *has* become their 'giver of life,' in all but name, and in more ways than you can imagine. He certainly *preserved* their lives and has not only allowed, but nurtured the awakening of true consciousness among his warriors. They have gained an understanding of this, and are grateful. Kurokawa, the Chooser, even General Esshk were wrong. Their experiments sought to develop better defensive fighters by allowing the less predatory hatchlings to survive. It worked, to a degree, but it was not as much the 'as born' nature of the hatchlings that made them what they wanted as it was the training they received. And the training—and maturity—this army has earned at great cost far surpasses that ever achieved by any Grik army in history. Or so I would imagine. This army is . . ." Niwa paused a moment, considering. "It is *aware*," he finally said. "Its isolation had much to do with that, I'm sure, as did the fact that it was battling an enemy the likes of which the Grik have never faced. It was *losing*, General Yikkit, and General Halik simply couldn't afford to continue wasting warriors in headlong assaults, nor could he afford the luxury of sending his older, more seasoned veterans to the cookpots! What gradually resulted is a *real* army, not a mere mob of mindless, suggestible killers. This has become an army of *people*, individualistic to a degree, that not only wants to survive, but knows it will have to fight for the chance to do so. Perhaps most amazing of all is that it has developed a fierce loyalty to the one who protects its desire, its chance!"

"It has become its enemy, then," Yikkit murmured.

"To a small but growing degree," Niwa agreed, looking at Yikkit, then all of them. "So this is when you must decide if you can accept that or not. General Halik preserved this army for General Esshk." He focused on Halik. "But in all honesty, how do you think he would feel if he saw it now? What do any of you think he would do if he truly understood what it has become, fully appreciated the threat it poses to Regent Shighat, regent Ragak, and all the others? Even him?" Niwa stared intently at Halik. They'd discussed this briefly, from time to time, but Halik never wanted to follow the thread to its conclusion. Niwa knew he had to, and so must Yikkit. Shlook and Ugla already had. Niwa shrugged. "Personally, I think he would use it. Esshk is no fool. But he would use it—use *us*—to death. And once the need was past, if any of us remained, he would destroy us. Those are the stakes, and that is what each of us must decide. Do we blindly follow a corrupt, life-consuming path, or do we blaze a new one? If we're not willing to do that, then we may as well let Shighat destroy us after all." He looked back at Yikkit.

"So before we give you twenty thousand troops, very few of which remain what Shighat hopes they are, by the way"—he nodded at Halik—"and before anyone does another thing to prepare for the battle to come, *everyone* must agree, at last, upon what it is we actually fight to save this army *for*! Do we fight merely to exist? To let Esshk use us as he will and then discard us like a broken sword?

Or will we fight for the future of your race, to *smash* the tyranny of the past that oppresses and consumes all life as though it has no meaning? The past is death. You all have seen it. The future might hold meaning, hope, *dignity*! That is what your army craves, General Halik, as do you: that thing called *honor*!" He took a breath in the silence that ensued. "If not for that, then what? General Esshk? Still? No." Niwa looked at the others again. "I will fight for the army we have built and for General Halik, who leads it. I will fight for him and the future he represents. I will not fight for General Esshk!"

Halik looked at him and slowly blinked his eyes. Never had he felt . . . whatever it was he felt. He couldn't describe it, other than as a profound sense of gratitude, but even that word was grossly insufficient. It would have to do. And whatever sentiment Niwa's words had stirred within his breast, it was good. "So be it," he said very softly. "I am no 'giver of life,' but I will be regent of this army, if that is what is required. Beyond that, we will see. General Yikkit? What say you?"

After the slightest hesitation, Yikkit suddenly cast himself on the ground at Halik's feet. "I serve you, Lord!" he said, his voice . . . sincerely reverent. He was in, with his eyes wide-open.

"Oh, do get up, General Yikkit!" General Ugla snapped gruffly. "We do not do that here!"

Central Madagascar
October 4, 1944

"This isn't what I expected at all," Courtney Bradford said, removing his wide sombrero and mopping sweat from his forehead with his sleeve. "It must be the different weather on this world, across the surrounding sea. The wind often blows north and south, for instance, not just from the east." He sat on a jagged stone, still puffing in the rarefied air, and gazed out upon the lowland to the west through his glass. Chack hopped up beside him, his Krag in the crook of his arm. Lawrence, who'd suffered terribly in the high-altitude cold, was feeling better and was casting ahead to scout the trail. Silva just stood humming softly and leaning on the Doom Stomper like a great, deadly walking stick. Petey's big-eyed reptilian face peered over his shoulder.

After days of toil, strenuous climbing, bone-numbing cold at night, and now a treacherous descent, they'd finally crossed the jagged spine of Madagascar to view a land that none of them had been prepared for. It was flat, as expected, but instead of the thorny desert Bradford had described, there was a broad savanna of tall grass with clumps of vegetation rising around the occasional utterly enormous tree. "They *are* baobabs, of a sort," Courtney insisted, pointing. "Look at the size of the trunk. But the limbs are much more conventional—and they're as large as galla trees!" Galla trees were sacred to Lemurians in the Alliance to varying degrees simply because they'd all originated here, on their ancestral homeland. That the Grik had used them so profligately to construct a kind of mountainous wall around their city in the north had struck most 'Cats as sacrilegious, even though the dense forests of the island were thick with them.

"Well, one thing's sure," Silva said, nodding at the near distance, where a herd of monstrous, long-necked beasts, like giant brontosarries, munched along, their heads close to the ground. "Things ain't as sparse here as we figured. Good thing I brung my usual armory." In addition to his Doom Stomper, a Thompson SMG was slung over his shoulder, riding in the small of his back. His 1911 Colt, Navy cutlass, 1903 Springfield bayonet, and an ornate if somewhat battered long-barreled flintlock pistol dangled incongruously from his belt. Chack and Courtney had expressed concern over Silva's load of weapons and ammunition, in addition to his share of the communal supplies, on the long climb because, for the first time anyone could remember, the burden seemed to drag the big man down. He blamed it on "lolling around, doin' nothin' for so long" while healing from wounds received in taking the Celestial Palace, but he wasn't bouncing back as quickly as he always had in the past. He still adamantly refused to part with any of his weapons, though.

"All that shit's slowing you down," Miles criticized, looking at him as he joined the group. "And that idiot lizard too."

Silva regarded him coldly with his good eye. "Petey's less of a drag on me than you are, Miles. An' what's your excuse for laggin' along behind? He nodded at the Allin-Silva "trapdoor" rifle the Marine carried. "That thing better be clean. Not like you've used it for nothin'."

Miles swore, looking at his weapon. "This piece of crap? Why couldn't I have had a Springfield? There were two on the Seven boat."

"Because Nat an' his 'Cats'll probably be fightin' their way all the way back down the river, five guys short. They need it more—and it'd be wasted on you."

Miles bristled. "And all that shit isn't wasted on *you*?"

Silva sighed and Chack grew tense, expecting trouble. He began to tell the two men to pipe down, but there was something indefinable between them that they needed to work out and he didn't understand. "Look, sonny," Silva finally said. "Every single weapon I'm carryin' has saved my ass or somebody else's more than once. Prob'ly save yours—if I don't use one of 'em on you first. So shut the hell up."

"Mr. Silva is right, though," Courtney chimed in as if oblivious to the tension. "This land will support quite a large population. Perhaps these Shee-ree predominate, and we can make friendly contact with them."

They all hoped so. The 'Cats that shadowed them up from the river had clearly been waiting for a chance to strike, but the party was always alert and the natives feared their "magic." It had still been tense. Then, suddenly, there were no more watchers. Granted, the weather at the top of the mountains had been unpleasant indeed, with all the party donning the peacoats and blankets Bradford had insisted they bring. But once they were gone, the natives hadn't returned.

"That reminds me," Silva said, pulling the heavy peacoat out of a pouch at his side and throwing it away. "Won't be needin' that again."

"You don't know that," Bradford objected.

"Sure I do. I wish we could've made contact with our people at the top of the mountains. Perfect place. But there was no way we were waggin' that hand-powered generator along. Too heavy an' bulky. Should've brought one o' the wind-powered jobs. Anyway, my point is we ain't goin' back over these mountains. Whatever it is, our way home lies ahead, not back, an' I'm sick o' waggin' the damn thing around."

Miles seemed to consider this and finally tossed his coat as well. Chack's fur protected him somewhat, but he liked the peacoat. Still . . . shaking his head, he pulled his out of his pack and let it fall.

"Well," Courtney sniffed. "I shall keep mine, and I highly suggest Lawrence do the same!"

"Do what you want. I don't care," Silva said, nodding

out across the prairie, "but we're gettin' thin on rations. We're gonna have to kill somethin' now an' then to keep on." His voice had returned to its usual, good-humored tone. He looked at Chack and winked. "Finally gettin' to the fun part o' this idiotic trip! Anyway, we'll need to pack more food than we can eat, most likely, so we'll have to make room."

"Eat?" Petey asked hopefully. Silva ignored him and took the blanket out of his pack, looked at it, but put it back. "It don't weigh enough to make a difference," he said.

Lawrence suddenly appeared, panting lightly in the thin air.

"How do you *do* that?" Silva demanded. "You must be the sneakiest critter there ever was. An' it ain't like you blend in! Anybody should be able to see a stripey-assed orange lizard hoppin' from rock to rock."

"Sneakiest Critter," Petey chirped disapprovingly.

"I just do," Lawrence replied patiently. "And not kick rocks and roar all day."

"Well, if we weren't pals, you'd give me the creeps," Silva confessed. "Hell, you *still* give me the creeps. What did you see?"

"A . . . ripher, down out of the 'ountains, heading . . . yest."

"There should be no rivers here, heading west or anywhere. Not really," Courtney grumbled.

"Good." Silva laughed. "For once, you're just like the rest of us: no idea what to expect! What else, Larry?"

"'Cat tracks." He nodded at Chack's sandaled feet. "New tracks. Ten 'Cats together, cross ripher down yonder." He pointed down to the west, northwest.

"Are they heading this direction?" Courtney asked.

"Not directly. They just cross, I think. 'Ut us could see they. Us head down soon."

"Well, we're goin' down." Silva looked thoughtful. "I dunno, Mr. Bradford. Maybe we want to sneak along a little farther before meetin' any more locals. Keep our heads down for now, so to speak. We'll have to follow the river for water and critters to eat anyway. Plenty of time to meet new folks after we have a better idea what's what on this side of the mountains."

"Chief Silva may be right," Chack agreed. "It might be better to search out a village, perhaps, than simply present ourselves to what might be a war or hunting party that may be particularly wary or prone to violence. We may be less likely to get in a fight among their homes with young-lings about." The notion of females being noncombatants never even occurred to him.

Courtney put the sombrero back on his head and stood. He no longer had a paunch, the mountains had seen to that, but he was a bit over fifty and his joints ached. "We might be *more* likely to provoke them if we just march right into a village unannounced," he said gloomily.

"I don't think so," Chack disagreed. "Consider a moment. We've already speculated about this a great deal. The river folk to the east are clearly related to my ancestors or we couldn't have communicated. Yet they look nothing like any Mi-Anakka I've ever met. Perhaps the same language and some customs prevailed all across this land at one time, but the people, the races, maintained their various territories. But why are there no 'Cats like we met in the East elsewhere in the Alliance? I say it is because they never left. None of them. They said the Grik are not there. Perhaps they never were, in numbers? We know they avoided the denser forest of this land except to stock it with specimens of their conquests and for sport." He blinked deep interest. "If I am right, then the Shee-ree or others like them, always closer to the Grik across the Go Away Strait and who see the Grik all the time, might be more closely related to my ancestors who escaped. If true, then some of our customs regarding the rights of guests and strangers may remain among them as well."

"It's a stretch," Silva said, frowning. "But them little guys on Diego, them La-laantis, were polite enough."

"A stretch indeed, but not a bad notion," Courtney said. "So, what you're saying is that if we locate a village or band along this river heading west, we should"—he glanced at Silva—"after observing them long enough to ensure they don't engage in cannibalism or other such unpleasantness, just march in among them, demanding to greet their High Chief?"

"Exactly. It's the most ancient of our social rites, and

something like it *must* still exist here! It might even have worked with the Erokighaani."

"You forget they was tryin' to kill us?" Silva demanded, then rolled his eye. "Never mind. Maybe you're right. But with them other fellas, even if we got past their defenses an' said howdy to their High Chief, I figure they would'a ate us anyway."

Chack reluctantly nodded, and Silva suddenly felt a twinge of remorse for his friend's lost . . . optimistic innocence. Something like that. He was proud of the "new" Chack who'd risen from the ranks to become the seasoned, maybe even brilliant battlefield commander who'd inspired the loyalty of 'Cats and humans—and Imperial humans at that!—alike. In spite of this little jaunt, he had a brigade of his own. If the war lasted long enough, he'd have an army, and he'd use it right. But Dennis couldn't help but miss the cheerful young 'Cat who'd once scampered all over *Walker* with such unabashed wonder and an ingrained trust that all people—*real* people—human or Lemurian, could generally be relied upon to do the right thing. Silva guessed that it had been fighting the Doms that had knocked that out of his friend for good.

"Well. Indeed," Courtney said, pulling at the short whitish beard he'd allowed to flourish. "Quite sensible, all of it." He looked at Lawrence. "Can you track these hunters, or whatever they are?"

Lawrence shifted uncomfortably. "Yes. 'ut these aren't city 'Cats. They're likely good at not getting sneaked on. Like that old 'Cat sergeant."

"Moe." Dennis nodded. Lawrence nodded back. "Yes. They'll catch Lawrence, I get too close."

"Then don't get close," Chack said, deciding. "Just ensure they don't get too close to us. And stay prepared for other . . . opportunities."

Silva hoisted the Doom Stomper to rest on his shoulder. "Sounds like a plan. This ain't gettin' us anywhere. Might as well move along."

Lawrence cut his eyes at Chack, then turned and trotted away down the trail he'd returned by. Chack and Bradford followed. Finally, Silva motioned Miles to precede him.

"What, don't trust me behind you?" Miles smirked.

Silva barked a laugh. "No, I don't. But if I thought I had to *worry* about you, for me or them"—he nodded in the direction his friends had gone—"I'd feed your sorry ass to the worms here an' now. You may've heard, but I don't like worryin' about stuff."

Miles's face clouded. "Just what the hell is it with you? With everybody! What've you got against me?"

Silva cocked his head. "It ain't so much what I've got against you, it's just that I got nothin' *for* you, and I think that's all that matters to you. You toadied up to that snoop Commander Herring all the time to a mighty unnatural degree. Now he's dead an' you got nobody left to toady to."

"You like Gunny Horn, and he was tight with Herring."

"Horn's a right guy," Silva agreed, "an' he respected Herring. But he kept things proper, see?" Silva shrugged. "An' Herring might've been okay too, for all I know. We had a talk or two from time to time about . . . things. While I was healin' . . ." He stopped and looked at Miles. "Even talked about *you* once, an' I got some o' the dope on why you're such a toad. Anyway, my point is that you don't sweat, and if things go in the crapper, you won't *bleed* for nobody. Nobody but Ian Miles."

Miles scowled. "And why should I? I've been through enough. I was a prisoner of the Japs before I ever even wound up here. . . ."

"Wah, wah. Yeah, the Japs had you, an' that was tough. But they had Horn, an' Herring, an' a buncha other guys too. Guys who didn't wind up with a heap o' chips on their shoulders. They didn't quit hatin' Japs, but they learned the Grik are just as bad, or worse. An' the Grik are the ones the Japs on this world shacked up with. Not hard to figure who the real enemy is, you ask me. So they pitched in. Now Horn's hurt an' Herring's dead, but they took theirs for the goddamn *team*, see?" He shook his head. "That's what I don't get about you. You're in one piece, mainly because guys like them ain't, an' instead o' hankerin' to even the score with the ones who did your pals, all you do is mope an' groan. The war marches on, but you still just slide."

"A man's got a right to take a break," Miles insisted stubbornly. "And your Captain Reddy's got no authority over me. He's got no real authority at all, ever since you came to this screwed-up world. And that bastard McFarlane sent me on this trip. Just *sent* me, like I have no rights at all!"

Silva suddenly grabbed Miles's shirt and shook the man. "You listen to me, you piece o' shit! Captain Reddy's *the* authority on this planet, far as I'm concerned. Why? Because he kept everything together when it should'a fallen apart. Spanky may be a bastard, I don't know, but far as *you're* concerned, he sits at the right hand o' God. *Do you understand?*" Silva pushed him away. "And yeah, Spanky sent you because he flat didn't want you around—and he wanted me to find out if you were worth feedin'. So far, I say no, but that's up to you to change." He grinned, but the expression wasn't born of humor. "He also said—just between him an' me, 'cause the Skipper'd never approve— that if you really ain't worth a hole in a chicken's ass, he never wants to see you again. Savvy?"

Miles's lip remained curled. "Yeah, I 'savvy.' Basically, if I don't do what you say, you'll try to murder me."

"Yep. 'Bout the size of it. Except for the 'try' part. Might anyway if I figger you ain't reformed."

"Awful sure of yourself, aren't you?"

Silva just looked at him with his one good eye. "Yep, I am. I seen guys like you all my life—in the Navy, in the Corps, it don't matter. I was a lot like you once myself," he added with a smirk of his own. "Grassburrs in the watermelon patch was all we were. All *you* are. But I'll level with you. If I can change into somethin' less useless than what I was, anybody can. So I'll give you a chance. You shape up an' we'll, well, maybe we won't get along, but I won't kill you. If you don't . . ." Silva shrugged.

"So that's it?" Miles asked quietly. He was watching Silva very carefully. Had he actually been listening, thinking about what Silva said, or was he just figuring his odds? His rifle was on his shoulder, his pistol buttoned down. He carried a cutlass too, but couldn't have any illusions there. Silva was no fencer, but he was pure murder in a fight with *his* cutlass, and could have it out and slashing before Miles even touched a weapon.

"Yep. Pretty much," Silva finally said, motioning Miles down the rocky slope. After another hesitation, the man cautiously turned to follow the others. "Just one more little thing," Silva added. "I know some of what you an' Herring were up to, with that 'Killer Kudzu' weapon Bernie Sandison cooked up in Baalkpan. I know what that shit does. I discovered it myself on Yap Island, as a matter of fact." He considered. "I guess Mr. Cook actually *discovered* it, him gettin' the thorn in his finger an' all." He looked at Miles. "But I had to cut that finger *off*. From one little tiny thorn. So I believe I'd go ahead and tell me the rest of Herring's scheme, if I was you."

CHAPTER 16

Indus River Valley
October 6, 1944

Geneeral Yikkit was very nervous indeed, marching forward with a small escort beneath a single shot-torn banner, to meet a delegation of Shighat's generals. They were approaching beneath a small cloud of snakelike pennants of their own. Behind him was what looked like a ragtag, fidgety mob of hungry warriors gathered together in a massive blob as if for mutual assurance, apparently teetering on the very edge of turning prey. That was certainly understandable considering what they'd been through, and was no less than what the head of the delegation marching to meet him fully expected to see. Behind *his* party, choking the tight mountain pass, was the uncountable horde of Shighat's "finest" warriors; his elite "Guard Swarm." Enaak's and Svec's reports—and Yikkit knew them to be true in this case, so was more inclined to believe the rest—numbered the Guard Swarm at just over forty thousand. They were all dressed alike in red leather armor—Shighat had been taken with how proper warriors dressed, if not by how they behaved—and though they had that hard, lean look of having marched a great distance, they were obviously well fed and equipped. Yikkit had once considered them a match for anything they might meet. Now, though they were an intimidating sight, even bunched together as they were, filling the curving pass as far as Yikkit could see, he knew that they were doomed. The Guard Swarm wasn't what concerned him. He was worried about what lay beyond it: a force four times as large, if not quite so pampered. And he was more than a little worried that he might be just a bit too close when the first blow fell in this—*face it*—rebellion.

He wasn't afraid to fight. He'd been a sport fighter too, just like General Halik. He enjoyed personal combat, and had never expected to feel that particular thrill again. He looked forward to that aspect of the coming battle with a pleasant anticipation that surprised him with its intensity. But if General Niwa and the special detachment of civilian Hij under his personal supervision had miscalculated, the blow that should soon break the vanguard of the Guard Swarm might very well break General Yikkit as well. He took a deep, calming breath and marched on. If it did, there was nothing for it, and chances were, he'd never know. "Greetings, General D'ga!" he called, raising his hand. "Greetings, General Suluk! And you, Chooser! I trust you are well this day?" He mentally berated himself. He'd never been friendly with Shighat's chooser, or General D'ga either, for that matter. He hoped they'd write his enthusiasm off as relieved eagerness to return to the comforts of the host.

"Greetings, General Yikkit," D'ga said, drawing near. He glanced disdainfully, significantly, at the mob gathered behind him. "I am surprised you could scrape up so many. Chooser, you likely have a long day ahead of you, regardless."

"No doubt," the chooser said, glancing at Yikkit. "This one has little notion of the difference between warriors and fodder. I expect to pass no more than one in five of that huddled vermin." The delegation apparently hadn't noticed the way Yikkit's escort, under the command of Captain Sigg, began spreading out.

"My dear Chooser," Yikkit said, laying the sarcasm heavily, openly now, "I suspect you will find a much higher percentage than *that*!" He dropped his hand. When he did, the banner also dropped. General D'ga looked at him uncomprehendingly as Yikkit's hand rose once more, grasping his sword, and slashed downward at D'ga's neck. At that moment, the earth shuddered beneath their feet.

Ever since they'd crossed the Indus River, Halik and Niwa had put the large number of Hij they'd rescued to work making whatever they could to replenish their combat stores. Much had been accomplished. They couldn't make new artillery pieces or the multitude of other things that required vast quantities of metal, but strange metal artifacts of some previous civilization were frequently discovered. Not nearly enough had been gathered to make even a few cannon, but there'd been sufficient quantities to repair swords and muskets and make thousands of crossbow bolts tipped with copper or iron. That, and the incendiary "Grik Fire" they'd improvised, gave Halik's army individual parity with any Grik force it was likely to meet. It had been Niwa's personal project, however, that would give them the edge today. They'd made canister, both stone and metal, for the much reduced arsenal of artillery they'd brought away, but more important, they'd continued making gunpowder far beyond Halik's army's ability to use it in its remaining weapons, or even transport it. This surplus, tons of it, had been strategically placed in the rock face on the northeast side of the narrow gorge that Shighat's Guard Swarm now packed.

The "other small favor" that Colonel Enaak had granted Halik—over Svec's thunderous objection—was the platoon of combat engineers attached to his 5th Maa-ni-la Cavalry. They'd very uncomfortably (considering the company they were in) rigged the explosives Niwa's sappers had emplaced with their demolition gear, consisting of two miles of wire and two cases of electric primers of the type used by the navy to fire their great guns in salvo. All this terminated at a boxlike, plunger-type blasting machine they'd never let out of their sight. As per their agreement, no Grik ever came within fifty paces of the nervous, heavily armed platoon of Lemurians.

Then they'd waited, expectantly watching for the dropped banner as their signal to activate their detonator, pack it up, remount their me-naaks, and ride like hell. Neither they nor any other member of the Grand Alliance would take further action in the battle that day. Ultimately, the effect of their small contribution was disproportionate, to say the least.

The sudden shudder beneath Yikkit's feet presaged a tremendous serial thunderclap that pounded his senses so hard that he didn't even feel his blade chop deep into General D'ga's chest. Nor could he keep his feet. Off balance, he crouched low and watched as the entire northeast slope of the gorge vomited a great gray cloud of powder smoke mixed with granite dust. Inside the cloud, thousands of tons of gravel, rock, boulders, entire trees, all spewed or tumbled down upon the Grik army underneath. And even as the echoes of the terrible blast and the rumble of falling debris began to fade, the screams of thousands rose.

"At them!" Yikkit roared, jumping up and hacking the chooser down almost without a thought. The dust cloud was billowing toward him, and he knew he must face it—and the enemy—with a solid front. "Now!" he bellowed again, even as the "mob" of warriors behind him began to morph into something . . . extraordinary. Halik had told him it was a "shield wall," something he'd learned from his human/Lemurian enemies, and something that could advance through the coming chaos and still keep together.

"Proceed," Halik said simply, peering down at the tail end of the horror wrought by the explosives. It was impossible to tell how effective the stroke had truly been through all the swirling smoke and dust, but most of the Guard Swarm had been thrown into disarray at the very least. Now it was time to infect the follow-on forces, already heaving back against the tide of their comrades, with yet another terror. Shouts relayed Halik's command. In moments, dozens of flaming spheres of Grik Fire were catapulted into the air from the southwest rim of the gorge, immediately followed by more from the other side. The sputtering spheres arced down amid the milling mass of warriors and exploded with gouts of flame, roiling black smoke, and whistling shrieks of agony. What the human members of the Grand Alliance had dubbed "Grik Fire" for reasons Niwa had explained, and Halik thought appropriate, could be made from virtually any flammable substance, as long as the vapor wasn't too combustible. Some substances were better than others.

The fuel they'd incorporated locally came from a mixture of the sap of a tree similar to a gimpra, and an oily resin easily distilled from a prickly native shrub. Both were combined in crude clay pots wrapped in ropes soaked with the resin. The ropes were lit just before the torsion-powered bomb throwers were activated so the spheres had their own ignition source when they impacted and ruptured, spewing burning fluid in all directions. Judging by how quickly the fluid ignited and how persistently it burned, it looked like they'd come up with a particularly good batch.

More bombs arced in, just as quickly as the machines could be prepared, and Halik watched intently as fire washed across the panicking horde, sticking to and burning anything it touched in the confining space below. He found himself amazingly detached for once, almost like an ordinary Grik general that merely planned a battle and set it in motion. Those plans often involved a few refinements beyond simply lining up and bashing at an enemy, particularly when fighting other Grik when "style" was more important. Flank attacks were common, even obligatory to a degree, being reminiscent of an earlier age when small packs used them to bring down prey. But showing off was part of the ritual when Grik fought Grik, and flank attacks and other flourishes were usually displayed for the opponent to see and admire. Halik had never fought like that, and the greatest difference between what he'd planned and what any ordinary Grik general was capable of imagining was that he'd learned to hide his embellishments from an enemy as perceptive as General Pete Alden, and he had troops he could trust to carry them out. Last, of course, he'd soon be in the thick of it, up to his neck.

"Lord General!" cried a runner, suddenly gasping at his side. "General Shlook sends his dearest worship, and the Guard Swarm is ripe for harvest! Perhaps a quarter of its number was crushed when the mountain moved, and the rest are pressed between the fire and the attack Sixth and Third Divisions make. It teeters on the sword edge of turning prey entirely! He begs can he join the rout with his Second Division!"

The thousands below, not yet under the firebombs, were already recoiling back up the gorge. "By all means," Halik said, "but wait a moment before you return to him. Signalers!" he said, raising his voice over the holocaust below, speaking to a section of Hij huddled near bearing bright pennants. Another trick he'd learned from his former, most esteemed foe. "Communicate to General Ugla that we will quickly begin our sweep!" As soon as a clear gap had formed between the forces dying below and the rest of Shighat's army, 1st and 4th Divisions, both under Ugla's command, would follow a cannonade by their few guns and a blizzard of crossbow bolts down the cliffs on either side and surge up the gap behind the fleeing foe. "Keeping up the scare," as Niwa had so eloquently put it. "Now," Halik said, turning to Shlook's runner, "as soon as Generals Shlook, Yikkit, and Niwa have destroyed what remains of the Guard Swarm, they must quickly race to follow General Ugla's advance. I go now to join Fifth Division to attack Shighat's field palace directly. Resistance will no doubt stiffen whether I am successful or not, but they must not give the enemy a moment's pause; they *must* grind through! Fifth Division will serve as the anvil for their hammer blow. Any delay and the enemy *will* realize he still has the numbers to shrug us off. Now go!"

Yikkit's shield wall, now strengthened by Niwa's 3rd Division, which had hurried to join it from beyond the enemy's view, churned up the rubbled slope against the frenzied but disorganized resistance of what remained of the Guard Swarm. The dust was still thick, but visibility had improved enough to see that the red leather armor of their foes had turned a dull gray, and the once clear water of the shallow stream to their left was now a muddy, boulder-strewn seep. There were boulders everywhere, in fact, which made it difficult to maintain their murderous front, but Halik had trained his troops at this unmercifully, and the training was paying off.

"Are you enjoying yourself?" Orochi Niwa asked General Yikkit, suddenly appearing beside him in the jostling, roaring line. Niwa spoke English, but with his elevation, Yikkit had been taught enough of the "scientific tongue" to understand quite a bit of what he said. Yikkit chanced a glance at the strange "Jaaph." The man was supposedly still recovering from very serious wounds, but if that was the case, he showed no sign. He had no shield, but was making swift, efficient, lethal strikes through the shields around him with an unusually long, slightly curved sword. His skill seemed highly practiced, almost casual. Blood streaked the sword, as well as the dust covering his face. Yikkit had always wondered how humans and their Lemurian allies could've given his race such difficulty. Neither appeared particularly formidable or had proper teeth or claws. Now he knew. He wouldn't have wanted to face Orochi Niwa in the arena.

"Yes," Yikkit confessed. "Yes, I am. I have missed this," he said, realizing it was true. He didn't have the wind he'd once had, but his muscles remembered the strokes of their own accord.

"Halik enjoys it too," the man said, slashing lightning fast at a head full of ravening teeth that suddenly appeared before him. "As do I," Niwa continued conversationally when the head fell away, cut half in two. "Against *this* enemy. I did not enjoy fighting the Alliance, for a number of reasons. But do you not find an interesting contrast here? We are generals, yet fight right alongside our lowliest Uul." He almost spat the word "lowliest," and it was heavy with sarcasm. "That is good, for a time. It builds their confidence and gains their respect. Something 'proper' Grik have never imagined a need for. Yet, while we are here, enjoying ourselves so immensely, all we can do is fight. We can't influence the greater battle around us."

"You think we should stop?" Yikkit demanded, slashing a guard with his own sword and pounding it away with his shield.

"Fighting like this? Yes, for now. It's a sad but apparent fact that the appropriate place for a general in battle is somewhere between this and what 'proper' Grik do. We must quickly finish this, or the rest of Halik's plan may fail. To do that, we must step back and direct others to take advantage of what we cannot see from here. For example," he said, benefiting from a momentary lull to physically drag General Yikkit back from the shield wall. Yikkit resisted at first, but then followed.

"What?" he asked.

"Join me here," Niwa said, clambering atop a jagged slab of granite, seemingly oblivious to the occasional crossbow bolt or musket ball that whistled past. The Guard Swarm had some matchlock muskets, obviously, but was so tightly packed they were having difficulty using them. "Look," he said when Yikkit stood beside him, gasping and licking blood from his claws. The Swarm beyond the shield wall was attacking almost frantically now, even slowing its advance in places. They weren't attacking with the same . . . purpose as before, however. It looked like they were more urgently trying to get *past* the shields than to come to grips with those who held them. In an instant, from there, it was obvious why. Sheets of crossbow bolts were slamming into the enemy flank from high up to the left, and volleys of musket balls hacked at it as well, though the reports of the weapons were nearly drowned by the din. Behind the fire, shapes were hurtling down the slope through the trees, screeching predatory cries. Individually at first, then in increasing numbers, General Shlook's 2nd Division splashed across the creek and crashed into the faltering enemy right. Already shattered by the cataclysmic blast that brought a mountain down upon them and caught between the new attack, Yikkit's and Niwa's divisions in front, and the roaring flames behind, Shighat's elite Guard Swarm suddenly just . . . broke, and began "turning prey." Many turned their weapons on those around them, simply because they were there, blocking their flight in whichever direction they were facing. Others ran screaming through the fire behind them. Most tried helplessly to claw their way up the loose, gravelly slope to their left. In mere moments, the battle in the boulder field turned to a slaughter— with the enemy doing most of the work to itself.

"Forward now!" Niwa yelled in his very best Grik. "Push them! Kill them!" The cry was taken up and became a mighty, chanting roar. The shield wall lurched forward.

"How did you know?" Yikkit yelled over the noise, amazed.

"I've seen it before," Niwa shouted back. "Too often to our own, I admit, but I doubt they're susceptible anymore, after what they've endured."

"What should we do?"

"Keep pushing, of course. The flames will soon die out and we can charge onward. Do you hear?" A deep, pounding, thumping rumble reached them from farther up the gorge. "Those guns signal the beginning of Ugla's sweep. We'll join his charge up the road to link up with General Halik at Shighat's field palace."

"But . . . what should we do with these?" Yikkit waved at the panicked Grik. He'd never seen "Grik Rout" before.

Niwa looked thoughtful. "We can almost ignore them. They're finished. Or, they are easy enough to kill now that their senses have left them. I wonder, though . . ."

"What?"

"To my knowledge, no one has ever offered battle-panicked Grik their lives. I wonder what they would do if you simply spoke to them?"

Despite the fact that the battle had been underway for over an hour before Halik's 5th Division launched its attack, the surprise was near complete and it easily overran Shighat's field palace. Unfortunately, Shighat himself managed to escape within a mass of bodyguards that physically carried him into the protective embrace of the nearby swarm still choking the road, untainted by the panic in the gorge. Halik led attack after attack, but his diminishing force simply couldn't break through. Nor could it force its way through to the road and become the anvil he'd envisioned. By then he realized not only would Shighat have been carried safely away, but he'd bitten off a bit more than he could chew. He should've either brought a larger force to execute this part of his plan, or not attempted it at all. Fortunately, Shighat had apparently been sufficiently rattled by his very close call that he chose to draw back before his whole army was infected by the panic pouring back from Niwa's, Shlook's, Ugla's, and Yikkit's combined drive up the road from the bloody gorge. 5th Division took a strong defensive position to the south of the road but couldn't do more than watch the enemy stream past, back into the mountains. Toward evening, the flood became a trickle, then ceased altogether. And that's how Halik's generals had found him, at dusk, when the first elements of Ugla's 1st Division finally trotted into view, reptilian eyes casting about for threats. There were none. The last of the enemy that hadn't fled in panic had broken contact before it could be tainted.

"What now?" Niwa asked. He looked terrible in the light of the braziers burning in Shighat's great tent. He wasn't wounded, that Halik could tell, even if he was almost covered with blood, dry and flaky, more black now than red, but he was exhausted. The whole army was. Outside was the sound of lethargic but contented feasting. The army was spent, but it was also happy. As far as it was concerned, it had won a great victory—its first in a very long while—and there was plenty of meat. Halik would no longer countenance his army eating its own, even those killed in battle. Shlook and Ugla considered that a rather extreme overreaction to a time when he'd been forced to feed his warriors with other live warriors, but they didn't argue with his decree. And enough of the enemy had been slain that the army couldn't possibly eat them all before they turned unhealthy. They'd already prepared sufficient provisions for a long trek over the mountains, and the same provisions would serve if the trek became a campaign. The fresh meat they'd gorge on now was a bonus. Of course, then there was the question of what to do with all the "prey" they'd taken alive. Ordinarily, they'd be used as walking rations, but Niwa seemed to have other ideas. Halik shook that off. *Later.*

"We must rest a day," Halik said, annoyed with himself. "I should not have allowed the pause that resulted in the gluttony underway, but there is nothing for it now. A day of satiated rest, and we can resume the chase."

"Chase?" Yikkit inquired. He looked at least as worn as Niwa, but he'd certainly proven himself that day. All Halik's generals had. The only one that failed to achieve his objective had been Halik himself.

"Yes. The victory is not complete."

"But . . . why? Shighat is beaten. Ghaarrichk'k armies do not fight to exterminate one another. He will retreat back to his capital at Sagar, in the distant southwest of his regency! He will not return until he has gathered another swarm, or another army is sent to his aid. But he is old and he has failed. I doubt either will occur before his life is over, one way or another. You will not see him again."

"We will," Halik said, "when we move to take Sagar from him. I would rather destroy him now. I hoped to destroy him today." He looked around at his generals, his friends. "We have all decided what we are to become. But if we are ever to be more than just a wandering horde, we must have a home. That means we must take one, and Shighat's suits me well enough."

"Ahh. Indeed," Yikkit said, realization dawning.

"All of Persia," Niwa said softly, a small smile on his face. "General Halik, King of Kings."

"What?" Shlook asked.

"Oh, nothing."

"So," Halik continued. "Tomorrow evening, we resume the chase. That in itself should surprise Shighat. He still outnumbers us, but his warriors have no notion of defense, so we will pick at him, bleed him, drive him mad—until we can pin him and force him to give proper battle." He looked at Niwa. "Do you think Colonel Enaak, at least, will continue to scout for us? We will need his assistance now more than ever—and I would be very grateful for it."

"And he will remain skeptical of your gratitude," Niwa said. "He cannot be comfortable with a Grik leader of your skill gaining such power as you aspire to, but then this campaign, at least, will take you progressively farther from India. I will ask." He rubbed his chin, balling up the mix of sweat, blood, and dust he felt there. "Even if he agrees, you should not expect any further assistance from him—certainly nothing as dramatic as he provided today. But has it occurred to you that we may not be as outnumbered as you imagine?"

Halik looked at Niwa, his jaws opening slightly in what looked like a terrifying grimace but was actually a sign of amusement. "The 'prey' warriors?" he asked.

"Yes. I suppose General Yikkit didn't have an opportunity to tell you yet. Well, it seems that we might have made a rather profound discovery. What is it that officers ordinarily shriek at their warriors as they are turning prey? They tell them to stop, to fight, to continue the attack—something the poor Uul under their command have already decided is hopeless. General Yikkit and I attempted something different today, and though I remain unsure how successful it was, I have some hope."

"What did you do?" Halik asked, genuinely interested.

"General Yikkit very loudly, and still quite severely, I might add, began yelling for them to stop fighting and . . . lie upon the ground. Any who did so would be quite safe, accepted by their conquerors, and fed."

"And what did they do?" Halik asked, amazed.

Niwa shrugged, but his smile broadened. "Some, perhaps a third, who had not already completely lost themselves to panic . . . did as he commanded. Essentially, they surrendered."

"I saw it myself," General Shlook declared, his tone carrying an equal measure of disgust and wonder. "Never has such a thing occurred! Obviously, they can't be trusted."

"Why not?" Niwa asked. "They didn't lose their minds; they merely obeyed a sensible command from a general they recognized. I think they will even still fight—particularly if mixed with more mature warriors who can help them make sense of what happened and begin encouraging their awareness. I suggest that such a thing has never happened before simply because surrender has never independently occurred to any Grik Uul as an option."

Halik stared at his Japanese friend for a long moment, absently picking at a gobbet of something stuck to his blood-smeared armor with a finger claw before shaking his head in wonder. "We will . . . contemplate this matter, and I will interview the prisoners myself. But tomorrow evening, the army shall move. Shighat will not have fled far or fast. He won't expect pursuit." He looked at Yikkit. "The time may come, if we can make the enemy desperate enough, that we will attempt another, larger 'offer' such as the one you made. It could be quite interesting to see what happens then."

Central Mada-gaas-gar
October 6, 1944

Chack, Courtney, Silva, Lawrence, and Miles moved mostly at night, aided by a bright, growing moon. Courtney had reasoned that Lemurians here, like Aryaalans and B'mbaadans from long-established land Homes in the East, were most likely to associate the Maker of All Things with the sun since they had no need for sophisticated celestial navigation. It stood to reason they'd be most active when the sun could "see" them. This theory was supported when Lawrence, watching from a distance, observed the hunting party he shadowed climb into one of the great baobab-galla trees to spend the night. They even cooked their food in the high branches, though Larry didn't see how they did that. He saw only the fire.

There were other considerations that prompted them to stick to a nocturnal schedule. The hunting party was generally moving in the same direction they were, dispersing into pairs at dawn, and it was inevitable they'd eventually run into each other if they all traveled by day. Best to let them settle for the night and then move along. That left them to focus on avoiding the many predatory monsters ranging the prairies of this Mada-gaas-gar. Courtney was enraptured by their variety but wasn't so lost to reality that he wasn't concerned by how many there were, far more numerous than any natural environment would've evolved, and they fought and ate each other as often as they preyed on the abundant herbivores. Though always apparently on the hunt, most of the predators did seem more active in daytime as well, so Chack and Courtney elected to move at night as long as the visibility was good.

Silva didn't care. With Lawrence's help, they'd managed to avoid the really big "boogers" so far, and he'd killed a number of smaller creatures with his Thompson, the brisk breeze erasing the relatively light report before it traveled far. They had meat and water and were making good time. All were amazed by how much ground the 'Cat hunters covered each day, and soon the moon would fade. They'd eventually have to take their chances in daylight. But they *had* to be getting close to a village of some kind. The notion that the 'Cat hunters flat couldn't carry—or preserve—enough meat to justify so long a trip began to intrude upon their initial theory, and they started to wonder if the ten 'Cats might be some wandering band, or even a war party after all.

"Why don't we just try to meet them?" Miles groaned softly as they picked their way through the tall grass, staying as far from the river as they dared. "I mean, if they're friendly, we can team up. It would be safer."

"Could be," Silva agreed. Miles's griping annoyed him, but at least he didn't do it as much anymore. He had, in fact, managed to make himself marginally useful ever since their little "talk." He still didn't volunteer much, to carry extra stuff or help gut something Silva shot, but he didn't exactly shirk either. *Tell him what to do, he'll do it,* he thought. *Maybe he just still don't put himself forward 'cause he's afraid to screw up?* Silva shook his head. *Givin' him the benefit o' the doubt,* he decided piously. *An' everybody's got a right to gripe.* He frowned in the dark. *He takes to whinin', though, I'll just go ahead an' kill his sorry ass.*

"Could also be they'd try to kill us an' then we'd have to kill them. Every damn one, to keep 'em from stirrin' folks up against us. An' then, let's say we got 'em all, what if we wind up someplace where everybody's friendly as puppies—but ten members o' their clan just never show up? Even if they didn't take to wonderin' if it was us who rubbed 'em out, *we'd* know, an' that's a hard thing to keep on your mind. Even harder not to let slip. Nah, I used to be a 'kill 'em all, sorry if you didn't really mean no harm' sort, but I'm reformed, rehabilitated, an' reconsidered."

Up ahead in the gloom Lawrence had returned, just drifting back into existence, apparently, out of the surrounding grass. He stepped up to Chack and murmured something, pointing west, and the two went to Bradford. "Why, ever' time I look at poor Larry I'm reminded of my youthful unrepressibleness," Silva continued. "I actually shot him once, you know? Now he's one o' my best pals. Nope, I give powerful attention to whoever I just rear up an' kill these days."

"What have you decided about me?" Miles snapped.

"Still has my attention," Silva said seriously. "An' we still got a talk comin'. But goin' back to your first question, I guess we'll be meetin' those 'Cats pretty soon after all, one way or other."

"Really? Why?"

Silva snorted. "Pay more attention to what's goin on, an' less to what's aggravatin' you, an' you'll see a lot more in life." He nodded ahead. Down a long slope where the river jogged to the south was a large cluster of the enormous trees, dark against the almost silvery sheen of the tall, dewy grass. The trees seemed to sparkle as well, with dozens of orange fires high in their branches. Slowly it became clear that the trees were surrounded by lower, but still elevated artificial structures, and lights emanated from within some of those as well. Double-ended boats were dark against the gray water along the shore of the river, and a palisade surrounded the whole area, encompassing thirty or forty acres. "Hey, Chackie," Silva said a bit louder. "Looks kinda like a teeny tiny Baalkpan, first time I saw it. You reckon they have beer?"

Courtney chuckled quietly, appreciatively. "Indeed! Let us hope that's another common, um, tradition that's stood the test of time."

"What do we do now?" Miles asked, head swiveling toward every sound around them. They were suddenly uncomfortably close to the river in his view, where all manner of creatures, benign and malevolent, tended to concentrate.

"We shall move closer and wait for dawn," Chack decided, "and introduce ourselves to wakeful folk."

"Yeah," Silva agreed. "Bangin' on the gate o' that palisade in the middle of the night, wakin' folks up, prob'ly won't make the best first impression. Let's just hope they ain't grumpy risers."

Carefully, they eased down the slope, Lawrence occasionally returning from his scout ahead to report drowsing herds of herbivores they should avoid. He saw no predators, causing Courtney to speculate that dangerous carnivores might possibly avoid the village. Finally, they stopped to rest amid a clump of brush on a little rise a mere few hundred yards from the palisade. Lower down and closer, the village was even more impressive. The trees were huge, bigger even than the great tree in the center of Baalkpan that Adar's Great Hall was built around. The palisade looked more imposing as well, consisting of sharpened tree trunks ten to fifteen feet tall, densely woven together in a fashion that reminded Silva of frontier forts in Western pictures, but these were angled outward to defend against taller assailants.

"I imagine Baalkpan, Maa-ni-laa, or any number of Lemurian land Homes looked exactly like that for hundreds of years," Courtney whispered.

"Until the last few hundreds," Chack agreed, "when they had to grow larger with increased populations both on land and sea." The great seagoing Homes had existed virtually unchanged since Chack's ancestors first left this land uncounted generations before, but they'd grown in number, and the land Homes that built them, repaired them, and traded with them for the oil of the gri-kakka fish had expanded accordingly.

"Quite amazing," Courtney mused. "And surprising. Not only do the people here seem to have thrived to some extent, living much the same as they probably have for thousands of years, but the Grik haven't molested them. Why not? This land, on this side of the mountains, would seem to epitomize their ideal. It's generally wide-open, warm, and full of food beasts."

"We already know they kept Mada-gaas-gar as a preserve for 'worthy prey' they could hunt for sport in better times. How do we know these remain always unmolested? Might the Grik not also have preserved sufficient populations for larger groups to 'conquer' from time to time?" Chack surmised bitterly. Courtney looked at his dark profile and blinked. "Why . . . I expect that's exactly right. Before the current war, the Grik often fought battles among *themselves* for the sheer fun of it—and to curb their population. And that would certainly explain why these folk remain so apparently unchanged when it's all each generation can do to simply rebuild after the latest visit by some small Grik swarm bent on entertaining slaughter." He nodded at the village. "Perhaps we'll know soon enough. I do so wish Adar was here! He'll be insufferable with envy!"

The sky began to lighten, diffusing the three-quarter moon that still stood on the horizon, and the village began to stir. More smoke from cookfires drifted skyward, and a few sleepy sentries replaced others that had been hidden along the top of the palisade. Silva grunted at that with satisfaction. "Not just sleepin' lazy behind their wall. My guess is, we'd approached in the dark, we'd'a been porkypined with arrows before we ever reached the gate."

Lawrence slithered back into their midst.

"Dammit, Larry!" Silva hissed. "I didn't even know you was gone! Don't you ever sleep?"

"Just doing 'at I do. I *like* scouting."

"Well, you've got pretty good at *sneakin'*, that's for sure. What did you see?"

"The 'Cat hunters are co'ing in. They stayed out last night to enter 'ith the dawn—like us—and to decorate they like I'joorka's Khonashi did, I think."

"That's . . . interesting. Wanna make an impression an' look pretty for the dames after being gone awhile. How close?"

"Close enough to hear, you not quiet down."

Silva glanced behind them, at the first rays of the sun, then looked at Chack. "I guess we're up."

Chack started to nod, but something caught his attention. The palisade gate nearest them was opening. 'Cats came, fanning out with bows in their hands and arrows at the ready. Their only clothing was a leather breechcloth-type garment arranged like a diaper, but they looked alert and formidable. Behind them, flocks of fuzzy creatures like a cross between a sheep and a pig darted out, en masse, headed for the river just below the party's hiding place. Gangs of naked younglings armed with long switches they applied with a will flanked the herd, keeping it concentrated as it moved.

"Wilya look at that!" Silva said.

Suddenly, the tall grass below them just a short distance away seemed to . . . swell.

"What the . . . whoa! Goddamn!" Silva said, his voice rising. Less than fifty yards away, something almost perfectly camouflaged was rising in the grass. At a glance, it was still invisible, but the motion of its movement gave it away as it appeared to . . . flow toward the odd Lemurian livestock—and the younglings herding it along. Perhaps the most amazing thing was that the grass was only about three feet deep, but the creature was quite large. It seemed impossible that it could've remained hidden at eye level. No matter how well camouflaged, it would've looked like a new mound or something where none should be—unless . . . "Damn," Silva swore, "it's a puff adder lizard!" He started to stand, raising his Thompson. Well trained by now, Petey hopped down in the grass with a panicked chirp.

"Wait!" Chack hissed, pulling at him. Silva blinked incredulously. "That thing ain't a pup they let out for the night! It's gonna get them *kids!*"

"Wait!" Chack insisted more firmly. "Watch!"

The younglings yipped and scampered away from the lunging monster, slapping at the sheep pigs as they went, herding them back. Armed 'Cats converged with a shout and a rising trilling sound from the palisade behind them. Long, heavy arrows sleeted at the thing, some penetrating shallowly, but most deflecting off the thing's tough hide. Snarling, the big lizard paused and rose higher, confirming it was indeed considerably larger than mere arrows should have to contend with, and quickly *changed colors* to a menacing black, a frilly, reddening crest rising above its head. Mighty jaws reminiscent of a Komodo opened wide, and it lunged at the closest 'Cat. Even as it did so, however, several arrows slammed straight into its gaping maw, and it clamped its mouth shut with an incongruous squeal.

"Those guys are good!" Miles hissed with genuine admiration.

The lizard seemed to collect itself and charged again, swiftly galloping toward the same 'Cat it had seemed so fixated on. The 'Cat was quick, no doubt about it, dodging a lightning lunge, but he stumbled on something in the grass and fell on his back with a cry of alarm. His comrades redoubled their fusillade, but there was no distracting the thing. With an almost jaunty hop to the side, it changed direction to pounce on its victim.

"Now!" Chack shouted.

"Cold, cold!" Silva muttered, but he centered his sight on the big lizard, raised his aim a tad, and squeezed the trigger. Bullets pattered across its back and . . . it did! It *flattened* itself in the tall grass like a puff adder, its color quickly surging to green-brown stripes.

"Everybody!" Chack said. "Open fire! Chief Silva has startled it, maybe even hurt it, but I do not think he can kill it with the Thompson! Open fire!" His and Courtney's Krags fired almost as one. Courtney was much quicker on the draw these days. Miles and Lawrence both fired their Allin-Silvas, their big bullets striking the thing and causing it to spin around, snapping at the painful wounds. That's when it saw them, outlined above it against the rising sun. With an almost whimpering shriek, it charged, its hide quickly darkening once more.

"Damn, Larry! Don't you wish you could change colors like that?" Silva asked as he dropped an empty magazine and slammed another in the well. Twenty more rounds clattered out, bright brass arcing away and glittering in the sunlight. Lawrence fired again, almost keeping pace with the bolt-action Krags. "Break its bones!" Silva growled. "Break its damn head! That puff lizard makes a big target, but the vitals ain't so big!" That didn't come out how he wanted, but he figured everyone knew what he meant. Chack was empty, and he flipped the loading gate of his Krag to the side. Grabbing a handful of cartridges from his pouch in a well-practiced manner, he quickly trickled five of them into the magazine and slapped the loading gate closed. Tossing the Thompson on the ground, Dennis twisted his mighty Doom Stomper off his shoulder and brought it up. The muzzle bobbed as he found the monster's charging head in his sights, but it was getting awfully close.

"Dammit, Silva!" Miles shouted, his voice high.

Dennis fired. A jet of flame stabbed out amid a great white cloud and Silva's shoulder jerked brutally backward, the rifle muzzle rising nearly thirty degrees. The bullet hit the thing near the point of its bottom jaw, and the bronze penetrator acted like a piston, expanding the lead around it to twice its diameter. A Borno super lizard's jaw would've shattered into something resembling bloody salt but might've stopped the lead before it reached much deeper. That's when the bronze penetrator, itself the size of a .50-caliber machine gun bullet, would shed the lead and churn onward, deep in the skull and possibly out the back of the head. But this creature, though nearly as large as a Borno super lizard, wasn't as heavy or dense, and the entire projectile, radically expanded lead and all, turned the thing's head into a canoe.

Silva saw none of this through the smoke, the dust, the fluttering grass caused by the monster's high-speed impact, and the momentary vertigo he always felt after firing the big gun. Muscle memory took over, though, and even before the morning breeze could whip his smoke away, he'd flipped the breech open, ejecting the huge powder-blackened shell, and slammed another in its place. Closing the breech and cocking the hammer, he raised the gun again.

"Cease firing!" Chack called. "Dennis, stop," he added. As quickly as that, with a thunderous exclamation point, the attack was over. The monster lay twitching and lashing its tail a mere dozen yards away, its hide flashing through a riot of colors beneath the blood that spattered it and the grass all around.

"Take that, sucker!" Miles exclaimed triumphantly, nervous energy washing away to be replaced by the shakes. Lawrence lowered his rifle and, with uncharacteristic tenderness, patted Silva on the arm. For his part, Silva's face remained grimly set, possibly hiding the pain in his shoulder from the quick, awkward shot, but he lowered the hammer to half cock.

"Oh, look at it! Isn't it marvelous?" Courtney exclaimed, rising to gaze happily at the dead monster. Chack restrained him before he could step closer. "Look at *them*, Mr. Braadfurd," he cautioned. Only then did Courtney realize that five 'Cat warriors had rushed to encircle them, joined by ten others, beautified with paint, feathers, claws, and other adornments, who'd suddenly appeared from behind. All held bows with arrows nocked and pointed nervously in their direction. Petey reemerged from his hiding place in the grass and scrambled back onto Silva's shoulder. "Goddamn," he practically whispered.

"Oh. Of course, Colonel Chack," Courtney agreed dryly. "And our band of hunters is home from the hill as well, I see. By all means, let's see if we can reassure these fellows just a bit, first thing."

The 'Cat that fell had joined the others now, and judging by the white fur on his otherwise brindled face—colored remarkably like Chack, as were most of those nearby—he was the oldest present. He was also the only one not menacing them with a weapon, though he held his ready. Without hesitation, he advanced beyond the others.

Slowly, carefully, Chack slung his Krag on his shoulder, muzzle down, and took a step toward him. Raising his right hand, palm outward, in what he hoped remained the universal sign of the empty hand even here, he repeated much the same greeting he'd made on the river under strikingly similar circumstances. To Chack's relief, the 'Cat returned the gesture with a practiced familiarity and took a step closer. Then he hesitated and glanced at the dead monster. "Your meat," he said simply.

Chack looked at Courtney but waved expansively. "For all. We are happy to share it—and other things—with any friends we meet."

"So it is true?" the 'Cat asked, blinking with great interest. "You are of the Big Boat People who fight the Gaarieks in the North alongside the Aan-glis forest folk?" He looked at Silva, Miles, and Courtney, who, with their beards, would easily pass for Maroons. His gaze lingered sharply on Lawrence but moved back to Chack.

Chack was no longer surprised he understood the stranger, but was amazed by something else. "It is true," he confirmed. "But how do you know? How *could* you know?"

"We know many things, you will see, but first, be welcome! We have been expecting you! These others were sent to find you," he said with a scolding gaze at one of the ten 'Cats that had joined them. "Lower your weapons!" he ordered, and they did. He looked back at Chack. "That you could evade our finest hunters speaks well for you." He flicked his ears at the dead monster. "And your magic is just as great as we have heard." He grinned at Silva and carefully formed the words, in Maroon-ish English, "Gad . . . Maaskit!"

Courtney was flabbergasted. "But . . . but how?"

"We have some contact with the Aan-glis. They are very strange," he added, "but we are at peace with them. We know the eastern river tribes too, the Erokighaani and others like them. They are . . . even stranger," he said with a disquieted blink. "We are not always at peace with *them*, but they stay on their side of the mountains and we stay on ours—and tales must be passed. All peoples must have tales."

Odd that the Maroons haven't told us this, Chack reflected, *but then, the ones we're in contact with may not know these—whoever they are. Maroons have clans too.*

"Soon we will trade tales with you," the 'Cat said. "But first, my name is Kaam and I am, ah, 'cap-i-taan of the guard,' as you might say, of the Naa-kaani Clan of the Shee-ree people. Our High Chief is Ror'at-Raal." Kaam grinned again and blinked. "He is interestingly mad." Without further explanation of that, he proceeded to introduce the others present, some of whom had started skinning the great beast—but not before pausing to urinate on its shattered head. Courtney stared at that, eyes wide, but didn't protest. Miles snickered. A few of the hunters disappeared back the way they'd come, probably to get the rest of their gear. None seemed particularly concerned that their homecoming had been upstaged by the arrival of visitors, evidence they actually had been sent to look for them. Chack was intrigued by their names and particularly by the fact that Kaam had only one, a convention usually reserved for Sky Priests among his people.

"Come," Kaam said. "You must meet the Great Ror'at-Raal! Your questions will be answered—and perhaps you can answer some of ours." Noting their hesitation, he added, "Keep your weapons. You have already proven we have nothing to fear from them and that you will use them on our behalf." He turned and took a few steps, but paused to shift his breechcloth so he could urinate on the dead beast's head as well, and he seemed to do it with considerable satisfaction. When he was done, he glanced expectantly at them.

"Um, Colonel Chack?" Courtney whispered urgently.

"Beats me," Chack replied defensively. "I never saw anybody do that."

"Clear as day." Silva snorted out loud, in English, and regarded Chack with a half grin. "I swear, most of the time I forget that 'Cats ain't just regular folks—with tails—but then they do stuff like that."

"I don't!" Chack insisted. "Why would I? Why would *they*?"

Silva rolled his eye. "They're claimin' it by pissin' on the part they ain't gonna eat. Can't make it smell any worse. That booger's ripe! But I bet they piss on trees an' rocks wherever they go, markin' their territory. I seen 'Cats, hunters like Moe, do it sometimes." He nodded at the head. "They'll prob'ly leave it here as a warnin' to others too."

"That actually makes perfect sense," Courtney agreed, "and no wonder Chack's seagoing clan has abandoned the practice, as well as the more, um, civilized clans we're accustomed to."

"Yeah." Silva chuckled. "In Chack's case it'd be like ever'body on *Big Sal* pissin' on every fish they caught! I can see it now. Long lines o' 'Cats drinkin' water like crazy an' marchin' up to ol' Adar, standin' there in his Sky Priest suit holdin' a flasher fish in each hand by the tail—"

Chack growled and Courtney interrupted impatiently, "But what does he expect of us?"

"Piss on it. It's part ours, right?"

*   *   *

A larger group of younglings and females had emerged from the gate in the palisade to help round up the sheep pigs that had scattered. Many stopped and stared at the procession making its way to the village. Chack continued speaking to Kaam, but Courtney waved enthusiastically at the gawkers. "Goodness gracious! How exciting!" he enthused. He glanced back behind them. "A great pity they're dismantling that amazing creature so quickly, but perhaps they'll allow me to examine its skull." His expression turned bleak. "What's left of it—and after it's been cleaned, of course," he added distastefully. He brightened. "I wonder if they'll let me boil it. But really, Mr. Silva, you should try to be less destructive to the more scientifically pertinent features of the various specimens we encounter, in the future."

"I'll try, Mr. Bradford," Silva replied dryly. "It just seems that them 'most pertinent parts' are always the ones most int'rested in gettin' us."

"Indeed." Courtney frowned, but his smile quickly returned. "Still, quite exciting! Was this how it was when you met the Khonashi in North Borno? I so envied you that!"

Silva looked at the broad prairie surrounding them and the isolated, mountainous clumps of gigantic trees dotting it here and there as far as he could see, but they seemed most common along the meandering river. He thought about it. *No, this has been a cinch. A lot shorter trip, an' we haven't run into near as many bad boogers. An' maybe we discovered more unfriendly folks this time, along the other river, but we didn't have to fight 'em. I feel pretty good,* he suddenly realized, his aches having begun to diminish once he'd descended from the mountains, *an' I been eatin' decent grub—instead of raw grubs an' other bugs.* "Not so much," he finally replied. "The trip's been easier so far, but folks here seem just as friendly as the Khonashi. We'll see about that. Seems they know stuff about us too, but they ain't had any direct contact we know of." Unlike the Khonashi, who'd made a lost, crippled destroyerman named Tony Scott their *king.* Silva didn't mention that. He didn't know if Tony had turned himself in yet. *Prob'ly has, an' got treated like a hee-ro. But he was afraid they'd hang him for a deserter, an' I promised not to blow.* "Other than that," he continued, "we gotta still be the better part of a hundred miles from the west coast of the island. We're smack in the middle of it now, about as secluded as we can get. So I don't think there's been any direct contact with our old world here, an' we ain't as likely to wind up in a full-blown battle alongside natives armed with bows an' arrows against a Jap destroyer full o' murderin' maniacs." He grinned back at Courtney.

The first evidence that Silva was wrong on at least one count was revealed almost as soon as they entered the gate, for there, perched atop a wooden scaffold like the centerpiece of a town square, was the battered, weathered carcass of a medium-size aircraft. The scaffold was largely covered with animal skins, and bright birds and lizardbirds swirled around the dingy thing, streaking it with their droppings.

"Well, shit," Silva muttered with a sinking feeling. *Have we scattered that much junk around this world? An' ever' time we find some, things go straight in the crapper.* "Looks like one o' those new Army B-Twenty-fives," he said resignedly. That B-25s would no longer be "new" back on the world he came from was immaterial, but what remained of the plane, the forward fuselage, the inboard wings and engines, was similar. The port engine, propeller, and landing gear looked intact, but the starboard nacelle had been savaged behind a bent-back prop, and its lost landing gear had been replaced by part of the scaffold. The Plexiglas was mostly gone from the nose, although there was a rust-dusted machine gun there, pointed as if guarding the gate. Both wings beyond the engines were gone, as was the tail behind the wing roots. Courtney was walking hurriedly around the plane, gazing at it in amazement as more and more 'Cats gathered around.

"No," Courtney said over the growing hubbub, "it's a Bristol Beaufort, I do believe. British made, though they were beginning to make them in Australia as well. And look!" he said, pointing at half a faded roundel, split when the tail came off. "That's the orange, white, and blue of the South African Air Force!"

Kaam and several others hastened to catch him. "How

do you know that?" Kaam demanded, then realization dawned. "You are not Aan-glis of the forest! You are Sowt-Aaf-i-caans too!" Kaam's dialect was unfamiliar, but Courtney understood him well enough. He smiled. "No, no, my dear fellow! I'm Australian! And that monstrous bugger there and his smaller companion are Americans. But we're friends of those who flew this plane! Where are they?"

Kaam shook his head, blinking. "Aus-traal . . ." He looked at Silva. "Amer-i-caans . . . You were friends of these?" He pointed at the plane.

Courtney hesitated, suddenly wondering if the plane was less a monument than a trophy. It seemed to occupy a place of honor, but it wasn't like they'd been keeping it clean and polished. "Well, yes. We were," he said. "In our . . . quite distant land. Their people fought alongside ours against evil powers."

"Jaaps?" Kaam asked, and even Chack blinked amazement.

"Why, yes indeed. The Japanese, Nazis, Italians . . . Please, were the men who flew this plane friends of yours? Are they still here?"

Kaam blinked something Courtney couldn't decipher. "Friends, yes," he said at last, "of the one who lived when the magic left the machine and it could fly no more. The other three were put under the ground," he added with a still incredulous whip of his tail, "where the machine fell. The one called 'Lef-ten-aant' insisted that was their way," he added skeptically. "Lef-ten-aant was hurt, but recovered and told us many tales once we learned to speak together. Strange tales," Kaam added with a troubled blink. "At first he told us this land belongs to the Vee-shee, and he was a scout of the Sowt-Aaf-i-caans for . . . *other* Aan-glis who those here do not know. He said they meant to take this land from the Vee-shee to keep the Jaaps away." He looked at them. "No one, not even the great Ror'at-Raal, could understand. At first we thought 'Vee-shee' sounded enough like 'Shee-ree' to frighten us, but Lef-ten-aant said they were very different. He tried to explain better, that Vee-shee were outcasts from a tribe of friends, but though he lived with us many months, we never fully learned to speak together without some confusion, so uncertainty still remains. Tell me, is 'Vee-shee' your word for 'Gaa-rieks'?"

"Ah, no," Courtney said. He looked at Silva and spoke to him quietly. "Apparently, our forces where we came from were at least considering trying to expel the Vichy French before they wittingly or otherwise allowed naval access here to the Japanese. What a disaster that would've been, with them positioned to interdict our supply lines to India, or any other territories in the region that may've remained to us." He looked back at Kaam. "It was a, um, different war. A different world. Do you understand that?"

Kaam blinked hesitant acknowledgment. "We think so, though we do not know how that can be. But Lef-ten-aant tried to explain it as *he* learned it, listening to the talking machine in his aar-plane."

Silva understood that much, and his head whipped around to stare at Kaam with his one eye. "That heap's got a *radio*?" he demanded. Kaam looked at him curiously. "That is what Lef-ten-aant called the talking machine," he said, but looked back at Courtney. "He heard things from the world, tales of how other people, people like us, have joined together to fight the Gaa-rieks! He heard of great battles far to sunrise-ward at strange-sounding places, but most stirring to us, he heard of victories!"

"Where is he now?" Courtney almost pleaded.

Kaam cast his eyes to the ground. "He has passed into the Heavens whence he came. He was recovered from his hurts, but then took a terrible pain in his side that no magic or medicine could cure. He tried to tell us how to cut the pain out, but by then his fever was too great and his words too few to fully describe the rite. We did the best we could," Kaam added.

"Appendicitis," Courtney surmised. "After all the poor bugger went through, he died of appendicitis." He looked at Kaam. "No doubt you *did* do your best. Without the, um, 'rites' he required, there was no saving him."

"He did not tell us to put him in the ground, so we sent him to the sky in the proper way," Kaam said. Apparently, the Lemurians here still practiced cremation. "Did we do right?"

"I'm sure that was fine," Chack assured him. "The spirit flies to the Heavens from the ground or the fire—or from beneath the sea," he said. He glanced at his friends. "This *we* believe."

"But what about the radio?" Silva pressed, looking at the plane. "I hope they didn't piss on it," he added aside to Lawrence.

"Sadly, the magic of the talking machine died with Leften-aant," Kaam said. "It grew sick and weak even as he did, but he was very afraid we would talk into it after he was gone, that we would talk to Jaaps and they would come, so he killed it."

"Shit." Silva grunted, then shrugged. "Battery must'a croaked anyway."

"We could've charged it," Miles suggested, and Silva looked at him questioningly. "The generator in that port engine," Miles clarified. "And maybe we can fix the radio. Tear the generator out, find some way to spin it . . ."

"Maybe. We'll see later." He gestured around. Nearly the entire village had to be gathered now, staring in wide-eyed silence at the exchange. There must've been four hundred of them.

"Are there really Jaaps out there?" Kaam demanded. "Yet another menace besides the Gaa-rieks?"

Courtney nodded. "There are, and others perhaps just as dangerous. Your . . . 'Lef-ten-aant' was probably wise to do as he did."

Kaam seemed to consider this, then motioned them onward. "Come," he said. "It is not right that we linger here so long. You must meet Ror'at-Raal. He will be impatient."

CHAPTER 18

***Aboard the NUS* Congress**
The Caribbean
October 7, 1944

"Holy smoke! Would you look at that!" Fred Reynolds said, practically pounding Kari's shoulder and pointing over *Congress*'s starboard rail to the north, northeast. Looming large across the morning sun-dappled sea between the steam frigate and what Lieutenant Hudgens had told them was the *only* "Cayman" Island lying about ten miles away, were two large three-masted sailing steamers. They looked a third again more massive than the Allies' latest *Scott* Class steam frigate/DDs, and nearly as large as the biggest Dom ships of the line they'd ever seen. Screening them were four frigates identical to *Congress*, at a glance. Their sails had been sighted at dawn, rounding the western point of the island, and Fred and Kari had been amazed that no alarm was sounded when so little of the ships were visible. But somehow, in that indefinable way sailors had, Captain Willis had immediately declared the approaching squadron as friendly.

"Just look at the cut of their sails," he'd told them, as if that explained everything. Of course, the *color* of their sails was significant, even to Fred and Kari. Warships of the Dominion almost always sailed under red canvas painted with the garish gold cross of their twisted faith. But Fred remained suspicious. "What if the Doms used white sails to trick us?" he'd asked. Willis had smiled. "They have tried that before, as we have attempted the reverse from time to time. It even works occasionally, from a distance, or when done by a prize. Ordinarily, though, the cut tells the tale." He'd paused, still smiling at Fred and Kari. "And besides, I am certain that is Commodore Semmes's squadron. The vicinity of Cayman Isle is his station."

"Does it belong to your people?" Kari had asked.

"Cayman belongs to no one, at present. Cuba is ours," he added with satisfaction, "wrested from the Dominion in the last declared war we fought them, twenty-three years ago. I was a midshipman then and participated in the decisive Battle of Santiago, likely the last battle we will ever fight with more sails than steam. I was aboard the old *Texas*," he said proudly. "She was pounded to an irreparable hulk," he admitted, smile fading, "as was half our battle fleet. But though the Doms outnumbered us three to one, they were beaten soundly enough that they've never made a serious attempt to retake the island." His brows had furrowed. "Until recently, that is. For the last several years, they have been amassing a truly enormous fleet that we have been endeavoring to counter with quality if not quantity. Not so successfully, I might add. Their labor pool is so much greater than ours, you see. It was obvious they meant to return to Cuba, and perhaps press even farther." His eyes had gone wide, and he blinked at Fred and Kari. "And then their fleet just . . . went away, presumably crossing westward through the Pass of Fire. Further substantiating the tale you brought us."

Fred had remained skeptical after Captain Willis left them, at least until the ships drew near. Now he could see details—and the strange five-starred flags. The "heavies" boasted two gun decks apiece, and their black-painted sides were pierced for fifty or more very large guns. Twin funnels, both forward of their mainmasts, implied multiple boilers. Lieutenant Hudgens noted their interest and joined them at the rail.

"That first one, with the long blue pennant, is the *Zachary*

Taylor. Perhaps you have heard of him?" Fred nodded vaguely. "We call her '*Old Zack*,' of course," Hudgens added with a smile. "The second is *Eric Holland*, named for the commander of one of the ships that brought us to this world, and our first director of the Navy."

"What do you call her?" Kari asked.

"Oh, a number of things." Hudgens chuckled. "She's known through the fleet as '*Holly*,' but the names her crew calls her change from time to time. She's reputed to be rather cranky under a full head of steam. Still, both are fairly new. The first sisters in a new class of ten, in point of fact. There are five others of them so far. They're armed with fifty-four guns, the largest being six-inch, eighty-pounder rifles, and they can make twelve knots under steam alone."

"Our 'Scotts' are faster, and their guns are bigger. Seven and a quarter inches," Fred boasted. He didn't mention they were smoothbores and only fired fifty-pound balls.

"Oh. Indeed."

Fred laughed at the man's suddenly crestfallen countenance. "But 'Scotts' aren't as big," he consoled, "and they mount only twenty guns, I think. Now, USS *Walker* only has *four* guns, and she could blow *Old Zack* and *Holly* to smithereens from nine miles away!"

Hudgens's face reddened, then he snorted. "Ha! Ridiculous! Now I'm sure you are teasing me!"

Fred's smile faded and his expression turned serious. "Nope, Lieutenant. I'm not pulling your leg about that at all."

Hudgens waved his arms. "Then . . . with such a ship, why would you need our help at all?"

Fred sighed. "Because *Walker*'s only one ship. Others like her are being built; they may already be in service, for all I know. But right now they're all fighting the Grik on the other side of the world. We're here. Just you and us."

With a flurry of signal flags whipping up and down her halyards, *Congress* eventually joined Semmes's squadron and slowly approached *Zachary Taylor* under her lee. The sea was calm and Fred, Kari, Captain Willis, and Lieutenant Hudgens were rowed to Commodore Semmes's flagship in short order. They were met courteously enough, but with many suspicious looks, especially at Kari. The barge carrying Don Emmanuel and the Dom prisoners followed them across. They were greeted correctly enough as well, it seemed, but the Dom's reception included a heavily armed Marine detachment that escorted all but Don Emmanuel below. The Dom emissary and Captain Willis were escorted directly aft, where they descended a companionway, but not before Don Emmanuel sent hateful glares at Fred and Kari. Lieutenant Hudgens remained behind with the two young aviators, while *Old Zack*'s curious crew gathered around them.

"So, what've you caught yourself this time, Sam?" asked a tall lieutenant with bright red muttonchops, angling through the crowd.

"There you are, Ully," Hudgens exclaimed with a grin. "I thought perhaps the commodore had thrown you overboard at last, when I didn't immediately see your foul, flaming face." He turned to Fred and Kari. "May I present Lieutenant Ulysses Locke, one of my more bothersome roommates at the Mobile Naval Asylum. He's really not as frightening as he appears. Ully, please welcome Lieutenant, Junior Grade, Fred Reynolds and his fascinating companion, Ensign Kari-Faask. They are both aviators"—he paused, considering—"ah, crew, of that splendid flying machine you see dominating dear *Congress*'s deck, amidships. They represent the great alliance to the east that has been giving the damnable Doms such fits. It was they who captured that rascal Don Emmanuel, in point of fact, and cheerfully handed him to us."

Lieutenant Locke stared at the Nancy aboard the other ship, then examined them more closely, his eyes lingering longest on Kari. But he, like Hudgens, seemed more amazed by the plane than by Kari's appearance, making her and Fred suspect anew that these people had had some contact, at least, with people who looked like her. Belatedly, he nodded a greeting. "Indeed?" he said. "You must tell me all about it."

For the next two hours, Fred and Kari entertained their hosts with tales of their adventures and the war in the West. Except for Hudgens and Locke, their audience changed from time to time as sailors were called to their

duties and replaced by others. Probably a bit giddy by the
sociable, if still occasionally somewhat suspicious, reception after their long, harrowing journey across a land that
wouldn't have welcomed them at all, Fred realized several
times that he'd probably revealed too much. He didn't
know nearly as much about these people as he was telling
them about his—but he was sure they shared far more than
just the superficial things he'd seen, including a terrible
enemy. *It isn't always true that the enemy of your enemy
is your friend,* he knew, *but anybody as committed to resisting the damn Doms as these "New Americans" seem
to be don't ever actually have to be our "friends" to become
potent . . . cobelligerents, at least.*

Finally, Don Emmanuel was escorted back on deck and
taken forward to another companionway on the fo'c'sle,
probably to join his companions in captivity. The hatred
behind his seething stare at Fred and Kari was undiminished when he was hustled past them. Shortly, a young
midshipman who looked all of twelve fetched Fred, Kari,
and both lieutenants aft. *Old Zack*'s layout below was similar to *Congress*'s. The gunroom they passed through was
a little larger, but not as much so as they might've expected
given her size. Fred suspected her second boiler and doubtless larger engine probably accounted for that. Soon, they
were brought to a door guarded by a Marine in blue and
white. He nodded at their approach and knocked on the
door before opening it. "The, ah . . . gentlemen you sent
for are here, Commodore."

"Enter," came a deep, robust voice, and the Marine
stepped aside and waved them in.

Again, the great cabin looked much like Captain Willis's on *Congress*, but it was substantially larger, occupying
the entire space from beam to beam, and from the door
to the large, square windows set in the curving stern of
the ship. A fascinating gimbaled bunk arrangement dominated the starboard side of the space, and a line of closets
stood to port. In the center was a large table surrounded
by chairs, but only Captain Willis and another man, as
tall and gaunt as Willis was round, sat near its head. *That
must be Commodore Semmes,* Fred thought as the man
gazed at them with piercing eyes beneath a pair of truly

outstanding dark eyebrows nearly as impressive as Courtney Bradford's. A bushy mustache swept aside to join the
muttonchops that seemed to try—and failed—to add an
impression of width to his narrow face. Otherwise, an
enormous cigar was clamped in his teeth, and by the smell
of the smoke in the cabin, Fred Reynolds realized it was
rolled from a variety of real tobacco. *That takes the cake,*
he thought. *Those weird "Mice" guys have fought so long
and hard to turn Aryaalan tobacco into something they
could smoke—and here I just stumble across the real thing,
and I can't stand the stuff!* Both men stood as the visitors
stepped inside.

"Lieutenant Hudgens," the gaunt man greeted, returning the man's salute. Belatedly, Fred and Kari both saluted
as well, and announced themselves as formally as they
knew how. Semmes blinked in surprise and allowed a small
smile before he spoke. "I am Captain Michael Semmes,
serving as commodore in command of this squadron. Captain Willis has told me a great deal about you two, and his
account is . . . astonishing, to say the least. Interestingly,
not only did my interview with Don Emmanuel actually
confirm a great deal of what Captain Willis said, I happen
to be in possession of . . . certain corroborative intelligence
of my own."

Fred's thoughts spun wildly with the implications of
that statement while Semmes instructed them to take seats
around the great table and they waited for refreshments
to appear. Fred politely refused the offered cigar, but Kari
actually chose one from the humidor and puffed it to life
with all appearance of relish. Fred did accept a glass of
something very strong, and he greedily gulped it down
with a cough. Semmes chuckled darkly when they were
settled. "Not that the Dom bastard *wanted* to help your
cause," he continued, "but his description of you as 'criminal spies, cowardly saboteurs, agents of a demonic force
bent on the destruction of humanity'"—he looked directly
at Kari—"and 'animalistic monsters' couldn't have more
thoroughly endeared you to me." He smirked. "A more
suspicious man, who hadn't already met Don Emmanuel
during several negotiations between his people and mine,
might almost be tempted to believe that his condemnation

was actually calculated to achieve that end. But as I said, I know the man, and know his attempt to defame you, if nothing else he said, was sincere. He really is arrogant enough to think we might credit his report against your character."

He nodded at Willis, then looked back at them. "And I *do* credit it, in your favor. That is largely due to my conversation with Captain Willis and his account of how forthcoming you have been to almost any question asked of you. It is his opinion that you are either telling the absolute truth about everything, or you must be the most accomplished, most deceitful 'demons' under heaven." He smiled at Fred's concerned expression. "I don't believe that, of course. Willis says you have told him all about your war against the Doms—and other possibly even more terrible foes—and have attempted to explain far more than he can understand about your amazing flying machine and your perhaps even more valuable communications equipment. I cannot believe you would have been so willingly informative about those two things in particular if you wished us ill."

He puffed his own cigar speculatively for a moment, then sighed. "And, of course, I have heard of you before, in a manner of speaking."

Fred was thunderstruck.

"Do you . . . Does that mean you know Cap-i-taan Anson?" Kari stammered.

Semmes gazed intently at her. It was the first time he'd heard her speak. He cleared his throat. "Ah, no, I don't, personally. Nor have I heard that name. I suspect it is more than likely an alias, as a matter of fact. But whoever he is, he is quite real, and if all you have reported to Captain Willis is true, I would certainly enjoy making his acquaintance. He is clearly a most formidable asset," he mused, knocking an ash into a tray on the table. "In any event, word has indeed spread in certain circles that one of our army's ah, 'covert scouts,' shall we say, was in contact with, and experienced numerous adventures alongside, a certain young 'pilot' of a flying machine and his . . . 'Lemurian' friend—did I say that correctly? It was also reported that these individuals represented a more recent 'relocation' of people from our own parent nation, allied with the Empire of the New Britain Isles. Suffice to say, the implications of that meeting have generated considerable excitement in some. There is caution as well, however, for various reasons. The excitement, I share, as a matter of fact—especially now that I have met you and know the truth of the matter—because it promises us the greatest opportunity to utterly defeat the vile Dominion that we have known. The concern—understandable, I suppose—stems from your association with the Empire, and the level of your technology. Your flying machine, for example, reflects a stunning achievement in a field that remains wholly theoretical to us. The wireless communication gear, though understandable in principle, is equally spectacular, but also possibly frightening to some. Still, it is likely that your association with the Empire is the cause of greatest concern. As Captain Willis has explained to you, we have had good reason to keep it at arm's length."

Fred cleared his throat, elated that someone at least knew about the first meeting they'd had with Anson. But there was also a growing anger deep inside that Anson's promise of assistance had apparently been meaningless—or quashed—by officials more worried about the Empire and preserving the status quo than they were about the Doms. "Sir, may I speak?" he asked hesitantly, somewhat concerned himself by what he might say once he got started.

Semmes nodded. "Of course."

"Okay. Well, the way I see it, if you know all that, then you may know our forces in the Pacific have been operating under the assumption that Captain Anson's commitment to an attack from this direction, following our destruction of the bulk of the Dom fleet on the other side of the Pass of Fire, was sincere. *I* thought it was, and told them so. Governor-Empress Rebecca McDonald, High Admiral Jenks, and Admiral Lelaa-Tal-Cleraan acted on that, and fought the biggest naval battle you ever saw." His voice began to harden. "We lost a helluva lot of ships, planes, and people to hammer *your* enemy, only to find out that Anson's—or whoever he is—word isn't worth a frog fart in a whirlwind." He absorbed the shocked expressions on Willis, Semmes, and even Kari. *Good,* he thought. *Got their attention.*

"That's why Kari and I flew all the way here in the first place, to find you and see what the holdup is. So forgive me if I'm a little sore to find out that there isn't any attack in the works, and only a few people even know we ever met." He took a deep breath and stared at the two officers. "So here's the deal," he continued harshly. "You can let us contact our people; tell them we're all happy as hell to be working together and you'll finally jump in and help us finish off the Doms—or not. If you do, you'll get all the fancy technology some of you are so afraid of, just like we've given it to all our other friends in this war." He looked at Kari, then shrugged. "If not, our people're eventually going to kick the Doms' asses anyway. It'll be a longer, harder slog, and a lot more of our people will die than would have if we seized this opportunity to work together now, but we *will* win, in the end, because we've got the guts to finish the job. When we do—when the Governor-Empress and Saan-Kakja, who's the western representative of the new Union we've established based on the *Constitution of the United States,* and"—he paused and grinned unpleasantly—"when *Captain Reddy* finds out you just sat out here with your thumbs up your asses while we did all the fighting—you *won't* end up with powerful friends all the way from here to the other side of Africa. You'll wind up with people who kicked the hell out of the Doms—who you couldn't lick in a hundred years—sitting in your backyard with all their scary technology saying, *'Lumaya ka sa harapan ko!'* the next time *you* get in a jam!"

Semmes's expression darkened, and Captain Willis shifted uncomfortably. "What does that mean, Lieutenant Reynolds?" he asked, then nodded at Kari. "Is that her language?"

"No," Fred told him, practically simmering. "Just something I used to hear a lot in Olongapo. It means 'Get out of my sight.'"

CHAPTER
19

Central Mada-gaas-gar
Naa-kaani Village of the Shee-ree
October 7, 1944

The "Great" Ror'at-Raal was not what they'd expected. It didn't matter that there'd been so many exceptions; the first High Chief they'd ever met was the gruff, bear-shaped Keje-Fris-Ar, and the second had been Nakja-Mur, whose obesity had been equally imposing in a way, when none of Matt Reddy's destroyermen had ever seen a fat Lemurian before. Even if more slightly built, Saan-Kakja was stunning to behold and possessed the most mesmerizing gold-and-obsidian eyes. Safir-Maraan was equally striking in her silver-washed armor and bright silver eyes, ebony fur, and black raiment. So they'd come to expect Lemurian High Chiefs to be . . . visually exceptional in some way. Ror'at-Raal, however, in his brindled fur and simple leather breech-cloth, looked enough like Kaam that they might've been brothers. Or, since Ror'at-Raal was clearly younger than Kaam, he might've been the Captain of the Guard's son. *Maybe he is,* Courtney speculated.

The High Chief's Great Hall was constructed in a circle around the largest tree in the village near its center and was elevated above the ground just like Adar's had once been at Baalkpan. Obviously, that design feature was as

old as Chack's people's last association with their possible
ancestors here. But where the portions of Adar's Great
Hall still dedicated to entertaining were decorated with
carvings and paintings, and hung with embroidered tapestries, this hall boasted none. It was more open, with wide
skylights beneath the eaves of the thickly thatched roof,
but there was almost no ornamentation. There was color,
however. Bright lizardbirds darted through the skylight
and frolicked in the rafters above, along with very bizarre
varieties of "regular," feathered birds. The most surprising
thing about them, that everyone noticed at once, was that
none of the flying creatures were trying to murder each
other. That was almost unprecedented in their experience.
Maybe there were sufficient insects infesting the thatch
above to keep them content? There was no special chair
or "throne" for the High Chief either, or really anywhere
easy to sit at all. The Lemurians they'd known favored
stuffed cushions, but here there were only bundled piles
of dried prairie grass. They weren't invited to sit, in any
event. Apparently, that wasn't the way here. All were expected to stand in the presence of the High Chief, just as
he stood to greet them.

Kaam introduced them, along with a brief description
of how they'd saved him and others from near-certain
death. His praise for Silva and his Doom Stomper was
high enough to make the big man shift uncomfortably
with an "aw, shucks" expression on his face. Then he
spoke of their reaction to the carcass of the Beaufort and
what had been revealed there. Ror'at-Raal studied them
with wide, curious, nearly perfect yellow eyes, but even
the yellow didn't distinguish him from others of his clan
since most had the same, even Kaam. What finally did
emerge, however, was a sense of amusement flickering
within the bright orbs.

"You came searching for us while we looked for you,"
the High Chief said at last. "The fatefulness of that is most
intriguing." He motioned for a servant to approach, an old
female with large, pendulous breasts, who brought a
wooden basin with a horn ladle. With his own hand,
Ror'at-Raal dipped the ladle and handed it to Chack,

gazing at Chack's fur and amber eyes with interest, but
also the garb he wore and the weapons he carried. "Take
water," he said. "You are welcome here."

Intuitively, Chack realized that a form of inviolate hos-
pitality was being offered, and he nodded gratefully, sipping the sweet water. He was surprised. This was not the
muddy scoop from the river he'd expected and they'd been
subsisting on. Passing the ladle on, Chack was glad to see
everyone take a modest sip, even Miles, but his ears flicked
in annoyance when Silva managed to produce a slight
slurp—and then offered the ladle to his ridiculous pet!
Lawrence seemed equally annoyed that the little lizard
drank before him, but solemnly lapped at the ladle when
it was his turn. Ror'at-Raal studied Lawrence intently.
"Not a slave, then?" he asked, blinking at him.

"Absolutely not, Your Excellency," Chack stated as
Lawrence bristled. "He is not even Gaa-riek, or Grik, as
we call them. He is from a tribe far across the sea whose
people are as committed as we to the destruction of the
Grik scourge. He is our friend and companion, and a
mighty warrior for good."

Ror'at blinked interest—and that same amused irony.

"You doubt?" Chack asked.

"No," Ror'at confessed. "But again, the fatefulness of
it all is most compelling." He looked levelly at Chack. "We
hear tales—strange, amazing tales, and this is a time like
has never come to my people. Two passings of the Sun
Brother ago, tales came of a great host of Gaa-rieks gathered on the shore to sunset of here. All feared it was a time
of harvesting, when they would swarm inland to kill us, eat
us, and throw those who survived back into starvation and
despair. This has happened many times," he added solemnly, and Courtney realized that at least part of his and
Chack's theory was correct. "But this time they gathered
in numbers unimagined before and all expected the final
harvest to begin." He blinked. "Some among us determined to fight them, my clan and several others, even if it
was hopeless." He grinned. "Most called us mad and fled
across the mountains to be enslaved by the Erokighaani
and their vile allies." He snorted. "Those who were of no

use to them, the old and infirm, were slain and eaten." He looked at Chack's horrified blinking with a curious twitch of his tail. "You did not know their nature?"

"No. We had . . . anecdotal evidence," Chack confessed, remembering the state of Sergeant McGinnis's corpse, "but assumed what we saw was the work of a single band—if it was the work of people at all." He suddenly felt a sense of even greater concern for Nat Hardee and the Seven boat.

"The Erokighaani and those like them are hardly people," Kaam retorted. "They are little better than a pale reflection in cloudy water of Gaa-rieks themselves. But they did not represent certain death, so many went to them." He shook the thought away. "Some stayed, and we prepared." He blinked in astonishment. "But the Gaa-rieks did not come! Instead, they got back on their big boats and sailed into a mighty storm. After some time had passed, tales began to return that they had been destroyed by the Aan-glis and other folk like us who came from the places Lef-ten-aant tried to tell us of, on great iron boats, with machines that fly! What was even more amazing, the tale insisted that these strangers had already destroyed the Gaa-rieks that have always lived beyond the mountain of rotting trees and were defending their conquest there!" He blinked intently at Chack and all the others. "Is this true?"

Chack took a deep breath. "Yes," he almost chorused with Courtney. Bradford smiled at him. "I understand him perfectly well, you know. You have gotten us here. Time for me to do *my* job." Chack nodded with a slight blink of concern but then just shrugged and grinned at Silva, who was watching him with an amused expression.

Courtney looked at Ror'at. "Indeed, it's quite true, and we come from that distant place. We, and the Grand Alliance of many peoples that we represent, have pushed the Grik back from their farthest conquests to their ancient nest itself. But before I continue I simply must know—how did you know we were coming? I mean, to actually send people looking for us, you had to not only know we were coming, but when, and from where!"

Ror'at blinked intense amusement then. "Trade in tales

is our greatest asset, and we are very good at it. We are also at the very center of the world—this, ah, 'island,' Lef-ten-aant called it. Our boats travel the river, and other rivers that touch it. Our tellers of tales range far—and move very quickly when the tale is urgent. They speak to other tellers of tales, wherever they go, but all must come through here." He managed what actually looked like a smug grin. "This is like the center of a spider's web when it comes to tales. Payment in tales or other goods come from those who hear the tales—or they get no more."

"I swear!" Silva barked. "It's like the Pony Express—with 'Cats! An' I bet you get a kickback from everything that comes through."

The Lemurians blinked at him uncomprehendingly, then Ror'at somehow seemed to grasp the gist of what he meant. "We hear all the tales, and can pass them on to others who will appreciate them."

Courtney was glaring at Silva. "Indeed," he grumped. He turned back to Ror'at. "But how, specifically, did you know to expect us?"

"We rarely know the origin of a tale, only that it must be true or no payment is sent. In your case, word of your preparations to come to us must have originated with the Aan-glis you fight with. They may not have even been part of the web, but would have told others who are. From there, the tale quickly spread. We did not know you were coming *here* until tellers of tales came from the other side of the mountains." He blinked. "We knew you would not be welcome there and if they did not kill you, you would either leave or come to us. That took little deduction."

Courtney had heard of the Pony Express. There'd once been something similar, briefly, in Northern Australia. With a communications network as sophisticated as the one Ror'at described, he saw how news of their intentions, departure, and approach actually could've gotten here ahead of them, since they'd spent so long at the mercy of a storm—and then creeping up the river. "But . . . ," he protested, "if the Grik buildup west of here two months ago—I mean . . . Oh, never mind. But why didn't that tale reach our Aan-glis allies?"

Ror'at blinked almost primly. "Some Aan-glis do not

think the tales of others have value. I would guess that those who fight with you have not always rewarded tellers of tales in the past."

"So we didn't get the word because our friends stiffed the mailman," Silva murmured.

"And we never dreamed such an arrangement for sharing information even existed," Chack agreed.

Courtney cleared his throat and addressed Ror'at. "Then perhaps you already know our reason for coming to you, and how costly the fight against the Grik has been for us—though I suspect it has taken more lives than you may be able to imagine. Still, we have reached the shores of victory at last." His bushy eyebrows arched. "But the Grik retain a final, greater shore across the sea to, um, sunset-ward. That swarm you heard of came from there to throw us off this land. It was destroyed," he confirmed, "at further great cost. That is, in fact, what prompted our mission here: to find Mi-Anakka, Aan-glis, *anyone* of honor who craves safety and freedom and will join us"— he paused and blinked irony of his own at Ror'at-Raal— "in our mad effort to destroy this evil forever." He caught the Lemurian gazing at the weapons his companions carried. "Those who do will be given training and war leaders experienced at fighting Grik, and arms like those we carry so long as they swear never to use them against anyone *but* Grik." With the apparent diversity of tribes and clans and ancient animosities on this island, Courtney wasn't so naïve as to believe modern weapons would never be used to settle old scores, but they could at least be careful who they armed—and who they didn't.

Ror'at-Raal blinked stunned amazement. "You will give us magic weapons? And come here to help us fight the Gaa-rieks?"

Courtney blinked back in consternation. "Um, yes, we will arm you, and do all the things I said, but we can't possibly do that here. We need you and your people to come to us, to help us fight the Grik where they continue to attack us—beyond the, um, 'mountain of rotting trees.'" He considered, then added, "And eventually beyond even that, on the final Grik shore itself."

Ror'at blinked alarm. "We cannot go from here!" he

said. "Even without the Gaa-rieks, other clans will take our lands while we are gone! The web of tales would tear, and we would return to find ourselves outcasts in our own lands!" He looked longingly at the Krag on Courtney's shoulder. "No," he said sadly. "Not for any magic could we do this. We will fight to protect our lands, but we cannot fight to lose them!"

Courtney frowned. "I understand your concern. But we need all the people of this land. Hopefully, none would remain to take yours."

"Even if that were so, that you could get all the clans of the Shee-ree and others to agree, the Erokighaani would never go. None of us would *want* them to go," he added with a bitter blink, "and they would come here at last."

"*I* swear we would return with you and help regain your lands from such as they," Chack assured with certainty. Courtney looked at him, surprised by the vehemence with which he'd openly contradicted the conditions for arming these people. Then he understood. Learning the full truth about the eastern river folk at last, Chack had equated them with the Grik. They were probably even worse, in his eyes, just as many humans considered the Doms worse than Grik as well. He sighed. Were they doomed to fight wars upon wars *within* wars for the rest of his life? Most likely, he supposed, given the nature of the world they lived in. *The nature of* any *world,* he conceded ruefully. But a confrontation with the Erokighaani was for the future and would be a ridiculously insignificant affair compared to the current conflict. "I will swear that also," he said. "For myself and the entire alliance I represent. If any tribe dares take the land of another that has left it to help us, to help *all* people everywhere against our common enemy, as the Allied plenipotentiary at large, I hereby commit the full power of the Grand Alliance to the utter destruction of anyone so cowardly as to do such a thing." He looked squarely at Ror'at. "Let your traveling tellers of tales carry *that* warning."

Ror'at blinked, then his eyes narrowed in deep concentration. "I will have to consider this. The scale of the Alliance and war you describe is hard to imagine, but since you five alone could probably keep your pledge, armed as you are, it carries great weight indeed." He paused. "But even if we agree to leave here, to join you in the war, we cannot do so now. The war is already here again. That is why *we* went looking for you!"

Courtney blinked incomprehension.

"The Gaa-rieks gather another force, larger than the last—and different. It is farther inland as well, somehow pulled upriver on big, flat boats by other boats that smoke. Perhaps they hide from your scouting boats and flying machines? But they are here, and more come with every night. They are even closer to my people than before, near a village of the Khot-So Clan of the Rik-Aar. We are at peace with the Rik-Aar, but are not allied to them. If we were, we would have gone immediately to their aid," he hastily added, trying to assure them—and possibly himself. He blinked regret. "We must assume the Gaa-rieks can only be preparing to come against us here or against your people once more."

"Have you sent this, um, tale to the Aan-glis, who might pass it to our leaders?" Courtney asked, alarmed.

"Yes, and we sent it to be told without reward."

"How long ago?"

"Five suns. As soon as we learned of it. But it took that long for the tale to reach us." He paused. "At the same time, though, we also heard the tale that you were crossing the mountains, and sent a party to find you."

"Fatefulness indeed," Courtney mused. "So, a new Grik army has been gathering for a fortnight or more. And you say it is already bigger than the last. How is it different?"

Ror'at made a strange face and blinked. "The last was like the flock of herdbeasts you saw when you approached. They surged back and forth as directed, but lived packed together in their own filth except to strip the land of animals and people to feed themselves until they left. These, the tale goes, move together in groups, and build night lodges in groups as well. And one group can attach itself to another, and all move as one." He blinked. "They are visited by flying machines of their own," he added, almost reluctantly, "if that part of the tale is true. It is difficult to believe, since it is said they look like horrible great fishes that swim in the sky!"

The visitors looked at each other. *Zeppelins.* "I fear it's true," Courtney said. "We've seen these machines ourselves."

Ror'at just stared at him, but then continued, "They strip the land around them as before, but use the stronger people they have taken—several clans, it is said—as slaves: to dig trenches for their filth, erect their night lodges, and unload great heaps of things from the big, flat boats. They eat the weak, of course," Ror'at growled. "But using slaves is strange and new for them—and disturbingly sensible. The slaves will all die in time, of course. Some are probably Shee-ree," he added bitterly.

"How many?" Courtney asked quietly.

"The tale tellers could not count them any better than the Gaa-rieks, but many hundreds."

"It sounds like Halik in Indiaa," Silva said grimly, "except he didn't have locals to enslave. Prob'ly would've, if he did, but it sure sounds like his style of army."

"It does," Courtney agreed, and took a deep breath. "So, General Esshk's army, the *real* army our reconnaissance to the mainland has had glimpses of, is mustering in the south by night and apparently just far enough inland to avoid the few reconnaissance craft we can spare to inspect the coast. This General Esshk is very shrewd. Apparently, he's guessed—correctly—that the last place we'd expect another attack is from a similar staging area as before. The next question is, will the army attack as before, or march overland?"

"A *part* of his army, at least," Chack agreed. "And overland, I suspect. With *this* part," he stressed. "It sounds like what they're preparing for. And though they're apparently slipping ships past our patrols, they could never gather a sufficient transport fleet, or move it toward Grik City, without being observed. Let us hope the tale tellers reach Captain Reddy in time, before the army advances into the jungles to the north and are completely lost to view." He scratched his furry nose. "But we can't wait for that, and certainly can't count on it."

"What do you propose?" Courtney demanded. "We're stuck here. We could try to fix the radio in that Beaufort, I suppose."

"We could do that," Chack agreed. "We *should* check to see if it is possible, at least," he added doubtfully. "How did, ah, Lef-ten-aant 'kill' it?"

Kaam pointed at the holster at Chack's side. "With the thunder weapon he carried like that."

"Oh. Indeed," Courtney said. "You *do* have another proposition?" he asked Chack hopefully.

Chack looked at Silva. "They've got smoking boats."

"Obviously steamers," Silva agreed. "But how many? Just two? A dozen? It'll make a difference." He turned to Lawrence. "How's your Grik lingo, Larry, ol' buddy?"

"Sufficient, I think," Lawrence answered calmly.

Courtney was increasingly *less* calm. He'd seen these three act this way before, and it was particularly unnerving that they all seemed to have the same idea at once.

"You will fight them?" Ror'at demanded, his yellow eyes brightening. "You can defeat them all alone?"

"Not alone, Your Excellency," Chack confessed. "And I doubt we can beat them. But with your help, and all the help you can quickly gather, we can hurt them, and maybe stop them long enough for our people to get their shit in the sock and hit them from the air while they're still in the open. We might even be able to get some of the, ah, 'slaves' out. More important, I want to get all *your* people out and away, where they can join ours and we can all fight the Grik together."

Ror'at looked from one to the other. "Very well," he said. "The fatefulness of the circumstances and the flowing together of purpose cannot be ignored." He let out a long breath. "We will join you—based on the promises you gave. What choice do we have? If we do nothing, the slaves are doomed. If the Gaa-rieks come here, we are doomed. If they destroy your people—our first, last, and only chance of resisting them—we are still doomed to at best continue as we always have. That is not enough. I will send word to the other clans of the Shee-ree who joined me before, and you will lead us to war."

"Oh, swell, here we go," Miles groaned under his breath.

"What's the matter?" Silva whispered at him.

"Gunny Horn always told me to stay away from you. Said you attract crazy trouble like a magnet."

"He was right," Silva said, "an' he should'a listened to himself. Horn's barely livin' proof there's such a thing as a useful *China* Marine." He'd stressed "China," glancing at Chack. "Old world" rivalries didn't always translate perfectly. "But he always was a idiot. You think *I'm* nuts? I could tell you a thing or two about Gunny Horn, from before the war . . . but you ain't earned them tales." He shook his head. "Don't matter now. I got you, an' you're finally gonna rare up on your hind legs like a man an' turn into a real live Marine if it kills you." Suddenly, he flashed his signature gap-toothed grin at Courtney. "Say, how many machine guns does a Bristol Beaufort carry?"

CHAPTER 20

1st Fleet (TF Alden)
October 9, 1944

"**D**amn, I love this ship!" Commander Perry Brister grated, smiling, leaning back in his captain's chair, bolted to the forward bulkhead of USS *James Ellis*'s pilothouse. The chair was just like Captain Reddy's on *Walker*, but considerably more comfortable. For one thing, it was padded with cushions that, like almost every item made of cloth aboard the entire ship, were embroidered with the ship's name. Not that Perry would ever admit to having "tested" Captain Reddy's chair. . . . It was a gorgeous dawn, with kind seas and a clear sky, exactly the kind of morning any destroyer skipper with a new, fast ship steaming at twenty knots would adore. A cool breeze whipped through the pilothouse and the gentle pitching of the ship threw steady, concave curls of water away from her sharp bow.

"That's not what you was sayin' last night, Skipper," admonished Taarba-Kaar (Tabasco), the ship's Lemurian chief cook, as he handed Perry a cup of monkey joe. His kind of almost coffee was far better than Earl Lanier's and particularly his mentor, Juan Marcos's, had ever been, and it was served in a proper Navy cup without a handle. The skinny, dark-furred 'Cat had thrived out from under Earl's, and even Juan's, thumbs, offering up what was probably the best chow—for humans and Lemurians—in the Navy, and Perry wouldn't trade him for anybody. *Well, nobody short of Spanky, or maybe Tabby,* he thought with a trace of disappointment directed at Lieutenant (jg) Johnny Parks. Parks was a decent engineering officer, but *James Ellis*, the first of her class and the first steel-hulled destroyer the Lemurians had ever built, had a lot of idiosyncrasies that sometimes needed an . . . imaginative engineer to sort out. Parks was competent but not overly imaginative. *Hell,* Perry thought. *I'd settle for one of the Mice!*

"Last night, we lost the feedwater pump to the number three boiler. Again," Perry said, as airily as his damaged voice would allow. "I thought you 'Cats were good with pumps," he goaded. "But now it's fixed, and all's right with the world!"

"You called *Ellie* a 'piece of shit,'" reminded Lieutenant (jg) Paul Stites in an aggrieved tone, without taking the Imperial telescope from his eye. He was staring out forward, far beyond the busy fo'c'sle below them. Once one of Dennis Silva's chief minions aboard *Walker*, the rangy Stites had risen to the post of gunnery officer on *Mahan*, and now *James Ellis*. It was he, in fact, who'd coined the diminutive *"Ellie"* for their ship. The loss of Jim Ellis still stung, and the use of the ship's proper name was a constant, stiff kick to their grief. *"Ellie"* lightened that a bit.

"I was just frustrated. I get that way when one boiler's on its third pump repair in as many days. I didn't mean it, not really," Perry said. "And I still love her. With four boilers, she's faster than *Walker*. We've had her up to thirty-five knots with pressure to spare more than once, and she didn't rattle her guts out. She's got four *dual-purpose* four-inch-fifties, and eight fully operational torpedo tubes—with decent fish in 'em—in her two quad mounts. They ought to put quad mounts on every ship we have," he added seriously. "I hear *Tarakan Island*'s got a pair of them for Captain Reddy. Other than that," he continued, "she doesn't leak, she doesn't bitch, and she's *clean*. I miss *Mahan*, and wish we could've gotten her back in action." He frowned. "Say, I hope those yard apes don't catch hell when word spreads that they're still tinkerin' with her in their spare time." He shook his head. "But I'm mighty glad to have *Ellie*." He rubbed his chin, gazing out the windows at the sea ahead. *James Ellis* and her sister, *Geran-Eras*, were casting about, ahead of the task force, blasting the depths with their sonar. Their purpose was to not only frighten any mountain fish that might cross their path, but to make sure there weren't any other undersea threats. Nobody really expected that, but they hadn't expected the strange sub that sank *Respite Island* and a DD either. As the morning progressed, they'd slow to match the convoy's speed.

"Look," Perry said after a moment. "She does have problems—everybody knows. Nothing we can't handle," he added hastily, "but she maybe . . . wasn't quite as ready as *Geran-Eras* was. A lot of improvements went into her sister." He nodded at Tabasco. "The 'Cats did a swell job on them both. *Ellie*'s hull is sound. Hell, it's way tighter than *Walker*'s. And after all the trouble they had tooling up to make turbines—and reduction gears, by God"—he shook his head at that, still amazed—"I bet her engines are better too. The gun and torpedo directors are probably the most complicated gizmos on the ship, and they made those *perfect*, down to the smallest detail." He shrugged. "It's the little things, mostly, things they didn't take as much—or took *too* much—care with that're giving us fits. And the little things always affect the big things."

Stites took the glass away from his eye and looked at him, grinning. "Yeah. Like the 'Cat's inclination to decorate every damn thing they get their furry little hands on. They understand the notion that form follows function, but can't seem to get it out o' their fuzzy heads that plain form is usually better than fancy form on machines!" He shook his head and chuckled. "It's like that lathe operator in Baalkpan who kept turning wedding bands on all the recoil cylinders for the new 4"-50s during his lunch breaks. Kid got tired of polishing all those straight, smooth pieces without doin' a little somethin' to doll 'em up. He didn't know what they were *for*, that they *have* to be smooth to work right. He only knew they weren't pretty. Lord knows how many he trashed before they caught him, an' we even had a few aboard here, packed as spares. It wasn't really his fault; that's just the way 'Cats are. They're proud of what they make an' want it to look nice. Last I heard, they set him up makin' more complicated stuff so he wouldn't get as bored—along with a warnin' to make 'em *exactly* like his templates!"

"That's what I'm talking about," Perry agreed. "Some stuff is so crude it barely works, and some is so fancy it *can't* work right. Think of the mixed signals they get. Somebody tells 'em to forget polishing the outside of some cast casing, because it doesn't need it, but then tells them the mating surfaces have to be perfectly smooth. Things like that. They wonder why they shouldn't finish out the whole thing, and when somebody tells them to let part of it slide, they think, *What the hell?* and do a half-assed job on the critical stuff." He grimaced. "And there are things like that all over the ship." He looked at Tabasco. "The feedwater pumps are just one example." He nodded at the brass compass binnacle, standing in front of the wheel in polished, blazing glory. The most striking thing about it, though, was the deeply engraved, heroic tableau of Jim Ellis, Bernard Sandison, and several 'Cats standing on the sinking stern of *Mahan* during the Battle of Baalkpan Bay. *Amagi's* shattered, burning silhouette loomed large in the background. "Look at that thing. It's a work of art! And it works too. But Ronson says the wiring running all over the ship is the worst nightmare he ever saw." Ronaldo "Ronson" Rodriguez was Perry's XO. He shaved his head because his hair grew in clumps around some old burn scars, but wore an enormous Pancho Villa mustache. He'd started as one of *Walker's* electrician's mates. "Says, from what he's seen so far, it looks like a pile of spaghetti, on paper. He's busy right now, as a matter of fact, tracing circuits with all the EMs, drawing new diagrams for damage control. Apparently, the builders threw the whole wiring diagram out the window and just ran everything however it made the most sense to them." He nodded back at the binnacle. "The light in there? It's not on an independent circuit, with the other instrument lighting on the bridge. It's spliced into the power for the comm shack, the chart house, and the wardroom!" He rolled his eyes. "All that's going to have to be rerun, eventually."

He stood, stepping out on the starboard bridgewing, and the wind whipped his shirt. Stites followed and caught his captain gazing fondly back at the Lemurian bridge watch. "But you know," Perry told him, "as much as I gripe, griping's all it is. I do love this ship, and she's got a fine crew, even if it's a little human-heavy." *James Ellis* had more "old" destroyermen aboard than *Walker*. That was largely because *Mahan* had needed them, and they'd just shifted, en masse, to the brand-new ship. Now she needed them almost as badly as *Mahan* had, Perry thought. "Maybe they should've worked out more of the bugs before they sent her out here, but it's not like we haven't had plenty of practice doing that for ourselves. And she's damn sure needed. *Walker*'s been on her own, in a lot of respects, for an awful long time. It always seems to fall on her to save everybody's ass. And who knows? Maybe it's our turn."

He looked aft, past the familiar four funnels, the amidships gun platform, and the seemingly distant aft deckhouse, to the broad, foamy wake. He glanced left to see *Geran-Eras* steaming about five miles away, leaving a similar wake, and it was easy to imagine they were all alone on the wide, empty sea. *Geran-Eras* had an all-'Cat crew, and Perry still thought politics may have been involved. But even if it was true, he doubted Cablass-Rag-Laan had anything to do with it. He and Perry had become close friends, and Cablass had turned into one of the very best skippers they had, even if most of his experience had been in sailing steamers. Many of his crew had time in *Walker* or *Mahan* and had therefore dealt with an amazing variety of battle damage and mechanical casualties. *He should be okay,* Perry judged, somewhat protectively, but it was probably just as well that Cablass had drawn the "better" ship of the pair.

He turned aft again, and there, stretching to the horizon, was the bulk of the task force, steaming at a respectable fourteen knots. Four great ships dominated the scene: The Fleet carrier *Baalkpan Bay* was paced by *Andamaan*, the former Grik battleship–turned–giant seaplane tender. He had a hard time thinking of it as an AVD. Behind them steamed *Sular*, the other Grik battleship that had become a protected troopship, and beside her was the SPD *Tara-*

kaan Island. Clustered around them were the *Scott* Class oilers and transports, along with a large number of smaller auxiliaries. Screening the formation on either side were the sail/steam frigates (DDs) of Des Ron-10. Some of those had seen a lot of action—*Bowles, Saak-Fas, Clark,* to name a few.

"I *hope* it ain't our turn to save everybody's ass," said Chief Bosun's Mate Carl Bashear, joining them on the bridgewing. The blond-haired and -bearded fireplug could've had his own command by now, but like Fitzhugh Gray, lost at Grik City, he was a Chief Bosun now, and that's all he ever wanted to be. Trying to get him off *James Ellis* and away from Perry Brister would've been as difficult—and pointless—as taking Gray away from *Walker* and Captain Reddy.

"I hope not, Boats," Perry agreed, nodding aft. "And with that much combat power, it's hard to imagine. But stranger—and worse—things have happened." He looked at Bashear. "I thought you were helping Ronson chase wires."

Bashear shrugged and spat a yellowish stream of Lemurian tobacco juice over the rail, covering his mouth with his hand like he would to shout. Then he grinned. "I guess it's like Spanky McFarlane on *Walker.* He's Captain Reddy's XO now, but you'll never get his heart out of her engineerin' spaces. Ronson—'Mr. Rodriguez'—will always be an EM in his bones. I figure we're all like that, in a way, slippin' back to what we know best from time to time. Kinda comforting. Anyway, he got tired of my 'suggestions,' I guess. Said he didn't need me."

Perry grinned back. "Well, then I'm sure you can find something else to do."

"Aye, aye, sir. Lots of somethin' elses."

Perry turned to Stites. "God knows what'll turn up next. I'm surprised they didn't cast heroic scenes on the anchors. I don't care about that sort of stuff, aside from the loss of time that could've been spent on more important things, but we all have to keep our eyes peeled for . . . weirdness that affects function."

"Ah," Bashear said, shifting.

"What?"

"You mean . . . you haven't looked at the anchors, Skipper?"

USS Baalkpan Bay *(CV-5)*

General of the Armies and Marines Pete Alden was on *Baalkpan Bay*'s hangar deck watching several III Corps company commanders exercise their Lemurian troops. I and III Corps had no Imperial regiments attached yet, and there were only a very few observers or liaisons. For such a big ship, the space was incredibly cramped with all the troops and aircraft crammed in, and the soldiers and Marines had to take turns with what room there was. Pete scratched his dark beard against the phantom itch of whatever they'd been that had infested it during the siege of his perimeter east of the Rocky Gap. The lice-like vermin were long gone now, but he still "felt" them sometimes. He didn't know what had kept the 'Cats, with fur all over their bodies, sane. Muln Rolak had been a wonder, never even deigning to scratch, as if the cooties hadn't bothered him at all. The old Aryaalan was like that, and Pete missed his company, but he'd—appropriately—embarked on *Sular* with the bulk of his I Corps.

Baalkpan Bay's skipper, Commodore Kek-Taal, was himself a Sularan. That reluctant member of the Alliance produced generally kind of snotty 'Cats, in Pete's opinion. At least the high-ranking ones. He apparently didn't like guys running around on his flight deck during daylight, even though there were no flight operations underway. His reasoning was that daytime was when they were most likely to have to get things going in a hurry. Pete wasn't sure he agreed, but despite "commanding" the task force, he would *not* get wrapped up in the day-to-day operations of Kek-Taal's ship. The pilots and support crews didn't like guys running around on the hangar deck either—not ever—especially when the pilots were frustrated that they couldn't fly, and the support personnel were annoyed that most of their planes weren't doing anything. They did launch the occasional Nancy, and recover it alongside, but though they might still theoretically launch the improved

P-1Cs, there was no place for them to land with Ben Mallory's eight P-40Es strapped to the flight deck. That was their problem, Pete thought, regarding the feelings of the support personnel. His troops had to stay fit, one way or another.

He glanced at his watch. The task force would briefly slow to a crawl in just a few minutes when one of the Clippers returned from its scout and was taken aboard USS *Andamaan*. Another would be lowered into the sea, and take off for its own long scout. It had been his call, but Pete still wasn't sure they shouldn't have just filled *Andamaan* with Nancys and flown the Clippers down to Madagascar. It was done now, though, and he liked watching the operation.

"Morning, General," Ben Mallory said, saluting.

Pete looked up and returned the salute. "Good morning, Colonel. Where are the rest of your Flashies?" he asked, referring to the other human and Lemurian P-40 pilots in Ben's 3rd (Army Air Corps) Pursuit Squadron. They usually all stuck together.

"They're at chow. I gave 'em the slip. Thought I'd look you up."

"Here I am," Pete said. "I'm heading over to the starboard side hangar bay to watch the Clipper turn around, then I'm going to go get some chow myself. You're welcome to join me."

"Thanks, General." Together, the two men weaved through the parked planes, busy crew-'Cats, and jogging troops until they stood in the huge rectangular opening. The sky was almost cloudless and the sea quite calm. Almost immediately, they heard the thundering crackle of four double-stacked radials.

"Right on time," Pete said as a big blue-and-white, four-engine aircraft with a deep, boat-shaped fuselage rumbled into view from the south and began circling as way came off the four ships in the center of the formation. The auxiliaries slowed, but plodded on. As usual, the screen both contracted and spread out, depending on their relative positions. The plane tightened its turn and descended on *Andamaan*'s port quarter, in the half-mile gap between her and *Baalkpan Bay*. Without hesitation, the PB-5D slapped the water and skimmed to a stop roughly even with *Andamaan*'s bow, and about fifty yards off her beam. Almost immediately, the two inboard engines wound down and the plane turned toward the ship and began to close the distance.

"It's a wet ship, I'm told," Mallory said, referring to *Andamaan*. "It sits up higher in the water now, with all the guns and junk torn out, but takes a lot of water over the front when the sea's up."

"I thought you'd be more interested in her big planes," Pete retorted.

"Sure. I've even flown them. They're good ships. Hell, I'd fly nothing else if that was the only way I could get back in the fight."

"You'd give up your P-Forties?" Pete asked, amazed.

"I haven't gotten to use them much lately, have I?" Ben asked bitterly. "I did more actual fighting in that old PBY before I flew its wings off than I have in those high-performance hangar queens strapped down topside," he added.

"That's about to change, looks like."

Ben shrugged, nodding across the water. "Anyway, that setup is kind of interesting." The plane was almost alongside now, and the big crane on the port side near the front of the casemate was turning outward, preparing to lift the plane. When the hook was secured, the outboard engines finally spun to a stop. "I wonder how well that thing would handle a real blow, though," he speculated. "A lot of water goes over the front, through the hangar doors—they can't be watertight, can they? The next thing you know, it just fills up and sinks."

"Kind of like a car ferry, huh?"

"I guess."

"You'd think they would've thought of that."

"I hope so."

They watched in silence while the dripping plane swung inboard. Unnoticed until then, they realized that another plane had been set down in the water off the starboard quarter. They knew only because it suddenly accelerated forward, past the ship, skipping across the wave tops until it lifted completely free and soared away.

"Nine minutes," Pete said, surprised, glancing back at his watch. "Pretty slick."

Ben rubbed his chin. "Yeah," he said. "They know what they're doing, at least. Question is, what am *I* doing?"

"What do you mean?"

Ben snorted, then waved around. "All this."

Pete waited expectantly.

"Okay." Ben sighed. "Here's the deal. My P-forties were a technological godsend, no question. I mean, the 'Cats have learned so much from them—their manuals, construction techniques, performance characteristics, even just looking at their lines—that they've started making honest-to-goodness pursuit ships of their own. Granted, P-Ones and even P-One-Cs are pretty primitive, but I'd say the Cs are nearly on a par with anything we had just fifteen years ago. And that was all from scratch! They carry real machine guns in their wings, along with a decent load of ammo, and their double-stacked radials give them better performance, even with the extra weight. They can carry guns *and* a couple of bombs, easy—even if they're no faster or maneuverable than a Nancy, then, but why do they need to be? Better pursuit ships might come in handy against the Dom's Grikbirds, but the first model P-Ones were already hell on Grik zeps. The Cs will go through 'em like castor oil."

"So what's your point?"

Ben closed his eyes, then opened them, blinking. "I guess I worry a little that, given the fact that my planes are still a couple of generations, at least, ahead of the Cs, Captain Reddy might be expecting miracles from them," he finally admitted. "From *me*," he added. "Sure, we helped turn the tide at Second Madras, but we didn't do anything the new D-model Clippers and C-model Mosquito Hawks couldn't do now." He paused. "And we've just got *eight* of the damn things left, not counting the two still in Baalkpan! To make matters worse, and to underscore the reason they *have* been hangar queens, fewer than half the ones we've lost were the result of enemy action. The rest just crapped out and fell out of the sky, or cracked up on takeoff or landing. No fault of my pilots and ground crews," he hastened to add. "That's a helluva lot lower percentage of losses due to mechanical failure or pilot error than you'll find in any other outfit. Any prewar P-Forty squadron, for that matter, I bet. But I guess my point is, maybe Adar was right, way back when we first found the things, when he wondered if we were spending too much effort on something of dubious value that we couldn't maintain and damn sure couldn't replace. We've been saving my planes and pilots back, like they were some kind of super weapon, when there's nothing out there we really *need* the planes for. And the pilots—*I*—might've been better employed training and leading other squadrons."

Pete stared out at *Andamaan*, watching as the task force accelerated smoothly back to its standard speed and the screen slowly shook itself back out. "You're preaching to the choir, Colonel," he said at last. "And while none of us really knows what's out there that we might *really* 'need' your hot ships for someday, I've been saying the same thing for a long time." He waved around them at the planes crowding the hangar deck. "They've been building these things faster than we could put qualified pilots in them for a while, and experienced leaders and instructors would've probably saved a lot of lives." He looked at Ben, his eyebrows narrowed. "But that's beside the point, isn't it? Even bigger than your frustration over being kept on the sidelines so long is your concern that your carefully reserved wonder weapons can't hack whatever stunt Captain Reddy might cook up for them. You think, whatever it is, it's liable to be a doozy." He snorted. "And it may well be. But did it ever occur to you that maybe there won't be anything 'special' about it after all? That Captain Reddy just finally wants to mass as much firepower in one place as he can? And whatever else your planes might be, with all six fifties back in 'em, and their bomb payload, each one equals a whole squadron of P-Ones in good, old-fashioned ground attack."

His stern expression softened. "Look, son, I know a little how you feel. Along with Second Corps, which has been whittled down time and again, First and Third Corps are the cream of the crop. We can't replace them either, not soon. Don't you think I love them too? Don't you think I'm frustrated that they haven't been with Captain Reddy at the very tip of the spear? And don't you think I worry sometimes that, because they're the 'cream,' Captain Reddy might someday expect more from them than *I* can handle? Not the army; it can handle anything. I mean *me*." He grunted at Ben's surprised expression, and unconsciously scratched his beard again. "Yeah," he said. "Look, all of us started somewhere. You were just a green Air Corps butter bar when we got here. Captain Reddy himself was a junior skipper of a worn-out tin can. Hell, that murderin' devil Chack was a goddamn *pacifist*!" He shook his head. "And everybody seems to forget that I started out in this world as a gimpy, homeless Marine sergeant, with nothing but a forty-five." He looked Ben up and down. "You'll do what you have to do, *Colonel*, when the time comes. All of us will, and you always have before." He grinned. "Now let's go get chow before they throw it to the fish."

"Sure, *General*," Ben said with a slight smile, stressing Pete's title as well. "And . . . thanks."

CHAPTER
21

The Highlands
West of the Indus River Valley
October 11, 1944

The morning was bright but cold, this high, and General Shlook's troops had been torpid and listless in the predawn gloom when the general and his staff, warmed by fires, roused his division as quickly as possible from the huddled mounds they slept in. Despite sharing many physical characteristics, Grik weren't exactly reptiles and didn't rely entirely on ambient temperature to regulate their body heat. It helped, though, and they were highly specialized to the equatorial environment in which they'd evolved. Over time, they'd adapted to somewhat milder climes such as prevailed in India, even if quickly traveling from hot to "cool" required acclimation. There existed tales of similar races that thrived in colder climes, but "proper" Grik didn't do particularly well in them—and "cold" was pretty much anything below fifty degrees Fahrenheit. Their aviators suffered terribly if they weren't warmly dressed and almost ridiculously well fed.

A flood of hot, meaty soup and an hour of vigorous exercise had brought Shlook's division around by the time the expected solid mass of enemy Grik swarmed down the road. The road was much broader here, winding through a sloping meadow between two peaks, and the attack would descend on a front of approximately a quarter of a mile. Strange bipedal creatures, heavily furred, fled before the swarm, scattering to the sides, bright sunlight flashing from whitish antlers on their heads and spikes on their tails.

Apparently, Shighat had prepared his warriors the same way Shlook had done, and without the timely—if somewhat disdainful—warning by a troop of Colonel Enaak's 5th Maa-ni-la Cavalry, his strike would've caught 2nd Division completely unprepared. As it was, Shlook's troops were already braced for the coming impact behind its shields and hasty breastworks.

"A close call," Shlook murmured to himself. "Very close indeed. Shighat can't *defend* himself any better than a fresh hatchling, and our aggressive pursuit tears great, bloody morsels from his flanks," he murmured aside to Captain Sigg, who'd increasingly become Halik's eyes in the various divisions. "But he can still attack, and his attacks grow disturbingly more imaginative." He suddenly shouted at a runner over the rising flood. "Apprise Lord General Halik of the situation here, along with my worshipful suggestion that such attacks may serve our enemy just as well as a strong defense! Go!" He turned back to Captain Sigg. "I do hope our reluctant scouts saw fit to make the same warning to our other divisions this morning, though I would not be surprised if they didn't."

"Why?" Sigg asked as four light guns spewed canister into Shighat's swarm, just as it slammed into the breastworks. The shield wall bulged back, but frenzied fighting reestablished the position—for now. Shlook tore his eyes from the collision and looked back at him. "They still hate us," he said. "Make no mistake. They want us to destroy Shighat's force, and will help us do that to a point, but they would not be the least distressed if we destroyed ourselves in the process." He watched the growing, blood-drenched struggle for several moments, gauging the weight behind the swarm with a practiced eye. He suspected perhaps twenty thousand warriors confronted the eight thousand or so that he had left. It was a sizable fraction of Shighat's army, perhaps a quarter of what remained, but the difference in quality should even the odds. Unlike his companion generals in Halik's army, even General Ugla, who was born a general just as surely as he, Shlook had no desire to personally join the fight. He could have, and had before. He was fully trained. But his satisfaction came from watching his warriors, his *troops*, fight well. For most of his life, that satisfaction had been dependent upon how their performance reflected on him. That was no longer the case.

Arrogance was not new to Shlook, or any Grik Hij, but he'd come to know that arrogance, particularly that of the Grik as a race, was based on little more than an illusion. Pride was different in a very fundamental way, and Shlook had learned to feel genuine pride in himself and in what he'd helped Halik accomplish. But the army was their greatest accomplishment, and a source of satisfaction to them all. Lately, however, he'd gained a growing, *special* sense of attachment to his division. That was what generated his greatest pleasure—and at the moment, his most severe anxiety. It was almost as if his own body were wounded with a blade or blow for each of "his" warriors he saw fall.

"It is well that Shighat is too fearful to combine boldness and imagination. This"—he gestured grimly at the shield wall—"will be close. I am tempted to ask for reinforcements, in fact. But a larger force might have already swept us back on 5th Division, and if it was still afflicted by the cursed night cold of these unpleasant mountains, the confusion would have been difficult to overcome."

General Halik himself trotted up within a cordon of guards, accompanied by the runner Shlook just sent. "Lord General!" Shlook and Sigg chorused.

"Good day to you both," Halik replied, gazing at the forming battle, his crest half raised in . . . curiosity. "I am glad to see that our erstwhile allies chose to warn you as well," he said.

"We were just wondering if they came to *you*," Shlook informed his commander. "Apparently so. Most obliging of them."

"Actually, they did not, but they came to General Niwa several hours ago. Interestingly, he immediately roused his division and marched toward a place in the riverbed south of the meadow"—Halik pointed—"and sent word to me."

He paused, seemingly baffled. "He also sent a personal message from Colonel Svec." Halik's eyes were wide when he looked back at Shlook. "Included were the usual words of insult, so I know that it was genuine, but it proceeded to assure me that Shighat will be 'served up to us' this day, if we can refrain from defeating this attack so quickly that we send the, ah, similar insulting words that must apply to our enemy, 'running for his life again' before they—and I assume Svec must mean his and Enaak's cavalry—are 'ready.' I have no idea what he meant by any of that, nor am I sure that he wanted me to be certain. I suppose he harbors a concern that we might capitalize on some vulnerability of *theirs* if we knew exactly what they meant to do." He huffed frustration. "Cooperating with enemies can be *so* tiresome! But Niwa is convinced that we will know when they are ready, and our response will be obvious." He shook his head. "Such annoying, enigmatic creatures! But the point, I suppose, is that we must allow Shighat to believe his attack here is succeeding, or is likely to with a greater push." He measured Shlook's reaction. "That means, while everything else *is* coming up, I must hold it back from your support so we do not destroy the illusion we must create. Your division will suffer sorely, I fear. Hopefully, not for long. Another runner just informed me that Niwa is almost in place."

Shlook opened his mouth to speak, possibly to object, then closed it. Whatever happened that day, his pride in his division would surely grow. He and Halik, followed by Sigg and their respective staffs, began to pace, staring at the battle at the shield wall. Guards protected them from crossbows as best they could, their shields soon festooned with dark-feathered bolts. Whether the group was deliberately targeted or not, guards occasionally fell, mostly victims of musket balls that respected no Grik shield. But Halik and his party kept moving slowly, their unspoken agreement being to stand behind the entire line at some point in the fight, so their warriors might at least sense their presence, know they were there. And they watched. They'd seen it all so often now: the rabid roaring, frantic hacking, the shrewd stab through an unprotected gap. Blood splashed and spritzed everything near the line, and coils of intestines spilled on the ground, churned in the dust, making a gruesome red mud. Shields banged together and pounded enemies in the snout. Warriors lost their weapons and reverted to the ones they were born with, using claws and slashing teeth. They were usually quickly slain, without the extra reach a sword or spear afforded them. Of course, there were also archers and musketeers on both sides, who killed beyond the reach of any handheld weapon with a startling, impersonal ease. Now and then, the shield wall briefly parted and a gun rolled into the gap, spewing canister with a great, smoky thunderclap that shredded dozens and felled scores.

They could have closed their eyes and seen it all just as well, smeared across their memories of a hundred fights. This was different, though, in one specific sense: one way or another, even as more of Shighat's warriors stampeded to join what they must've believed was a fine chance to eliminate the annoyance that had nagged them all the way up from the valley below, Halik and Shlook both knew they were going to win. And their warriors, now engaged, clearly believed it too. It was a bitter, costly struggle, but they were holding. And just as their leaders had confidence in them, they had equal confidence that General Halik would soon "do" something . . . interesting, with the *four* other divisions not yet in the fight.

"Second Division is fighting superbly," Halik shouted at Shlook.

Shlook straightened and almost visibly puffed out his sides. "Yes, Lord General. But it grows weary. The line grows thin."

"It can persevere awhile longer yet. The heap of enemy dead makes it difficult for Shighat's warriors to reach the shields. There is some respite in that, I think."

"I agree. But I do wish that . . . whatever is meant to happen, will happen soon. And I hope it will be worth it," he added with a tone of distress.

Halik looked at Shlook. His friend. "General," he said, "I remain unsure what our former enemy means to do, but I do believe Enaak and Svec have proven they can be trusted. As least insofar as our current cooperation is concerned." He took a long breath. "And General Niwa trusts them. That, and my understanding of the phrase 'served up,' makes me confident that not only will we destroy this force completely today, but their plan likely includes furnishing us with Regent Consort Shighat himself, in some way. Remember, they have proven to be amazingly competent scouts, and likely know exactly where he is." He looked back at the battle just as a low, rolling *boom* sounded, echoing down from the far side of the long, climbing meadow. It went on for a long moment, each report distinctly spaced.

"I counted twenty cannon shots!" Sigg cried.

"Twenty-three," Halik corrected. "Shighat still has some artillery, but has not been able to use it. I doubt they could fire with such precision in any case. The Allied cavalry has four batteries of light guns, six guns per battery. Perhaps one is damaged, or they reserve it for something else, but I do not think the number is coincidental." He turned to face Shlook. "I believe we, and General Niwa, now know 'when.' Colonels Enaak and Svec must have worked around beyond the enemy, and doubtless hold a commanding position, blocking their escape from the ground ahead. Captain Sigg? Have Generals Ugla and Yikkit bring up their divisions at the trot. They will deploy from columns into files behind Second Division. As soon as General Niwa makes the flank attack I expect, the First and Sixth will pass through the Second, and sweep all before them. General Shlook? You will follow with the Fifth, keeping your Second Division as a reserve." His crest rose in satisfaction. "My *friends*," he said, stressing the word, "we made this army, our very *selves*, from nothing. We have suffered countless hardships, betrayals, and defeats." His eyes narrowed. "We have also benefited from strange, unexpected mercies, on occasion. But without those things, and the wisdoms they taught us, we would none of us be here upon this plain of decision. Of destiny. One more great battle, my friends, and we—this army—could be the masters of all Persia before the night comes again."

"You took *prisoners*, General Halik," Colonel Enaak observed as he reined his me-naak to a stop in front of Halik, Niwa, Shlook, and Yikkit. General Ugla had been wounded in the fighting, but the healers—charged with actual healing now—said he would recover. The others had been waiting for Enaak, and the full company of the 5th that now deployed around them all in the center of the meadow where the last, fiercest fighting had taken place. With very strict instructions, no other Grik approached. Ironically, Svec and Enaak's cavalry had been quite active at the end of the battle after all. In addition to bottling up the primary escape route, they'd swiftly moved their artillery and engaged Shighat's panicking swarms from carbine range to help herd them to their destruction. That they had, essentially, fought at Halik's side to achieve the victory wasn't lost on any of them, and their feelings about that were . . . complex.

The high mountains to the west were clawing at the sun and the air was cooling fast. Fires were sprouting here and there, the smoke joining the evening haze that had begun to form. "I guess you're going to eat them," Enaak accused lightly. "Stop that, Aasi!" he scolded his mount, which was snuffling a Grik's head that had been impaled on a spear in front of the Grik delegation. "It's not polite to eat in front of people—or lizards!"

Halik spoke, and Niwa translated. "Your animal might grow ill if it ate that; it is Shighat's head."

"Really?" Enaak looked closer. It could've been any Grik's head, for all he knew. He'd never seen Shighat and could barely tell any Grik apart, for that matter. Halik was easy because he was just, well, big. Other than things like that, they all looked the same.

"And we did take prisoners," Niwa confirmed for Halik, nodding at him. "They might eat some," he confessed. "But not all." He cocked his head to the side. "It seems no one ever thought to offer surrender to Grik warriors that were in a real 'jam,' as our American friends might say. It appears that, when properly motivated, they can surrender after all. Actually, it's more like joining a stronger, rival swarm or pack, but the result is the same."

Enaak blinked and his tail swished behind him. "You don't say? We don't get much news," he said. "It might've happened before. Geerki kind of surrendered, and the last word we got was that some civilian Grik may have sort of surrendered at Grik City. I'm not sure about that. Interesting, though." For a long moment, they all just stared at one another, the only sound the creak of leather and the moans of wounded Grik. Finally, Halik spoke, and Niwa interpreted for him.

"General Halik wishes to . . . thank you, Colonel Enaak, and Colonel Svec as well. He is very much aware of what you and your people did for his army this day."

Enaak blinked a very complex expression that Niwa couldn't catch. He hadn't spent enough time around Lemurians to learn much beyond the basics. "Okay," Enaak said curtly. "Tell that to the eleven troopers I lost, fighting *with* Grik at my orders. *Don't* tell that to Svec. He lost twenty, and he's mad as hell at me right now for talking him into this." He waved. "He's gone off, chasing Grik that got away, on his own hook. I couldn't have stopped him if I wanted to." He looked hard at Halik, his wide eyes bright in the last rays of the sun. "I damn sure never thought we'd be fighting on the same side," he almost whispered. Then he shook his head. "I wonder if they'll can me for it. Doesn't matter. My guys died fighting Grik. If you'd lost, we'd have had to fight the same ones anyway. Glad to help, I guess. Better the Grik you know than one you don't." He leaned forward in his saddle. "The question is, what are you going to do now?"

Halik spoke to Niwa for quite a while, and when he finished, Niwa looked at Enaak with a strange expression. "We may have to meet again, when we can write things down," he said. "But for the moment, ah, 'Lord Regent General Halik' desires that I tell you this: the Gharrichk'k Empire, as it is, is doomed, whether you destroy it or not. Whether that doom will even come in our lifetimes, no one can say. The Empire is vast and will not die easily. But even as you flay it from without, it is dying from the inside as he"—Niwa looked at Yikkit—"and others recognize what their race can become if *they* will allow it." Niwa raised his eyebrows at Enaak. "This is Halik's regency now, from here to Arabia. There will be more fighting as the army nears the populated regions, no doubt, but there can be little left to stand against us. The conquest of Persia *will* occur, and the entire regency shall remain at peace with the Grand Alliance, as long as it remains at peace with us."

Enaak's eyes had grown ever wider while Niwa spoke. "Halik knows what a *treaty* is?"

"I have explained it to him. But he already understood the concept of agreements between warring powers, as you may recall. He will honor the treaty I described, and I will write the particulars myself."

"Write all you want," Enaak said incredulously. "*I* can't sign anything like *that*!" But instead of turning and bolting off like Niwa half expected, he merely sat scratching the fur under his chin. "But I'll tell you what," he said at last. "If he really means it, I'll take it to somebody who *can* sign it—along with my opinion that it sounds . . . pretty good."

CHAPTER 22

Above the Zambezi River
October 11, 1944

A raw dawn found Lieutenant Commander Mark Leedom and the aircrew of his "borrowed" PB-5D bundled gratefully in their peacoats against the high, sharp air. Moments before, as a step in what seemed a fairly momentous undertaking in Mark's opinion, they'd crossed the dingy fan of sediment streaming from the Zambezi river delta into the Go Away Strait, five thousand feet below. Against all expectations, this Zambezi, on this world, had a well-defined entrance, more like the mighty Mississippi than the countless mazes of rivulets, mangrove swamps, and flooded lowlands it "should" have had. That hadn't surprised Mark Leedom. Theirs wasn't the first reconnaissance to reach this far. They were the first to have a plane with sufficient range to probe more than just a few miles inland, however. And that was their mission: to follow the Zambezi as far as their fuel would allow, in hopes of discovering where the Grik were marshaling whatever fleet they must be preparing to carry their armies back across the strait. So far, it had eluded them, but they knew it had to exist. Even the "civilian" Grik prisoners taken at Grik City seemed to confirm it.

Mark snorted, not nearly loud enough to be heard over

the four droning engines above and behind, but he still earned a questioning look from his Lemurian copilot, Lieutenant Paraal-Taas. Paraal was a brown-and-tan-striped 'Cat from B'mbaado who'd flown Hij Geerki down from Madras. That meant he'd—probably—cracked the record for the longest ever nonstop flight on this world. Mark smiled and shook his head, returning to his thoughts. *Not that the Grik prisoners have a helluva lot of information.* All that survived were "Hij," supposedly smarter than the Uul laborers they'd eaten before they finally surrendered. Geerki was in charge of them and now used them as laborers themselves. Mark had actually been surprised by how smoothly that transition went. *Of course, any one of them would've obediently cut his own throat if a superior told him to. If they put such little value on their own lives, I guess they wouldn't gripe much over a little extra work, now, would they?*

Still, everyone knew there were "smart" Grik, but these, Hij or not, knew virtually nothing of the Grik Empire past their shore. They had no idea how big it was, or even vaguely how many inhabited it. A few knew the names of the other two, now abandoned, cities on Madagascar: Ajanga, just a short distance down the west coast, and Ghassgha, a little farther south. That was only because there'd been occasional commerce back and forth, and some had made the perilous trek through the predator-rich jungle between them from time to time. Otherwise, they'd been so completely absorbed in their slavish, almost ant-like lives of servitude to their Celestial Mother, it had apparently never even occurred to them to wonder about the world beyond the Celestial City. But they did agree that the Allies hadn't destroyed a tithe of the ships they'd seen coming and going at their port before the battles that wrested it away.

It's possible, Mark imagined, glancing down at the clustered, adobe-like warrens constituting numerous small villages bordering the mouth of the river, *that they counted every ship they ever saw, not understanding that ships don't last forever. Even if they just counted how many might've passed through on their way to destruction in other battles, it could've been a lot.* He changed hands on the plane's control stick and scratched his brow. *But none were ever built at Grik City. They all came from somewhere else.* Captured charts aboard half-sunken ships in the harbor had revealed a few details about continental harbors and coastal population concentrations. Even a few shipyards—vast, nightmarish hives of clear-cut timber and ghastly swarms of laborers—had been discovered. Those had been systematically firebombed by marauding Nancys off *Salissa*, *Arracca*, or raiding AVDs. But even as large as those yards were, they couldn't have made all the ships the Allies had already sunk in this war by themselves, not to mention all the machinery, guns, and armor they'd required. *There have to be other places.*

Doubtless, more shipyards and industrial centers still operated in the north, near where Zanzibar ought to be, and beyond. The Allies simply didn't have the capacity to explore or raid that far from Madagascar *or* Madras. They could keep close watch in that direction, though, and the possible existence of shipyards and harbors there was the main reason TF-Alden was keeping its distance from the coast on its way down. But that region would have to wait. Particularly since every single Hij prisoner had heard of *one* place on the African Continent, virtually assured to be a major hub of Grik industry and war-making potential. In most cases, it was the only city name familiar to them at all, beyond their own, and each knew of and revered Sofesshk.

From what they'd gathered, Sofesshk was the most ancient Grik city and it surrounded their holiest shrine, a structure much like the huge, granite, cowflop-shaped Celestial Palace that rose like a dark mountain in the middle of Grik City. There was even reason to believe Sofesshk actually surpassed the Celestial City in size and population. It was the cradle of their civilization, such as it was, and the birthplace of the Celestial Bloodline that had ruled them since the beginning of time. None of the prisoners knew why their Giver of Life had moved her throne to Madagascar; such was beyond their ability or desire to understand. She could do whatever she pleased. But Sofesshk still existed and had remained the heart, if not the capital, of their empire for thousands of years.

Geerki had roughly translated an old saying that went, essentially, "All life comes from the Celestial Mother, but all things come from Sofesshk." The allusion certainly supported the theory that Sofesshk had, at least at one time, been the center of Grik industry. Since all of Geerki's charges agreed that had the Giver of Life escaped her doom, she would've gone straight to Sofesshk to rule as her ancestors had, chances were, nothing had changed. And the captured charts showed what they *thought* must be Sofesshk, approximately a hundred and fifty miles up the Zambezi River. Hij Geerki hadn't been positive since Hij mariners, though careful draftsmen and obviously more intelligent than the average Hij, were notoriously paranoid about recording place-names. *They* knew the names of the symbols on their charts, after all. Why write them down?

It had always been a supreme frustration to the Allies that, try as they might, they'd never secured a Grik ship captain—or general, for that matter, if you didn't count Orochi Niwa—alive. *Sure,* Mark thought, *we've gotten our hands on a few who weren't exactly dead. They'd been conked out, or trapped under stuff, or something had kept them from knocking themselves off. But they always managed to get the job done, sooner or later. They'd jump in the water, chew off an arm and bleed to death, or just . . . die, somehow.* But their charts sometimes remained, and the drawings showed a major city on both sides of the Zambezi, just downstream from a very large lake that hadn't been on *Walker*'s meager chart of the region, or even in a moldy old atlas aboard *Santa Catalina.* It seemed the perfect place to hide a major industrial center—and a fleet.

Mark Leedom looked at the 'Cat beside him, and then contemplated the rest of his crew. Captain Enrico Galay had been a Philippine Scout during the old war. Now he was in Chack and Risa's 1st Allied Raider Brigade. He came because, for the first time, if they saw something worth expending some of their very limited supply of large-format film, they were going to take pictures. A teenage Galay had worked with a photographer for the English-language *Manila Times,* and photography had been an interrupted passion. He'd been a natural to entrust with the Graflex Speed Graphic, which had come to this world with *Mahan*'s dead surgeon. It was the only surviving large-format camera they had, and Galay already knew how to use it. There were a lot of other cameras, brought by *Walker*'s, *Mahan*'s, and S-19's crews, but few still worked and all were cheap, compact, 35- or 46-mm specimens preferred by sailors, and there was little film for any of them. Besides, until they came up with a better way of transferring images than the salt-paper process they'd reinvented in Baalkpan, the larger format gave more detail for reconnaissance purposes when printed on contact—detail that could be enlarged by Lemurian artists.

Leftenant Doocy Meek, the liaison from the Republic of Real People, had come as an observer for his kaiser, Nig-Taak, despite Captain Reddy's objection. He'd countered that he had orders, and now that Matt had direct communication with the Republic, he wasn't really essential anymore. Leedom thought that was kind of dumb, but he'd used a similar excuse when his XO, Lieutenant Araa-Faan, said he—as Grik City's Commander of Flight Operations (COFO)—didn't have any business making the trip either. His argument that she could run flight ops as well as he was true, but saying he was better suited than she for this mission was probably stretching things. He'd based that solely on the fact that he had more hours in seaplanes, and he did, but only in Nancys. He had a grand total of *six* hours in PB-5s. *Shoot,* he thought humorously, *I've almost doubled that, just since we left Grik City! And Paraal can take over if we have to make a hairy landing.*

He didn't know the two 'Cats in the waist, whose main duties were to load and unload cargo, help with refueling, and—now—man the two .30-caliber machine guns there. Nor did he know the wireless operator, though the young 'Cat seemed enthusiastic about the trip. Lieutenant Paraal-Taas was the navigator as well as copilot, and Mark would be his own bombardier if they found a target worthy of the three two-hundred-pound bombs under each wing. Normally, the plane would carry a couple more crew, but the wireless operator could man the front top gun and Galay could certainly manage the one in back. There wasn't any point in risking more people than they had to.

Mark wasn't afraid—exactly—and he trusted the big flying boat. The D model, with its stacked radials, fixed wing floats, impressive fuel capacity, and defensive armament, was a major improvement over its predecessors in every respect: speed, range, payload, and reliability. The cockpit was even fairly comfortable with the pilot's wicker seat shifted all the way back. It was the first adjustable seat in any Allied aircraft, making it equally controllable by humans or Lemurians. But the added range the plane afforded them also quite literally allowed them to push irretrievably deeper into trouble than anyone had ever been in an aircraft on this world before. Mark was confident they'd be okay even if they lost an engine, especially now that they'd burned enough fuel to lighten the ship. They'd topped off at a hasty depot established on the southernmost of the Comoros Islands, but that was six hundred miles ago. Sadly, they couldn't feather the prop if an engine crapped out, but the D model was equipped with a cable brake to the shaft that would prevent it from windmilling and causing even worse drag than a still propeller. If they lost *two* engines, however, or anything else went wrong to force the big plane down, they might as well eat their pistols. Being the very first humans and Lemurians to find themselves on the ground in the middle of a continent at least largely dominated by hungry Grik wasn't the most pleasant thought to contemplate.

"Welcome to Africa!" shouted Doocy Meek over the roar of the engines and the swirl of wind whipping down from the gunner's position above. Mark had noticed before that the man's British accent had been interestingly colored by others over the years. He had thrust his head up between Mark's and Paraal's, and his white-streaked blond beard was split by a grin. "Plan to stay long?"

"Not any longer than we absolutely have to, this trip," Mark shouted back. "We're only here on business. I hope to come back when I can stay longer. See the sights."

Meek nodded southward. "My people're less than six hundred miles that way. They'll be coming as well, before long. We'll get together an' see all the sights in this sodding, dreary place."

"I look forward to it."

Captain Galay squeezed up alongside Meek. "I take it you didn't want any pictures from back there," he stated, referring to the villages they'd passed. "Looks like they've put up a few big guns where the river starts to narrow a little."

Leedom shook his head. "I saw 'em, but they haven't changed since Nancys off *Big Sal* scouted the coast. The cartographers have 'em pretty well plotted on the maps they're making at HQ. Don't waste film on stuff like that, and just draw pictures if you see more of the same." He turned slightly to look at Galay. "You've just got two more film packs. That's a total of eighteen pictures you can take. Orders were to take two shots of anything worthwhile because the developing process still has kinks."

Galay was nodding. "I know, and nobody out here has ever done it before. Have to follow the directions they sent. Good thing the process isn't much different from what I'm used to. I won't screw it up"—he grinned, his dark eyes sparkling—"as long as you get me back in one piece. But that just leaves nine shots, for all intents and purposes, if we stick exactly to orders."

Mark thought about it. "We'll see," he said at last. "If we start running into lots of important-looking things, we'll see. Just make sure you keep drawing pictures, to back you up."

"You bet, Commander. I'm heading back there now, with my pencil behind my ear. Just let me know in plenty of time to get the camera ready." Galay backed away, and then teetered toward the observation windows in the waist. Mark glanced aft and saw the 'Cats were staring down, making drawings of their own. Galay must have told them to do that, and it was a good idea.

"How did you get nabbed for this in the first place, Commander?" Meek asked him, genuinely curious. "Flying, I mean. Word is you began aboard the submersible that was lost at Second Madras."

Mark nodded. "Yep, I did. Here, anyway. I was a torpedoman, striking for . . . well, it doesn't matter." He grinned. "I guess I always wanted in the air, though. My first rating in the Navy was Airship Rigger, of all things, but the Navy had already done away with the big, rigid

jobs that made me sign up. Nothing but gasbags—blimps—
by then. So, this idiot buddy of mine talked me into subs.
Don't know why it never occurred to me to try to become
a naval aviator. It just didn't. Anyway, I learned to fly right
after Fred Reynolds, and here I am."

"A higher rank than he, if I'm not mistaken."

Mark shrugged. "His bad luck . . . and mine, I guess.
I'm a lot older, not that it matters, but until recently, we've
been flying—and losing pilots—on this side of the war a
lot more. I guess I've seen more heavy action than he has,
though I sure wouldn't trade it for what he's been through.
And maybe him being younger matters after all, the way
he and Kari-Faask just flew off on their crazy lark to God
knows where, on a hunch."

"Like we're doing now?" Meek asked innocently, but
Mark shook his head.

"Not the same at all. We know what we're looking for,
we've got a pretty good idea where it is, and we're going
to do our damnedest to get back!"

"Glad to hear it, Commander," Meek said, then with a
pat on Leedom's shoulder, he disappeared aft. Mark and
Paraal grinned at each other and flew on.

For the next hour or so, the river squirmed and twisted
lazily beneath them, its width averaging about a third of a
mile. They saw few dwellings of any sort for quite a while,
no doubt because it was clear that the land often flooded.
There were great herds of beasts, however, too distant to
easily describe, apparently roaming freely among the
clumps of forest that topped low mounds of higher ground.
Huge swarms of flying things, also too low and indistinct
to identify, surged across the landscape like fast, dark
clouds. *In that sense,* Leedom supposed, *this place is still
kind of like I always imagined Africa.* He'd known it was
a continent of contrasts, just like any other. There were
jungles and deserts, certainly, but he'd always pictured the
broad savannas, teeming with game.

"Co-maander," said Paraal suddenly, pointing forward.
Mark looked. Instead of narrowing, as they'd expected,
the river was broadening out once more. *That doesn't make
much sense,* he thought. *Sure, this world isn't exactly like*

*the one we left behind—the sea level's lower, for one thing.
There probably really is at least a little "ice age," just like
Courtney Bradford says.* That was fairly obvious, considering the relative temperatures everywhere but in the tropical
zone. It was probably *hotter* than they remembered at the
equator, but colder everywhere else. *But with lower sea
levels, the Zambezi ought to be smaller. . . . Shouldn't it?*
He thought about that. *Unless a wetter inland climate
poured enough rain upstream over the eons to dig the river
deeper. Or maybe the Grik keep it dredged.* That was a
disturbing thought.

He gradually noticed something else as they flew. There
were habitations along the riverside again, growing larger,
more congested. There were ships now too. Most were
anchored close to shore, but some were tied to docks along
the south side of the river, alongside large warehouses like
they'd seen at Grik City. A few ships were underway, sailing westward, mostly. Then Mark saw the first steamer. It
was a double-ended side-wheeler unlike any Grik ship
he'd seen before, chuffing across the river from south to
north. Progressively more docked steamers appeared, and
at least a few were the massive ironclad dreadnaughts
they'd grown so familiar with, but there weren't very many
of those. Certainly not enough to constitute an invasion
fleet bound for Madagascar. He frowned.

"Look ahead there!" Paraal said, pointing.

"We've found a city, all right—a real one," Mark said
with a slight edge. They had indeed. Abruptly growing
out of a brownish morning haze, and stretching a great
distance, mostly to the south, sprawled a city far larger
than Grik City itself. As they passed the outskirts over
the city proper, Mark began to wonder how many Grik
were down there. *Tens of thousands, at least,* he imagined.
*Maybe hundreds of thousands—all looking up at us by
now, at the strange noise in the sky. The big, fat, loud bird.
Probably wondering what it tastes like.* The thought gave
him the creeps.

"Whoa! What's that?" he asked, banking slightly toward
the north side of the river. The city looked . . . different
there, and a broad tributary of the river abruptly veered

north as well. There was also something else, something familiar. "Are you drawing all this?" he shouted back behind him.

"Sure!" Galay replied. "I don't know if anybody will ever know *what* I drew, though. Even me. It's kind of bumpy and shaky in this thing for making masterpieces. Any pictures yet?"

"Not yet, but pretty quick. Better get the camera ready."

It was soon apparent that the architecture on the north side of the river was quite different from any they'd ever associated with the Grik. There was an almost geometric angularity, not only to the structures themselves, but to the way they were arranged. Real streets, probably paved in stone, or possibly brick, crisscrossed one another just as they would have in any modern, well-planned urban area. Most of the buildings appeared to be constructed of stone or brick as well, without the dingy, muddy look Mark had grown accustomed to. There were the ubiquitous adobe structures, true, but even those looked more . . . refined, better finished. And there was genuine ornamentation! Granted, most seemed to consist of awnings, flags, and banners, with dark "Grik red" predominating, but even that was unusual for anything other than Grik ships. This high, it was hard to tell, but there even seemed to be a little architectural decoration on some of the buildings. No columns or domes, nothing like that, but just . . . superfluous things, like ledges and protrusions. *Maybe like gargoyles,* Leedom fancied. The comparison to a "modern" city struck him as particularly weird, however, since the part on the north side of the Zambezi also practically radiated an impression of profound antiquity.

The rigid angularity was subtly eroded, and despite the dense habitation evidenced by the throngs of Grik they now saw, filling the streets and looking up, there were crumbling ruins here and there. Most telling was the single massive structure that quickly dominated their attention. Confirming their conviction beyond any doubt that this was, indeed, Sofesshk was a great monolithic structure rising in the center of what Leedom had already dubbed "Old Sofesshk" in his mind. Like a mountainous, round-topped, soft-cornered pyramid, it did indeed resemble a slightly smaller version of the Celestial Palace in Grik City on Madagascar, down to the very color of the stone it was constructed with. This "Cowflop" looked so ancient, however, that Leedom had to wonder if the corners, even the top, had once been sharp. Given the distinct geometry of the city around it, he suspected they might have been. Hij Geerki had told him his translation for the structure, and Mark tried to remember what he'd said. *Oh yeah, the "Palace of Vanished Gods," or something like that.* He snorted. *No wonder their gods took off, if the Grik had them living in a giant cow patty.*

"You can take pictures now, Captain Galay," he said. "Just a few, though, and try to get as much of the city in each one as you can. I'll circle the Cowflop so you can get different angles, then we'll head across the river. Save most of your film for when we get to that lake beyond the city. We can always take more pictures on the way back." He *hoped* they could, at any rate. So far, nobody had shot anything at them, but he doubted that had as much to do with capability as surprise.

He finished his wide orbit of Old Sofesshk while Galay worked his camera, then flew across the river, above "New Sofesshk." The contrast was striking. The structures there were typical Grik, like really crude pueblos, stacked haphazardly all around and on top of one another. And they stretched for miles. Considering how many Grik had inhabited Grik City, he reluctantly revised his previous estimate upward exponentially. He now suspected there were upward of a million of the damn lizards in Sofesshk. Not all would be warriors, maybe not even most . . . but there'd be a lot.

"I took four pictures," Galay reported from aft, his normally exuberant voice somewhat subdued. "Eight total, now. You think I should get more?"

"No. That's plenty. We're heading west, toward the lake." Leedom eyed the wide tributary leading north, but decided against following it yet. Maybe on the way back. They *knew* there was a lake to the west.

The confluence of the rivers—and they soon realized there was yet *another* tributary, angling northwest—created a virtual lake all by themselves. And they finally saw, if not actual shipyards, at least heavy industrial and repair facilities on the outskirts of the city. Smoke streamed from tall, lumpy towers more like crayfish chimneys than proper smokestacks, rearing high alongside numerous large, squat structures. More of the massive dreadnaughts and cruisers were moored nearby, amid clusters of tall, gangly cranes. Leedom wasn't ready to go lower for a better look, but the ships looked different from others they'd seen. Paraal glassed them with his Imperial telescope and confirmed they were "weird," but couldn't say how. They'd get a closer look later.

The first response to their presence came in the form of a gaggle of zeppelins, rising from a broad field southwest of the factories. Probably more than a dozen were beating their way into the sky. Paraal pointed them out.

"They're no threat," Leedom said. "Vulnerable as they are coming up, we could probably shoot them all down by ourselves. But that's not our job today. Not yet," he added. Then he frowned, doubting this could possibly be the source for all the zeps that came at Grik City every night. It was just too far, and they hadn't seen a field big enough to gather them all together. *But maybe they build them here*? "Take two pictures back toward that industrial park and zep strip, Captain," he hollered back. That would leave them just eight shots, Mark realized uneasily. Doocy Meek wedged himself between him and Paraal once again. His earlier grin was gone.

"I don't like the look of it," Meek shouted. "I saw Grik City before it was destroyed, and it was intimidating enough." He pointed his thumb back over his shoulder. "But there's heavy industry back there, on a scale—if not sophistication—similar to that found in a few Republic cities. Close to what's been described to me of Baalkpan. I never dreamed the bloody *lizards* could have a city that big, and it can't be the only one, can it?"

Leedom looked at him, concerned. Not for Meek, but what he'd tell his kaiser. "Getting cold feet?"

Meek shook his head. "Not in the least. I'm convinced that the Grik menace will only grow and must be destroyed. But Kaiser Nig-Taak and General Marcus Kim need to know that, whatever they estimated they'd face when they start their show, they'd better double it."

"Coming from you, that might help," Leedom replied seriously. "One of Bekiaa's biggest frustrations is that your people just don't seem to get how many Grik there are, or what it'll be like fighting them." Major Bekiaa-Sab-At was doing all she could to prepare the Republic's Legions for what they'd face. She'd reported that the Republic was—finally—"all in," but retained deep reservations about what they expected that to entail. "And I wouldn't worry as much about their industry as I would about how many warriors they can crank out." He jerked his head aft, indicating the zeppelins and dreadnaughts. "If that's the best they can do, build big-assed targets like those back there, I figure we've still got the edge."

Very shortly after Leedom made that statement, less than thirty minutes, in fact, he was forced to consider the possibility he was wrong. Very abruptly, the river suddenly fattened and became the lake they'd been told to expect.

"There's where they keepin' all their cruisers," Paraal said darkly, and at a glance, there appeared to be more than thirty of the things, moored near the northern and southern shores. Several dreadnaughts were there as well, which made the total number that they'd seen more than a dozen. Just as ominous, there were great, long sheds, hundreds of feet long, extending out over the water along the shoreline. Leedom had no idea what they covered, but they were similar to the "wet" Nancy hangars near Kaufman Field, north of Baalkpan. Except Nancy sheds were only about thirty feet wide. These would accommodate something a hundred and fifty to two hundred feet long.

"Damn," he murmured, remembering the bombs under his wings. He'd been awful tempted to drop them on the palace at Sofesshk, but knew they wouldn't have any more effect than Grik bombs dropped on the Cowflop back at Grik City. And now . . . his six bombs seemed hopelessly inadequate for the target-rich environment they'd discovered. There were the warships, obviously, but there was also whatever the enemy protected beneath the sheds. Added to that were tents, *real* tents, like a dusty white sea of choppy, wedge-shaped waves, utterly uncountable, stretching as far as the eye could see. And closer in were hundreds of zeppelins, moored across the plain surrounding the wide, deep lake.

"Holy smoke," Leedom said. Just then a thin streamer of white smoke rose among the tents, followed quickly by a score or more just like it.

"Rockets!" Paraal warned. Leedom nodded, but wasn't too worried. They were at six thousand feet. He'd examined the rockets captured at Grik City, and Tikker told him the ones he ran into over the Seychelles would barely reach five thousand. Those had been provided with contact fuses, and had to hit you to hurt you. They'd been more of a menace to troops and equipment on the ground when they inevitably fell to earth. These kept rising, however, and even though they all missed, they shot up *past* the plane. Meek had jumped up to look out the top gunner's position and suddenly flinched back. "Gawd blimey!" he shouted. "They bloody *went off*!"

"What?" Leedom demanded, craning his head around.

"About a hundred feet above us!" Meek confirmed, stuffing himself back between the pilots. "An' look there! More of 'em!"

Leedom couldn't count how many white towers of smoke were rising in their path. Instinctively, he pushed the stick forward.

"New fuses!" Galay bellowed behind them. "They've got *time* fuses now, just like we do, that set 'em off at whatever altitude they pick!"

Leedom couldn't believe it—but it had to be true. His subconscious mind had figured it out first, as a matter of fact. That's why he put the plane into a dive. They heard the explosions this time: a staccato bursting of dozens of small warheads going off—he looked up—amazingly well concentrated around where they would've been if he hadn't evaded. "Get your pictures now, Captain!" he shouted. "Out the starboard side. I'm turning left." He looked at Paraal—just as several streamers rose in front of them and detonated with white puffs of smoke. An instant later, the plane was hammered by a terrible clatter like a pile of boards dropping on the ground.

"Number four engine's hit!" Paraal cried, staring out and up to the right.

"Hey! We're smoking!" Galay called from behind.

"Cut fuel and power to number four," Leedom shouted at his copilot, reaching up to cut the throttle. "Hit the brake!"

Paraal twisted the knob on the appropriate fuel line and flipped one of the knife switches beside his knee. The plane started bucking as the engine coughed and died, then started crabbing to the right. Paraal pushed one of two long levers forward and locked it into place. The prop stopped spinning. Mark advanced the throttle on number three and pushed on his rudder pedal. More rockets burst, above them again, mostly, but a few more of what they used for shrapnel struck the plane.

"We gotta lose our bombs," Leedom ground out, glancing below. They were down to about four thousand feet and a dreadnaught was directly in line, bow on. Good enough. He would've liked to drop at least one bomb on the sheds, and maybe see what was under them, but that was pointless now. And all his bombs might kill a couple hundred Grik in their tents, but what was a couple hundred? The zeppelins were tempting targets, but as many as there were, they were too far apart to set more than a few alight. He pushed the suddenly very annoyed stick forward again with his right hand, caressing all six bomb-release levers with his left. At twenty-five hundred feet, the massive dreadnaught nearly filled his windscreen when he started dropping bombs—port, starboard, port, starboard . . . then he stopped. The last two would clearly miss—and the sheds were coming up. A group of rockets burst alongside, on the right again, and he felt something in the rudder. Without a word, Paraal grasped his right arm with his left hand and it came away bloody. The sheds were just ahead. Staring through the crude gun sight in front of the windscreen, Mark lined up on the post mounted off center near the nose. But now he needed three hands! He gave up on the machine gun—and dropped his bombs at eighteen hundred feet.

He pulled up and to the left, out over the zeppelins. Surely even Grik wouldn't shoot off rockets over *them*. They would and did, but the big plane was too low and fast now for accurate rocket fire, and nothing else even came close. The plane was balky, draggy, and felt like he was driving a big car in thick mud. But finally, as they passed beyond the zeppelin field and he began to climb once more, the rockets ceased entirely.

"What now?" Paraal asked, his voice strained.

Leedom felt strained as well. "Did you get pictures of *that*?" he roared at Galay instead of answering.

"Ah, yeah. Mostly. I think the last shot was of my feet, but the two before it are probably no good either. I . . . sort of dropped the camera and cracked the lens. But what I got should be good enough. And if it isn't? I figure we can draw it. None of us are likely to forget that mousetrap for a while!"

"You didn't happen to see what was under those sheds, did you?"

"No. But we hit that Grik heavy pretty hard. At least two bombs. I can still see her burning."

Leedom looked back at Galay as Meek joined them again. He wasn't about to go back for another look at the sheds. "You okay?" he asked.

"Sure."

"Mr. Meek, would you have a look at Lieutenant Pa-raal's arm?"

"Of course. I'm as curious as he was what you plan on doin' now, though. I rather doubt you intend to fly back over Sofesshk."

"No. We've lost our one engine," he said, oblivious to the fact he hadn't discussed his earlier thoughts with the rest of the crew. "After you make sure the lieutenant won't bleed to death, would you please ask the wireless operator to send what we saw and what happened, as well as a request for a ship, *any* ship, to head our way if he can. We might need a pickup if we're losing fuel. But we won't see Sofesshk again, this trip. We'll swing south, around the city, and then cross the river heading northeast. Time to get the hell out of here."

CHAPTER 23

Grik Sofesshk
The Palace of Vanished Gods

"It would seem that the enemy has found us at last," said Lord Regent Champion Esshk, Guardian of the Celestial Bloodline, and First General of All the Grik. His tone was one of anger, leavened with bleak resignation. He stood on the slab-paved entrance walkway to the great, arched ground-level entrance to the Palace of Vanished Gods—*his* palace now, in a sense—looking at the sky to the west where the enormous blue plane had gone. Like nearly everyone in Sofesshk, no doubt, on both sides of the river, he'd raced outside to see what was causing the frightening thunder in the sky. Unlike most, however, he'd immediately suspected—and then known—what it was, remembering the great "PBY" flying boat the enemy used to help break the Invincible Swarm at the place they called "Baalkpan." This thing appeared to be almost as large and had even more engines.

He began to pace, rapidly clacking the claws on his hands and practically hissing with frustration. His guards bolted out of his way as he swept the massive, age-worn paving stones with his whipping, feathery tail and long Imperial Red cape. It was disconcerting enough that his enemy—former prey!—could make things like that, but even more so that it should pass overhead with impunity.

They'd devised defenses against such incursions, but he hadn't really expected to need them. Certainly not so soon! The enemy was weak and battered after the recent battles, and Esshk's campaign of misdirection had seemed to be succeeding. He'd never dreamed the enemy—*Captain Reddy!*—had the wherewithal, or even the inclination, to continue his searches just yet. And Esshk's own complacency had undoubtedly fed that of his generals commanding the rocket batteries around the city.

He finally released the building, furious hiss he'd been restraining and turned to face his one confidant in all the world. The Chooser, now "Lord Chooser of All the Ghaarrichk'k," was puffing slightly from his effort to keep up with his pacing. He was shorter, certainly poorly exercised, and garishly dressed beyond all reason. His cape wasn't as long as Esshk's, but was much more ornate. Tiny gilded bones were woven directly into the dark fabric, and they glittered as it moved. More gilded bones dangled and clattered from necklaces and other . . . suspensions about his person, including the ornate dagger he wore in a studded white baldric. His claws were painted red, and the downy fur around his eyes and snout had been colored to hide the white encroaching there. He'd even begun weaving the dark crest that stood up on his head into a rigid fan he couldn't lay back if he wanted to. Esshk generally disapproved of such things, but the Chooser was prone to fits of . . . unease, and his crest always betrayed them. Under the circumstances, what he'd done was probably for the best.

And Esshk needed him, not only for his advice, but for the forbidding authority the Lord Chooser brought to their new regime. Choosers, as a class of Hij, were not only the keepers of ancient wisdoms, rites of succession, and elevation, but were the ultimate arbiters of life and death. It had always been they who determined, based on mysterious criteria guarded by their order, which hatchlings would be elevated to the status of Hij, which would remain Uul, and which would be raised as the most abject laborer Uul—available for the cookpots at any time—and which could simply be eaten at birth. It had been this chooser, attendant upon the Celestial Mother herself, who'd reluctantly blessed a suspension of the cullings for the duration of the current emergency so sufficient armies could be bred to meet it. The experiments that followed—largely aided by General of the Sea Hisashi Kurokawa, Esshk had to admit—not only resulted in more warriors than had ever existed before but, with the new training and indoctrination Kurokawa introduced, far *better* warriors. With that superiority, however, came great advantage and equally great risk. Both stemmed from a capability for independent thought that had, until recently, been reserved entirely to the Hij. That capacity made bad warriors worse, but it was more than balanced by making good warriors better. The real danger lay in the fact that it was now quite obvious to Esshk, at least, that the greatest "mystery" protected by the choosers was that there *was* no qualitative, observable difference between one hatchling and another. Their order had existed solely as a means of artificial population—and thought—control.

Absent that control, the "new army" Esshk had been nurturing (and reserving, for the most part) should be more similar to the armies of his enemies than to most other Grik forces elsewhere on the continent. They were better trained, more disciplined, better able to act on their own initiative (notwithstanding the lapse of Sofesshk's missile batteries), and—again, thanks to programs instituted by Kurokawa—almost instinctively more loyal to Esshk than to the new Celestial Mother they'd recently elevated. For now, for Esshk's current purposes, that was good. But similar programs had been initiated in at least two other regencies. He still controlled them, in the name of the Celestial Mother he protected, and they cooperated willingly enough. But what of General Halik? He still had no idea what had happened to his most promising protégé, or if he and his army still existed. The world had grown quite complicated indeed.

He glanced away from the Chooser, contemplating the western sky once more, as a backdrop for the teeming, *seething* city and its multitudes. Regardless of the skill and ingenuity of his race's greatest enemy, he couldn't really imagine defeat. One day, the war would end and the current emergency would pass. What then? As he'd long feared, it would be no simple thing to return his race to its proper path. In the meantime, the Chooser had endorsed and assisted the steps Esshk had taken to secure absolute power, in fact if not in name. In return, Esshk supported the legitimacy of the Chooser and his order. Their original purpose would be required again someday. And the Chooser had risen above a lifetime of laziness and court privilege to become Esshk's most discreet advisor and confidant, the necessities inspired by the way the world had turned finally forcing him to cultivate a latent but extraordinarily keen and conniving mind. That was something they both would need.

"Lord Regent Champion," the Chooser said tentatively. Esshk looked back at him.

"Yes?"

"They could have dropped bombs. I think I even *saw* bombs, suspended beneath the wings of that monstrosity."

"As did I, but they did not," Esshk assured, but his voice turned grim. "They will probably use them on the forces we gather at Lake Nalak." He jerked his head diagonally. "One craft, even such as that, can do little damage there. The greatest damage will come from what they will and have already seen. The full measure of surprise we had hoped to achieve has been lost. Only the timing and method of our attack can be kept from them now. We must look to ways of growing those assets."

"True," agreed the Chooser, "and any damage they might do to the swarm at Lake Nalak is insignificant . . . compared to what they might have done here, to us." He took a few paces himself. "Our race realizes it will be a great while before our new Celestial Mother is fit to lead." Both of them had already decided that would never happen. Henceforth, the Regent Champion—and the Celestial Mother's Chooser—would forever hold supreme authority behind the Celestial throne. That was how it had to be, but for as long as they could manage it, they must maintain the fiction that all would one day become as it had been for all of time. There was no reason either of them shouldn't live another twenty years or so. By then, few enough who remembered things any other way, or in a position to challenge the new order, would remain. "A warrior reaches fighting age in a year and a half. Your 'new' warriors are proficient in two. Their officers, even elevated from older, experienced warriors, need that long as well. But a female just achieving breeding age cannot be expected to choose which claw to clean her nostrils with in that time. We have five more years, perhaps a decade, to fully effect all the changes we have discussed, before the higher-ranking Hij might consider that our stewardship has lingered overlong. Until then," the Chooser continued, "you are recognized as the utmost authority. But for the first time in memory, that authority is dependent to some degree upon the submission of the Hij you rule. I . . . do not know what will happen if bombs fall upon Sofesshk."

"You fear *rebellion*?" Esshk demanded, red eyes wide and blinking.

"No, of course not. And the masses may react more with fury at those who dared such a thing than with dissatisfaction toward you for not preventing it. But *some* would be dissatisfied—just as Regent Ragak was."

"Now that the enemy knows where we are, I do not know how we can prevent a single bomb from falling on Sofesshk, regardless how effective our defenses might be. Our airships take grave losses, surely, but even the enemy cannot prevent us from bombing *them* at will."

"Then move the army here. If the bombings are severe, we may lose small numbers of it, but it is most loyal to you. It can effectively deal with any who may grow . . . dissatisfied."

Esshk considered. "Very well. The army can be embarked as easily here as at the lake, when the time comes to launch the Swarm. And camped in the open, it would take more losses to raids there than here, at any rate."

"Even better," the Chooser ventured, "would be to embark on it now. *Attack* now, before the enemy has time to gather against us."

Esshk snorted with renewed frustration. "We are not ready! The force we gather to strike the enemy from behind is only now beginning to deploy. It is too small and unsupported. The army you suggest moving here *can* do that, but it would not yet be a certain thing." He glared at the Chooser. "I *want* a certain thing! And I want the rest of our warriors that are yet to arrive from the south. The rains have hampered their movement." He began to pace again himself. "The cursed rains! They have slowed *everything*, from corralling, slaughtering, and drying provisions, to the construction of transports. Provisions!" He snorted, suddenly distracted. "What general ever had to concern himself with *preparing* provisions, beyond what was needed for a few days? Swarms of the past always gathered them as they advanced, or from the land or prey they conquered. But we, unable to count on the prey to provide them, must take them with us!"

With some effort, he stopped pacing and lowered his voice. "Our warships are almost complete. Their hulls were made before the rains, and they are fitting out now. And they will be better than any that Kurokawa's race ever gave us," he said proudly, accusingly, neglecting to add that the designs for the improvements they'd incorporated had been left behind by the Japanese when they bolted for Zanzibar. "But the transports! They are made almost entirely of green wood that we cannot cure or fit in the rain! Barely two-thirds of what we need are complete, and the shipmakers tell me that they will likely not last a year before they rot away."

"We will not need them for a year," the Chooser soothed.

Esshk glared at him, then waved angrily at the sky. "And the *one* day the sky is clear . . . !" That's when he noticed one of the zeppelins that had risen near the city was approaching the palace and he paused his rant. Motors revved and fluttered as the great airship, already descended to barely a hundred feet, crept toward them from downwind. Just short of the palace, which reared high above it now, the airship came to a stop and a line tumbled down from the forward gondola. An instant later, an air warrior snaked rapidly down the line until he touched the ground, then raced toward them. Esshk waved his guards back as they moved to stop the intruder, and the flier hurled himself to the paving stones at Esshk's feet.

"Lord Regent Champion!" he practically squealed.

"Report!" Esshk demanded, already recognizing that the air-warrior before him was one of the "superior" ones he was so proud of—and made him fear for the future.

"We tried to fly after the blue enemy. They was too fast to catch. We seen what they did, though."

"Well?"

The aviator swallowed and groveled more energetically. "They flyed west, and we seen rockets rise over Lake Nalak. They bursted, many, but then there was smoke rised up high. We turned to report here, but seen the fast blue enemy fly back east, south of Sofesshk. It go away."

Esshk took a long, deep breath. "You did well," he said. "And even better to report what you saw." Not many would have, he realized, and the contrast between the value and danger of initiative struck him once again. Better to encourage it, for now. "What is your ship?"

"*Pouncer*, Sire."

Esshk nodded, though the name meant nothing to him. Unlike naval squadrons, which were always organized in threes, airship squadrons were organized like the land forces: by groups of ten, within groups of a hundred named for their commander. An example would be "second of ten, eighth of Lashk's." Esshk didn't know air-warriors had begun naming their ships. *More initiative,* he thought. "Very well. You will be rewarded. Now return to your ship." The aviator dragged himself a short distance away, then jumped up and sprinted back for the line still dangling from the airship, which hovered somewhat lower now.

"So they did bomb something, after all. And escaped to tell what they saw."

Esshk whirled back to face the Chooser, and the shorter creature took a step back in the face of his fury. "We are *almost* ready. Perhaps they will bomb us, and I will follow your advice and move the army here. But they can do little to us in a month—and a month should give us the time we need. Then we will finish this 'Captain Reddy' and his Grand Alliance of prey animals once and for all!" He seemed about to continue, but stopped and gurgled something that sounded almost like laughter.

"What is it, Lord Regent Champion?" the Chooser ventured.

"It is only that, in the time until then, our 'ally' Kurokawa is poised to give them something more immediate than our presence and preparations here to think about.

We would not have moved until that occurred regardless. That it will take us slightly longer to move than I led Kurokawa to believe should allow *all* our enemies a little more time to rend one another."

"You planned that from the very beginning of your renewed contacts with the Jaaphs!" the Chooser guessed aloud, his rigid crest trembling with its effort to lie flat in admiration.

"Of course."

CHAPTER
24

West-Central Mada-gaas-gar
October 11, 1944

Every warrior of the Naa-Kaani Clan of the Shee-Ree followed the river west, paced by all the boats from their village, and more with each village that they passed. The boats were kind of beamy, shallow-draft dhows equipped with oars and single masts upon which high lizardbird wing–shaped sails could be raised. There still weren't enough boats to move everyone, so the warriors marched on shore while all the very young and very old went by water. Chack was serious about getting everyone out that they possibly could, and the boats would also prove useful if the warriors had to cross the river.

They were joined by groups of warriors from many clans, some quite distant from the river. Most were still Shee-Ree, or from allied clans, but the tellers of tales had ranged far enough, quickly enough, to bring 'Cats from clans that Kaam and Ror'at-Raal had never heard of. These represented every imaginable color and physique, but all were armed with the powerful bows the visitors had grown used to. Their clan names were so varied and even unpronounceable, to the humans at least, that it was difficult to keep track of them. Silva didn't even try. He simply referred to them as "the red ones, the white ones, the stripey tails," etc. All shared the same purpose, however, and recognized this could be the only chance they'd ever get to resist their ancient enemy.

How they'd do that, exactly, remained a mystery. At least until they viewed the dispositions of the Grik. A conventional pitched battle was out of the question. Regardless how "magical" the weapons of the five visitors, they had limited ammunition and no artillery. Three Vickers GO (gas-operated) guns had been retrieved from the Beaufort, and Silva and Lawrence had gone through them as well as they could, removing rust, grime, and dried grease. All three had been restored to reasonable functionality, but their ammunition was limited as well, consisting of only ten serviceable drum magazines with around ninety-five carefully cleaned rounds of .303 in each. The Shee-Ree were excellent archers, and their relatively short (compared to those of the Erokighaani) composite bows were easily as lethal as a .45 auto, but they weren't skilled at hand-to-hand fighting. For that they carried only "hunting" clubs with long wooden handles and blue-gray chalcedony heads attached with rawhide. Those heads were napped to a fine, murderous edge, but Chack hoped their new friends could avoid getting "stuck in."

Ror'at-Raal was in nominal command, but it was understood that "Col-nol" Chack and Kaam were his designated war leaders. Kaam, apparently, was renowned enough as a warrior that even the unknown clans had heard of him. Chack, of course, was a "warrior shaman" of the Big Boat People. That was enough for most. But Chack constantly stressed that their curious force wasn't an army by any definition and it was impossible to mold it into one on the march. Regardless, he also swore he'd devise a plan that, combining the native archery with the magic weapons his people bore, would allow them to strike a heavy blow. Some may have noticed he didn't promise *victory*, but did seem confident they could accomplish their objective—whatever an "objective" was.

The objective remained merely a general desire, even to Chack, Silva, and Lawrence: to cause enough confusion among the Grik to steal a ship and get their band of fighters, their dependents, and hopefully the "slave"'Cats as

well, out and away to the north. It couldn't seriously damage the Grik army in Mada-gaas-gar, beyond causing as
much pandemonium as possible, or bring a significant force
to Captain Reddy, even if they all made it out. But it would
bring warning—if he didn't already have it by then. And
word would spread among all the peoples of Mada-gaas-
gar, south of the great jungle, that everyone who wanted
to join the fight against the Grik was welcome, and that
one hardy band had actually fought to do so. It might wind
up being only a bloody propaganda stunt, Chack thought
grimly at times, but surely it would be worth it?

"Col-nol Chack!" Kaam cried, edging through the mob
that surrounded Chack, Silva, and Miles as they trekked
along the river in the hot, muggy, mosquito-infested air.
Bradford was with Ror'at–Raal, and Lawrence was . . .
somewhere else. The land cover was changing here, even
as the climate became more oppressive in the lower elevation, from the tall grass of the savanna to a kind of prickly
brush that Silva had compared to a stunted hackberry.

"Here," Chack called back, and Kaam joined them.

"Scouts have returned, your Laaw-rence among them,
and bear reports. They observed the enemy this very day.
Indeed, we are that close at last."

"We'll be right there," Chack assured. He glanced at
Silva. "Are you ready for this?"

"Born ready, Chackie." Silva shrugged. "If our main
goal is to raise a ruckus, why, that's what I do best!"

Lawrence squatted and began briskly drawing a map on
the ground, the other scouts watching supportively, making suggestions. Obviously, using a stick and dirt to convey
images and ideas wasn't an unusual expedient among
these plains 'Cats, at least. The leadership of their combined force, including Ror'at, Kaam, Chack, and half a
dozen other clan chiefs, looked on, as did Silva, Courtney,
and Miles. Surprisingly, one of the scouts explained what
Lawrence was drawing. *Maybe not so surprising,* Chack
considered. They'd all been concerned the natives would
fear Lawrence because of his similarity to their enemy,
but lethal as he undoubtedly was, Lawrence had always
maintained an air that somehow inspired a trust similar

to what one might feel toward a particularly helpful youngling. He'd never understood it, but Lawrence just had a way about him. *And part of that is a surprising vulnerability,* he supposed, *always evident by the self-consciousness with which he speaks around strangers. He understands English and the apparently almost universal Mi-Anakka base language perfectly, and has even learned a great deal of Grik, but it painfully frustrates him that he just can't say certain words. He often substitutes, sometimes imperfectly, but in this situation, with clarity so important, he's obviously agreed with the other scouts that they should speak, not he.* That encouraged Chack, even as he felt for Lawrence—and he suddenly realized that was another way their Grik-like companion did it. He hid a blink of secret admiration.

"The greater portion of the Gaa-riek army has gone," the scout said, blinking what looked like a mix of relief and alarm, "leaving a wide trail pointing toward the great jungle."

"North," Lawrence hesitantly clarified. They'd begun to realize the Shee-Ree, at least, didn't have words for "north" or "south." With the river that ran through their territory running east and west, "sunrise-ward" and "sunset-ward" were all they really needed, and north and south were described as being in the direction of various prominent features, the farthest point north being "toward the wall of rotting trees," and the farthest south simply "toward the cold."

The scout blinked at Lawrence and continued, pointing at the map on the ground. "A large group remains near the Rik-Aar village, still unloading things and putting them on carts." He glanced up. "Slaves pull the carts away but none return, according to what other watchers told us."

"Other watchers indeed," Courtney said with interest.

"We met some Khot-So warriors who escaped the Gaa-riek. They watch to see what happens to their families, and to send tales, of course. They watch for us now as well."

"How many slaves remain?" Ror'at-Raal asked.

"Four hundreds. Maybe more. It is hard to count them since they are penned on both sides of the river like the herdbeasts the Gaa-rieks consider them. They . . . are not in health," the scout added darkly.

"And the enemy?"

"That many, three or four times," the scout replied.

"Call it fifteen hundred. Half again as many as us," Silva murmured thoughtfully, and Lawrence nodded at him. Silva grinned. "That's not so bad. Seen a lot worse odds."

"How is the enemy disposed?" Chack asked. "Ah, how placed?"

Lawrence pointed at a semicircle he'd drawn south of the river, and the scout answered, "They guard outward here, on this side of the river, with four big . . ." He paused and looked at Lawrence.

"Guns," the Sa'aaran supplied. "Artillery." The scout blinked appreciation and continued.

"They have landing places for their smoking boats on both sides of the river and warriors and supplies unloaded on this are floated to the other in smaller boats, but then they follow the greater Gaa-riek force. The outward guard is not so large on that side, and they have no . . . guns."

"Sure," Miles said, suddenly and surprisingly engaged. "That's the way their army went, gobbling up everything in their way. Why watch there?"

Silva looked at him, speculating a variety of things, then nodded.

"They do watch," the scout stressed.

"But that may be our best bet," Silva suggested to Chack, who nodded slowly. "How many smoking boats and barges—I mean, square boats—are there now?"

"Three," the scout answered. "One on this side and two on the other side of the river. There were four, but one came and two left even as we watched. The other watchers say they always come or go under the sun," he added. "And it will be quickly reported if more come or go." He blinked uncomfortably. "There are now two of the great flying fishes as well," he added. "A second arrived yesterday, we were told. They somehow . . . float near the ground, tied to it like boats."

"Which side of the river?"

"This side . . . Col-nol," the 'Cat said.

"Where the larger force can protect them," Courtney mused. "And we might also assume that's where their headquarters—and leadership—would be."

"A fair assumption," Chack agreed. "And regardless that the main army has already marched, the staging area remains active, so we must move quickly. Another single boat and barge could change the equation by half a thousand warriors. Did the Khot-So watchers say when the main Grik army marched away?"

"Four days," the scout said, "But five hundreds have gone each day since. With the carts," he reminded.

Chack looked at Ror'at-Raal. "I must see the ground myself," he said, "but Chief Silva and I have discussed many scenarios, several of which might work based on what we have heard." He nodded at Dennis with an ironic blink. "He and I both have faced . . . difficult situations in the past. But it sounds as though speed is essential to our success, so as I go forward, you must move the rest of our force as close as the scouts deem safe and we must all be prepared to go into battle tonight."

Ror'at's eyes bulged amid the rising clamber of objection. "We cannot fight in the dark!" he sputtered. "Only under the eyes of the Sun can we do battle, where He might witness our glory—or gather the souls of the slain!"

"My dear Ror'at-Raal," Courtney interjected, "we respect your faith and traditions. Many of our people, B'mbaadans and Aryaalans, share them, in fact. But they understand, as you should, that the Sun, God, the Maker of All Things—however you wish to describe Him—sees ALL. Do you feel free to behave in such a way that He wouldn't approve of at night, simply because He's not then watching from the sky? Do you commit evil deeds in the shade of the trees?"

"Some do," Ror'at snapped. "The Erokighaani believe the trees of the jungle shield them from His view and His wrath."

"Do you believe that? Are you like the Erokighaani?"

Ror'at's fur bristled with rage, but then he blinked. "No," he finally grudged. "But it is not the same," he added weakly.

"Of course it is," Courtney assured gently. "And even by the strictest interpretation of B'mbaadan and Aryaalan faith, the Sun Brother—the Moon, we call it—remains to watch the night even as the merest sliver, or even resting entirely behind the curtain of stars. Is it not the same with you?"

"It is," Ror'at admitted. "But He . . . misses things that do not interest him when the curtain is drawn."

Courtney beamed. "Then I assure you that the Sun Brother will find whatever Colonel Chack and Chief Silva come up with to do to the Grik quite interesting indeed! He will be most anxious to report it."

Ror'at hesitated. "But why can't we wait? Something like this should be better planned."

Silva snorted. "Plans are swell. I love 'em myself. Kinda like pretty pictures on the wall. Trouble is, they tend to go all to pieces when you whack a Grik on the head with 'em." He grinned. "Me an' Chackie have a few plans, but they ain't complicated pictures, they're clubs. Simple an' easy. That's all this mob can handle, and you know it," he stressed. "An' Chackie's right about another thing. The longer we wait, maybe just hours, the more likely there'll be a heap more lizards to fight." He nodded at the scouts. "They say the tugs an' barges show up during the day. That means they're crossin' the Go Away Strait between here an' Africa at night, prob'ly to avoid our patrol planes. It's likely there'll be more here tomorrow."

"Your Excellency," Chack said seriously. "I will view the disposition of the enemy, and if it appears that anything might be gained by delay, we will certainly wait and plan as long as we must. But whether it is tonight, tomorrow night, or the night after that, we must attack in the dark. By all accounts—those we had before we came here and others you have told us—these Grik are disciplined troops, not the mindless hordes we've fought thus far. I believe we're still smarter and more flexible," he assured, "but we're too few, too disorganized, and honestly, with your dependents to consider, far too . . . cumbersome to attempt anything else. In the dark lies our only chance for success, so you must embrace it—or go home."

Sovereign Nest of "Jaaph" Hunters
Zanzibar
October 11, 1944

Diania gently shook Sandra awake, hissing, "Min'ster Reddy! Do wake up, Min'ster Reddy! Sompin's goin' on!" Sandra sat up immediately in the near dark stateroom she and Diania had been imprisoned in for thirteen days, ever since *Amerika* was destroyed. She'd been out of it only once, except for twice-daily excursions down the short passageway to a nearby head, escorted by extremely disconcerted-looking guards. The dinner she'd attended the evening after their capture, along with Adar, Horn, and Lange, hadn't gone any better than their first meeting with Admiral Laborde. His captain, a man named Dupont, had even seemed intent on aggravating the tension. Sandra ate nothing, and when the strained conversation inevitably veered back to the atrocity of the day, Sandra had implacably launched into another furious, threatening rant. She couldn't help herself.

The dinner had abruptly ended, and she had no idea if Adar and the men had been invited again. She hadn't been, and since then, hers and Diania's meals had been delivered to the stateroom. It was just as well, she'd bleakly realized. If she'd continued dining with their slimy, murdering captors, she probably would've done something incredibly rash at some point. Secreted inside a small pouch of medical supplies she and Diania had quickly stuffed in the bag they'd brought aboard was a lovely little ivory-handled Colt Model 1908 Pocket Hammerless in .380 ACP. Her father had given her the weapon, always a favorite "officer's" pistol, on her last visit home to Alexandria, Virginia, before the war began. She'd carried the gift across the gulf of worlds, stowed among her dwindling possessions.

It really wasn't much of a weapon, and would probably consume the entire single magazine of ammunition she had for it to kill a single Grik. Her hands were small, but she'd learned to handle a 1911 Colt and the local copies well enough. That's what she usually carried when the need arose, and she'd wished for the little .380 only once before, when she'd been taken—along with then-Princess Rebecca Anne McDonald—by the HNBC criminal Billingsly. She hadn't had it then, and hadn't expected to *keep* it this time, but despicable as she considered Laborde, his surprisingly chivalric gesture of countermanding Dupont's orders that she and Diania be searched may well save her life. On the other hand, if she'd been subjected to Laborde's company often enough, she was sure she would've eventually taken the pistol and murdered him, Dupont, and as many others as she could—before she and everyone else was killed.

She still wanted him dead for what he'd done, but her fury had dulled enough for reason to reassert itself. As long as she and her friends—and the baby inside her!—were alive, escape remained a possibility. She'd use the little Colt for that when the time came. Her husband and the Grand Alliance could be relied upon to exact revenge for *Amerika*'s dead.

"What's happening, Diania?" she asked, quickly whipping her long, sandy brown hair into a knot behind her head. Glancing out the single porthole in their prison, she could see it was nearly dusk. With nothing else to do, nothing to even read for almost two weeks, she and Diania spent most of their time either exercising or asleep. The exercise had been an eye-opener. Sandra had always kept herself fit, but the diminutive Diania, even shorter and more slightly built than she, had been teaching her a number of disabling moves she'd learned from Chief Bosun Fitzhugh Gray. In addition to all his other duties, Gray had always considered his primary task to be protecting Captain Reddy. Since Diania was so devoted to Sandra and meant to stay always at her side no matter what rating she ultimately earned in the Navy, Gray had suggested that she serve Matt Reddy's wife in the same capacity. It hadn't much complicated things when the gruff old "Super Bosun" and the tiny, dark-skinned Impie gal fell in love, but Diania had been devastated when Gray was killed. Sandra was gratified that their "exercises" not only gave her more confidence that she could physically protect herself, but despite their confinement, they also seemed to be helping Diania crawl out of the shell Gray's death had built around her. She remained a long way from the happy, cheerful soul she'd become in Sandra's company before, but she was getting better.

"I don't know, m'lady," Diania replied. "Sompin'. The engines ha' stopped."

Sandra stood and stepped to the porthole and peered out. "Uh-oh," she said darkly. "This doesn't look good at all." Outside, in the light of the setting sun, she could see that they were in a tropical port of some kind. She had no idea where, but quickly recognized most of the ships anchored nearby. All were of a design she'd come to associate with the Grik. There were quite a few of the "Indiaman"-type square riggers, but also several of the things Matt called "cruisers." Worse, she thought, were a number of ironclad Grik "battleships" like the captured ones she'd seen at Madras. Those appeared to be undergoing various alterations, but she couldn't tell exactly what was being done in the failing light. Most concerning of all was the pair of modern ships steaming into the harbor to anchor alongside *Savoie*. One was a beat-up-looking, smallish tanker, but the other was a two-stack destroyer, considerably bigger than *Walker,* and armed with twice as many guns. Sandra couldn't see the flag on either ship in the gathering gloom.

There was a brisk knock on the wooden door, and it

opened to the light in the passageway. "Come, please," said one of their guards in rough English.

"Where are we going?" Sandra demanded. The guard motioned helplessly at their few things neatly arranged around the stateroom and made a gathering gesture.

"Come, please," he repeated. Sandra and Diania looked at each other, then quickly complied. Sandra was concerned that if they didn't, they'd be rushed out anyway, losing what little they had—including the Colt. In less than five minutes, they were being led topside. With a mixture of joy and dread, she saw Adar, Gunny Horn, Becher Lange, and the crew of their small boat. All were gathered near a gangway leading down to a rough-hewn but substantial dock, already lit by torches set in iron brackets. She realized with a surge of terror that many of the figures she saw on the dock and beyond were Grik. Then she saw with equal dread that several humans were waiting for them as well. Contre Amiral Laborde and Capitaine Dupont joined them, walking briskly, followed by a security detachment. Laborde looked at her and paused ever so slightly before Dupont and the first half of his security preceded him down the stairs that had been rigged out.

"Minister Reddy, Miss Diania," Adar said quietly, "I am so glad to see you well!"

"We're both fine, Mr. Chairman," Sandra replied, looking more closely at her friends. Adar looked harried, and Lange had started a beard. Horn's was longer and more bristly. Otherwise, they seemed healthy. The Lemurian sailors didn't look so good, however. 'Cats didn't do well in confinement. All three said they were fine as well, however, when she asked them how they were.

"Any idea where we are?" Sandra whispered when their guards urged them toward the stairs, but Adar shook his head, glancing skyward at the stars just beginning to appear.

"I have not viewed the Heavens since we saw you last," he said, his tone pained. Apparently, Adar's captivity had worn on him as much as the other 'Cats. Maybe worse in some ways, since he was, above all, a Sky Priest. "At a glance I can only say that we must again be as far west as

Liberty City, and somewhat north as well." "Liberty City" was his name for "Grik City," and despite the universal objection, he stubbornly persisted in calling it that.

"But . . . how far north?" Sandra pressed.

"Shh," Horn breathed as they waited at the top of the steel steps. "Later," he whispered. "The less they think we know about anything, the better."

Unexpectedly, they were forced to wait a considerable time while the men on the dock carried on a lengthy, animated discussion. They used that time to catch up a little, talking quietly among themselves. When they were finally prodded forward, all fell silent as they stepped to the dock and advanced toward five men, still locked in what sounded like a heated debate. As they drew near, someone hushed them irritably, and three men stepped past Laborde and Dupont to stand before them. Confirming her first wild suspicions concerning the people here, Sandra saw that one was clearly Japanese. Was this the madman Kurokawa at last? She had no idea, but judging by his body language, he was obviously in charge. One of the other men was taller, dark haired, with a thin mustache. She suspected he was French simply because that's what it sounded like the argument had been in, and his uniform, very similar to Laborde's, seemed to confirm it. *Odd*, Sandra thought, looking at his rank. *Laborde outranks him, but this man is apparently his superior.* She couldn't tell as much about the third man since he'd stayed slightly back, the others blocking the torchlight.

"Ladies and gentlemen," the Frenchman began in a deeply sorrowful, near-perfect English. "I am Capitaine de Fregate Victor Gravois, ranking representative here of the League of Tripoli. Before I say another word, please accept my most profound apologies for the loss of your ship and the nobly wounded troops embarked aboard her. I am . . ." He allowed a glare to fall upon the silent, stiff Laborde. "I am *stunned* to learn of her dreadful fate. Allow me to express condolences on behalf of myself, my mission here, and my government. To say that Contre Amiral Laborde exceeded his instructions by even confronting your ship, much less destroying her, renders the term 'understatement' grossly inadequate. Furthermore,

I also deeply apologize for the . . . limitation of freedoms you have since endured. That is nearly as unforgivable as the circumstances that brought it about. We shall discuss those 'circumstances' and the relevant . . . aftereffects in a moment, but first allow me to present my colleagues."

Without waiting for a response, Gravois motioned the man behind him forward. "I am pleased to introduce my particular friend Maggiore Antonio Rizzo, of the Aeronautica Italiana."

Rizzo stepped forward and snapped to attention, then bowed specifically before Sandra and Diania, sweeping his hat from his head. "A poignant pleasure to meet you, indeed, dear ladies," he said, a great frown beneath his equally large mustache. He nodded curtly at the rest. "And you all as well, of course. I wish it had occurred under more pleasant, ah, conditions."

Gravois nodded somberly, then turned slightly, somewhat hesitantly it seemed, to indicate the bespectacled Japanese officer standing beside him. "And not least, by any means, is His Excellency, General of the Sky Hideki Muriname. He is second in command of all the, ah, 'people' on this island, and is currently in charge while his superior, General of the Sea Hisashi Kurokawa, is away. He speaks English," Gravois hastened to add, "but perhaps not as well as I, and has agreed to allow me to greet you and . . . acquaint you with the further unhappy restraints you must bear."

Sandra had been squinting into the darkness and saw several other Japanese—and Europeans as well. She wondered who they were. Obviously more members of Gravois's "mission," but why hadn't he named them? That's when she caught the part about Kurokawa and restraints. Furious horror surged again, and she gathered herself to speak, to voice some objection, but Adar beat her to it.

"I cannot accept your apology," he ground out. "Certainly not without an explanation." He flicked his ears at Laborde. "A vessel under the control of your 'League,' a power that has already displayed a great deal of antagonism toward us and our cause, not only blockaded a port and nation allied to us, but destroyed a hospital ship loaded with wounded troops. It then proceeded to transport us against our will into the custody of our deadliest enemy." He glared at Muriname. "Such behavior can only be described as acts of war."

Gravois looked at him. "Ah, and you are Adar, High Chief of Baalkpan and chairman of the Grand Alliance! Your accomplishments, and those of your people, have left me in a state of amazement. I am a great admirer of yours."

Adar's eyelids blinked so rapidly in surprise, they were almost a blur.

"And normally you would be right, of course," Gravois continued. "But we, under the instructions of our government, have already taken what small steps we are able, in order to rectify the situation as best we can. *Savoie* has been cast out, her actions disavowed. Her crew will be evacuated to the two other of our vessels you may have seen, bound for their homes, and her senior officers will be dismissed from the service of the League of Tripoli! Observe." He motioned their attention to *Savoie*. Her amidships arc lights had been directed at her mainmast, and even as they watched, her French Tricolor and the other strange flag she flew bowed away in the darkness as they rattled down their halyards. For a giddy instant, Sandra thought they were actually *surrendering* the battleship to them as reparations. Then, with a rush of dread, she saw another flag flutter to the top of the mast: the Rising Sun of Imperial Japan.

"Oh my God," she moaned. Then she spun to face Gravois. "You appalling, unspeakable bastard. You're giving that ship to *Kurokawa*? Whatever crazy agenda you think you're advancing, if you know so much about us, then you've got to know he's a maniac!" She looked at Muriname, half expecting to be struck for her statement, but the Japanese officer remained impassive.

Gravois regarded her. "My dear Lady Sandra," he said, his tone aggrieved. "I must confess that I admire you above all others in your cause. Your devotion to healing, and to your formidable husband, is sufficient to inspire us all. That you have followed Captain Reddy in all his mad adventures—and indeed, he is quite mad in his own way, is he not?—does you enormous credit." He paused and cocked his head. "Your fidelity, even to the point of carrying his child into harm's way, strikes tremendous envy of the man into my heart."

Sandra nearly panicked then, but steeled herself. How could he possibly know that? Of those present, Adar and Diania knew she was pregnant. How could they not? Otherwise, fewer than a dozen people in all the world had been informed. Some of those were in Baalkpan, though, notified via coded wireless. Alan Letts, for one. And if he knew, so did his wife, Karen, and . . . *Well, it isn't as if we'd intended to keep it secret forever,* she mentally defended her friend, *but this means they've either broken the Allied code for sure, or they have spies everywhere.* She started to deny it, or point out that she and all the rest aboard *Amerika* had been leaving the war zone when they were attacked, but realized that would be pointless.

Gravois interrupted her thoughts. "Of course General of the Sea—and whatever else he calls himself—Kurokawa is raving mad." He nodded at Muriname. "That is no secret to anyone here. But having disavowed *Savoie,* as my government and conscience demand, I cannot simply entrust her to her former officers once again, the very ones who caused so much embarrassment and consternation to the League." He shrugged helplessly. "Nor can I scuttle her, or cast her adrift." Glancing at Muriname, he wryly raised his eyebrows. "I honestly do not believe our generous hosts would allow such a thing. So, as you can see, I have no choice but to turn her over to them. I do fear she may yet pose further problems for your Grand Alliance in their hands"—he smiled sadly—"but never again in ours."

"You are a monster," Becher Lange stated simply, speaking for the first time.

"I think that's the biggest load of steaming bullshit I've ever heard in my life," Gunny Horn said, almost wonderingly.

"Most colorfully put. Do you really think so?" Gravois asked cheerfully, suddenly dropping all pretense of remorse. "I shall fine-tune the explanation considerably, I am sure, but the fundamental truth does remain." He looked seriously at Adar, then back at Sandra. "Contre Amiral Laborde *did* act against the express wishes of the

League of Tripoli when he engaged and sank your ship. He *has* been dismissed from the service for his act. The League truly does *not* want war with you—or your enemies, even the Grik. *All* that is true. The fact remains, however, that *Savoie* did what she did, and there were survivors in the water. Believe what you like, I am thankful for that fact. In any event, some will be rescued. They probably already have been, and will report what they saw." He looked at Muriname and sighed. It was probably the first genuine gesture of regret that he'd made. "I do not *want* to turn over *Savoie*. She is not the most capable League vessel by any means, but is still quite powerful and is likely to upset the careful balance of power that we have struggled so diligently to achieve in this sea. Yet I simply have no choice. Only with her flying the flag of your already avowed enemy can we plausibly deny responsibility for what these"—he waved at Laborde and Dupont—"imbeciles have done."

"But our people know where she came from," Horn said stubbornly.

"Of course," Gravois agreed. "And it will be my regretful duty to report that, following her rudely rebuffed efforts to prevent the Republic from joining your misguided war against the Grik, *Savoie* proceeded here on a mission of goodwill." He gestured at Muriname. "Unfortunately, and entirely unknown to her commanders, these people were already engaged in the very same struggle, on the other side, and seized her for their own ends. It was they—perhaps flying her former flag to confuse the issue, should the subject arise—who destroyed SMS *Amerika*. Not the League."

"So how will you spread this bullshit?" Sandra snapped. "Obviously, you won't send us to tell my . . . Captain Reddy this fantasy."

"No," Gravois agreed. "As much as it genuinely pains me, I must consign you to the custody of General of the Sky Muriname." Sandra's fear reached new heights, and she saw Gunny Horn stiffen. She'd expected as much, but to hear it at last . . . "I do wish I could take you with me, but it is quite impossible—and unnecessary in any event." Gravois addressed Adar. "Contre Amiral Laborde informed me of what you said: that you are not as important to your alliance as one might initially suspect. From what I understand of the fledgling nation you are building, I am forced to agree. Pity." He looked back at Sandra. "And you, my dear, I absolutely *cannot* take—when I personally bear my 'fantasy' tale to Captain Reddy on Madagascar."

Sandra was struck utterly speechless, and without another word, Gravois smiled, bowed slightly, and turned to go. Rizzo followed, still wearing what appeared to be a genuine frown. Laborde, Dupont, and the other Europeans chased after them, leaving the stunned prisoners alone on the dock, surrounded by Japanese sailors with rifles.

"This world is full of madness," Hideki Muriname said softly, surprising them. His English was heavily accented but quite understandable. "I went mad long ago, I fear, but it is that fear, I think, that allows me to continue to behave as if I am sane. I *pretend* sanity to avoid tumbling into the same pit as Lord Kurokawa. *He* is dangerously mad, as you know, but he does not know it. Therefore, nothing . . . balances his insanity." He managed a pained smile. "Still, he has preserved us this long and I am bound to serve him." He nodded in the direction Gravois went. "That one knows he is mad, I am almost sure, but actually seems to enjoy it. It . . . liberates him from his conscience, and any small compulsion to speak the truth. He will leave us soon, to do what he said, but I think he leaves also because he has finally accomplished his mission."

"What mission is that?" Becher Lange asked, finding his voice first.

Muriname nodded at *Savoie*. "I suspect even he must realize how important all of you truly are to your people in general, and your Captain Reddy in particular. He gives us a battleship that Lord Kurokawa will find it impossible not to use at once, but also brings you here as a lure for your people. What better way to bring about our complete mutual destruction?"

Sandra gulped, realizing at once that Muriname was probably right. Gravois would go to Madagascar and tell his lies. Whether anyone believed them or not, they'd believe it when he told them that she and Adar, Lange and Horn, Diania and three Lemurian sailors, were being held by Hisashi Kurokawa. He'd seen them and could describe them all—down to her pregnancy!

Adar cleared his throat. "So, what will happen to us?" he asked.

Muriname looked at him, eyes narrowed in curiosity. "I have never spoken to one of your kind before," he confessed. "I did not know it would be so like speaking to . . . anyone else." He shook his head. "To answer your question, however, I do not know. I personally do not believe you have tainted yourselves with the sin of surrender. No shipwrecked crew, even of an enemy warship, truly surrenders when they are plucked helpless from the sea. But it is not for me to decide. I will try to protect you, but I . . . cannot risk the wrath of Lord Kurokawa. Sometimes only I am left to stand between his rages and my people here. I must do my duty to them. I promise you will be well treated until he returns, and perhaps he will let that stand. But it will be up to him."

"Where has he gone?" Sandra asked.

Muriname looked at her, and despite his mild manner, his eyes held . . . hunger for her, as a woman, she realized with a dreadful chill that twisted her insides. He quickly conquered his expression and pointedly looked away, as if disgusted with himself. "He has taken a portion of our fleet to destroy your convoy steaming down from Madras," he said simply. "Your 'Task Force Alden,' I believe it is called." He finally looked back at her. "The one transporting all your reinforcements for Madagascar."

1st Fleet (TF Alden)
140 Miles NE of Mahe Island (Seychelles)
USS **James Ellis**
Dawn, October 12, 1944

"What the hell's that?" Chief Bosun Carl Bashear demanded, shading his eyes and staring into the rising sun. He'd been standing on *James Ellis*'s aft deckhouse, observing the 'Cats on the number four gun go through their morning drill exercises as another pleasant day began, when something . . . strange caught his eye. The gun captain, a burly Lemurian with a gray-streaked brown coat, initially called "Hopalong," and then just "Hoppy" for reasons Bashear couldn't fathom, tilted his helmet down and squinted as well. "I not know, Chief. I not see nothin'."

"Hmm." Bashear grunted. "I don't see it either now. Too goddamn bright. Just caught a glint. Maybe it's the night patrol Clipper comin' in. They don't usually scout *behind* us, though."

James Ellis was steaming at the very rear of the task force that morning, escorting *Sular* back into formation. The big ex–Grik troopship had blown a steam line late the night before, forcing her to secure the four boilers in her forward two firerooms, slowing her by a third. Nobody had been injured when the line let go, and the repair hadn't been difficult, taking only a few hours—just long enough to let the boilers and lines cool off enough to do the work, and then raise steam once more. But instead of slowing the whole task force, Commodore Kek-Taal had ordered *Ellie* and *Bowles* back to shepherd *Sular* along until she could rejoin. Bashear doubted General Alden would've been happy about leaving most of I Corps behind, even with protection, but then Kek-Taal was kind of a turd and probably wouldn't have even told him until Pete noticed *Sular* was missing from the formation.

That sort of thing had become more and more common in First Fleet, and it wasn't only Kek-Taal. Just as the shipboard clan structure that had always prevailed aboard seagoing Lemurian Homes had reignited age-old abovedecks and belowdecks rivalries on individual ships, an interservice competitiveness had begun to take root as well. Things of that sort weren't all bad, Bashear reflected, and often even improved performance as chiefs berated their "deck apes" or "snipes" not to screw up in front of the other faction. And the enthusiasm of the various services to show the others how it's done wasn't necessarily bad either, as long as they didn't keep one another from doing so through subversion or misinformation. Bashear suspected that a dose of the latter was starting to creep in. It hadn't been bad when Captain Reddy or Keje had been directly riding herd on the fleet, but he'd seen more and more of it since First Fleet (South) had split away to begin its campaign against the heart of the Grik Empire on Madagascar. *Just wait until Captain Reddy and Keje see how it's gotten. Guys like Kek-Taal'll wind up skipperin' harbor ferries, I bet.* He squinted again.

"Hey," he murmured. "That ain't no Clipper! There's . . . Shit! Whatever they are, there's a *bunch* of 'em!"

The general alarm began to sound. Unlike *Walker*'s new acquisition, *James Ellis* had no bugler. Nor was there an electronic alarm. New/old traditions had been combined, based on simple things that worked, and the crude, pipe-shaped alarm gongs first used on Lemurian warships had been superseded by bells situated strategically around the ship. The first one started aft of the bridge, urgently ringing as a 'Cat rapidly whipped the dangling cord back and forth.

Another sounded atop the amidships gun platform and an air division 'Cat raced to answer with the bell at the base of the mainmast/aircraft crane. A studiously calm but insistent Lemurian voice joined the ringing, coming over the crackly speakers tied into the shipwide circuit:

"All haands! All haands! Maan you baatle-stations! Staand by for air aaction!"

"Air action! Jesus!" Bashear swore. All the new 4"-50s were on dual-purpose mounts designed to allow the guns sufficient elevation to engage aerial targets. They were even theoretically capable of hitting them. But the need to do so had seemed confined to the ability to hit Grik zeppelins that got past the fleet's air cover, or maybe shooting in among flocks of Grikbirds once the new gun system made its way to the war against the Doms in the East. Even then, each weapon was still expected to fire in local control since they hadn't come up with a gun director for antiair purposes yet, relying on range, elevation, and speed *estimates* by the gun's captains. They'd practiced— a little—shooting at high angles, expecting plenty of time to correct their aim or change their fuse settings off shell bursts relative to the slow-moving zeppelins. But the things Bashear saw speeding in from the east weren't zeppelins, and he doubted they'd give them any time to correct their aim at all.

"Oh, hell," Lieutenant Rodriguez said, climbing up the ladder from below to take his place at the auxiliary conning station at the front of the platform. He was staring aft. The flying shapes were in the dozens now, clearly conventional aircraft of some sort.

"You said it, XO!" Bashear snapped. "Somebody loaded the dice on us. Where'd the goddamn Griks get airplanes?"

"They aren't zeps," Rodriguez agreed.

"Nope. Congratulations, sir! We're the horse's ass, and you're at the tip of the tail! Guess who gets first crack at those bastards? I'm headed forward," he said, running for the ladder. Sliding down the rungs, he waited while the observation Nancy, its engine already roaring and its catapult just completing its turn out to starboard, suddenly rocketed away in a gush of prop-whipped smoke from the impulse charge. Making the little floatplanes ready to go in an instant, at GQ, had been a hard-learned and costly lesson. The highly flammable aircraft were dangerous to have aboard in combat, and throwing them over the side whenever things got hot was a terrible waste. Bashear didn't even wait to watch it gain altitude before racing forward, passing 'Cats preparing machine guns and scampering up from below with belts of shiny ammunition. Running past the galley beneath the amidships gun platform, already breathing hard, he hit the stairs to the bridge at a leap and thundered up. He was gasping when he entered the pilothouse, finding a scene of controlled tension, excited voices calling updates on readiness and the general situation.

"The Clipper was just circling in and saw a formation of unidentified aircraft coming up behind us," Captain Perry Brister told him. "Its observer counted maybe a hundred of the damn things and no ships in sight! No land either, so who knows where they came from."

"They gotta be Griks, Skipper." Bashear breathed heavily.

"Must be. That damn Kurokawa must've had 'em building planes for years. Anyway, they're here, and we have to keep 'em off the heavies."

"Mr. Rodriguez aasks, can he shoot now?" cried a Lemurian talker. Perry paced to the bridgewing and looked aft. The leading formation of planes was about a mile astern, perhaps a thousand feet high, forming a ragged V. They were still just dark silhouettes against the rising sun, but their intention was clear. They weren't from the task force, there was nowhere else friendly planes could've come from, and there'd been no attempt at communication. They couldn't be good guys. Then he looked at *Sular*. The big ship was starting to pull away, accelerating *past* fifteen knots, steaming through the tail-end ships of the task force. Several more Nancys were already in the air, flying off other escorts, turning to intercept the oncoming planes. Some had been armed with .30 cals in their nose, but not very many. Most would have to rely on their observer/copilot shooting a Blitzerbug SMG from its aft cockpit—for whatever good *that* would do.

Bashear joined his skipper. He hoped the ready fighters on *Baalkpan Bay* would get up quickly enough, not that there were very many of them. They'd started keeping six P-1Cs near the carrier's two catapults, as soon as they were in range of the Seychelles. The new airstrip on Mahe wasn't finished yet, but it was better than nothing. They could launch more fighters—slowly—as they brought them up from below. The strapped-down P-40s were still in the way. *Crap! The P-40s! Ben Mallory's babies are sitting ducks!*

"Very well," Perry called. "Come right twenty degrees to unmask the battery to starboard. All ahead full. We'll zigzag up alongside *Sular*. Tell her and *Bowles* what we're doing. Guns one, three, and four, commence firing!"

The ship rocked as the guns stuttered, their shells *shhhsshh*ing away on high trajectories. Black puffs of smoke, widely scattered, erupted in front of the oncoming planes.

"*Sular* opens fire!" called a lookout to port. The big troopship had four 4"-50s of her own. There were more black puffs, even as *Ellie*'s guns spat again. The blooming black clouds were popping at a fairly impressive rate—but they weren't hitting anything. *What did I expect?* Bashear wondered bitterly. *We've never even thought about shooting at anything fast!* He stared aft. The fire was having *some* effect, apparently at least scaring whoever was flying those planes. They tended to jerk away from the shell bursts, and the closest formation was breaking up. Two Nancys, then a third, roared by overhead, closing with the enemy at a combined speed of somewhere around three hundred miles an hour.

"Dammit!" they heard Stites yell from the fire control platform above. "All guns, check fire! I repeat, check fire until our guys are past, then be damn careful what you shoot at!"

This is crazy! Bashear thought. *We can't hit the bad guys* on purpose. *How do we* aim *to miss the good guys?* But they had to try. There were a *lot* of planes coming in, and they had to assume they carried bombs or something else dangerous to surface ships. Why even attack otherwise?

Perry Brister's thoughts mirrored his Chief Bosun's.

"Resume rapid fire," he called up to Stites. "Our guys'll just have to take their chances. But keep reminding your gunners to adjust their fuses! Don't let them get too carried away for that!"

"Our planes gonna try an' cut off the second formation, or get aroun' behind 'em," the talker cried.

"Very well," Perry said, moving through the pilothouse to the port bridgewing. They'd caught up with *Sular*, but *Bowles* was lagging. Fifteen knots was as fast as she could go. *Nothing for it,* he realized. *Ellie* had to add her protective fire to *Sular*'s. "Come left, thirty degrees," he ordered. "Bring us up to about three hundred yards off *Sular*'s starboard beam, then come right ten. We need to keep a little wiggle room."

"Ay, ay, sur!" answered the Lemurian quartermaster's mate, spinning the big brass wheel. "Comin' lef, turty degees! Right ten at tree hunnerd yaads!" The guns ceased firing for a moment until the first turn was complete, then numbers one and four resumed, joined by number two. A cheer sounded as one of the approaching aircraft disintegrated within a cloud of black smoke and debris fluttered down to the sea. Another plane, veering sharply, slammed into a third. Both crumpled and fell spinning toward the water. Staring through his binoculars, Perry finally got a good look at the enemy. "They look just like our Fleashooters!" he called. "Send it out! The enemy planes look just like ours, but they're green and gray. Maybe a little bigger." He paused, watching the Nancys blast through the first group, scattering it further, but a clump of at least a dozen enemy planes were diving now, apparently targeting *Sular*—and *Ellie.* "Standby secondary armament!"

James Ellis had eight brand-new water-cooled copies of the .30-caliber M-1919 Browning Machine Gun that could be emplaced at various points around the ship. *Geran-Eras* was similarly armed, as were all the large ships in the task force. Even some of the sailing steamers had a couple of thirties now, as more and more of the wonderful weapons finally found their way to the fronts. They'd been a long time coming. The ammunition had been perfected for some time, feeding the older weapons on *Walker* and elsewhere, but making good enough barrel steel to sustain prolonged firing of high-velocity jacketed bullets had been the major holdup. Once solved, the machine guns began pouring out of the Baalkpan and Maa-ni-laa arsenals. It would be a while before capacity reached the point where the Allies might focus on producing heavier machine guns or updated small arms. They still hadn't even caught up with the demand for the single-shot, breech-loading Allin-Silvas yet, and too many Allied troops in the East still carried *muzzle-loaders*. But it was hoped the current focus on light MGs would give all their troops the much-needed support they'd lacked so long. And of course, though machine guns had originally been issued to the navy as the antipersonnel weapons they'd needed so often, now at least a few ships in TF Alden had some close-in protection against aircraft as well. Based on the number of attackers and the fact that his machine gunners hadn't practiced shooting at *any* flying targets at all, Perry had to wonder how effective they'd be. Stites must've been similarly concerned. The cry, quickly passed, of "All machine gunners, *lead* your targets! Watch your tracers! Aim where the planes'll *be* when the bullets get there, not where they *are*! It's just like shooting at ships in the distance, but these targets'll be a helluva lot faster!" came from above.

"*Sular*'s maanuverin'," shouted the talker. "She zigzaag. First turn away!"

"Acknowledge," Perry said. "Helm, maintain this interval. Boats, tell Mr. Stites the secondaries may commence firing at his discretion."

The dozen planes apparently targeting *Sular* swarmed down in a gaggle, getting closer, closer, hurried shells still bursting around them. And they carried bombs. Perry could see them now, one under each wing. And he saw something else: large red "meatballs" painted on their wings. "Son of a *bitch*! They're Japs!"

Some of the thirties opened up with a chattering roar, and white tracers arced up toward the diving planes. More tracers rose from *Sular*, crossing *Ellie*'s stream of bullets. Amazingly, some started hitting almost at once. Pieces tumbled away from one plane, and another coughed smoke. Still, they bored in. The cacophony of machine-gun fire intensified as the rest of the MGs joined in, just as the first enemy plane swooped low over *Sular* and released its bombs. Immediately, its left wing tore away and it spun crazily into the sea, just as its bombs threw up large water-spouts in *Sular*'s wake. The rest of the planes came in close together, and how none of them collided was some kind of miracle. Another fell as two lines of tracers sawed it in half, but ten planes dropped their bombs almost at once, and eight flushed upward in all directions like an exploding covey of quail. Two wouldn't make it. One flew away, still smoking. Another pulled up too late, its landing gear catching a wave top, and it somersaulted onto its back in a spray of foam. But twenty bombs exploded around—and on— *Sular*, raising sheets of water that scoured the ship as high as the top of its casemate. At least three blasts shook her, and they were respectable, but she steamed through the towers of spray, her guns chasing the fleeing planes.

Perry stared at her through his glasses. "She looks okay," he said loudly as his own ship's machine guns tapered off amid Stites's shouts for them to cease firing. "A bunch of her landing craft got clobbered, but her armor shrugged it off. If those bombs were designed to punch through, they dropped 'em too low to get a head of steam." He looked at the sky. The scene above was . . . surreal. He'd heard the term "dogfight," referring to aerial battles, but this looked more like a swarm of flies zooming every which way. Actually, it was more like when flocks of lizardbirds engaged in combat over some morsel, swooping, veering, flaring out, attacking anything they saw without their own peculiar plumage. There appeared to be no real strategy anymore, beyond "attack," ever since the formations had been broken by the antiaircraft fire and a few determined planes. The six P-1Cs of *Baalkpan Bay*'s ready squadron had jumped in, and had apparently already knocked down a couple of enemies. Pretty good, considering the only "training" they ever had against aircraft with similar performance to themselves was when they chased each other around the sky for fun. That practice had been discouraged as pointless and dangerous at Kaufman Field near Baalkpan, at least since Ben Mallory and Walt Fisher left. Now it was saving their butts.

At least some of them, Perry amended bitterly. A Nancy was burning, falling to the sea, with three enemy planes still shooting some kind of wing-mounted machine guns at it—again, just like their new C-model Fleashooters. And not all the Cs were safe. A plane had skillfully evaded one, and came roaring up behind it, spitting fire. The Allied plane burst into flames and spun downward. Another suddenly roared by trailing smoke, very close to *Ellie*, with a green-and-gray pursuer right behind. It was the closest he'd seen one yet, and he noted that it *was* bigger and more subtly different than he'd thought at first. They passed near enough that Perry saw the Lemurian pilot in the P-1C struggling to keep it in the air . . . and a *human* in the fighter chasing him. Two more planes followed, drawing tracers, and just before one exploded and fell to the water, Perry caught a flash of a distinctive long, toothy snout and large, reddish eyes behind the windscreen.

Realization dawned. "Get this off!" Perry shouted to his talker as another gaggle of enemy bombers swooped down at *Sular*—and *Ellie!*—and the guns roared again. "Most of the enemy planes are piloted by Grik—repeat, *Grik*—based on the way they're acting, and the fact that I just *saw* one! God knows how they taught them to fly, or built something they *could* fly. But there's Japs up there too, at least a few, who've trained to shoot down planes! So tell our guys up there to watch their asses!"

"Cap-i-taan Brister!"

Perry turned to one of his Lemurian lookouts on the starboard bridgewing, and saw her pointing forward, eyes blinking in horror. He looked. He'd been so caught up in the fight around his ship that he hadn't noticed much of what was going on beyond her and *Sular*. They'd been the center of his attention, but apparently hadn't received all, or even most, of the enemy's. Now he saw that several ships were burning—at least one oiler, by the thick, black smoke. Worse, another tall, heavy column of smoke was erupting into the sky from one of the principal members of the task force. They'd closed to little more than a mile, but with the angle, he couldn't tell which one it was. It didn't much matter. All were vital to the war effort—and Captain Reddy's campaign.

"Here they come!" Bashear growled, and Perry looked up. Several planes were diving directly at *Ellie* this time, and the banging of her guns reached a fever pitch. He glanced at *Sular*. The top of her casemate fore and aft of her two funnels was wreathed in fire and smoke as she lashed the sky as well. He couldn't affect how things went with *Baalkpan Bay*, *Andamaan*, or *Tarakaan Island* until they closed the distance. But there were eight thousand troops and maybe four hundred crew on *Sular*, and she was under *Ellie*'s protection.

"*Sular* turns haard right!" the quartermaster's mate called.

"Very well, match the turn, but bring us in closer alongside her this time. Stand by for emergency flank." He glanced at Bashear. "We'll add our guns to hers as best we can. *Bowles* is coming up on her port side now. The zigzagging let her catch up. But even if we can't turn sharp to get out from under those bastards' bombs, maybe we can still *jump* out from under them!"

USS Andamaan

"Get the lead out! Let's go!" roared Lieutenant Walt (Jumbo) Fisher as he and his remaining flight crews heaved the big PB-5D out through the forward hangar doors onto *Andamaan*'s tracked fo'c'sle. Walt was a big man, maybe the tallest human in the Grand Alliance. How he'd ever managed to dodge the height restrictions that should've kept him out of P-40s in the old world still remained a mystery to most who knew him. Now, of course, there weren't enough P-40s to go around, and he flat wouldn't fit in a P-1. So even though he technically remained XO of Ben Mallory's 3rd (Army) Pursuit Squadron, he'd been left to run the flight training program at Kaufman Field until finally asked to bring all but two of the P-40s left there up to join his skipper. Even then he hadn't been needed to *fly* one, since Ben had more veteran pilots than planes—and Walt had happily agreed to switch to the far roomier PB-5D, and command of Pat-Squad 22. It had seemed like a fun, exciting assignment at the time, commanding and formulating cooperative tactics for the largest concentration of long-range, heavy-payload, bomb-and-torpedo-capable aircraft in the Alliance. Not only that, but he got to fly a lot. That all went in the crapper that morning, and he *hoped* he still had one other plane out there, circling the battle—and running out of gas, by now. Two had been destroyed by a bomb that fell through the open hangar doors aft, and two more were about to burn. He was damned if the enemy would get *this* one too.

The steam winch that usually moved the planes had lost pressure, so they had to do it by hand, and despite the help of eleven 'Cats and two Impie midshipmen assigned to his squadron, Walt, his dark brown hair sweat-plastered to his head, was probably doing most of the work. *Andamaan* was nearly dead in the water and already low by the stern. The steepening angle made it even more difficult to shift the heavy flying boat. "Just a little more!" Walt croaked. Fire was spreading forward inside the cavernous space behind, and smoke gushed out above them to join a great, gray-black pyre mounting to the heavens. 'Cats dragged hoses, directing them at the flames, but water pressure was dropping as well.

"There's no steam for the caat-a-pult!" Walt's flight engineer warned. Sergeant Aanse-Ar-Mus wore a brown pelt with almost-yellow blobs that looked suspiciously like spots. Instead of the inevitable nickname, he'd been dubbed "Moose." There was already a "Spot" in the squadron. "The crane neither," he added, suspecting Walt would try to set the plane in the water.

"We can work the crane with the hand winches," Walt gasped. It was possible. The ship's cranes were designed with that capability in mind, but it would be tough. Walt looked up to see that they'd finally cleared the overhang, then glanced back. The guns at the top of the casemate hangar were still blasting away, but the ship had slowed to a complete stop. He was horrified to see the landing craft dories, just like those covering *Sular*'s sides, sliding down to the sea, filled with troops and crew. "And that's what we'll do," he decided. "I don't know what kicked us in the ass. The bomb that fell in the hangar wasn't very big, and it shouldn't have hurt the hull. But there were those other thumps, whatever they were, and this big bastard's going *down*. Take charge of the winch detail, Moose. Hook her on and swing her out." He looked around. The whole squadron's air and ground crews were there now, having joined the others in time to give a final push. Some of the ship's crew was gathering as well. In addition to the dozen 'Cats Moose quickly gathered, there were maybe twenty more, and two other men. "The rest of you guys, get in the plane!"

"We'll be too heavy to get in the air!" a young Impie midshipman named Reese warned him, eyes searching for attacking planes. Unsaid was how helpless they'd be just bobbing around.

"We got no ordnance. We'll get her up, and we're not leaving anybody who'll fit. Period. Now load up!"

Quickly and professionally, several of Moose's detail climbed to the top of the big plane and hooked the cables onto the three lifting points. There were two on the wings, between the inboard and outboard engines, and one on the fuselage, halfway to the tail. "Watch those taglines when she's up," Walt warned. It was going to be very tricky indeed, as the stern dipped lower and the bow rose. *Andamaan* was sinking fast. It had been impossible to make the transverse bulkheads the yard added completely watertight, but they should've kept the flooding down to something the pumps could handle—unless multiple compartments were wide-open to the sea. And, of course, without steam pressure there'd be no pumps. Walt still wondered what hit them. There'd been no word, or even any official announcement to abandon ship. Comm must be out as well. He climbed in through the hatch in the side of the plane as the last 'Cat ducked inside. "Make way! Make yourselves small!" he shouted, squirming up through the packed fuselage. "We need room for a dozen more in here! Start the engines!" he called ahead. Ordinarily, they'd never run the engines while the plane was suspended from the crane, but they were out of time. In mere moments, the angle would be too extreme to allow the plane to clear the crane or the casemate.

Finally reaching the flight deck, he stepped up the two-rung ladder and settled into the left wicker seat. Reese was in the right seat already, feverishly completing the preflight check, even as he flipped the ignition switches on the overhead. Walt glanced at him, then nodded. His usual copilot was in the circling Clipper.

"Contact," Reese reported.

"Wind 'em up!" Walt yelled through the open hatch above and behind the cockpit. The detail still on the wings spun the geared cranks protruding from the rear of each superbly maintained engine, and all four quickly roared to life. "Hang on!" he bellowed up at the detail as he fiddled with the throttles. The ten cylinder radials always missed for a while until they settled down and the noise was deafening. Whether they heard him or not, the detail stayed put. They'd have to be ready to unhook as soon as they settled on the water. The plane bounced and swayed as the crane lifted them, and much more quickly than he would've imagined possible, they rose above the fo'c'sle and started swinging out to starboard. He couldn't see them, but he imagined Moose's detail must've been doubled or tripled up on the winches, spinning the handles as if their lives depended on it—which, of course, they did. Reese, twisted around to see, was watching them, and the expression he wore when he looked back at Walt told the big man all he needed to know. Just then, the right wingtip banged into the tilted crane, sending a grating shiver through the Clipper's rigid bamboo bones. The plane performed a drunken pirouette, rotating slowly clockwise, as taglines snaked loose behind it in a tangle. Walt hoped nobody had been jerked over the side. Things went even faster then, as Moose must've realized that the best thing to do was to get the spinning plane in the water as quickly as possible. He apparently timed it exactly right too, because it boomed onto the waves and squatted down with the left wing nearest the stricken ship.

"Thank God the sea's calm," Walt growled, staring at the 'Cats by the crane. "Unhook and get in!" he yelled at the topside detail and felt them pounding down through the aft top gunner's opening between the trailing edges of the wings. Then he advanced the throttles slightly and eased closer to the ship. "Thank God for 'Cat agility too!" he barked with genuine humor when, not even waiting,

Lemurians started hopping lightly from the ship to the wing and racing toward the same opening the cable detail used. In moments, Walt saw Moose bringing up the rear, but he was pointing up behind them and waving at him to go. Walt got the message. "Somebody get on the guns!" he bellowed over his shoulder, and pushed the throttles to their stops. In addition to their other advancements, PB-5Ds had five .30-caliber machine guns. There were two on top, mounted on pivots in the openings they'd just used. Two more were on either side in the waist, and one in the nose, fixed, so even the pilot or copilot could fire at targets in front of them. The two top guns started chattering as the engines roared and the big plane churned forward.

"Look out!" Midshipman Reese cried urgently. USS *Geran-Eras* was charging past in front of them, from right to left, with a huge bone in her teeth. Dark smoke streamed from all four funnels, and her guns—all at high elevation—twisted and bobbed as their pointers and trainers madly spun their wheels. Some of her machine guns were pouring tracers up and over the Clipper. The plane heaved when something struck the water close alongside, and the hull rumbled with the impacts of pieces of whatever it had been. There was a sharp cry from aft.

"We get one!" Moose roared exultantly. He'd taken the gun behind the cockpit as he jumped down.

"Or they did," Walt shouted back, nodding at *Geran-Eras*. The plane was still accelerating despite Reese's concern. Walt was confident they'd miss the fast-moving destroyer. "And it nearly got us," he added beneath his breath. "Keep your eyes peeled!" he warned loudly again.

They must've been a tempting target for their attackers, and the guns hammered frantically twice more before the big plane finally bounced and clawed its way into the air. But both times, the attacks broke off as the swooping enemies overran them, almost hitting the water. Walt suspected either his gunners hit them or they just gave up, not confident enough to aggressively strafe something so low and slow. He stayed low for that reason, also counting on the fact that the top side of the Clipper was painted nearly the exact same color as the deep water and they'd

BLOOD IN THE WATER   327

be hard to see from the air. Carefully, he circled around toward *Baalkpan Bay*, hoping he was right. He'd been right about what the Clipper could carry, loaded with nothing but fuel and a little ammunition. There must've been more than thirty people crammed inside. Granted, most were 'Cats who weighed barely two-thirds as much as a grown man, but that had to be some kind of record on this world.

Still banking left, he saw burning ships all over the place, and his heart felt sick. *Sular* was finally coming up, apparently unharmed so far, with *James Ellis* and a steam frigate close alongside. But a new attack was falling on them, and black puffs blotted at the smoke-smeared sky. And then there was *Andamaan* at last. Her stern was underwater all the way up to her aft funnel now, her bow jutting high in the air. The fire aft had dissolved into an enormous gout of steam, but flames now gushed out the forward part of the casemate they'd just escaped. All around the sinking ship were motor dories filled with people, bobbing on the dark blue sea. "My God," he murmured.

"Commodore Kek-Taal says us get outa here! Head for Maa-he, in Saay-chelles," called a comm.-'Cat who'd fired up the wireless and TBS gear. "We gonna get hit by *somebody*—theirs, or ours in mistake—we keep flutterin' aroun'."

"Where's *our* other plane?" Walt demanded. "The scout that was coming in when all this started? I doubt it has the fuel to make Mahe Island."

"It go too . . . but us better keep eyes for it, on water."

Walt frowned grimly. "Okay. God, I hate running from the fight, but that's what we'll do. Nothing else we *can* do." He raised his voice again. "Call out any fighters you see back there," he warned, then snorted. "Goddamn Jap-Grik *fighters*," he swore. "I can't believe I just said that. Can't believe I had to."

USS Baalkpan Bay

"Get the lead out, Sergeant!" Colonel Ben Mallory shouted at his ground crew chief as he trotted up, pulling on a leather helmet and adjusting the goggles on his forehead. He caught a glimpse of *Andamaan* burning off the starboard side and losing speed. "Damn! Bombs. Now!"

"Commodore Kek-Taal wants your aar-craaft off this ship at once!" cried a Lemurian lieutenant commander, practically running to keep up. "There is *no time* for bombs!" he added nervously, straightening his white tunic, when Ben reached the plane Dixon was helping to arm. His head swiveled constantly and his large, brown eyes flicked back and forth at swarming specks in the sky.

"We're hurryin', Colonel," Cecil Dixon replied to Ben, his voice strained as he stood out from under the P-40's wing, shaking his hand in the air, with a pained expression on his face. 'Cats immediately scampered away with the bomb cart. Others were already positioned under the rest of the planes. Two 'Cats climbed up to the cockpit to start the fighter's powerful engine. "We're done with yours."

"Fuel? Ammo?" Ben demanded. They'd kept the planes armed and fueled since they left Madras—just in case—and their engines were run up every day.

"I checked the guns myself, and all the tanks are topped off."

"Colonel! I must insist!" the Lemurian snapped, his voice rising to be heard over the 4″-50s mounted on the carrier's island that had just opened up. The source of the noise apparently just occurred to him and he jerked his face to the sky. Clouds of black smoke appeared very high and aft, exploding among several clustered planes. One inexplicably pitched up and stalled, before beginning a long, tumbling fall to the sea. The others quickly dropped their bombs and scattered. Ben could tell immediately that all the bombs would miss and looked down at the 'Cat, still staring up and blinking . . . fear. He didn't have time for this, and the officious Lemurian naval officer was slowing them down.

"There is a great deal of shooting—and missing—by both sides, it seems." Lieutenant Conrad Diebel observed over the rough whine accompanying the suddenly spinning prop on Ben's "M" plane. The blond Dutchman had joined them when they weren't looking. Diebel had fought the Japanese with the ML-KNIL, essentially the Air Corps of the Royal Netherlands East Indies Army, and found his way to this world aboard the Japanese prison ship *Mizuki Maru*—along with Gunny Horn, Ian Miles, Captain Reddy's cousin Orrin, and even Cecil Dixon, to name a few. He was a strange, stoic man, but a damn good pilot.

"Having tasted the fire from the first ships they encountered, the enemy seems to have gained a rather unfounded respect for our antiaircraft efforts," he added dryly.

He was right, Ben reflected, as his engine roared to life amid a cloud of blue smoke. He remembered the transmission he'd just heard from Perry Brister on *James Ellis*. A few enemies still bored in, alone or in pairs, but most dropped their bombs from as high as they could.

"It is very strange," Diebel continued, louder. "Fearful Grik, flying airplanes. Both unprecedented—and apparently mutually exclusive. Or do they follow the example of likely Japanese flight leaders? What could *they* still fight for? The mad Kurokawa? I find that difficult to believe— unless their cause is fear of him." He grinned at Ben. "Or they all just follow orders to be careful with valuable aircraft."

"Several good points, Lieutenant," Ben allowed. "And aside from the hit on *Andamaan* and a number of auxiliaries, the attack's been almost as amateurish as the defense— so far," he added cynically, with a glance at the Lemurian commander.

"We cannot launch our planes fast enough to defend the task force with *your* planes blocking the aft elevator!" the 'Cat repeated as a squad of very uncomfortable-looking Lemurian Marines jogged up to stand behind him.

Ben stared at them, then shook his head in frustration. "Keep loading the bombs, Sergeant Dixon," he ground out. "On the double."

"Three're up, Colonel," Dixon said, taking a chew and folding his arms. Holding his ground. He stared hard at the 'Cats. "The kids're doin' fine without me now. I'd just get in the way."

"If you do not fly off this ship this instant, I will . . . I will be forced to arrest you," the Lemurian officer said almost shrilly, but emboldened by his reinforcements.

Ben laughed. "That'll sure speed things up! You'll never

get them off then." One of the braver enemy pilots swooped to strafe them, his bullets flinging splinters from the flight deck near the confrontation. Machine-gun tracers from the ship's island and various emplacements around the flight deck chased the enemy plane, but it flew away unscathed. Its bombs fell late, however, hitting the water between *Baalkpan Bay* and the slowing *Andamaan*. Ben ignored it all and pointed at the forward elevator, rising with two P-1Cs. "You've already got six more than the ready squadron in the air. There are two more—and how much faster can you recycle the catapults? Not much. Listen, Commander, those Jap-Griks came from *somewhere*. Not from Africa, and not from any island. We're too far from anywhere like that where they might be. That means they have carriers." He pointed at the sky. "More than one, to carry so many planes. *Carriers*," he stressed again. "Just like this. We've got to find them and hammer them!" He waved at his planes as the rest of his pilots quickly gathered round and more engines coughed to life. The humans wore aggressive frowns, and the 'Cats were blinking furiously. "We're talking *minutes* here, Commander! We're practically done! I started my guys loading bombs as soon as the Clipper sent its first warning. Kek-Taal refused to have any of *Baalkpan Bay*'s planes armed with bombs"—he shrugged, looking at his fliers—"so we're it."

"That is a fine argument for later," the Lemurian said with false patience. "Right now you must obey Commodore Kek-Taal's command." Ben rolled his eyes and started to respond, but a gruff voice cut him off.

"No, Commander—obeying *my* command," General Pete Alden said, striding up behind the Marines. "As will you and Commodore Kek-Taal. This may be his ship, but it's my goddamn task force!"

"Gener-aal!"

"Shut up, you, and get the hell out of my sight. You're holdin' up the war!"

"That was fun to see," Ben said, watching the Lemurian naval officer scurry away, followed by much more satisfied-looking Marines.

"Yeah, well, we've wasted enough time." He waved at the sky as the air defenses opened up again and more bombs exploded alongside, heaving spray down on them. The two P-1s had been hooked to their catapults, and their engines were running up. "Those bastards might get lucky any minute," he yelled over the noise. "How many planes are ready now?"

Dixon glanced aft. "Five, General. Six in a second."

Pete looked at Ben. "Go now. The rest'll follow as they're ready. The elevator's locked, and we're turning more into the wind and speeding up to give you as much help as we can, getting those heavy bastards off." He stuck out his hand. "Good luck, Colonel, and go get 'em! I'll see you on Mahe."

Ben shook Pete's hand and saluted, then turned to his plane. "Keep an eye on that man," he said in Dixon's ear. "If this ship gets hit . . . well, we can't afford to lose him."

"I'll do my best, sir. Good huntin'."

Ben pointed at "Shirley," the smallest Lemurian pilot in the squadron, and one of the best, even if she had to sit on two parachutes to fly. Then he pointed at the plane next to his as he strode around the wing and clambered up to his cockpit. Hopping in, he waited while the tie-downs were removed and the two 'Cats helped with his straps. When they jumped down, he looked at Shirley's plane to his left and mashed the Push to Talk button. "Okay, Shir . . . I mean, Flashy Four, I know we've never done this before, but remember what we talked about. I'll go first, then you, then Conrad in Flashy Two, etc. Staggered take-offs, but we flush as quick as we can. There's only about four hundred feet of flight deck in front of us, but we'll be starting with almost thirty knots of airspeed, with the ship steaming into the wind. Don't forget to use about one-quarter flaps," he added, pushing his own flap lever down a little and squeezing the button on his stick. They weren't entirely sure that was a good idea, but it had shortened their takeoffs on the rough ground at Flynn Field. "And get your tail up, fast," he added. "Stand on your brakes and give her full throttle, then let 'er rip. Got it?" Out in front of them the two P-1C Mosquito Hawks were hurled off the end of the ship in a cloud of steam. *The new steam catapults for the latest carriers are swell,* Ben thought. *Too bad we can't use 'em.*

"I got it," replied Shirley's tiny voice. Ben nodded to himself and took a deep breath. "Here goes," he muttered. He quickly ensured that the red fuel selector knob was pointed at the fuselage tank. He'd change it to the belly tank once he was in the air. Then he made sure the mixture was set to "Auto Rich" and ran the engine up to 2,300 rpms to check his magnetos. Satisfied, he did a practiced, three-second check of all gauges and switches and saw that his cowl flaps were already open. Then, with another glance at Shirley, he stood on his brakes and pushed the throttle full forward with his left hand. The Allison engine roared, and the plane shuddered. He held it there for five full seconds, then relaxed his legs. The P-40 seemed to bolt down the flight deck like a racehorse out of the gate. In just seconds, it seemed, he'd passed the ship's island and was halfway to the end of the deck. He was almost surprised when the tail popped up so soon and he actually lifted off with about forty feet to spare. He breathed a sigh of relief as he raised his flaps and landing gear, and eased back on the throttle. The rest of his squadron should be okay.

Quickly climbing to five hundred feet, his eyes sweeping, searching for threats, he finally shut the canopy, switched his fuel selector knob, and closed the cowl flaps. Then he banked right to have a look and wait for the rest of his planes. *Andamaan* was doomed, he realized with a churning in his chest. The ex–Grik ironclad had fallen behind *Baalkpan Bay*, and her bow was rising in the air beneath a fiery, smoky pall. He did a double take. Somebody'd dropped a Clipper in the water beside her and was trying to get it in the air, even as several enemy planes dove at it. Fortunately, the new DD, *Geran-Eras*, seemed to be charging in to help. He started to join her—but was stunned to see a . . . different . . . pair of green and gray planes arrowing in toward *Baalkpan Bay*. They looked a lot like the other Jap-Grik aircraft, only bigger, and they had *two* radial engines, one on each wing. He kicked his rudder over and pushed his stick forward, lining up on the low-flying bombers—*They have to be bombers*, he realized. *Or could they be . . ?* It was damn sure possible, after everything else they'd seen that day. He flipped the switches on the right side of his instrument panel, arming his guns.

"All stations, all stations!" he shouted in the clear. "This is Flashy Lead. Watch for low-flying twin-engine planes. I think they're *torpedo* bombers! High fliers might be a diversion!"

"I'm right behind you, Flaashy Lead!" came Shirley's squeaky voice. "I see 'em too."

"Flashy Lead, this is *Geran-Eras*. We see 'em. They's a bunch of 'em, all comin' in about tree hunnerd feet, from multiple quaaters. That's prob'ly what get *Andamaan*. Cap-i-taan Cablass-Rag-Laan is get us closer to *Baalkpan Bay*! He think she's they main taagit."

Of course she is, Ben realized furiously, wondering bitterly which other advantages the Allies had thought they held over their enemies would suddenly evaporate that day. He fired. Six streams of tracers arced away from his plane with a juddering thunder. The plane closest to the carrier literally fell to pieces as his bullets tore it apart and kicked up spray in the sea beyond. He released the trigger and lined up on the second attacker, already straddled by bullet geysers sent from the carrier's defenses only a few hundred yards away, just as something long and heavy dropped from the plane and splashed in the water.

"Torpedo inbound, *Baalkpan Bay*!" he yelled, sending tracers down to eat the second bomber. Its left engine flipped over the top of the wing, the spinning prop shredding the fabric, and it winged over and slammed into the waves.

"There's more!" Shirley cried as Ben pulled up and over the carrier. He glanced down in time to see Diebel's ship taking off—and a towering spume of white water, much taller than the splashing bombs, rocket into the air alongside *Baalkpan Bay*. His plane jolted from an accidental near miss from a 4"-50, but he didn't even notice. What he did see was how many columns of smoke were rising over the task force, and how many wispy, lingering tendrils marked where a plane—who knew whose—had fallen from the sky. He also saw that what remained of the task force was beginning to both clump together—and split apart. *Sular* and *Tarakaan Island* were turning east, steaming at full speed and making smoke. The deliberate, billowing black clouds probably added a great deal to his impression of disaster, and he hoped they had the same effect on the enemy. A gaggle of other ships were racing to join the fleeing heavies. *James Ellis* was already close in, and her intentional smoke screen was augmented by more smoke streaming from an apparent bomb hit aft of her funnels, but it hadn't slowed her down. Other ships were closing on *Baalkpan Bay* as well, for mutual support, but the carrier—and *Geran-Eras*—was turning west.

It made sense. Such a move might invite defeat in detail, but just as First Fleet hadn't (hell, nobody had!) developed effective anti-air tactics, its attackers obviously weren't very good at this either—yet. They'd had some success against slow-moving targets with insufficient and inept protection, but even then it was costing them. Commodore Kek-Taal, or more likely General Alden, had apparently ordered the task force to separate, to split the enemy's attention and lure it from the ships carrying the most troops and equipment so essential to Captain Reddy's strategy and his force's very survival. And they were using the very best bait they had. Just as Ben was wild to get after the enemy carriers, there was no doubt in his mind that *Baalkpan Bay*, the only Allied carrier in sight, would now draw the enemy's greatest concentration.

"I'm up!" cried Lieutenant (jg) Suaak-Pas-Ra, better known as "Soupy," over the radio. "I mean, Flaashy Two's up," he added hastily. "Daamn! That was hairy! An' *Baalkpan Bay*'s startin' ta' list. She's not slowin' down, though!" Soupy was probably the best of all of them, a better natural pilot even than Ben. He still didn't have the air-to-air training Ben had received and had never really expected to need again. And only Conrad Diebel and Captain Reddy's cousin Orrin, attached to Second Fleet, had real combat experience against frontline Japanese fighters. Diebel got his in Brewster "Buffaloes" over the Dutch East Indies and Orrin's was in P-40s over the Philippines. Orrin still used his training and experience to some degree, fighting Dom Grikbirds in the East. Diebel was about to get a refresher course. The only air battle Ben ever fought, besides shooting at Grik zeps, was when he'd dueled a nimble Japanese spotting plane in a battered PBY Catalina. . . .

"Okay, Flashies, we'll circle the carrier until our last

plane is in the air, see? Keep your eyes peeled for more torpedo planes."

"There's three!" Soupy called immediately, startling Ben. "They's comin' in on *Bee-Bee*'s staar-board side again!"

"Get 'em, Soupy! Shirley, follow him down."

"I have it, Colonel," Conrad Diebel sent. "Ah, Flashy Five is airborne, and I see the targets."

"Okay, Five. Four, you stay up here with me." He paused, his stomach churning. "Check that," he said. "Two more are coming in from aft of the ship, curving around. Follow me, Four—but don't get between the planes and the ship! We're liable to get shot up by our own people."

General Pete Alden was back on *Baalkpan Bay*'s bridge, watching the developing air-and-sea free-for-all with his III Corps commander, General Faan-Ma-Mar. The stalwart, middle-aged Lemurian had been in every action in Indiaa since making the crossing from Saay-lon. And if he and his Corps' contributions had rarely garnered spectacular attention, they'd been extremely critical to keeping Rolak's I Corps from being eaten alive on more than one occasion. III Corps had always been the reserve, the diversion, the anvil for Rolak's hammer, and General Faan had always quietly, competently, managed to be right where he was supposed to be when he was needed most. Now, like Pete, and with a fair-size chunk of his beloved Corps aboard the ship he'd agreed might have to sacrifice itself, all he could do was watch.

"I do not think the commodore was much pleased by your order to separate our force," he said dryly, glancing over his shoulder where Kek-Taal stood, broodingly silent, staring forward.

"Nope," Pete agreed, as a fifth P-40 flew off *Baalkpan Bay*'s tilting deck. The torpedo that hit the ship's starboard side hadn't been particularly big or powerful as such things were reckoned on the "old world." The real stunner had been that the enemy had them at all. It had been inevitable, Pete supposed. The Japanese helping the Grik had the technology to make better torpedoes than the Allies could. It had just been a matter of time. That didn't make it any easier to swallow. Still, the light weapon might not have done much damage at all to a heavier-hulled ship like *Big Sal. Baalkpan Bay* was a purpose-built carrier, however. More capable in some ways, including watertight integrity, but smaller and lighter built. The torpedo had split a fuel bunker and flooded the starboard shaft alley all the way from the aft engine room to the steering gear. The engine room itself was taking water as well, but the pumps were keeping up, and the hit hadn't slowed them. But Ben Mallory and *Geran-Eras* had reported at least a dozen more torpedo planes, all headed for *Baalkpan Bay*.

"Sulky bastard, ain't he?" Pete continued, then shrugged. "Well, as my grandmother always used to say, 'He's got the whole rest of the day to get glad.'"

"Perhaps not," Faan said, pointing. Three of the twin-engine planes were boring in, past the sprinting *Geran-Eras*, heading right for them. Tracers filled the sky, and water geysered around them. Two P-40s stooped and chopped at them from above. One suddenly blew itself out of existence, its torpedo probably going off. The other two dropped their "fish" and thundered over the flight deck, still drawing fire. Pete grabbed the rail and looked down at the water. One wake had gone squirrelly, beginning to circle away. Another was clearly going to hit.

"Hang on!" Pete growled, but nothing happened, and he relaxed slightly. "A dud!"

But *Geran-Eras* was still blasting frantically to port as she raced down alongside *Baalkpan Bay*, fore to aft, and several things suddenly happened at once. The new destroyer's stern lurched up amid a roiling cascade of foam, rising high enough that they saw her churning screws for an instant before she squatted back, abruptly logy and losing way. Pete wondered if she'd been hit by the errant torpedo. Then two more planes roared right over the stricken ship, charging in, impossibly close. One struck the destroyer's foremast in a welter of whipping stays and shredding fabric, losing a piece of its wing. The other dropped a torpedo and banked away unmolested, barely clearing *Baalkpan Bay*'s flight deck. The crippled plane was out of control, starting to spin. But instead of plowing harmlessly into the sea, it—and its torpedo—struck the carrier right at the waterline, directly beneath the island.

Pete and Fann, and everyone in view, were thrown to the deck by the close, heavy explosion. Smoke, fire, and burning debris spewed up from below, shattering the windows and spraying broken glass. And even as they shook their heads, trying to rise, the other plane's torpedo must have hit, because the ship shuddered yet again and a heavy gust of water drenched them where they crouched.

"Daam-aage report!" Kek-Taal roared.

"I think you're right, Fanny. I don't think he's going to get 'glad' after all," Pete quipped, helping his Lemurian friend to his feet. Faan was bleeding from several cuts, and Pete figured he was too. The ship was clearly slowing now, and steam gushed upward in hot, swirling gasps from the wound in her side. "That's done it," Pete grunted.

"There's fire!" a 'Cat talker practically screeched. "Fire an' floodin' in the aa-mid-ships fireroom! Boilers are out!"

"Calm yourself!" Kek-Taal said softly.

"Ah, ay, ay, Commodore," came the chastened voice. "Boilers are out, busted wide-open." He listened to the bulky headset beneath his helmet for a moment. "Lots'a caas-ul-tees. The plane blow right thoo, an' then the torpedo hit near right under. There's no way to paatch, an' nothin' to shore up. The space is *gone*. For-ard fireroom's floodin' too," he added. "Worst thing's the fire on the flight deck!"

"What fire?" Kek-Taal demanded, eyes blinking, then he raced to the port bridgewing and stared aft. A final P-40 had just cleared the deck, weaving as it rose, apparently still compensating for the shaking it took as it gathered speed. The other two sprawled amid the tangled wreckage of a bomber that had come in from aft. Whether it was shot down or its Grik pilot deliberately crashed into the tempting target like its zeppelin-dropped "suicider bomb" pilot predecessors would've done, there was no telling. And it didn't matter. It must've hit almost simultaneously with the other plane and torpedo, because they hadn't even felt it. They did now. Flames swept outward from the burning planes, carried by spreading fuel. 'Cats advanced with hoses, but a bomb or torpedo cooked off within the blaze and swept them away in sheets of searing fragments. Another detonation, heavier, shook the ship, and the tangled, burning debris heaved up—just as billowing flames and smoke roared out the side openings to the hangar bay. That, more than anything else, spelled *Baalkpan Bay*'s doom.

After the loss of *Humfra-Dar*, there'd been many improvements made to all the Allied carriers. At least those in First Fleet, and especially the new construction. Watertight integrity had been improved, magazines had been reinforced, and efforts had been made to isolate the aviation fuel. Much of this relied on the single most important protective measure they'd incorporated into the new *Baalkpan Bay* Class of fleet carrier: a barrier of armor plate between the flight deck and the hangar deck below. Too much armor made the ship top-heavy, however, and they'd only used enough to be proof, they thought, against the very light bombs the Grik had initially used. As Grik bombs got bigger, the vulnerability was recognized, but it was assumed the new dual-purpose armaments and improved pursuit planes would be sufficient to protect the ships. All that changed today, and either the crash or the powerful Allied bomb exploding on the deck had turned the flames loose below, where perhaps thirty more aircraft, fully fueled, awaited.

"General Alden," coughed Sergeant Cecil Dixon, racing up the companionway to starboard. The man's khaki clothes were scorched and smudged, and his beard had an uneven, crispy look. "We gotta get you and your troops, and all my guys, the hell off this tub. She's about to go up!"

"This ship is not finished yet!" Kek-Taal said severely, then blinked rapidly when they felt another rumble deep below. "But perhaps we should evacuate those not immediately involved in defending or saving her," he admitted reluctantly. The ship had slowed to barely four knots, and he stared out to starboard. "*Geran-Eras* seems to have difficulties of her own," he added. The proud new destroyer had made a gentle turn to come back alongside, but her stern was sagging and she was clearly struggling. For the first time they also realized she wasn't firing her guns anymore, nor was the gun platform aft of the bridge thundering and shaking with reports. Kek-Taal turned. "Instruct any planes we may have still in the air to proceed immediately to Maa-he Island in the Saay-chelles. We certainly cannot recover them. Then contact *Clark* and *Saak-Fas*," he said. "Instruct them to come alongside and begin taking our people off."

"They still pickin' up boats from *Andamaan*."

"The landing craft are quite seaworthy, and others can perform that duty. This ship"—his tail twitched slightly—"may soon become an inferno. I want no oilers or ammunition ships alongside her!"

"Ay, ay, Commodore."

"One last thing," Pete interjected, his tone mild, but his eyes ferocious. "Contact Colonel Mallory's Third Pursuit Squadron. I *hope* he still has six planes, and enough fuel for the job. Either way, he's to quit hangin' around here and proceed with his mission." He looked at Kek-Taal. "Tell him to follow the bastards who did this back where they came from and blow 'em straight to hell."

West-Central Mada-gaas-gar
Predawn, October 12, 1944

"Now *this* is kinda what it was like, foolin'
around with those Khonashis," Dennis Silva
grumbled softly, apparently to the tree-
gliding reptile clinging to his back as he, Courtney, Miles,
Kaam, and six hundred Lemurian warriors crept ever
closer to the Grik boma palisade on the south side of the
river. "You weren't there for that. Oochin' along in the
dark with a buncha overeager amateur warriors," he went
on, "sneakin' up on pre-pared defenses. Ow! Goddammit!"
he hissed when a thorn pierced his knee. At least he hoped
it was a thorn. Snakes were scarce as hen's teeth on this
world—at least where he'd explored so far. Too many things
would gulp them like worms, he supposed. But Kaam had
shown him a weird little lizard with poisonous barbs on its
back. . . .

"Goddammit!" Petey sympathized, mimicking Silva's
whisper. He'd finally learned there were times when keeping his voice down might prevent him from being thumped
on the head.

"But in that case, if I recall your account, the enemy
was Japanese, had modern small arms and machine guns,
and was supported by fire from a formidable warship,"
Courtney wheezed back, having obviously overheard. He

was in much better shape than Dennis had ever seen him but was having trouble with the low crawl as well. Particularly burdened by a thirty-pound Vickers gun that he was dragging along beside him on a leather sled. He'd surprised Silva and Chack by confessing, rather enigmatically, that he knew how to operate it—as long as it didn't "throw a wobbler."

"Details," Silva muttered distractedly, searching the gloom for a spiky lizard. He found something sharp with his hand. "Shit," he muttered, but in a tone of relief despite the new pain. "Thorns."

"What a baby," Miles scoffed. "I always hear stories about 'The Great Dennis Silva,' but you're just a whiny baby when it comes down to it."

"I'm gripin'. I told you, there's a difference." He looked back at Miles, who was dragging another Vickers. A 'Cat youngling, too small to handle one of the powerful bows, had been detailed to stay with him, along with a pouch of extra magazines, just as another trailed Courtney with a similar pouch and his Krag. Miles's Allin-Silva rifle had been given to Kaam, along with a two-day course in how to use it. He'd even competently fired a couple of rounds, but seemed most impressed by the long, triangular bayonet. A third youngling, an older female, had no other mission that night than to lug Silva's heavy Doom Stomper and its bandolier. Dennis hoped he wouldn't need it and had his Thompson in his hands. "An' we'll see how *you* do when the lead starts flyin'," he added. "Chack said these Griks have muskets, different from the matchlocks they've used on us before. Said they look like copies of the ones our guys carried ashore on Ceylon—which were caplocks!" He shook his head. "God knows how they cap 'em, with their claws, but they must somehow. Larry figured it out, so maybe they did too. Anyway, it's liable to get real noisy here d'rectly, an' if you run away"—his face hardened—"I'll plug you in the goddamn back. Clear?"

Miles bristled. "Maybe I'll beat you to it."

"Gentlemen," Courtney soothed, but there was a note of irritation in his voice. "You've been sniping at each other since this trip began, and I insist you put an end to it. At least until our current business is concluded!"

Silva slowly grinned that . . . unnerving way he had, visible even under the thin moon. "Sure, Mr. Bradford. It's just fightin' talk. Always comes out before a fight, when fellas are keyed up. Ain't that so, Miles?"

"Indeed," Courtney puffed doubtfully as they pushed on, keeping up with the line advancing on either side of them. He couldn't recall ever having seen Silva "keyed up," and knew he wasn't now.

"They don't like each other," Kaam whispered, and Courtney jumped, betraying how nervous *he* was. "Oh. I didn't see you edging closer. I was distracted, I suppose."

"Those two, not Aan-glis, but . . . men like them, like you, like Lef-ten-aant."

Courtney nodded in the dark. "Yes. All men," he agreed. "We—at least some of us—call Mi-Anakka 'Lemurians.'"

"Why?"

For an embarrassing moment, Courtney was at a loss. "Well, when my people first met Colonel Chack's, we didn't speak the same language—except for a *different* language that few of either of our people knew. . . ." He stopped, realizing how absurd that sounded. How to explain that his limited Latin and the corrupted version that Adar had learned from his Sacred Scrolls had formed the foundation of their early communications? "In any event, it's a long story. But that's what some of us called the Mi-Anakka. Among other things," he added truthfully. "It's been a great advantage since that so many Mi-Anakka still understand one another after having been so long apart. There must be something about your base language that discourages corruption over time," he thought aloud.

"I do not know," Kaam said, but then flicked his ears at Silva and Miles. "I do know men. I met some Aan-glis traders long ago, and I knew Lef-ten-aant. I learned, like Mi-Anakka, there are good men and bad, so though they were men, they were still people. Only those who think *all* bad, like Gaa-rieks, and some Erokighaani, are not people. Do you understand?"

"Yes, I think so," Courtney gasped, dragging the Vickers over a large rock, and believed he did. *How profound!* "There are men like that," he confessed. "And by your

definition they would certainly *not* be 'people' either."
Adolf Hitler and Joseph Stalin come immediately to mind. . . .

Kaam flicked his ears at Silva and Miles again. "What
about them?"

Courtney had to stop and stare at Kaam in the darkness. He needed a rest anyway. "You can do that? Judge
whether individual members of a, um, clan or species are
people or not?" *Why not? I just did.*

"Yes. Among the Shee-Ree, those who are found not
to be people are . . . not allowed to live among us. They
are dangerous and must be made to go."

"If they won't?"

"They are killed."

"A sensible solution, I suppose," Courtney said, rubbing his nose and starting forward again.

"Then you see also why I ask about them, since they"—
Kaam paused thoughtfully—"and your Col-nol Chack are
the most dangerous people I have ever seen. If they are
not really people . . ."

"Oh! I see," Courtney exhaled, glancing quickly back
to make sure the two men hadn't heard. *What if they did?
Miles doesn't understand the language well enough, and
Silva wouldn't care.* "Then rest assured. All of us are people, even dear Lawrence," Courtney whispered firmly. After a brief pause, Kaam seemed to take him at his word.
Oh, I do hope we all remain people, Courtney thought. *This
dreadful war has torn us so! But it's interesting that even
though Grik aren't "people" in Kaam's eyes, he doesn't
question Lawrence's personhood. Or mine.* He considered
more carefully. *There doubtless lingers some bad in Dennis
Silva's heart, but there's a great deal of good there as well.
It's like he suffers from a kind of behavioral Tourette's syn-
drome. Isn't there a name for that? And paradoxically, the
worse the war gets, he alone seems to spiritually thrive, revealing more and more good all the time. But what of Miles?
Silva probably explained that best himself. He sees a lot of
his old self in Miles, and probably loathes him for it. In
Miles's case, he sees in Silva a man he can never measure
up to.* He frowned. *I think. I really haven't paid nearly
enough attention to the man, particularly considering his*

long association with Commander Herring and the dreadful weapon the two of them literally smuggled into the war zone. I wonder how many know about that. Has Adar even told Captain Reddy? That thought made Courtney extremely uncomfortable, and he vigorously shook his head. *I've been directly involved in few enough battles, but I'm sure the last thing I should be doing just now is pondering things such as that—and analyzing my companions.* He took several deep breaths. *It does keep my mind off this tiresome, undignified advance, however, and this bloody great gun I so foolishly volunteered to operate! Perhaps I should've allowed others to move it....* "How much farther?" he gasped.

"We are nearly close enough now," Kaam replied. Ahead through the tangle of brush was a clearing about a hundred yards wide. Beyond it was the boma, densely packed with the brush that had been cut. Firelight flickered beyond it, from camps, Courtney assumed, and torches threw enough light to silhouette two of the gun embrasures before them. Occasional movement betrayed a Grik sentry, but there'd been no pickets, and it really didn't look like there was a great deal of tension or expectation on the other side of the palisade. He felt a thrill, but at the same time a sense of resentment threatened to overcome him. "They *are* ridiculously arrogant, aren't they? But all the better for us. I do believe we've achieved the element of surprise," he murmured.

"The cleared area Col-nol Chack described before we parted is there," Kaam confirmed. "The thunder weapons he saw must have a similar range to our bows."

"If they are what he thinks, they should have a similar *accurate* range," Courtney reminded, "but they're still lethal considerably farther away."

"Either way, we have almost reached our attack place without discovery." Kaam moved a bit farther, glancing right and left. "Here," he said. "Place your weapon. Corporaal Miles," he whispered louder, "here is the place!" Miles and Silva crawled forward.

"Looks like we caught 'em nappin'," Silva said. "We'll wake 'em up soon enough." He looked at Kaam. "Whenever you're ready, Cap'n o' the Guard, but remember, as soon as we overrun the palisade, ever'body has to hit the brakes." He watched the yellow eyes disappear behind uncomprehending—and frustrated—blinking. "I mean *stop.* 'Raise a ruckus,' remember? We gotta give Chackie an' ol' Roar-at-Y'all a chance to do their thing. If we can do more beyond that, swell, but our main chore is to make a lot of noise an' keep it up for a while."

Emaciated Lemurians plodded listlessly along in the dark, carrying burdens of dry wood on their shoulders that would've been impressive for strong, healthy 'Cats. These were anything but. Yet they staggered on like a line of ants from the remains of the Khot-So village to the hastily constructed pier on the north side of the river. Chack had seen this through his Imperial telescope during his sunset observation from a small rise on the far side of the river, there to scrutinize the disposition of the enemy for himself. That's when his desperate plan, employing a few hypothetical scenarios he'd discussed with Silva and Lawrence, took its final shape. He didn't much *like* the plan, and feared it would be quite costly, but he simply couldn't think of anything better in the limited time they had.

The village had been dismantled, even the great trees cut down, all to feed the boilers of the Grik transport tugs that came and went almost every day, according to the scouts. Slave work parties moved constantly to shift all that wood, and they weren't even that closely guarded. What could they do? They were too weak to run far, and any who tried was shot by what looked like exact copies of the Allies' own first-generation muskets. *They must have gotten captured specimens of those out of Say-lon or Indiaa,* he'd realized. Occasionally, a slave simply dropped under its load. When that happened, a Grik guard eventually approached, cut its throat, and flung the corpse on one of the carts, also loaded with wood, drawn by other slaves. That burned his heart, but when he saw the grim procession pass through the lighter defensive circle, through the smaller encampment, and directly to the moored steamers and barges with no notice at all, the opportunity was obvious. Particularly when he studied the tugs. They were unlike anything he'd seen the Grik make. Double-ended sidewheelers, like he'd seen in the Empire of the New Britain Isles, and about fifty or sixty tails long. They gushed woodsmoke from a single tall funnel, he noted, which meant they kept steam up all the time, but they had no masts for sails at all; fairly ambitious considering how unreliable Grik engines had been thus far. Just as important as the tugs, however, was what he saw secured behind each one: a high-sided rectangular barge a hundred tails or more in length. Obviously, the Grik used them to bring troops and supplies to this place. He'd use them to get people out.

Now he and a dozen Shee-Ree waited in a clump of brush, burdens of wood concealing weapons close at hand, and watched one of the Grik guards swagger casually closer as if to make a cursory inspection of their hiding place. The 'Cats around Chack nocked arrows on bows they would leave behind and tensed.

"Wait," he hissed. "Let him get closer."

The Grik paused barely ten yards away. It was dressed in light leather armor dyed a dull gray and wore an iron-plated leather helmet just like all the other Grik. This was unusual in itself since they'd only ever seen a few Grik regiments wear actual uniforms. Over its shoulder was a cartridge box exactly like the Allied model, and it carried a sword and a brightly polished musket, complete with a socket bayonet. Chack sighed with relief when his closer inspection revealed the weapon to be an Allin-Silva rifle.

"Colonel Chack," Lawrence hissed. "Hurry. The, ah, coast is clear."

"Let's go," Chack ordered, and the 'Cats dropped their bows, shouldered their loads, and darted out to join the column of hopeless misery that trod before them. There were a few exclamations of alarm but these were quickly silenced by hasty, whispered explanations. Chack tensed. He'd told his comrades what they might have to do if someone drew too much attention, but fortunately that didn't happen. Chack joined his raiders—he was already thinking of them that way—and Lawrence stepped close enough to whisper, "This ar'or stinks."

"Its owner won't be found?"

"Not tonight," Lawrence assured. He wrinkled his

snout. "The goo the Shee-Ree used to stain I to look like a Grik stinks too," he complained wryly.

"It will wash off. Probably," Chack tried to reassure him. Several of the closer Lemurian slaves were unnerved by Lawrence's proximity—and by the fact he spoke their tongue. "Do not fear. He is one of us . . . in disguise." He figured that would be the easiest explanation just then, and it was true enough.

"Loose!" Kaam cried, his voice carrying in that distinctive Lemurian way. With a great, long, whickering rush, six hundred invisible arrows rose high in the air.

"Go, go, go!" Silva roared, racking the bolt on his Thompson and leaping forward. Petey squeaked but held on. "We gotta get amongst 'em just after the arrows hit! Watch our asses," Silva shouted back at Courtney and Miles. "An' don't shoot us in 'em," he added ironically.

Kaam gave the order to charge and a great, trilling roar went up.

"Just go," Courtney cried back, sighting on the gun embrasure through a lane left open for Miles and him. Their jobs were to ensure that no Grik could fire those guns, if they were loaded and waiting for something like this. Silva sprinted forward.

Glancing from side to side as he ran, he saw the whole force charging the palisade and the sound they made sent a chill down his spine. Like many other things, apparently, Lemurian battle cries hadn't changed very much, and not for the first time he suspected they were a lot like what the oldsters he'd grown up around had described as a "rebel yell." That cry had stricken fear into the hearts of their enemies, he'd been told, and this one probably did the same. It sure gave *him* the creeps. He heard the stutter of a Vickers gun and felt bullets pass him in the dark. For an instant he wondered if Miles was shooting at him after all, but dull red sparks sprayed from the cannon in front of him and he saw a shape pitch backward. Then he was at the embrasure itself, huffing and yelling, and he climbed up on the brush in front of the gun's axle. There in the flickering firelight he saw a Grik staring at him in wide-eyed astonishment, and he fired a short burst in its face. Wet . . . things pattered against him. Leaping across the axle, he almost fell, but regained his balance in time to spray another pair of Grik hurrying toward the gun. They spun and crashed to the ground. With his longer strides, he'd been the first to reach and breach the palisade, but now 'Cats were pouring through after him. Kaam was shouting for them to hold, and most did, though a few raced onward, lured by the near-perfect surprise they'd achieved.

"Turn these guns!" Silva yelled, slapping the one beside him. "Here, you three on this wheel, you others on that one. Heave it back! Now, you three hold on while the others push! Get over here and lend a hand!" he shouted at some other 'Cats just staring. "Get on the trail—that thing sticking out the back—and move it right . . . no! *Its* right, goddammit!"

"What's 'right'?" one of the 'Cats screeched in frustrated anguish. Silva, somewhat chastened, quickly showed them, and a few moments later the gun was turned and pointing back at the camps. A quick glance up the line revealed that the other three guns were turning as well. No live Grik remained near them, and a fair number had been pinned to the ground by the initial arrow volley. Any that survived that had been hacked apart. A growing tumult from the camps made it clear the Grik were starting to stir, however, and he looked at the vent at the breech of the big gun. "Somebody take that staff and shove it down the barrel," he roared. "Yeah, that thing! Stick it in the hole up forward—in the end there, dammit! Put your hand on the staff where it stops and show me." One of the 'Cats, blinking something like desperation to please, drew the rammer and showed him. "Yeah, it's loaded. Check these bodies. Look in their pouches! One of 'em's gotta have a priming horn or somethin'." Another 'Cat showed him what looked like a handful of paper tubes. "Yeah! Gimme one o' those!" He took a tube and, after squinting at it in the gloom, broke it in two. A little powder leaked on his hands. "Break 'em," he instructed. "One for each gun, an' stick 'em in these little holes. Tell everybody to stay behind 'em—but not *right* behind 'em. They'll sqwush you when they go off—an' point 'em at the enemy!" The

Grik were practically swarming now, in confusion, but weren't advancing; they were *forming up*. "Tell 'em to wait for my command, then light their tubes with a torch." He hurriedly looked around and saw there were still a number of torches nearby.

"Yes!" the 'Cat cried, and bolted.

"Oh my," Courtney gasped, picking his way through the embrasure, lugging the Vickers in his hands. Miles followed, as did the younglings with the small arms and ammo—and Silva's Doom Stomper. "You've already turned the guns, I see. Most impressive!" Courtney squinted. "Most impressive indeed," he continued. "The Grik are forming into ranks! I do believe they mean to fire a volley at us!"

"That's my thinkin'," Silva agreed. The Grik line was firming now, warriors forming ranks two deep the entire length of the palisade. What could only be Grik officers— real ones—frantically roared and snapped and chivvied the Grik into place. "We need to break 'em up fast."

"Where do you want us?" Courtney asked.

"Here. On the ground. Kaam!" Silva called aside. "When we open up, I need your archers to pour it in. We can't stand here an' trade arrows for musket balls. They'll eat us up." He didn't add that he doubted Kaam's undisciplined warriors would stand under the withering fusillade these Grik seemed prepared to deliver. "Hurry it up! Are those other guns ready?"

The shouted replies of "Yes!" were anxious—and uncertain. These 'Cats had no idea what they were about to unleash, had no idea what they were about to *endure*, but they were willing and highly motivated. Silva hoped that would be enough.

"Fire!" he roared, reaching over the wheel of his gun and touching the primer with his torch. Conditioned to know what would happen next, Petey clutched his neck more tightly and cringed.

None of the guns had been well aimed—they'd just been pointed in a general direction—but when three of the four big weapons spat fire and smoke amid thunderous, stuttering roars, the effect probably couldn't have been much more destructive. Obviously, the Grik finally had canister now, and hundreds of musket balls spewed from each gun.

They flailed the sky with a sheeting rush or churned the ground and skated upward, warbling into the darkness—or the enemy. But the vast majority, at a range of about sixty tails, brutally slashed into the once-neat ranks of Grik warriors that were preparing to fire. Bodies tumbled back, flinging weapons in the air. Others simply dropped to the ground. Arms, legs, and heads were pulped by the canister balls—or the secondary projectiles they created when they struck equipment. Three great swaths of mangled heaps of dead and screaming wounded had been hacked out of the Grik ranks with that single stunning barrage—and that wasn't all. As soon as the cannon fired and the smoke was whipped away by the night breeze, Courtney Bradford and Ian Miles opened with their Vickers guns, sweeping their aim back and forth across the still-standing foe. Kaam had apparently been a bit stunned himself, but his belated roar sent dozens, then hundreds of arrows arcing in. More Grik went down, like wheat before the scythe, screeching cries of agony and terror.

Silva suddenly realized that for all their "professional army" appearance and discipline, these Grik weren't veterans. That they hadn't cut and run immediately, falling prey to Courtney's "Grik Rout," bore testimony to how tough they'd be once they *were*, but he'd worry about that later. They were tough enough already. And those that hadn't fallen suddenly leveled their muskets as one. The fourth gun fired, spewing more canister into the carnage—just as the Grik fired their own volley at last.

Blood sprayed, flecking his face, and two of Silva's new gun-'Cats yelped and went down as dozens of balls shattered wheel spokes or smeared lead down the iron barrel of the cannon he stood by. Other 'Cats—a *lot* of 'Cats—went down on either side of him, wailing in pain and fear. Most kept shooting arrows, but quite a few wavered already.

"Stand fast!" Silva roared. "Kaam! Keep 'em at it! Get those other guns reloaded. You 'Cats, we gotta load this thing!"

"How?" several chorused desperately.

Silva hesitated, never having taught field artillery before, and certainly not in the middle of a battle. "I'm teachin' raccoons to dance in a hurricane," he muttered to himself. "In that chest," he shouted, pointing. "Some o' you dopes watch how we do this an' go show the others. Heave that chest over here behind the gun." One Shee-Ree opened the lid as others picked it up. "This?" he cried, raising what looked like a four- or five-inch-diameter tin can about eight inches long, with a cloth bag tied on. *Grik are really starting to get their shit together,* Silva thought. *Now they have fixed ammunition!* "Yeah," he shouted back. "Ram it in, bag first. Use that staff, the same one as before. Push it all the way down." Cursing, he raced to the chest himself and found a vent prick and another handful of primer tubes. "Keep 'em coming. As soon as one fires, slam another down—but watch yourselves!"

"Watch for what?"

Silva ignored the question. He had no time to describe how many ways there were to die while operating a muzzle-loading cannon. "Mr. Bradford, how's your ammo?" he asked instead.

"What?"

"Your ammo."

"Oh. Well, as you can see, I'm changing magazines now," Courtney replied distractedly. Dark blood glistened all over the back of his left shoulder, but there was a dead 'Cat lying next to him. Silva hoped the blood wasn't Courtney's. "I have two more left. Battles are quite amazingly loud, you know, even without the shooting." He blinked. "Of course you know," he said, and continued what he was doing.

"Mr. Bradford, you an' Miles hold your fire a second, then hose 'em good right after we shoot this off, wilya?" Courtney was still trying to lock his drum in place and didn't seem to hear, but Miles nodded. Another volley clattered at them, and more screams rent the air. *The second rank,* Silva realized, even as he glanced to see its effect. More 'Cats were down, and a few seemed ready to hop back over the palisade, but far more now fought with that hard, blinking, savagely determined . . . *way* about them he'd learned to recognize in countless fights when Lemurians had settled into what he considered the "killing zone." They'd hold a while longer.

The rammer staff thumped against the load in the gun,

the 'Cat seemingly determined to pound it through the breech. "That's good enough," Silva yelled. "Now stand clear! You and you, help me shift it a little to the right. No, dammit! If you move the *trail* right, it points the gun *left*, see? There! Hold it—I mean, stop!"

Piercing the powder bag through the vent with the prick, he broke a priming tube and stabbed it down the hole. Stepping outside the wheel and retrieving the torch from where he'd stuck it in the ground, he yelled, "Git out o' the way!" and spanked the breech with the torch. *Hisss—BOOM!* The gun roared and leaped back seven or eight feet, narrowly missing running over one of the 'Cats that hesitated too long. Piercing screams erupted beyond the smoke and the Vickers guns opened up. "Load it again," Silva shouted. Obediently, the "rammer 'Cat" snatched another canister out of the chest, carried it to the muzzle, slammed it down the barrel with his staff—and disintegrated when the charge found a lingering spark at the breech and ignited.

Even Silva was stunned by the unexpected detonation, and Petey scrambled down inside his shirt with a panicked chirp, claws digging into his skin. It could've just been the latest assault on his damaged hearing, but near silence appeared to prevail for just a moment and Silva looked around. All that was left of the rammer 'Cat—Silva never even knew his name—was legs, tail, and torso below the chest. The rest was just . . . gone. Belatedly, Silva realized he should've at least thumbed the vent. There hadn't been time to teach his pickup crew to sponge with water, or anything else for that matter, and stopping the vent was something *he* could've done that might've made a difference. He took a deep, acrid breath. "Oh well," he snapped aloud to himself, but he knew the young rammer 'Cat would join the long list of regrets he kept bottled up and tried to visit as rarely as possible. It didn't always work, and they often came to him when he least expected it, but now was definitely not the time. Short bursts from one of the Vickers guns snapped him out of it. "Load it again!" he snarled at the 'Cats standing around, blinking at the gun in obvious fear. "But treat that staff like a sore pecker. Don't go poundin' on it like that poor bastard did."

*B*right flashes lit the night on the far side of the river, punctuated by booming thumps and a tearing, crackling sound. Some of the weary, starving 'Cats in the line of slaves stared across in wonder. Most didn't even raise their heads. They just kept putting one foot in front of the other, incapable of willing themselves to do more.

"The show has begun," Chack whispered to his Shee-Ree comrades.

"Shh," Lawrence cautioned. "Guards ahead, at the gate."

It wasn't much of a gate, just a section of the boma that had been pushed aside for the slaves to pass. But it was open. Three Grik stood silhouetted against the campfires and the flashes across the river, staring at the "ruckus" Silva and Kaam's force was raising. Another commotion was rising in the camp just ahead as horns sounded, different from those Chack had heard so many times before. These were not as loud, but were capable of combining notes to give more detailed instructions. Chack wondered what they looked like; then he saw one illuminated by a campfire. It looked oddly like a bagpipe, such as some Imperial troops were so fond of, but the notes were changed by sliding something across the face of a small box between the bag and the horn that jutted up alongside the operator's head. Grik officers roused their troops with harsh cries, and some were already trotting, in columns, down to the water, where wide, shallow-draft boats awaited them.

"It is working!" one of the raiders hissed.

"Silence!" Lawrence cautioned more insistently.

One Grik turned to watch Lawrence approach, even as the first slaves were already past it. As they drew closer they could see a crest rising from the back of its helmet. An officer, then, most likely. The other two continued staring at the fight over the water.

The officer spoke to Lawrence with a series of harsh *clicks*, *clacks*, and guttural tones. Lawrence stopped and stood straight, replying with something that sounded similar, at least to Chack, but his hand tightened on his Navy cutlass, concealed in the bundle of wood on his shoulder. He had no choice but to move along, however, as the rest of the slaves trudged onward. Soon Lawrence was lost to view behind them in the dark. He faced ahead, looking at the camp while trying not to appear too curious. What he saw amazed him. There were what appeared to be squad tents arranged in neat, ordered rows, and cookfires were regularly situated. Muskets stood in tripod stands—at least until rushing warriors snatched them up and raced down toward the dock. There was growing chaos of a sort, but it was an orderly, purposeful chaos like he'd never seen Grik demonstrate before. Even General Alden had never reported anything quite this . . . unsettling from General Halik in Indiaa. It was like they'd not only copied the weapons of the Allied Army, at least as they'd been introduced to them during the invasion of Ceylon, but they'd also imitated the army itself, in form, function, and practice.

These Grik are clearly different from any I've *faced. More like the "smart" Grik Halik somehow created.* And thinking back, he realized that Safir had told him that she'd seen a few like this at Grik City, though not armed with muskets, and there hadn't been enough to make a difference. Now he was seeing the rear echelon, a mere *support battalion* for an entire army patterned after their own. He had a chilling thought. *Could we defeat the army we once were, which they seem to have copied? Yes,* he decided after a moment. *We have better weapons now, better tactics. And we're far more experienced—and ruthless—than we were. Reaching parity with the force they'd emulated, wedded to and limited by linear tactics, should make these Grik roughly equivalent to Doms. So, all other things being equal, we can still beat them. But things aren't equal, are they?* he argued somberly with himself. *They never have been equal in numbers, and the only things that have saved us are discipline and superior firepower. They seem to have caught us in the discipline department. How "superior" is our firepower now? Still enough to make up for their numbers?* He simply didn't know. Lawrence caught up with him at a trot.

"You had quite a long talk," Chack said. "What did he want, and, more important, did he buy what you had to say?"

"I don't know," Lawrence confessed. "He asked the unit, the . . . 'phack' I in. I told he the Second, ah, 'Eaters.' That's the unit this Grik"—he tugged at his armor—"is in. He thought I talked strange, and I hold I throat like it hurts. Then he asked how I didn't get chosen to get cooked, since I so short." He shook his head, blinking irritation in the Lemurian way. "Not sure he 'ought it. He let I go, though, saying the Second is headed across the ripher and I need to join it, go down there." He cut his head toward where Grik were piling into boats. Some had already shoved off, and oars were rising and falling. "I ran that direction, then this again. He could'a seen."

"We're almost to the dock," Chack said, nodding forward. Just ahead now, the first of the two steamers loomed in the darkness. It had a two-level superstructure between the paddle boxes and a small, blocky pilothouse positioned just forward of the funnel. Chack was relieved to see occasional sparks flutter upward from the funnel and glow in the stream of smoke the breeze carried away. *Steam's still up,* he thought. Behind the steamer was the barge, empty now except for heaps of wood—like the slaves carried—and it was toward the barge they were being directed by another pair of Grik sentries. Barely visible in the gloom beyond was the other steamer, also receiving a load of wood.

"All still depends on you," Chack reminded Lawrence.

Lawrence jerked a nod and strode toward the sentries. "Not a sound, if you can help it," Chack hissed at his raiders.

Both sentries were taller than Lawrence, but they never had a chance. He merely stepped right up to them and stabbed the bayonet on the end of his Allin-Silva rifle deep into the first one's eye. He stepped forward as he jerked the bayonet out and slammed the rifle butt into the other Grik's astonished face. The first fell without a sound, flopping and kicking spastically even as Lawrence reversed his weapon and drove his bloody bayonet through the second Grik's throat. It tried to scream, but there was only a harsh hiss and a thick rush of blood. Chack and his raiders dropped their loads of wood, their weapons tumbling out. A raider immediately sent a heavy arrow straight through the head of the closest guard, just beginning to stir in response to the commotion. Chack was again impressed by the power and accuracy of the Shee-Ree bows. Two raiders bolted into the night to hunt other guards while the rest tried to quell the growing uproar among the slaves. Some quickly recognized what was going on, but many were stunned, even terrified by the sudden turn of events. They moaned and cried, and a few dashed away in panic.

"No!" Chack hissed in frustration when he saw one of these running blindly back the way they'd come, through the camp and toward the first Grik sentries. "Try not to hurt them, but get the rest of them on the barge, whatever it takes," he ordered, his voice rising to be heard. He nodded at the remaining ten raiders before stooping to retrieve his gear from the pile of wood he'd dropped. "Two with Lawrence, to the engineering spaces—Lawrence will lead you there. Two with me to secure the pilothouse. The rest of you, and the others when they return, will clear the superstructure—the, ah, house above the deck—and defend the ship at all costs. Mount the Vickers gun at the top of the ramp and see if there are other weapons aboard. But don't fire unless you have to. Use arrows as long as you can. Let Chief Silva's ruckus draw as many Grik into the river as will go." He finished latching his pistol belt, affixed the bayonet on the end of his Krag, and hefted the rifle. "Let's move!"

"What about the other smoking boat?" a raider asked, and Chack hesitated. "Ror'at-Raal will take it when he comes." At least that was the plan. "And Lawrence or I will get it underway once it's secure." Of course, if they couldn't take it—or operate it when they did—they'd have to disable it. Somehow. "Follow me!" he cried, dashing up the gangway and aboard the steamer. His two raiders quickly followed, arrows nocked. Four more 'Cats banged through a hatch into the superstructure, leaving four to finish killing Grik guards and herd the slave 'Cats onto the barge. Lawrence's party brought up the rear, then darted aft as soon as they were aboard. Almost immediately, both groups met a companionway, one up, one down. "The Heavens watch you!" Chack called to Lawrence. "Good luck!" the Sa'aaran answered, then bounded down the wooden stairs. Chack went up.

An uncomprehending Grik face, toothy jaws wide with surprise, met him at the top of the stairs, and Chack drove his bayonet into the open mouth. The thing screamed and tried to slash him with its claws as it tumbled back, but Chack kept it away with the long rifle, driving up, forward, and down on the deck. Jerking back, he stabbed down again, nailing the Grik's neck to the planks and twisting savagely. An arrow whisked by over his head, and another startled Grik staggered back and fell down to the fo'c'sle below with a dead-meat *thunk*. "You guys are *good* at that," Chack complimented as he rushed onward and up the next companionway to the pilothouse. Flinging open the door and rushing inside, they found three Grik— and these had realized something was up. They weren't armed, but with their vicious teeth and wicked claws, no Grik is ever truly unarmed—and bows and arrows are not the best choice for fighting in confined spaces. Chack led with his bayonet again, taking what might've been the captain in the chest and slamming him back. A second Grik pounced from the side, teeth flashing, but one of the raiders jammed his bow in the thing's mouth and shoved hard. The string snapped and shivered the bow from the 'Cat's grasp, but the effect momentarily stunned the Grik as well. The third one clamped its jaws on the back of the raider's head and slashed his throat with its claws. Chack withdrew his bayonet and turned in time to see his third raider, still in the doorway, drop his bow and grasp the hatchet at his side. He'd never raise it in time. The second Grik had already tossed their dead comrade aside and was lunging, jaws agape. Chack stabbed it in the back, bowling it forward against the pilothouse wall while the raider, blinking furiously, practically leaped over him and brought his hatchet down between the third Grik's eyes. It made a *huff!* sound as the stone head bit deep, crushing bone and brains, then sprawled thrashing on the deck.

Chack and the raider stood gasping for a moment in the cramped pilothouse. Blood was everywhere, spattered on the walls, the deck, the wheel, and them. The sharp reek of blood and voided bowels—*Nothing stinks like Grik shit,* Chack mused numbly—was thick enough to taste. At that moment, the speaking tube beside the wheel wheezed dully, totally unlike the piercing whistles Chack was accustomed to. Without thinking, he stepped to the tube. "Bridge, ay, Chack speaking."

"Colonel Chack," came Lawrence's voice, very formal. "The engineering s'aces are secure. There's only one gauge," he added, his tone growing somewhat incredulous. "They *say* it's a gauge. There's just a line not to go o'er. It says there's enough stea' to get under'ay."

"Very well," Chack replied, equally formal. "But who's 'they'?"

"The Grik 'lack gang." Lawrence paused, then simply said, "Us didn't e'en need to kill any o' they. They're not, ah, 'soldier Grik.' Just sailors. I told they that us . . . own they now, and they act like that's okay, like it's natural." There was a slight pause. "Usual."

Chack blinked amazement. What next? At that moment, the Vickers gun on the gangway opened up, and cries of alarm reached him through the glassless windows of the pilothouse. "Very well," he said. "Make all preparations for getting underway. The Grik are wise to us."

Wham! Wham! Silva's cannon, and another, fired almost as one, canister sweeping bodies away like a great, terrible broom. He squinted through the smoke. *Finally,* what was left of the Grik line seemed to be wavering. They were no longer dressing ranks or loading and firing as mechanically as before. Some just stood as if stunned, incapable of doing anything, and Silva wondered if that was the price they'd paid for this new army. They apparently didn't run away, turn prey, like their . . . less sophisticated predecessors had done on occasion. Maybe they didn't know how, had in fact been conditioned not to even recognize the option of fleeing from danger? *Quite a stunt, if true. But when they snap, they just stand there. Run away in their heads, maybe.*

"We gotta charge 'em," Silva shouted at Kaam.

"But Col-nol Chack said not to get, ah, 'stuck in.' Said our main task was to cause alarm among the Gaa-riek, draw them to us." He looked at the carnage around them, blinking deep distress. "We have done that too well," he practically accused.

"He also figured we'd be runnin' amok in amongst 'em by now. I did too," Dennis confessed. "Never figured they'd stand like this when we surprised 'em so, an' even hammered 'em with their own guns. But they did, an' now we gotta charge 'em to break through—so we *can* run amok, see?" Also nibbling at his mind was the fear that the Grik officers might bolt aboard the steamer and shove off—or board it with enough troops to defend it—before they could seize it themselves. It was always hoped they could manage that, but the plan hadn't relied on it. If they couldn't pull it off they were supposed to withdraw after doing all the damage they could and wait for Chack downriver. But Chack was supposed to get *both* boats from the other side, plenty of space to carry everyone away. What if he didn't? Silva didn't want anyone left behind, least of all himself and Courtney, and that's what would happen if Chack only got one boat. Besides, honestly, he *wanted* that boat, and wanted to burn the zeppelins too.

"We can't stay here," Silva insisted. "We've hammered these guys an' they're ripe to bust, but pretty quick there'll be more, from the other side. When they get here, they'll be fresh. They'll chase us off—an' chase us down. So we either gotta go for broke, charge through, burn the zeps, and take the boat, or haul ass. An' we gotta do it right goddamn *now*."

Kaam looked at him, blinking something Silva couldn't decipher, dark or not. "This fight"—he gestured helplessly around—"*this* is war? As you know it?"

"Pretty much," Dennis said. "An' it's here to stay. All you can do is jump in an' fight like hell or run away. An' if you run, it'll catch you from behind an' tear your guts out. Guaranteed."

Kaam blinked again, but his ears stiffened with determination. "Then we jump in," he said. "I will not be brought down like fleeing prey." Silva nodded grimly back, remembering that despite his current distress, this was the Lemurian who'd charged a puff lizard. "Let 'em have a good rip," he called to Courtney and Miles, "then we're at 'em. Bring your guns if you can, bust 'em if you can't. I wish we could spike these," he said, waving at the cannons, "but I don't even know how to tell these little guys what that is."

"So, are we going already, or are you going to stand there jacking your jaw like some damn officer?" Miles snapped.

"After you, Miles," Silva replied mildly, and Miles snorted and started firing. Kaam raised his voice and exhorted his warriors to war.

A growing number of Grik were shooting at the raiders on the tug, and even at the released slaves trying to surge aboard the barge. One of the 'Cats they'd trained on the Vickers gun sprayed the enemy with admirable restraint considering the circumstances—and that he'd never been allowed to shoot his amazing weapon before. Just like Silva instructed him, he maintained short, controlled bursts but squealed with delight at the sight of bright tracers probing for and shredding his targets. For the moment, well-aimed arrows and the Vickers were keeping the enemy back. Most of the Grik troops on this side of the river—Chack had to grudgingly admit they *were* troops—had already boarded the boats and rowed into the darkness. Many might be returning even now, but there weren't many left, and the opportunity had been made. *Now, if only Ror'at will make the most of it,* Chack brooded. He was lying prone on the upper deck beside the pilothouse, picking off Grik marksmen with his Krag, drawn to them by their own muzzle flashes. Hardly any seemed to be shooting at him, and Chack's sharp eyes and accurate rifle made every shot count. Still, they didn't have much time. They were probably outnumbered ten or twenty to one, even if the Grik couldn't know that yet, and some of those that left *would* come back.

"Col-nol!" said the raider who'd stayed with him throughout. He was pointing north, where a few muskets were popping and flaring in the dark, first at the boma, firing outward, and then in seemingly random directions. Even over the fighting, Chack heard a trilling battle cry wash over the boma and into the camp. The distant musket fire all but ceased, and soon running shapes were visible, lit by campfires—and squad tents that began to burn.

"No!" Chack muttered angrily. "Don't waste time on destruction. Just get over here!" Ror'at's three hundred warriors couldn't hear him, of course, and their sudden frenzy upon breaching the Grik defenses was probably understandable even though he'd specifically warned Ror'at not to permit it. But in retrospect, what could Ror'at have done? He was High Chief of less than a third of the warriors here. And beyond that, the Shee-Ree and their allies were suddenly in a position to take vengeance, small as it was, on an enemy that had tormented them throughout their collective history. They proceeded to do so. More and more tents erupted in flames, sending sparks and flakes of burning canvas swirling into the sky. A thunderclap explosion heralded the destruction of what was probably a small powder magazine or armory. Grik screamed in terror and agony as they were mercilessly slain.

The Grik on the landing still fought, but their fire became sporadic as they were distracted by events behind them. The fire from the tug lessened as well, as raiders took greater care what shapes they shot at, and the Vickers went silent. Triumphant shouts and yipping cries preceded a sudden flurry of arrows that felled many of the Grik still standing, and Chack thought he saw two or three actually break for the dock where the boats had departed. It struck him, though, that they didn't seem to be mindlessly fleeing. They just left a hopeless position, carrying their weapons. Something else to think about later.

"Col-nol Chack?" came a shout from below as several dozen Shee-Ree emerged from the gloom. It was Ror'at-Raal himself who'd apparently led the spearhead to the dock.

"Here!" Chack called back. "This tug and barge are secure. You must take the other!"

"It is already being done." A block of large tents near the other steamer went up in flames, illuminating it clearly for the first time. To Chack's amazement, the tug had cast off its lines and was trying to get underway, its paddle wheels churning the river to froth at its sides. Almost comically, though, the barge was still secured to the shore and the towlines hadn't been cut. Someone would figure that out soon enough, and Ror'at realized that just as Chack did. "Come!" he shouted to the warriors standing by, and they raced off, toward the barge, Chack assumed. They'd have to board the tug from it, across the towlines, while keeping the Grik sailors from cutting them. A sudden thought made him stand and sling the Krag. "I'll have to go," he told the raider beside him, "to stop the engine once they capture the vessel. Even if the boarders figure it out, it will take time we don't have." He rushed toward the companionway.

"Send Laa-raance!" the raider shouted after him. "Your place is here!" Chack started to yell back that calling Lawrence up out of the engineering spaces and sending him over would take too much time as well, when he realized the 'Cat was right. With Ror'at running around, his place was here—and Lawrence might be able to "capture" another black gang to boot. All was rendered irrelevant, however, when something very substantial blew up. One of the burning tents alongside the other tug must've sheltered a large stockpile of ammunition meant for the army that marched away. It might've been *the* stockpile, judging by the size of the blast. Two hundred yards away, Chack saw an impossibly bright flash of yellow fire engulf the tents, slam the straining steamer on its beam ends—and blowtorch a strung-out huddle of rushing Mi-Anakka into oblivion.

The overpressure blew Chack to the deck and he saw the sky alight with flaming, fluttering debris. He jumped up and stared aft. The tug was still rolling, its port paddle-wheel spinning in air. Then its boiler burst when cascading water touched it and more debris, jagged, lethal, sprayed in all directions, some scything into the terrified slaves huddled in the barge trying to avoid the falling, burning fragments from the first explosion. A terrible, keening wail mounted from wretched beings that had already endured too much. Of the other barge that had been secured to the destroyed tug, nothing could be seen. Striding a little unsteadily back where he'd been, Chack helped the raider to his feet and roared savagely down at the dazed warriors that had begun to gather alongside.

"Ror'at-Raal is *dead*! *You* killed him with your senselessness! Now I command without question and will kill any who dares dispute that!" He waited a moment, gasping with rage at these . . . *idiots*. But he was just as furious with Ror'at-Raal, he realized, for leaving him in this position. And he was probably most angry with himself for creating the situation in the first place. What hubris! At that moment he wasn't interested in considering the fact that he really hadn't had a choice. When there was no challenge to what he'd said, he spoke again. "You." He pointed at a burly female 'Cat at random. "Take twenty and gather the rest of those . . . *herdbeasts* bent on destruction and bring them here immediately. You." He pointed at another 'Cat. "Take twenty more and search quickly for survivors over there." He waved at the destruction aft. Ror'at had said others were already nearing the other tug. Maybe some had survived. "The rest of you, other than those my raiders choose to help with security and guard against a counterattack, will go aboard the barge. Put out fires, check for damage, tend the wounded, and stay out of the way! There will be another day to kill Grik, I promise," he said, finally softening his tone. "We will kill them together. But first we must get those people out," he said, gesturing again at the barge, "and rendezvous with the boats carrying your families. After that, we have a long trip ahead of us that may be contested, and we can afford no more foolishness."

He was surprised by how quickly everyone in earshot suddenly moved to comply with his commands. *If only they'd been so willing before,* he thought. *Or maybe they were, but no one ever spoke to them like that: together, as one people.* He shook his head. *I should have. They do have a common cause, after all. The most fundamental cause of all: survival.* He caught the raider blinking something like amazement at him.

"What?"

"Nothing, Lord . . . Ah, Col-nol Chack. What can I do?"

Chack gazed across the river. The cannon fire had ended, but so, it seemed, had the organized volleys. The fighting had bloomed into what looked like a general melee, with firing everywhere. He even thought he glimpsed the distant sparkle of a Thompson. "Single up all lines. . . ." He paused. "I mean, take in all lines but one each at the front and back of the tug and barge," he said, hoping that was simple enough. He glanced back at the fighting across the river. "And then pray to the Maker."

West-Central Mada-gaas-gar
Predawn, October 12, 1944

*T*he firelit dark seemed alive with arrows and whizzing, warbling musket balls as four hundred and fifty or more Shee-Ree and their allies smashed through the faltering Grik line. Stone hatchets were a poor match for Grik bayonets, and it had been touch and go for a moment. But when it came right down to it, these Grik were just as new to this kind of fighting as their attackers. And disciplined as they were, the Grik simply weren't motivated by the same furious resolve that stoked the Lemurian charge. They didn't actually flee, just running for their lives as so many Grik had done before, but they did scatter, and that allowed Kaam's combined force to rampage deep into the Grik position.

Dennis Silva ran with the tide, trying to keep track of Courtney. He didn't know if Miles had joined the advance and didn't really care. Courtney seemed just as caught up in the charge—and the chase—as any of the 'Cats, and it was the first time Silva had ever seen him like that. His sweat-beaded face was red and set with an expression of utmost determination, and the thirty-pound weapon he lugged didn't appear to slow him at all. Occasionally, he slammed to a stop beside a crate or cart, and with something to prop the barrel on, hosed a gathering of Grik with .303 tracers.

"Blast!" he shouted when the Vickers coughed to a stop. "Another magazine, if you please," he instructed the wide-eyed youngling with the bag of ammunition and his Krag. A ball slapped into the crate Courtney was using as a rest, and Silva fired a burst at two Grik, charging together with bayonets leveled. Both dropped, writhing and squalling, and 'Cats hacked them apart as they raced past. Silva's bolt had locked back, and he released his own empty magazine. "You okay?" he shouted over his shoulder in his rough Lemurian at the youngling carrying his Doom Stomper. She'd stumbled under the load and seemed to be having trouble getting up. "Yes! Good!" she gasped back gamely, her high-pitched voice sounding much like Petey's. Petey remained hidden under Silva's shirt, but had shifted his grasp to the strap over his shoulder instead of his flesh.

"Well . . . quit doin' that. Thought you was shot." Silva slammed another twenty-round stick in his Thompson but hesitated, still looking at the youngling. "Aw, shit. Maybe you best just leave that damn heavy thing," he told her. "It ain't much good in this fight, an' they'll give me another. Not like anybody else wants one of 'em."

"No!" the youngling stated flatly, blinking irritation. "I *will* carry it. I have this far," she reminded him defiantly. "This is my . . . *mission*," she added, using the unfamiliar English word she already seemed to understand quite well.

Dennis shrugged. "Suit yerself, Squirt. C'mon, Mr. Bradford. We're drawin' a crowd."

"Yes, yes, indeed," Courtney replied, finishing attaching his final drum. "Most of our friends have passed us by, but there remain quite a few Grik filtering back into the fight!" They ran to catch up with their Lemurian comrades, hearing or feeling musket balls *voop* past from behind, and Silva had to be careful where he fired, lest he hit friendlies that had gotten ahead. There were still plenty of targets. The night had been replaced by a bright, swirling inferno as tents, carts, and equipment of all sorts were put to the torch, and Dennis was just beginning to realize just how big a supply depot the Grik position was. Burning canvas and heaps of wood were stuffed under guns arrayed in an artillery park, and their carriages crackled and hissed as the flames took hold. Explosions erupted here and there, probably small magazines or ammunition chests for the artillery, sweeping away friend and foe alike. Dennis fired at another group of Grik rushing to block them, raising their muskets. All went down.

Struck by a sudden notion, he shouted for his companions to keep going while he trotted over for a quick glance at the dead Grik. *Not like any I ever saw, a'tall,* he thought. *All dressed alike, workin' together, followin' orders. They're more like Tony Scott's Khonashi, or even ol' Larry; full o' vim an' vinegar, an' smart enough to gang up instead o' just runnin' at us all alone.* He quickly surveyed the corpses and wasn't surprised to confirm a theory. Judging by their crestless heads they were all about two, maybe three years old, the age at which Bradford had finally determined that the Grik reached physical, lethal maturity. *An' plenty o' time to teach 'em new tricks if they start as soon as their beady eyes open,* Dennis added to himself. Perhaps most disturbing, none had claws on the thumb and two fingers of their right hands, and it looked like they'd been removed at birth. Grik did that to young Hij destined to become artisans, and Larry had figured out on his own to keep several of his claws filed back strictly so he could handle weapons and ammunition better. But they'd never encountered "warrior" Grik like that before, prepared and obviously trained from birth to perform complex tasks with their hands. *Like pinchin' musket caps,* Silva brooded. *That must'a took a serious shift in Grik thinkin'.* Their claws and teeth had always been what made the Grik such lethal hunters—of all kinds of prey. And even after they'd taken up swords, spears, and crossbows who knew how long ago, their claws still symbolized their age-old image of themselves as the world's fiercest predators. Dennis had seen the first charts they ever captured from the enemy, and claw signs had even been used to show territory the Grik controlled. Claws were part of what made them what they were.

"I bet that damn Kurokawa kicked this off, givin' the idea to Esshk," he muttered grimly. "Weren't for that slimy bastard, we'd'a licked the Grik already and saved a lot o' lives. He's gonna pay for that."

A musket ball snatched at his pants leg, and he fired back at another gathering group before sprinting after his friends.

A huge pulse of fire throbbed across the river, illuminating the tugs and barges there. One tug had been caught in the blast, and it rolled swiftly onto its side. Moments later, it blew up. "*Thought* we'd need the one over here," he grumbled. But up ahead, it looked like they'd lose this one as well because the whole camp was going up in flames. "Dammit, Mr. Bradford!" he shouted, catching up. "Quit playin' soljer an' shootin' at whatever stray lizard you see. We gotta take the tug! An' you or me will have to raise steam if the boilers are cold, an' conn the damn thing too!"

"Quite right," Courtney agreed, blinking streaming eyes against the bitter smoke. Beyond him, fire arrows arced into the sky and fastened onto one of the hovering zeppelins. They were answered by a fusillade of musket shots, and no more arrows flew at the airship. For a moment, nothing happened, but then blue flames flickered for an instant before racing up the fabric sides to join a greater boil of burning hydrogen that suddenly pulsed inside the envelope and burst out the top to form a perfect mushroom of flame. The whole thing crashed to the ground—like the burning skeleton of the giant flying fish the locals likened it to—and ignited an enormous fire close to the dock. There were Shee-Ree around them now, and most stopped to stare at the amazing sight until a crackle of musketry toppled a few and the rest turned to face the threat from behind. Scores of Grik were rushing out of the smoke.

"Go!" Silva yelled at Courtney. "Find Kaam an' take that tug! We'll hold 'em back a minute 'er two, then come a'runnin.'"

"But . . ."

Silva looked at the youngling who now carried only Courtney's Krag. "Get him to that boat, hear? That's *your* mission now! Nobody's goin' anywhere if we don't get him aboard, at least." He nodded at the other youngling with his Doom Stomper. "Take her too. I want that gun *safe*!" he added for her benefit. Then he turned and started firing.

Some time later—Dennis didn't know how long, but the faintest hint of gray had finally touched the eastern horizon—it was almost quiet where he wearily sat, the hot Thompson lying across his lap. It was empty, and so was his last magazine. That was a shame, since there was still stiff fighting down by the dock, too heavy for him and his five surviving battle-worn 'Cats to break through. But it had apparently drawn all the remaining Grik, and there was nothing around just now but smoldering tents and corpses. Silently they watched the tug and barge pull awkwardly from the dock. It would be close. There was fighting on the barge itself, against Grik that had boarded to retake the vessels, but Silva figured Courtney and at least a few hundred 'Cats were clear. Probably more, since it looked like the slave pens on this side of the river, near where the burning zeppelin fell, were empty. Even so, he didn't know whether to cheer or . . . well, he wouldn't sob.

He just hadn't realized until now how badly he'd wanted back in the "real" war, back "home" with USS *Walker*—and now it looked like he was stuck. *It could be worse,* he supposed. *These Shee-Ree 'Cats're okay, and the ones that didn't get on the barge can use a hand.* "We'll catch our breath a minute," he said for the benefit of his companions, "then round up as many lost or wounded as we can find and make tracks while the lizards're focused on the river. . . ." Musketry flared on the water as boats full of Grik fired at Chack's tug and barge, maneuvering to take on the Shee-Ree families from the dhows now gliding downstream. Tracers from Chack's Vickers stitched the Grik boats, chewing them apart. Dennis wondered if some of them may've thought better than to reveal themselves. He wouldn't have imagined the possibility before.

He caught movement out of the corner of his eye and spun to his feet, leveling the empty Thompson, even as the 'Cats hopped up with bows ready.

"You going to shoot me now?" came Miles's flat voice as he stepped forward, leading fourteen Lemurians. Most appeared lightly wounded, and even Miles was covered in blood, but he seemed unharmed—physically. The firelit expression on his face left Dennis less sure. The China Marine was pulling a resentful youngling by the arm—who was dragging a huge rifle in the dust. "I found this little idiot over there, watching you," he added.

"Idiot!" Petey squeaked nervously, peeking around Silva's neck.

"You sent me away," the youngling accused Silva, "but I still do my mission! You might need the big magic maaskit!"

Silva lowered his weapon and groaned, then slung the Thompson over his shoulder to rest in the small of his back. "Ain't gonna shoot you, Miles." He looked at the Lemurian youngling. "'Cat broads. They're all like that, young 'er old. What can you do? Get over here, Squirt." He looked at Miles. The man still had his Vickers, resting heavily in the crook of his arm. "Don't know if I'll kill you or not, though. Might depend on what you been up to. Where'd you run off to?"

Miles motioned down toward the slave pens with his chin. "Kaam went that way after the breakthrough, and I thought he might need fire support. Good thing too, I guess. There were a lot of Grik." He shook his head and for the first time Silva saw tear tracks in the grime on his face. "We tore them up, but a lot were already headed for the docks. Then that zep fell on a bunch of them and burned the suckers alive," he related with intense satisfaction. "We had the place to ourselves for a while, so we opened the pens." He looked away, down toward the docks, where muskets still flared at the tug. Courtney, or whoever had the conn, was increasing speed, the paddle wheels churning. "Most of the poor devils caught on that we were here to help, but some went nuts. Even fought us," Miles continued. "I get that, after what they went through—after what they saw." He took a long breath. "Been there myself, you know? When the Japs had me . . ."

His red eyes glared at Silva. "The flames made it hard to see. There were lots of shadows, and I stepped in one. Only it wasn't a shadow. It was a pit." His face twisted. "A big goddamn *pit* full of bloody 'Cat bones, skins . . . other stuff . . ." He gestured helplessly at the gore covering him. "They've been butchering and *eating* these 'Cats, *right in front of the rest of them*, all this time. . . ."

"That's what they do, dammit," Silva snapped. "You knew that! I'll allow these lizards're different from any I've seen, but when it boils down to it, they're still Grik, bein' Grik. Even on their ships, they keep folks in the hold—doin' that!"

"But I never *saw* it!" Miles snarled back. "It wasn't *real*, see? I always thought what the Japs did to me, to Horn and Herring and all the others, was the worst—and it kind of . . . broke me, you know? I don't mean it made me helpless, like some of the 'Cats we saw, but it made me a . . . different man. Selfish. Damn near useless," he confessed, his tone now softer but even more bitter. "This never has been my war. You pegged me right off. I was just going along to get along, to be safe and get fed, and the hell with anybody else." He looked down at his weapon. "I have maybe half a drum left. That's it." He looked back at Silva. "But this is *my* war now, by God! These 'Cats . . ." He took another long breath, and new tears appeared. "They're *good* people, Chief, and they need me. Hell, they *want* me! I had a . . . hard time, down in that pit, but when I crawled out, Kaam was gone with most everybody else and the Grik were closing in on the dock. It didn't look easy getting through." He waved around at his Lemurian companions and straightened. "These fellas found me. Gave *me* a mission," he said, looking at the youngling with Silva's Doom Stomper. "They saved me," he added quietly.

"What mission?" Silva asked.

"Get as many of our people out of this mess as we can," he said simply, and Silva was surprised how closely Miles's plan reflected his own. "This *was* a mess," he stressed, "just like you and Colonel Chack knew it would be." He wasn't accusing, just stating a fact, and Dennis had to agree. "But we still won," Miles added, waving down at the destruction they'd caused and the two tugs and barges chuffing sparks near the middle of the river now. "We won the first victory against the Grik these people have ever seen. They know the Allies are fighting everywhere else, and winning sometimes, but now they know they can too. Word will spread, and 'Cat tribes from all over will come to fight." He shrugged, and his face grew animated with excitement for the first time since Silva knew him. "I want to help them, to keep chewing on the Grik every chance we get. Maybe just as important, that Brit bomber gave me the idea that what we—all of us—need down here is an airstrip! These people can build one pretty easy on the plain near the Naa-Kaani village. That'll let us stay in touch, get more trainers and weapons down here, and give us an air base to hammer these Grik in the ass!"

"That's . . . a pretty good notion," Silva allowed. "But how will anybody know we're doin' all that stuff, 'specially the airstrip?"

Miles looked at Silva, and his old smirk reappeared. "I thought 'The Great Dennis Silva' always had a plan, never gave up, and always came through," he mocked. "They'll know because *you'll* tell them. This is *my* show. I thought it up, and I don't want you meddling around."

Silva cocked his head and arched the brow over his good eye, his near-perpetual grin approaching that worrisome shape. This was definitely a different Miles from the one that went into the battle, but they still weren't pals. "It's a cinch I ain't hitchin' a ride with Courtney or Chackie," Dennis said. "They'll pick up whoever's already made it downriver, if they can"—he gestured at the five 'Cats and the youngling standing beside him—"but they'll be long gone before us that stayed fightin' can get there."

Miles snorted. "You're right—and you're stupid. Hurts to say the first, but I've been waiting a long time to say the other. And both are true. What we're going to do is help you get down behind the Grik before they wise up and start looking to their rear again. Then we're going to get you up in that," he said, pointing. Silva looked, and for the first time he really noticed the second Grik zeppelin still suspended above the ground, miraculously untouched by the flames.

"I'll be damned. I should'a thought o' that," he said, his grin changing, growing wider. "I really should, you know? Maybe I am a little stupid—tired." He nodded decisively. "Sounds like a hoot, if I can make it go."

"What? You never flew a zeppelin before?" Miles asked.

"Nope. But there's always a first time. I'm game, if we can get it." He looked at Miles, nodded, then pulled his battered 1917 cutlass with his right hand and his .45 with his left. "An' you're right too. Let's go before they figure out some of us are still runnin' around behind 'em. No shootin' unless we have to."

They scrambled closer to the docks and the preponderance of remaining Grik, keeping to the shadows as best they could. It wasn't easy. The flames lit the area pretty thoroughly, and the first rays of the sun had begun to emerge, turning the top of their objective a fluorescent golden pink. There was a lot of smoke, though, and the tugs and barges still held the Grik's attention, stopped in the middle of the river, transferring passengers from the dhows. Soon they were in sight of the mooring lines tethering the zeppelin to the ground, and there weren't any Grik in sight. The proximity of the fires had probably driven them away. A rope ladder dangled from the forward gondola. "I bet there's nobody up there either," Miles puffed, tired from their run. "Hell, with everything burning all around, *I* wouldn't go up there." He paused and grinned ironically, challengingly. "But I'm not Dennis Silva."

"You just watch." Silva grinned back. "Who's with me?" The five 'Cats who'd been with him for the rear-guard fight all volunteered—somewhat hesitantly, he noted understandingly—and the female youngling with his Doom Stomper defiantly stepped forward. "Oh, all right," he grumped. "Go! All of you, before the damn lizards see us!" The 'Cats rushed the hanging ladder, so similar to those they used to access their tree lodges, and scampered up. Dennis turned to Miles. "You're gonna have to cut us loose," he told him, "an' keep the Griks off us if they look this way, but haul ass as soon as we're risin'." He scratched his ear under his helmet. "Might take us a minute or two to figure out how the damn thing works, but don't wait for that, just scram."

"You won't have to tell us when," Miles assured. "We'll be long gone." Suddenly, hesitantly, he stuck out his hand.

Silva immediately took it. "I'm glad I didn't have to kill your sorry ass after all, Miles," he said lightly, "but I still gotta know one thing: did Herring ever tell you who he gave that kudzu bomb to?"

Miles shook his head. "He didn't trust me anymore. I don't blame him. But just between us, I figure it was Adar. Maybe even Mr. Bradford. I know they were sending messages back and forth about it after we headed down here in the Seven boat—and Mr. Bradford's not as opposed to using it as he once was."

Silva blinked thoughtfully. "Hmm. That may be. Even so, just between us, keep it to yourself."

"Sure," Miles said, looking at the waterfront when he heard a loud report. Apparently the Grik had finally moved a couple of cannon down from where they'd been stored ashore, waiting to be floated across, and were now firing at the tugs. The tugs themselves were gaining way, heading downstream. It was time to go. "I have just one more question for *you*, Chief Silva," Miles said, still looking toward the river. "If *you* had the kudzu weapon, or knew where it was, what would you do with it?"

Silva raised his brow, then slowly, that very disconcerting grin of his spread across his face. "That's a damn stupid question," he said. "Hell, I'd use it . . . first chance I got. If there was a button I could mash that'd kill every goddamn Grik on the planet, you couldn't kill me fast enough to keep me from punchin' it till it broke. So long, Miles!"

"Stupid question!" Petey cried back as the big chief gunner's mate ran to the rope ladder and hauled himself up.

"Good," Miles said quietly, grimly. "Good," he repeated more forcefully. Then he looked at his Lemurian companions. "Cut those lines, and let's get the hell out of here!"

CHAPTER 30

IRIS **Nachi**
260 Miles N, NW of the Seychelles
October 12, 1944

Generalof the Sea Hisashi Kurokawa paced the quarterdeck of his Grik-built "cruiser" flagship, the "Imperial Regency of India Ship" (IRIS) *Nachi*, as his strike aircraft returned from their attack on the American/Lemurian convoy in untidy clumps. *Not very professional,* he brooded, *the way they straggle about so. But then, this was their very first carrier operation.* He sniffed. *Their first combat operation of any kind, in most cases,* he amended. *They will improve.* His mood lightened again. *It feels quite interesting to be . . . pleased about something,* he reflected.

What he himself recognized as an uncharacteristic frame of mind was founded on a variety of things. First, of course, he was at sea and had a relatively decent ship under him. He rather liked his cruisers, particularly now they'd been significantly improved. Each was named after an "old world" cruiser and, despite numerous refinements, still resembled the old *Azuma*—Japan's very first ironclad warship—to some degree. Their rams (which he considered pointless, aside from the forward buoyancy and stability advantages they afforded) were much abbreviated, and their scantlings were uninterrupted except for gunports. He'd also done away with all but a vestigial, auxiliary sailing capacity now that his engineers had upgraded their machinery. The result was a small fleet of "pocket battleships," to borrow a term, which combined the heavy firepower and toughness of his monstrous yet vulnerably slow and clumsy battleships, with much greater speed and agility than they'd ever had before. A further personal attraction was that they were smaller, less prominent targets than his three great carriers. He'd learned that lesson long ago; one should always avoid commanding from the deck of the most conspicuous target. Of course, if he had a *real* battleship to wrap around himself . . .

He raised his 7x50 Nikko binoculars and watched the planes return to his carriers *Kaga* and *Soryu* to port, and *Akagi* steaming some distance to starboard. Except for the leaders of the Grik squadrons, he'd specified that all his Japanese pilots operate from *Akagi*. He was glad he had. Planes recovered aboard her successfully enough, though it took a great deal longer than he'd have liked. One damaged plane missed the arresting cables and slammed into the raised barricade protecting the aircraft already aboard. The result was a brief fire, but no real damage. It was different on *Kaga* and *Soryu*. Muriname's Grik pilots had apparently learned to fly fairly well, and even the newly promoted "Captain of the Sky" Iguri, so long Muriname's opponent on the subject, had finally agreed that Grik could be made competent in the air. The older ones, properly matured and trained, even seemed to have a certain knack for aerobatics. Their carrier landings left a great deal to be desired, however, and now, returning with damaged aircraft or flushed with excitement for this new kind of combat, many Grik were landing . . . poorly.

General of the Sky Muriname will be furious at the preventable loss of so many of his precious planes and pilots. Kurokawa almost chortled, and the occasional plane, cartwheeling into the sea or missing the big ship entirely and crashing in her wake, actually amused him. On one level he lamented the waste, of course, but it would take a great deal more than a few comically dead Grik and lost planes to ruin his day. And signals indicated that *Akagi*, at least, would soon be prepared to launch a second strike against the crippled enemy convoy.

He felt a growing thrill. "Crippled" was the word that lifted him, sent by Iguri, who'd led the raid in one of the twin-engine bombers. He'd been strictly ordered to avoid the actual attack so he could observe its effect—and risk a brief transmission on the radio they'd copied from the one in their old Type 95 floatplane. His was one of only three planes equipped with radio, and transmissions were dangerous things—a point driven home by the fact that intercepted *enemy* communications had made this day possible in the first place. Iguri had dutifully refrained from exposing himself to the surprisingly effective defensive fire and reported the sinking of numerous auxiliaries and at least one of the strangely converted Grik dreadnaughts. He'd also related that the enemy *carrier* was crippled and ablaze by the time the first strike was forced to return for fuel and more ordnance. For all their vast advantages over the zeppelin fleets of the past, the new planes had very short legs and a range of only about a hundred and fifty to two hundred miles if they meant to return. But most important to Kurokawa personally, Iguri had seen a steel-hulled destroyer—apparently very active in the defense—take one of their wonderful new aerial torpedoes! That ship was also crippled, and dead in the water as well. Iguri had been unable to confirm that either ship had sunk, but both were definitely badly damaged.

Kurokawa was ecstatic. As far as he or Gravois's spies knew, his enemies had exactly two steel-hulled destroyers, and one remained laid up at Madras. That meant USS *Walker* herself—and *Captain Reddy!*—must've steamed to meet the convoy at some point. It only made sense, Kurokawa supposed, if the convoy was as important to him as Gravois indicated it would be. But instead of luring his greatest enemy into battle in response to today's attack, Kurokawa had already caught him. Crippled him! Maybe even killed him! He grasped that hope with both greedy hands and continued pacing with a genuine smile on his round face.

"Ah, General of the Sea," said the slightly built Hara

Mikawa, approaching his lord with care. Mikawa was *Nachi*'s new captain, and he hadn't risen to the post from a mere ensign by being foolish. He was perfectly aware how volatile Kurokawa's moods could be. And *Nachi*'s first commander had taken great pains to remind him before leaving to command *Soryu*.

"Yes, Captain Mikawa," Kurokawa said with a . . . bizarrely benevolent tone.

"There are further reports now, signaled from *Akagi*, made by returning airmen who had different perspectives on the attack, Lord."

"And?"

"All concur that great damage has been inflicted," Mikawa stated hastily, "and the last returning Japanese pilots report that the enemy carrier is fully ablaze and listing heavily."

"Excellent news, Captain Mikawa!"

"Yes, Lord . . . but there seems to be . . . disagreement on a few small points."

Kurokawa's smile faded slightly and he blinked. "Explain."

"Lord, Captain Iguri said the enemy destroyer was struck by at least one torpedo from a staggered wave of bombers attacking the carrier from its starboard side, while the convoy was steaming eastward."

"Yes?"

Mikawa licked his lips. "Lieutenant Takeo, who led the first waves of fighters rigged with bombs, reports that he saw the enemy destroyer close alongside . . . *another* of our former battleships and a number of support vessels. Possibly more than half the convoy, all told. They were some distance away from the carrier, and after taking numerous bomb hits, those that could all steamed *west*."

Kurokawa waited.

"Lord," Mikawa continued reluctantly, "based on these conflicting reports, is it not possible that the enemy somehow managed to employ *Walker* and *Mahan* with the convoy, in some fashion?"

Kurokawa waved his binoculars. "A common error, Captain! Spatial orientation is often skewed in the air. I have often found it so myself. And it is natural for men, caught

in the exuberance of battle, to misremember details—
perfectly understandable for them to confuse the exact direction of a target they are focused on attacking." He smiled
again. "Don't you see? Despite which flight leader ultimately claims the credit, this is further proof that the American destroyer that has plagued us so long was very badly
damaged indeed, perhaps struck by bombs *and* torpedoes!"
He smiled even more broadly. "And even if there *were* two,
if they somehow managed to repair the other sufficiently
to send it down after all, then that's *both* of them accounted
for at last!"

"Yes, Lord," Mikawa agreed without inflection.

"Was there more?"

Mikawa took a breath. "Yes, Lord. Another sighting
by two of our human pilots"—no one even considered
taking reports from Grik—"confirms that at least a few of
the enemy's modern warplanes, their P-Forties, were on
their carrier when it was struck. Their destruction accelerated the flames aboard, in fact."

"More wonderful news!" Kurokawa said, almost giddy.
"I had wondered if Captain Reddy, having so wildly over-
extended himself, would send for them. I honestly doubted
he would. And now they are destroyed as well!"

"Lord," Mikawa added with in inward cringe, "though
some were definitely destroyed, others were reported to
have flown off the ship to engage our aircraft. They shot
many down before our planes broke off the attack."

Kurokawa's eyes narrowed, but then he smiled again.
"We can replace our losses, even with Grik. They can
never replace their modern warplanes. And where will
they land? They couldn't have landed on the carrier even
before it was blown from under them. I think we will find
that, as many planes as we may have lost today, their most
capable aircraft—and pilots—have been annihilated."

A Grik runner approached and hurled himself to the
deck at their feet. "*Akagi* is ready to launch its air-craht,
Sire. *Soryu* an' *Kaga* is re-ar'ing, and is soon ready to
launch, ah, 'reduced' skadrans."

"Very well," Kurokawa said lightly. It was the first time
Mikawa had ever seen him speak to any Grik without
a measure of abuse. "Still," he mused, looking back at

Mikawa. "Any surviving enemy planes will likely make for the Seychelles. Gravois tells me they have begun constructing an airfield on one of the islands in that group. I won't send *our* army away from Zanzibar just yet, but perhaps General Esshk would be interested in sweeping such a small enemy force away." He chuckled. "It might boost their reptilian morale, after all the reverses they've endured of late." He shook his head. "But the Seychelles are the only place. They can't possibly reach anywhere else."

"Lord?" Mikawa said, his voice suddenly rising in distress and his eyes flaring wide. He pointed up at the late-morning sun just as alarm horns began to roar. "There is *one* other place!"

"Flashy Flight, this is Flashy Lead. Looks like we caught 'em just like they did us, with their pants down and planes all over their decks," Ben Mallory said into his microphone over the roar of his engine. They'd also positioned themselves to approach out of the sun—just as the enemy had. Hopefully, it would work just as well for them. It definitely gave them a fine view of the enemy task force. The big carriers were as obviously made from Grik dreadnaughts as *Andamaan* and *Sular* had been, except they'd removed the casemates entirely and installed massive flight decks. Smoke hazed downwind from a cluster of funnels poking out their sides behind very small "islands." And just like the planes, all three ships had big red "meatballs" painted on them. For an instant, Ben felt almost as if he were back in the "old" war, just fighting the Japanese again. He scowled. *Not likely.* They'd had it bad, and hearing from guys like Cecil Dixon that the Japanese had caught, it only kept getting worse. But it was hard for him to imagine anything being worse than *this* damn war.

He didn't see any apparent auxiliaries, like colliers or . . . oilers. *Hey!* he realized. *Those ships are burning oil!* He didn't know how he'd missed the complete lack of telltale columns of black smoke. But where'd they get the oil—and gasoline for their airplanes, for that matter? With a sudden certainty that startled him, he knew Kurokawa must've cozied back up to the Grik in a big way. Wherever he'd holed up after their apparent break, only the Grik could get oil to him, or allow him to take it. But judging by all the meatballs, Grik pilots and ship's crews or not, this was a Kurokawa show, pure and simple. Wasn't it? Things had changed, but Kurokawa and the Grik were friends again. Friends . . . but not together. So what were the Grik up to by themselves? That was an important question—and information by itself.

Clustered around and between the carriers were about a dozen of their goofy "cruisers." He'd sunk a lot of those, but these looked different. Shorter masts and no sails, for one thing, and the armor sloped up and over the decks a lot more, making them less vulnerable from the air. *Well, we're not really interested in them today,* he thought. Those cruisers were bad news, worse than the big dreadnaughts in some ways, he understood. But they were far enough away from the split task force he needed to protect, and they couldn't fly.

"We've got six planes and twelve bombs," he said at last. "I wish we had the rest of the guys, but we're it," he added bitterly. "So here's what we'll do. Two pairs'll hit those two carriers steaming together. Flashy Two, you'll take the one on the right with Three. Flashy Five, you and Seven jump the one on the left. Chase your guns in and break 'em up. Keep 'em from shooting back if you can. If you get 'em, I'll hit the last one with Flashy Four. If you miss, we're the cleanup batters, see? So don't miss. I want all three of those bastards!" He paused. "Look," he said, "none of this is new. We hammered plenty of Grik ships when they were trying to resupply Madras. If anybody can do this, we can. Just . . . watch yourselves. Who knows what newfangled air defenses they've cooked up."

He was worried about that. Those rocket things the Grik had used weren't very effective—although there'd been fragmentary hints via wireless of something more worrisome from a scout up the Zambezi. He still didn't see how they could use rockets on a ship without torching themselves, but these guys, these "Jap-Griks," had aircraft carriers and *planes*. What else might they have come up with? They obviously had enough machine guns to arm at least some of their aircraft. He'd love to get a look at one and wondered what they were based on, as well as how accurate and reliable they were. It had taken the Allies a long time to re-create the technology required to field their own "new" machine guns. Then again, the Allies hadn't been willing to field them until they were *right*—and they weren't unique when it came to underestimating threats either. Grik antiair "canister mortars" had proven somewhat effective against slow-moving, low-flying aircraft. Maybe they'd stuck with them, confident their own armed planes would tip the balance. He'd know soon enough.

Soupy and Conrad peeled off with their wing-'Cats behind them. Ben wasn't concerned about the two leaders. They really did have plenty of experience at this sort of thing, against much smaller targets. The "new" guys in Three and Seven had almost as many hours in their hot ships, but neither had participated in the strikes he'd referred to. He doubted this was the best time to remind them, and they knew it anyway. They also knew to do what their leads did. He and Shirley rolled up on their starboard wings, looking down from five thousand feet, and watched their friends charge down at the enemy carriers. Puffs of white smoke appeared along each side of both flight decks. *So far, more of the same,* he thought, referring to the canister mortars. *There are a lot of 'em, though,* he realized. *Looks like twenty or more down each side. Plenty to knock down a couple of Nancys. But they're not used to shooting at anything as fast as a P-40 in a dive, and they're jumpy, shooting too soon.* His eyes narrowed. *Either way, there's going to be a lot of iron in the air that those planes have to fly through, and it won't make much difference if it's rising or falling when they get there.* He was too high to see the tracers darting from the attacking planes, but waterspouts galloped in from aft until they climbed the ships' sterns. Immediately, splinters and dust formed advancing clouds—and green and gray planes began to burn.

Now! he thought, just as the four planes pulled up, one after the other. Two high, heavy splashes rose behind the carrier on the right. One erupted close aboard and hurled a cascade of spume on the flight deck—just as the fourth bomb must've hit right in the center of a group of planes staging aft of the island. In an instant, several were tossed off the ship by the force of the blast, but it was the secondary explosion, fed by bombs and fuel, that appeared to ignite a floating volcano. Flashes sparkled amid mushrooming flames and blazing debris—and the ship was just . . . gone. All that remained was a burning stain of black fuel oil and a dark cloud spreading across the water, preceded by thousands of splashes, large and small. Ben whooped, then caught himself when he realized the carrier on the left had passed, unscathed, through towering columns of spray.

"Flashy Lead, this is Flashy Five," came Diebel's frustrated voice. "I, ahh, took a few hits," he said. "I fear they may have disturbed my concentration at a particular moment," he confessed dryly. "Seven dropped when I did. Not his fault."

"What's your status?"

"My windscreen is spalled, and there are holes in my right wing and aileron. I am losing fuel."

"Can you make Mahe?" Ben demanded, remembering another time Conrad had been forced to leave a fight. It couldn't set well with the proud Dutchman.

There was a moment of silence. Finally, "Yes, I think so. I am just switching from my belly tank now. If there are no holes in my other wing or fuselage, I should have no trouble."

Ben took a deep breath. "Roger that," he said. "How are you doing, Seven?"

"I think okaay. I heard some-teengs hit my ship, but don't see nuttin'. Intstaa-ments all aay-okaay."

Ben cringed. Some of the spare parts for his planes had been dispersed to *Tarakaan Island*, but most had been aboard *Baalkpan Bay*. Battle damage to his precious P-40s, already difficult to repair, might soon become impossible. "Very well," he said. "Both of you head for Mahe now. The Four ship and I will hit the same target before it has a chance to reload its canister mortars. Flashies Two and Three, good job. Now comes the traditional reward: you get to do it again. Hose 'em with your guns, and we'll follow you down. If we get the carrier on this run, we'll all try to at least shoot the other one up." Ben took another deep breath and shifted on his chute. "Let's go."

The four planes dove. The great ship below was turning ponderously, though probably as radically as it could. Soupy swept in, his wing-'Cat close alongside, and they both sprayed the ship with .50-caliber bullets that savaged planes and running Grik on her deck. Fire roiled suddenly, and black smoke gushed skyward as the Warhawks bored through, shocking the smoke into coiling tendrils with their propwash. It was Ben and Shirley's turn. Ben gazed through the sloped-lens head of his N-3 gun sight, trying to keep the lighted bead in the middle of the ring—and right on the big red "meatball" painted on the carrier's deck. Smoke darkened his view as he closed, but he never completely lost the target. Although a few white puffs distracted him slightly, there weren't very many this time, and the carrier was a sitting duck. With a profound sense of retribution for what had happened to *Baalkpan Bay*—and who knew how many of his friends still aboard her—he activated the bomb release and pulled back on his stick. Shirley would've done the same, probably less than a second later, and Ben clawed for altitude before banking left and looking back. Two bombs had hit the ship, maybe a hundred feet apart, hurling deck timbers and parts of aircraft far and wide. Fuel from ruptured planes met the existing flames, and an orange-black fireball rolled into the sky, consuming the abbreviated little conning tower/pilothouse as it spread. Two bombs had splashed alongside, close enough to look like torpedo hits, and the bursts of water pressure they'd sent against the carrier's hull had probably done almost as much damage as torpedoes. Steam billowed out from under the flight deck, and more rapid-fire explosions rocked the ship.

Ben looked to his right and felt a surge of relief. Shirley was with him, hanging tight, looking at him. He pointed up and made a circling motion, and they soon joined their squadron mates orbiting above. Ben glanced down. Another carrier certainly doomed. It hadn't gone up as catastrophically as the first, but it was clear the spreading flames were out of control. What's more, they'd probably killed everyone on its bridge, and it was circling now, slowing, but still too fast to lower any boats. Ben suddenly realized he hadn't *seen* any boats. Surely it had some, for its

Japanese crewmen at least? Maybe not. That would be consistent with Kurokawa's nutty philosophy, though *he'd* certainly escaped plenty of rough situations. Then it struck Ben Mallory that he'd never considered the possibility that Kurokawa might be on one of the ships they'd just destroyed. He still didn't. Somehow, he just knew. *If that Jap freak is on any of 'em,* he thought, suddenly looking for the third carrier, *it'll be the one that stayed apart from the others. One alone would be less tempting than a pair!* He finally saw the ship he sought, surprisingly far away already, steaming north at high speed. Away from the Seychelles. He also saw that most of the cruisers not still in the vicinity of the carriers they'd just attacked had gathered close around it, and they were a lot faster than those he'd seen before. He wondered if they had machine guns. They definitely had canister mortars, and clustered together, expecting attack . . . Then he caught a blur of motion and realized planes were flying off the carrier, rising to join others already orbiting above. He watched them for a moment, but when they didn't do anything other than circle their ship, he sighed.

As badly as he wanted that third carrier—wanted to at least slash through that flight of planes—he found himself considering the odds. He'd lost three of his available P-40s that day, maybe four or five, depending on how badly Flashies Five and Seven were damaged. That might leave him with only these *four* ships to face future surprises like the one that sneaked up on them today. And that, he knew then, was what his planes were really for. *Kurokawa—or whoever commands over there—flushed his planes knowing we're out of bombs, and shooting up his planes and starting fires on deck is the only way we might still seriously damage his ship,* Ben thought. *Add a likely much hotter antiair reception—and machine-gun-armed fighters that don't need a P-40's performance to swoop down and clobber us while we're on strafing runs . . .* He shook his head. It would be different if the Jap-Grik fighters came after them, or moved to make another strike against what remained of Task Force Alden. *We'd chew 'em up,* Ben thought savagely. *We still can't really hurt the carrier, though, and they . . .* know *both those things, dammit.* He toyed briefly with the notion of attacking the enemy planes, but there were already perhaps two dozen aloft, with more still joining the circle. *That's a tough formation to crack without somebody getting a shot at you—and they'll ram us if they can!* He abruptly understood that instinctively. He took one last look at the enemy, who seemed perfectly content to taunt him—and retire. *They can afford to.* Ben simmered. *We got two of their carriers and a lot of their planes, but* Baalkpan Bay *and all her planes—and people—were worth that trade alone. Add* Andamaan, *maybe* Geran-Eras, *and who knows what all else, and there's no getting around the fact that they kicked the absolute hell out of us today.*

"Flashy Flight, this is Flashy Lead," he spat. "C'mon, let's get the hell out of here. I want to check on TF Alden on the way to Mahe, though. We should have plenty of fuel."

"A pity they did not press their attack," Hisashi Kurokawa murmured, lowering his binoculars.

"They did us great damage," Captain Mikawa said hotly, thinking of all the *real* people, irreplaceable comrades, they'd lost. There'd been perhaps a dozen Japanese fliers and officers on *Kaga* and *Soryu*, including the latter's captain, whom Mikawa had admired a great deal. At least he'd probably died instantly when his ship disintegrated. *Kaga* was still burning fiercely, finally dead in the water.

If Kurokawa noted any rebuke in Mikawa's tone he didn't show it—which suddenly amazed Mikawa when he realized how he'd spoken. But his lord didn't explode, or even raise his voice. If anything, he appeared . . . satisfied. "You don't understand," he said at last, his voice rising, bordering on triumphant, as he indicated the surviving carrier. "*That* ship, with the largest number of our people aboard, is much more heavily armed than the others, with the new large-caliber, rapid-firing weapons emplaced. *Our* people man its planes in a strong defensive formation. My only regret about this day is that a fine opportunity to eradicate all of the enemy's modern aircraft may have been lost. On the other hand, we know we destroyed one of their carriers and a large number of other ships, possibly including their most dangerous ship of all, and the man who leads them. I would be wholly satisfied with the exchange based on that possibility alone," he confessed intently. Then he grasped his hands behind his back and straightened. "In addition, we can quickly replace our losses here. Two more carrier conversions are nearly complete, and with the resumption of raw materials from the mainland, the production of aircraft and Grik pilots has accelerated. We learned a great deal in this confrontation, and the price was not as high as I was willing to pay." He turned to stare at Mikawa.

"The enemy, on the other hand, is stretched to the breaking point. Despite their many alarming technical advances and the tenacity with which their ape-man lackeys fight, they are much, *much* farther from their base of supply, and we and the Grik have bled them white. Just as significant, we fight only one war. According to that outrageous Frenchman Gravois, the enemy has ridiculously allowed itself to be drawn into a second war in a distant land. We knew this already, but even I never imagined the extent to which that other conflict has diluted their potential combat power. We still have no direct contact with their other enemy, nor do I believe has First General Esshk. But Gravois's people, his 'League,' apparently has, and I hope to persuade him to introduce us." He scowled, his face clouding ominously. "I doubt he will, however. Any such direct association might make us too powerful to serve his aims," he mocked, but then quickly brightened. "Yet even without a coordinated strategy, we and the 'Dominion' do help each other a great deal. Once we make contact with them, which I intend to attempt, I expect that fact to weigh heavily in favor toward establishing a more cooperative approach"—he sniffed—"for as long as it remains in our interest to pursue it."

Mikawa nodded, but wondered why his lord confided in him. He was clearly pleased by the results of the day and perhaps just needed someone to express that pleasure to, to validate his impressions, his perception of the strategic situation. So far, Mikawa had to admit that Kurokawa's evaluation seemed plausible. Why did that surprise him? Like nearly every Japanese survivor of

Amagi, Mikawa accepted that his lord was mad. But the man was also amazingly successful at surviving. He and those he led had endured their banishment to this twisted, dangerous world, an unwholesome association with the savage Grik, and setback after setback at the hands of the Grand Alliance. Any one of those things might have destroyed them. Yet, in a way, they'd thrived. Zanzibar—secured for them by Kurokawa—was a true haven, and their productivity there, now that they were all assembled once more with a virtually unlimited labor supply, was nothing short of phenomenal. They still didn't have any women, and that was a source of a growing, frustrated near-madness for all their people, but Kurokawa assured them that, with victory, even that want would be met. Lost *Amagi*'s remaining crew still feared Kurokawa—Mikawa freely admitted *he* did, to himself—but they finally *believed* in him now. So, mad or not, General of the Sea Hisashi Kurokawa was also a genius of some sort, and his subjects would follow him to the death.

"So . . . what now, Lord?" Mikawa managed somewhat nervously, fearing Kurokawa might suddenly regret his openness or resent the presumption of a question.

"The fleet will steam north for the remainder of the day in case the enemy somehow manages to pursue us, or send a long-range aircraft to spy. After dark, we will shape a course to return to Zanzibar to rebuild our fleet. It is time for First General Esshk to do his part."

———

Ben Mallory's bad day wasn't over yet. It was easy enough to find the scene of the morning attack on TF Alden because of the dense columns of smoke marking the place.

"TF Alden, TF Alden, this is Flashy Lead," he called on the guard frequency, abruptly sure that "TF Alden" had been a stupid code name for the task force. They knew the enemy probably had spies, and were certainly listening to their voice transmissions. The mere name "TF Alden" would've told them all they needed to know about the composition and purpose of the force they'd attacked. He blinked. They'd been so complacent, expecting always to keep their tech edge over the Grik, that even as they knew things were changing, it was taking time to adjust. They had to think that through and recognize that even the little things, like stupidly descriptive task force names, couldn't slide anymore.

"TF Alden, this is Flashy Lead," he repeated glumly. "Flashy Flight is approaching you from a bearing of, ah, two, zero, zero, relative, two thousand feet, over. Pass the word that we're coming in. I imagine there are a lot of itchy trigger fingers down there."

"Roger, Flaashy Lead. This is *Saak-Fas*," came a tired-sounding Lemurian voice. "We are the northern picket. We see you and will repeat your warning."

"Thanks, *Saak-Fas*," Ben said, focusing on the sailing steam DD coming up below. Then, almost reluctantly, he lifted his gaze. For the first time the enormity of the disaster finally broke through his defensive shell when he grasped that the distant smoke had resolved itself into a terrible spread of scattered, burning hulks. Most had undamaged ships in attendance, either helping fight their fires with hoses or carefully taking off survivors. The latter was always a perilous task. It was instinctively ingrained in everyone on this world that the sea teemed with voracious creatures of all sizes, but just as the old saw, based on coincidence or not, that "land battles bring rain" was reemerging here, there was direct proof for the new axiom that "sea battles bring sea monsters." Fortunately, as the war raged on, lifesaving techniques and equipment had improved. Allied ships carried more boats and rafts than in the past, and ship-to-ship rescue drills were carried out in all weather. Ben thought the survival rate of the crews on all but the most shattered ships would likely be quite high, but many had been horribly mauled. Several of the oilers had erupted in flames so quickly and completely that he doubted anyone could've lived. A lot of boats had escaped *Andamaan*, probably saving most of the troops aboard, since their duty in the event of battle had been to assemble on the catwalks beneath the casemate adjacent to the boats. Not only did that keep them out from underfoot when *Andamaan*'s crew was fighting their ship, it gave them the best chance to survive, to fight their kind of battle. But *Andamaan* sank so quickly, most of her crew had probably perished.

The same might be said for *Baalkpan Bay*, Ben thought grimly as his flight finally approached and circled the heavily listing inferno. She still floated, burning from end to end, and no one could survive aboard her now. He noted with some relief that there was nobody left in the boats that eddied aimlessly around her corpse, and he hoped that meant most of her people had been saved. He also saw, however, that there were no other ships alongside, fighting her fires. *They've given up,* he realized sickly. *Of course they have. She's still got a lot of ordnance in her magazines. Just a matter of time before the fire reaches them, unless...* Even as he watched, four puffs of smoke swept aft, one by one, from the gray steel destroyer steaming slowly past *Baalkpan Bay*, about five hundred yards away. Splashes rose alongside her as the torpedoes fell into the sea. "My God," he mumbled, a huge lump rising in his throat, his heart going out to Cablass-Rag-Laan on *Geran-Eras*. He understood the necessity of what the Lemurian destroyer skipper had just done, but didn't know if he could've done it himself. Then his eyes narrowed, and he quickly scanned the area, almost frantic. "My God!" he said again, more forcefully. "That's not *Geran-Eras*!"

The new destroyer below was scarred by at least two bomb hits. It didn't look like the relatively light weapons had penetrated her decks, thank God, but they'd played hell above them. There was a jumble of debris just aft of her fourth funnel, and the fresh paint was scorched and blackened there and on her fo'c'sle. Damaged or not, she could still fight, and her guns were clear and manned despite the fact that her decks were otherwise literally packed with Lemurian troops and sailors. But what made him so sure she wasn't *Geran-Eras*, DD-23, was that she steamed easily, wasn't low by the stern, and wore the wrong number on her bows. *This* destroyer was DD-21: *James Ellis*. She must've sprinted back as soon as Ben reported that the enemy was retiring. But if she was here, all alone, that meant her sister must've gone down.

Just then, the first high waterspout jutted from the sea alongside *Baalkpan Bay*. Another followed, then another. Ultimately, all four torpedoes hit the stricken ship and exploded, the falling water snatching at the flames amid a boiling plume of steam. The great carrier, the first of her class and only the second carrier ever purpose-built on this world, rolled quickly on her side and began to settle. Flames roared anew from the hangar deck bays, but steam and rising water rapidly choked them out. The last Ben Mallory saw of *Baalkpan Bay*, proud veteran of Second Madras, was her death-stilled port-side screw and a hint of green from the copper sheathing that covered her wooden hull. Then she was gone. He blinked at the tears that suddenly hazed his vision. They came for *Baalkpan Bay*, of course, but also for *Geran-Eras*, *Andamaan*, and all the other ships and people they'd lost that day whose names he didn't even know. They came for the friends and planes he'd lost, all still technically under his command as chief of the Army and Naval Air Corps. *What a laugh!* he thought. *Jumbo has a better claim to that. I haven't been involved on an organizational level in a year!*

That's when it finally dawned on him how foolish and selfish he'd been. He'd wanted back in the fight and even dabbled in it from time to time, but hadn't really been *in* it up to his eyes, like Tikker, Mark Leedom, or even Orrin Reddy out in the east against the Doms, since the old PBY fell apart around him. He'd moaned and groaned about how "tied" he'd been to his "personal" squadron of "hangar queens." Now half of what remained of it was damaged or destroyed, possibly even including its support personnel—people like Cecil Dixon—who were probably more valuable than the planes! That's when the most bitter tears of all filled his eyes, tears for *himself*—for *his* loss and *his* bitter frustration at not being able to prove his squadron worthy of all the care, effort, and expectations lavished on it by somehow protecting TF Alden in spite of everything. Worse, it—*he*—hadn't even been able to finish the last enemy carrier and taste a full measure of revenge for . . . anything. It had been a terrible day indeed.

The last four airborne P-40Es of the 3rd (Army) Pursuit Squadron approached Mahe Island, largest of the Seychelles, at around 1500 hours. Mahe was a hilly, rocky thing, shaped like a crumpled trumpet, and wouldn't have been anyone's first choice for a place to put an airstrip if the Grik hadn't already cleared a diagonal crease through the center of the island for a zeppelin field. At last report, after just a few weeks of work and great effort, the field still wasn't ready for aircraft operations, but there was no place else to go. Ben's flight might still make Grik City on the north coast of Madagascar, but they'd be cutting it way too close for comfort. Still, he considered the option anew when they flew down over the ragged cut in the Mahe jungle.

"At least some of *Baalkpan Bay*'s air wing made it," Soupy called over the radio as they pulled up after their look. Ben was actually amazed to see so many of the lost carrier's planes. And a number of Nancys floated among the engineer's support ships anchored near a string of sunken, half-finished Grik dreadnaughts in the little harbor northeast of the strip. Those dreadnaughts—and others—had been placed at a couple of islands in the Seychelles as bait for a trap that very nearly worked. They'd been sunk to prevent their reclamation by the Grik before the decision was made to occupy Mahe.

"It looks like several cracked up, though," Ben warned. "There were some wrecks dragged off to the side. The strip looks clear but awful damn lumpy. Anybody see the Five and Seven ships?"

"I saw one of 'em," Shirley reported. "Close in the trees. The other's prob'ly under 'em."

"Flashy Lead, Flashy Lead, this is Flashy Five," came Conrad Diebel's voice, obviously speaking from his cockpit. "The engineers attached to the Austraal Marine regiment assigned here, as well as the pilots already down, have cleared the field as well as possible. They've been expecting you. Circle back around and land from the same direction that you approached. The wind is out of the west, southwest." He paused. "Bring them down one at a time and keep to the very center of the strip. It is smoothest there."

"Roger, Flashy Five," Ben replied. "Flashy Flight, I'll set down first. The rest of you, watch how it goes. If everything's okay, do exactly what I did. If not . . ." He gave his head a little shake. "Try to adjust accordingly." He curved around to the south, back over the hills. *They're almost mountains*, he thought, *covered with jungle to the*

very tops. It's actually kind of a pretty place, he unexpectedly reflected, *the way the water all around changes color
at random, and there are a lot of different greens in
the trees.* Colorful flying creatures swooped and swirled
among them. Coming back around, reducing his throttle
and beginning his descent, he saw the ships and Nancys
again. *Decent little harbor, with a good channel entrance,*
he observed. The variations in water color clearly defined
the shallows from above. With a sudden lift, he saw two
of the big Clippers squatting in the water near an APD.
Jumbo made it, he realized thankfully, *and so did the other
one, probably sucking fumes.* They were going to need
those big planes now more than ever.

Lining up on the gash in the jungle, he lowered his landing gear and flaps and unlatched his canopy. Wind buffeted
him, and the canopy clattered as his airspeed dropped.
The strip opened before him as he cleared the final trees
and saw that Conrad hadn't been kidding. The ground was
clear of rocks and debris, but was very wavy. The center
did look best, and he quickly chose what looked like the
longest stretch of level ground. He slid the canopy all the
way back and eased his plane down. The landing gear
rumbled and shuddered as he cut the throttle, and he
bounced and swayed for several moments until the tail-
wheel touched. It got even noisier then, and the level stretch
seemed to end abruptly. Suddenly the plane was pitching
and rolling like a ship in a storm. Very carefully, with gentle
taps, he started applying his brakes.

Gray dust he hadn't seen until then gushed up around
him when he finally came to a near stop. Looking around,
he saw the P-40 Soupy spotted from the air, separate from
an unkempt line of ten or eleven P-1Cs, partially covered
by low-hanging, sweeping branches. He kept looking but
saw only the one Warhawk. With a jolt of concern, he
turned his ship and gunned the engine. "Flashy Flight,
this is Flashy Lead. It's kind of rough at the end of the
strip, so set 'em down as soon as you clear the trees, and
watch your brakes." He listened until each pilot responded,
then bounced and rumbled over near the tree line. Quite
a few 'Cats were milling there, and he saw Conrad Diebel
step down from his plane. Pulling up close to the other

P-40, Ben spun his around and cut the engine. Even as he unstrapped his harness and the prop wound down, Diebel climbed up on the wing beside him.

"The Seven ship?" Ben demanded. Diebel looked down and ran fingers through his sweaty hair, then shook his head. "He didn't make it." His voice sounded . . . odd. Ben had heard the stoic Dutchman angry before, but never really sad. Maybe that's what this was. "How?" Ben asked, sick at heart, as he rose from the cockpit and stepped out, beginning to unfasten his parachute and watching the next plane land.

"He felt something hit his ship," Diebel reminded. "The antiair mortars. He must have caught one or more balls in his radiator." He looked at Ben. "His engine overheated and he attempted a water landing near the SPD *Tarakaan Island*. It went . . . poorly. Perhaps he was knocked unconscious on his gun sight, I don't know, but he didn't get out before the plane sank." He grimaced. "Which may be for the best, since the closest rescue boat was still some distance away at that time."

The Three ship came in, even as Two—Soupy's—veered off the strip and headed toward them, gusting a gray cloud away beneath its wings.

"That's just . . . swell," Ben ground out bitterly as they both hopped to the ground. Then he sighed. "How's your ship?"

"Fixable, I think. I would have no doubt, but we have no idea what we will have for spare parts or mechanics after today. The holes in the skin can be patched. There are patches already," he added wryly. "But patching the fuel tank is another matter I do not know enough about."

"We'll figure something out. Our ground crews should've gotten off *Baalkpan Bay*. I hope they did. . . ." His voice trailed off. Shirley's plane was touching down a little fast, it seemed. It wouldn't be a problem on a better strip, but she was coming up on the rough patch awfully quick. Her tail came down as she started to slow, then bounced as the Warhawk started pitching up and down in the wavy area. Suddenly, even as it looked like the plane was finally rolling to a standstill, the tail bounced high off the ground—and just kept going. With a clattering crash, like a broomstick thrust in a ceiling fan, the P-40 stood on its nose and slammed to a stop. Ben and Conrad were already running, angling around the other two ships taxiing toward the trees.

Shirley was climbing out of the plane when they reached it, quickly joined by a dozen Lemurian aviators who'd chased after them. "I so sorry, Col-nol Maal-lory!" she cried desperately, blood coursing down her face from a cut on her forehead. The N-3 gun sight had struck again. "I tried to brake easy, but when the tail come up, I slided forward on the brakes. I couldn't keep *off* 'em!" It made sense. The double-chute arrangement required to let the talented pilot fly the big planes had a tendency to settle, loosening her straps. Usually, she would've tightened them periodically during the flight, but after the day they'd had . . .

"You're okay?" Ben challenged.

"Yes," she assured him, dashing blood from her eyes. Ben stared skeptically at her, then gazed grimly at the damaged plane. The prop was ruined, and the chin and spinner were crushed. Hot, sweet-smelling Prestone was pooling under the ticking engine. The highly specialized coolant alone would be a grievous loss after today. They'd had a decent reserve, in drums, but how many of those had been lost? All of them? How would they make more? He doubted the stuff they were using in the liquid-cooled Nancys would cut it. He sighed and stepped forward, gently helping his friend down. "I soo sorry I broked the plane!" Shirley almost wailed then, tears mixing with the blood to stain the light-colored fur around her eyes.

"Not your fault," he told her softly, holding her close. "We should've come up with a better seating arrangement for our hottest pilot a long time ago." He looked around at the gathering faces. They didn't have a corps-'Cat to turn her over to, and Conrad ripped the sleeve off his flight suit to hold against her head. They didn't have anybody to turn their damaged planes over to either, Ben suddenly remembered. *Hell, we don't even have a can of gas!* That was when it returned to him that he wasn't just in charge of the 3rd (Army) Pursuit Squadron, but the whole damn Air Corps, Army, *and* Navy. It was time for him to start acting like it again.

"Who are the engineers here? Who's in charge?" he snapped, though it was easy to tell. The combat engineers wore the same helmets and tie-dyed combat frocks as the rest of the Austraal Marines garrisoning the island. Some of them raised their hands, blinking, and one with a single white bar painted on his helmet stepped forward. "You've got to have some water and chow around here, Lieutenant," Ben said. "Let's get these pilots fed and fixed up." He glanced at the sky. Dark clouds were beginning to gather for the afternoon squalls. "And under some kind of shelter. We'll improve that as we can. But starting tomorrow, we're *all* going to get to work on this damn airfield and make it fully operational as fast as possible. Grik City doesn't need us, and it's under constant air attack anyway. We're staying here." He stopped, considering. "All of what's left of Task Force Alden will likely be dribbling in over the next few days, as a matter of fact. You've got a wireless set? Current codes? Good. We'll stay off the voice radio from now on, or at least until we *are* operational, but I need you to contact *Tarakaan Island* and tell her we need everything they can give us: fuel, chow, bullets, more planes and pilots if Captain Reddy will okay it—the works. And we need whatever spares for these things"—he waved at the upended P-40—"that might be squirreled away aboard. The same for the other planes already here, at least." He frowned. "And find out the status of our ground crews. If they made it off *Baalkpan Bay*, whoever picked 'em up needs to get 'em here."

The Lemurian lieutenant blinked at him in surprise, his tail swishing back and forth. He glanced at the P-1C pilots. "We heard *Baalkpan Bay* was damaged, but—"

"She sank," Ben said brutally. "We saw her go down." He turned to the others. Virtually all the engineers and pilots had gathered by then. "And she wasn't the only one. Frankly, we got our asses kicked. And in addition to everything else, we now have Jap-Grik airplanes, aircraft carriers, and God knows what else out there. And no idea where they came from except—probably—northwest." He took a huge breath and let it out. "That's just a guess, but their base has to be somewhere between due west of here and west of India. Beyond that, I haven't got a clue. I do know this island, and the airstrip we're going to finish is a helluva lot more important now because it stands right between wherever they came from and Grik City. Right now we have"—he glanced at the line of P-1s—"eleven Fleashooters and five—*four*—modern planes left to fight with, but only if we get supplied. As things stand, out of fuel and ammunition, we couldn't chase off a duck!" He looked back at the lieutenant. "But we *will* get supplied, and we'll get more planes and people too. We'll finish this airstrip, and other ones on the islands west of here, and build facilities to handle Nancys." He pointed at the trees. "I want revetments with overhead protection and camouflage for fifty planes, to start, and concealed shelter for three hundred people."

The lieutenant stared around, eyes wide. "Y-yes, sur, but . . . how you know Maa-he an' those other islands gonna be so impor-taant? Get all that stuff?"

Ben smiled grimly. "Think about it. Right now we've got Grik City, *Salissa*, and *Arracca* to operate aircraft from. Zeppelins can't catch the carriers, but Jap-Grik airplanes can. We lose air superiority again, like we did today, and we'll lose the war," he said simply. "Mahe'll be our biggest effort, eventually the hub to supply the other islands closer to Grik City, the Africa coast, and probably wherever the Jap-Griks—and Kurokawa—are." His expression turned savage. "These islands are going to replace *Baalkpan Bay* with a *fleet* of airfields they can't sink."

"Do you think Captain Reddy will approve?" Conrad Diebel asked, his brows furrowed.

"That's exactly what he wanted to do, eventually. *Tarakaan Island* was going to be *stationed* here, remember? And after today?" Ben paused. "I expect Captain Reddy'll do his best to get us every single thing we ask for, as fast as he can."

West-Central Mada-gaas-gar
Dawn, October 12, 1944

"*H*uh," Silva grunted speculatively, gazing around the interior of the zeppelin gondola. In a somewhat bizarre contrast to the Grik sailing ships Silva had been on, the airship seemed very crudely made. More like the giant Japanese-designed ironclads, he reflected. Of course, the airship had been designed by Japanese as well. It was empty too, as they'd suspected. If anyone had been on watch they probably fled when the first zep burned. At a glance there wasn't very much by way of controls; a tall tiller protruded from a pivot on one of the frames supporting the double-thick wicker deck beneath his feet. Cables were attached down low, protected by light wooden boxes leading to blocks at the ends of the frames. From there, exposed cables ascended vertically or diagonally to pulleys in the top of the gondola and disappeared through the overhead. With little cries of alarm from the Lemurians, the gondola suddenly lurched, rising at an angle, until it lurched again and the stern of the airship began to rise. They were loose. "We are flying in the belly of the fish!" one 'Cat exulted, and the rest scrambled to look down. There was no glass in the windows, and Silva looked out over the rail as well, momentarily distracted by the view below.

Everything seemed washed in red: the sunlit smoke,

the burning camps, even the river and the coal smoke rushing skyward from the tugs. Grik were down below, still in their hundreds, some beginning to look up now. "Back!" Silva ordered belatedly. "Quit gawkin'! We're still in musket range. If they don't see us, they'll just think we're lizards goin' to chase the tugs—I hope."

"But . . . we go up, but how do we convince it to move?" the youngling asked.

"That's what we gotta figure out right off, Squirt. Say, what's your name anyway?" Silva countered, going to the back of the gondola. The engine mounted there seemed straightforward enough. There was a fuel valve, a hand crank, and a large knife switch on the wicker bulkhead. Small levers were probably the choke and throttle controls. Simple.

"Niri-Aani," the youngling replied.

"Well . . . Neery Annie, these controls . . ." He saw now there were four more sets arranged around the gondola, approximating the positions of the other engines mounted to the rigid envelope above. Near each station and alongside the tall tiller were speaking tubes that went . . . somewhere. "The controls tell it what to do," he continued. "You throw this switch, turn this valve, push these levers forward—and crank this handle." He spun the crank, and the little opposed cylinder engine behind the gondola *blap*ped to life with a noisy but satisfying ease. He adjusted the choke. "Now, you stand right here an' push this lever up if I tell you to go faster, down if I say to . . . slow down." He blinked. "Now that makes a scary buncha sense."

"What about these?" a 'Cat asked, indicating the four other control stations.

"Hell, I don't know. Don't see a way to crank the motors." He gestured at a light wooden ladder near the center of the gondola. "Maybe they got somethin' rigged up in the envelope, closer to the engine mounts. Why don't you . . ." He stopped. "*I'll* run up in a bit an' have a look. For now, let's just hope one engine'll get us clear an' we can worry about the rest later." The zeppelin had begun creeping forward as it rose, passing about two hundred feet, but it was headed toward the dense column of smoke. "Better keep us out o' that," Silva said, and returned to the tiller, shifting it experimentally. "We wanna turn to port. Let's see if this thing's as idiotproof as it seems." He leaned the tiller to the left.

The airship had tailfins, like the US Navy's *Macon* that Silva once saw before he joined up, but there was also a smaller rudder right behind the engine mounted on the back of the forward gondola. That made a lot of sense to him. It directed the thrust of the engine and turned the nose of the ship faster than tailfins alone. Ahead, and about 250 feet below them now, were the two tugs straining to pull their overloaded barges, one after the other. The river helped them gain speed, no doubt, while the wind was against the zep. Their friends were drawing away. For the first time he noticed that Petey had crawled up out of his T-shirt to stand high on his shoulder, peering out at the ground in apparent amazement. "Go ahead," Silva challenged. "Be the damnedest glide you ever had. But good luck survivin' down there, 'cause we ain't stoppin' to pick you up! No? Oh well. Don't say I didn't offer." He raised his voice so the others could hear. "Gotta have more speed." He snatched a 'Cat. "Hold this," he told him, placing him at the tiller. "Don't pull back or push forward, just ease it side to side to keep us pointed at our people. Savvy?"

The 'Cat jerked a nervous, wide-eyed nod, and Dennis raced up the ladder. Inside the envelope, he finally got a good look at the airship's construction. He'd poked around the debris of crashed specimens before, but had never had a chance to look at one like this. Very little light filtered through the painted fabric of the skin, but he could see a little. The framework was a kind of bamboo, related to the type so abundant on Borno that the Allies framed their aircraft with. The construction techniques weren't as sophisticated, and he didn't see any of the laminations that made Allied aircraft so stout, but there were quite a few stringers, and the diagonal bracing impressed him. The hydrogen bladders themselves were a patchwork of finely split skins that might've been stomachs, or even real bladders from some big land lizard for all he knew, but he'd studied their charred remains before. The skins—whatever they were—had been impregnated with some kind of rubberlike substance that sealed them amazingly well, even at the seams. One thing about Grik zeppelins: they didn't leak much gas unless you shot a bunch of holes in them. Again, he was struck by the combination of the slapdash and ingenious that characterized most Grik construction.

Carefully, he squirmed down the narrow catwalk toward where he hoped to gain access to one of the port-side motors. Sure enough, a transverse catwalk appeared ahead between the bladder he crouched beneath and the next. He turned left. Beyond an opening, supported by more light but sturdy struts outside the ship, was a motor. It was significantly brighter outside now, but the opening was so small he couldn't see much but the little engine. At least the daylight leaking inside provided better visibility, and he immediately noticed several things. First to catch his eye was a large, soldered-copper fuel tank big enough to hold maybe five hundred gallons. Some of the seams weeped a little, and the smell of a mixed fuel—mostly ethanol, he suspected—was strong. "Yikes," he muttered. "No wonder the damn things're so easy to burn down. It ain't just the hydrogen." Interestingly, a wooden lanyard handle dangled from a pulley overhead next to a speaking tube, and he followed the rope with his eyes. "I'll be damned. Motor's got a rope starter like a boat outboard, with a return spring like a Johnson Seahorse." He shouted into the speaking tube, "Hey! You guys hear me?"

After a moment's hesitation, a voice nervously replied. "Is that you . . . fish?"

Silva rolled his eye. "It's *me*, dammit. Just talkin' through a pipe. Look, flip all the switches an' turn all the valves, like I showed ya, an' hang on to that tiller. We're about to get up an' go."

After another moment, a tinny voice reported, "It is done."

"Okay. One o' you guys get up here pronto, an' see how I do this."

"Ah . . . where are you?"

"Straight up the ladder, forward—I mean, to the front." More quickly than he expected, based on the uneasy voice he'd heard, a tensely blinking 'Cat joined him, and Silva described what he was doing while he started the forward port-side motor, then the one to starboard. Each took a number of pulls on the lanyard before roaring to life.

"Runnin' like crap," he muttered. "I gotta go below and adjust the chokes an' throttles. There's two more aft. Start 'em just like I did these." He grinned. "You're chief engineer now, o' the very first zep in the 'Cat air corps! Stick close to the voice tubes an' holler if you need a hand."

"Chief Si-vaa!" came a cry through one of the tubes he'd just indicated.

"Silva here. What's up?"

"You come please? Quick?"

Silva slid down the ladder and dropped heavily on the wicker deck, then thumped Petey on the head and grumbled, "Shut up, you. An' now I'm a goddamn flyin' 'Cat wrangler too." At a glance, he saw they were considerably higher now, and moving faster. The wrecked Grik depot was safely behind them and the tugs steamed in column not far ahead, about six hundred feet below. He began to worry Chack might shoot at them, thinking they were Grik. He still had a Vickers. "Whatcha got?" he demanded while quickly adjusting the choke levers for the engines. They started running smoother but still rattled more than he thought was right. *Probably normal for them,* he thought. They *were* Grik motors, after all: crudely made almost by definition. *But they do run, and they must've made thousands of the damn things by now, considerin' how many we've shot down!*

Niri-Aani was practically hopping, pointing impatiently to the west. "Look! Look!" she said.

"Well, dammit," Silva said matter-of-factly. They'd beaten the day's run of reinforcements, but only barely. The rising sun had revealed another tug, barge, and zeppelin combo clawing their way upriver about three miles away. The zeppelin hovered just a couple hundred feet above the barge and was probably attached. They'd seen that before. But even as they watched, the zeppelin pitched upward and started to climb. Silva peered behind them and saw the tall column of smoke from the Grik depot slanting downwind. "The jig's up. They can't know we're not lizards, but they know somethin's up an' they'll come on careful." He had a sudden thought. Moving back to the speaking tubes, he called into each until he got an answer from the 'Cat he'd left above. "See if you can get down in the aft gondola and tell me what you find." A few moments later, the 'Cat's breathless voice came through yet another speaking tube. "There are six stacks of . . . smaller fishes, about a tail long. What are they?"

"Bombs," Dennis said. "Damn," he added in frustration. "If this one's loaded, I bet that one is too—and that's bad news for our friends below." He gauged the distance to the approaching enemy. "Steady as you go," he told the 'Cat at the tiller. "I mean . . . keep doin' what yer doin'. Maybe ease the stick forward just a bit, not too much. I need to get back there and see what's what. Two more o' you dopes, time to quit goofin' off an' gawkin' around. I know, yer flyin', an' it's a helluva thing, but we still got work to do! Come with me."

Dennis scrambled back up the ladder closely followed by two Shee-Ree. He still didn't know their names either but intended to get to know all his companions better if they made it through this. They hadn't had a clue what was going on from the start, throughout the fighting and now this, but despite his griping, they'd done well. He figured they were naturals for Chack's Raider Brigade. Reentering the envelope, he bounded aft under the bladder until he saw the expected ladder leading down to the aft gondola. Sliding down the rungs again, he found this one dimensionally identical to the first but much more cramped—with lethal devices. That only made sense, he supposed. The aft gondola was closer to the airship's center of gravity, the natural place to load the heaviest objects. Arrayed along either side was a pair of light swivels, breech-loading "jug" guns of a type they'd begun to see and with a roughly two-inch bore. He wasn't much interested in them. He needed to be forward, and there just wasn't time to teach these 'Cats how to use them, particularly when he still smarted from the accident that had killed a 'Cat on a much bigger but simpler weapon. There was also the fact that, with hydrogen overhead and a load of bombs in the center of the space, any accident would likely be fatal to them all. He regarded the bombs, betting they weighed about a hundred pounds apiece. They stood in six racks, three deep, pointed down. Directly below them, the deck was clearly intended to open like a trapdoor. *The bombs* do *look like fish,* he thought. Obviously cast iron, they weren't perfectly cylindrical. More like the zep itself, they were elliptical, with tapered ends. He didn't know what purpose that might serve other than to make them vane and fall erratically. But maybe that was the point? To make them spread out and impact a larger area? He didn't know, and it didn't matter just then. Each had fins on one end and a contact fuse on the other, "safed" by a pin that could be pulled out from the side with a little wire. He looked around and thankfully saw that everything else was fairly self-explanatory—to someone who knew what to look for. One lever obviously opened the trapdoor, and another on each rack would drop all three bombs in the stack. He quickly explained this to the two 'Cats that followed him, telling them to stand ready to "pull the pins, open the door, and shift the levers" in that order (he made them memorize the sequence and keep chanting it after he left), and listen for his command on the voice tube. With that, he took the "engineer" back forward but left him near the tube beside the first outboard engine they started. Then, breathing hard, he dropped back down into the control gondola.

"Crap!" he exclaimed. They were a little lower now, and close to passing directly over Chack's tugs. He had no doubt they were about to be fired on. "Gimme that!" he ordered, shoving the 'Cat aside and taking the tiller. Immediately, he wrenched it hard to the left. The airship pivoted when the rudder behind the gondola vectored the thrust of the engine just in front of it. "Stick yer stupid heads out now," he shouted. "Wave at our people, shake yer tails at 'em. *Piss* at 'em if you have to, but let 'em know we're the good guys, quick as you can!" Niri-Aani and the two other 'Cats started shouting and waving over the rails. Apparently, it had the desired effect, because no shots came, and Silva eased the tiller back to aim his zeppelin at the enemy once more.

The Grik airship was as high as they were, less than eight hundred yards away. The tug and barge were within two miles.

"What will we do?" Niri-Aani demanded.

"I'm calculatin' that now," Dennis replied.

"You shoot the big fish with your magic maas-kit?"

"Not sure where to aim that'd do any good. Never thought I'd need incendiaries for the ol' Doom Stomper. 'Bout all there is, though. Gotta get past it somehow, an' bomb that Grik tug. I don't know that our people can get past 'em by theirselves."

"*I* will shoot it!" Niri proclaimed derisively, hefting the big rifle again. "*I* will kill the flying fish!"

"You'll kill *yourself*, Squirt." Silva chuckled. "That booger thumps on both ends. Here . . ." He motioned to the 'Cat he'd taken the tiller from. "Get back over here. Hold it just like this. You know yer left from yer right? I guess not. Just hold it steady. I'll try to take a shot."

Hoping the 'Cat really could keep them steady, Dennis took his big rifle from Niri-Aani. "Hand me a round," he said, pointing at the huge cartridges in the bandolier the youngling still wore, slung across her body. "An' keep 'em comin' until I say stop." Obediently, the youngling pulled a cartridge from a loop. It looked even more enormous in her small hand. Silva took it and, after opening the breech, shoved it in the chamber. Snapping the breech shut, he rested the weapon on the forward rail and crouched behind it, considering. The approaching zep was pointed almost directly at them, but its crew still had no reason to expect they were hostile. It was clear something had happened to the depot, and they probably thought Silva's zep and the tugs below were attempting to escape whatever it was. That would change if they got a closer look at the tugs—which Dennis couldn't risk—and as soon as he shot at them, of course.

"Steady," he called, looking at the oncoming airship through his sights. He figured he could get several shots off, at least, before the enemy could react. Where to put them? A pair of one-inch holes near the tops of the bladders would release a lot of gas. How many of the five bladders would his big bullet penetrate, end on? All of them? At least three or four, he suspected. He also knew about where to aim to hit other things now as well, like the fuel tanks. But how to light them? He might not be able to. He shook his head. "I'm overthinkin' this," he grumbled. "All this responsibleness I been samplin' lately has dulled my edge." Adjusting his rear sight to the five-hundred-yard mark, he aimed near the top of the oncoming zeppelin and fired.

The gun rocked him back, and smoke coursed quickly through the open gondola. "Gimme another," he demanded of Niri, who seemed a little stunned. She blinked and yanked another fat cartridge from the bandolier and handed it over. Dennis opened the breech, ejecting the smoking shell, and slid the new one in. Taking aim again, he sent another big bullet on its way. He managed a total of six increasingly painful shots before the enemy zep began to turn to port, about two hundred yards away. "Ghaa!" Dennis said, shaking his arm and wiggling his fingers before reloading again.

"The fish flies lower," the 'Cat at the tiller observed excitedly. "It is dying!"

"Not yet," Silva said, imagining the effect of what he'd done. With luck, he'd opened the equivalent of a square-foot hole in each of the forward bladders, at least. The zep would go down, and probably fairly soon—but even as he watched, sand-filled ballast bags dropped from under the forward gondola, the nose came up, and the engines—now close enough to hear—roared louder. "They're tryin' to get above us," he realized aloud, "so they can blast us with their swivels! Pull back on the tiller a bit." The 'Cat complied, but they were going fast enough now that the nose came up more quickly than expected and the 'Cat lost his balance. With nothing else to grab, he hung on to the tiller, pulling it back to the stop.

"Whoa!" Silva roared, grabbing the rail while Niri tumbled toward the back of the gondola. "Level us off! You tryin' to loop us? Push that stick forward!"

Bracing his knees against the wicker deck, the 'Cat managed to comply, but it was too late. The big airship had practically stalled. Without the hydrogen that held them aloft, the elevators would only have increased the angle as they slid backward, straight into the river. As it was, the tail slowly began to rise, but for a moment they hung practically motionless, a sitting target for the pair of swivel guns the enemy could bring to bear. There'd be a double handful of half-inch balls in each, fired from less than a hundred and fifty yards. They'd instantly do as much or more damage than Dennis had managed, and probably hit some of "his" people as well. He shouldered the Doom Stomper and fired into the aft gondola, hoping to rattle the Grik gunners at least, and maybe get a hit on the bombs. It achieved the first objective, causing both gunners to fire wildly. They still hit the gondola, though, probably with the top of a pattern of shot, and a blizzard of balls and wicker fragments sprayed through the space. The 'Cat at the tiller cried out and fell, and Dennis felt a stinging pain in his side.

"Take that tiller!" Dennis roared at the other adult 'Cat. "An' bring my damn ammo back," he demanded of Niri. The youngling was on all fours, tail high and whipping back and forth, but she blinked big yellow eyes and scampered to his side. Dennis loaded again as quickly as she gave him a cartridge and aimed at the aft gondola again. Then he blinked when first one, then two more Grik just . . . jumped out. "Hey . . . ," he said, watching them fall. Only then did he realize they were trailing smoke from their feathery fur. "Hey!" he repeated louder, looking back at the zep. "Hard a'port!" he yelled. "Left! Left! *This* arm!" he roared in exasperation, flapping his own.

The dark interior of the aft gondola on the enemy zeppelin seemed to flicker with a pale, almost neon blue for several seconds. Then, with a rushing *whump!* the bladder above it exploded in fire, shattering the airship completely in half. The gondola fell free and plummeted toward the river below even as both ends of the wrecked zeppelin quickly burst into flames. Burning fragments wafted down, unnervingly close to Silva's zep, but they'd turned away just in time. A heavy detonation drew Dennis's eye down where the gondola—and all the bombs aboard—had exploded when it hit the water just a few hundred yards short of the first tug in Chack's little convoy.

"Ha!" Silva barked, incredulous, but shaking his massive weapon with glee. "Ha-ha! They lit up their *own* stupid-ass selves! Must'a swirled a bunch'a gas down in there when they pitched up so sudden, then the vent jets on their guns set it off! Ha!"

"You are hurt!" Niri insisted, raising his bloody T-shirt to look at a gouge along his ribs.

"Nah, I ain't hurt. Just scratched this time, an' that's a fact," Dennis said, glancing down at the graze. "My shoulder's a tad sore, though," he confessed ruefully, rubbing it. "Have a look at our buddy over there. Looks like he took one in the leg."

"What will we do now?" the 'Cat at the tiller asked while Niri examined their companion.

Dennis scratched his eye patch. "Well, first we're gonna climb a bit higher an' bomb the shit outa that Grik tug an' the barge behind it. If they ain't got anything more than muskets, we oughta be okay. We got six tries to hit 'em. Kaam said there ain't no flasher fish in the river this far from the coast, but there's other boogers. An' I never saw a Grik swim before. After that, I'll see what shape our 'flyin' fish' is in. If it ain't bad, we'll scout for our friends until they reach the sea, then hightail it to Grik City. If I don't think we can make it, why, we'll hitch a ride with Chackie. Either way, by air or sea, we're gettin' the hell outa here." Suddenly, he grinned. "Chackie lured me down on this little jaunt promisin' me a huntin' trip, an' I thought it was gonna be a bust, at first. Now I've sunk a super lizard with a torpedo, killed a puff lizard, an' shot down a zep— I mean a giant flyin' fish—with my Doom Stomper! An' I'm fixin' to sink another bunch'a Griks *from* a flyin' fish! Helluva time." To everyone's amazement, he began to sing with his dry, smoke-roughened voice.

*Oh! I come from ol' Grik City, an' had a helluva
   lot o' fun,
I killed two hundred Griks with my favorite
   Tommy gun!
But it don't make a dit o' bifference, to neither you
   or I,
Big Grik, little Grik, all run 'er die!
Oh! The Doms an' Griks are full o' tricks . . .*

He paused, shook his head in frustration, but began again as the airship rose, angling toward the enemy.

*Oh! I learned to fly, like a Air Corps guy, without
   the fancy suit . . .*

CHAPTER 32

USS **Walker**
Grik City Bay
October 12, 1944

"I t's bad, Skipper. Damn bad," Spanky said grimly, entering the wardroom with a sheaf of message forms in his hand. Matt had been staring out the starboard-side porthole at *Santa Catalina*'s dark form, silhouetted by the setting sun. The nightly air raid would likely begin in a couple of hours, but for now, all was peaceful. He and numerous others were gathered there, waiting for the latest. He turned and nodded at his Exec. He'd known it was going to be bad; reports had been coming in all day and it already was. Apparently, judging by Spanky's expression, things were about to get even worse. It was interesting, he thought. Everyone was gathered aboard *Walker* again, for a change. Admiral Keje was there, flown in from *Big Sal* by Captain Tikker, who sat uncomfortably on a chair beside him. Keje's red-brown eyes were blinking solemnly as he exchanged whispers with General Queen Protector Safir Maraan. Russ Chappelle had come over from *Santy Cat*, and Majors Risa-Sab-At and Alistair Jindal had just arrived. Leftenant Doocy Meek, effectively now the Republic's direct liaison to Matt, was sipping coffee with a frown, a sheaf of new maps lying on the table in front of him. Commander

Bernie Sandison, Lieutenant Tabby, and Surgeon Lieutenant Pam Cross had found places at the big wardroom table, and Chief Bosun's Mate Jeek stood behind them, saving the last chair for Spanky. Juan Marcos hovered expectantly near the curtain leading aft, a battered coffee urn in his hand. He suddenly thumped the curtain viciously when some listener lurking beyond it leaned too close. The muffled curse that resulted sounded suspiciously like it came from Earl Lanier. *After all we've been through, it's just like old times,* Matt reflected with a half smile at his crew's antics, for the benefit of the others, but he felt a sick feeling in his gut. It had been growing for days, as concern over *Amerika*'s "overdue" status seeped into his consciousness, and now the trickle that fed his apprehension had become a flood. *Walker*'s wardroom was crowded with old friends, though far too many were absent, and they'd gathered again as they had so often in the past to try to manage a terrible situation.

"What do you have?" Matt asked, holding out his hand as Spanky settled in the chair beside him. Spanky subtly held the papers back. "Why don't I just hit the high points, Skipper? The low points, I mean," he amended. "We can go over the rest of this briar patch"—he shook the forms—"after we adjourn." He nodded around the table. "Some of these guys need to get ashore or back to their ships."

Matt nodded. "Sure, Spanky. Good idea."

Spanky grimaced, flipping through the forms until he pulled one out and laid it on the stack. "In addition to *Geran-Eras* and that big-assed AVD *Andamaan*, *Baalkpan Bay* is gone," he stated flatly. Everyone already knew the carrier was doomed, but it hurt to hear Spanky confirm it. "*James Ellis* finished her with torpedoes," he added. "*Ellie* took a couple of bombs herself and had seven killed and twenty wounded, but Captain Brister says the damage was superficial. She'll be ready for action as soon as she can get her wounded and all the people she took aboard set ashore. She rescued *Geran-Eras*'s crew and picked up a couple hundred troops from *Andamaan*'s boats."

"Just how good are the new Jap torpedoes?" Bernie asked, probably talking out loud to himself.

"Good enough to sink *Geran-Eras* with one hit," Spanky

grumbled. "Of course, it opened her up near her keel right at the bulkhead between both engine rooms, so she lost just about everything all at once. We won't know more until we get a full report from her people." Spanky looked back at his list. "We lost nearly half the light auxiliaries: fast transports, oilers, ammunition ships—you name it. They weren't equipped for air defense at all and were sitting ducks. We're gonna be *damn* strapped for auxiliaries for a while." He looked up at Matt. "Losses in crews range from two or three, to, well, total, on one of the ammo haulers. Our worst losses were on *Andamaan*, which took nearly four hundred down with her, along with four of the big Clippers on board. And *Baalkpan Bay*, of course. Commodore Kek-Taal got almost all the troops off her, including General Alden, thank God, but early estimates are that close to a third of her crew was lost. Nearly everybody in engineering. Probably around another four hundred. Of course, her whole air wing is gone too, except a few Fourteenth Pursuit Fleashooters. They're on Mahe with Colonel Mallory, his five remaining P-Forties—two of which are damaged—and maybe a couple dozen Nancys off all the ships that carried 'em. Talk about a hash-up squadron! Jumbo Fisher's two remaining Clippers are there. Jumbo wanted to get back in the air immediately and go looking for that last carrier, at least see where it came from. Ben told him 'no go.' He'd be easy meat for those new Jap/Grik fighters, even if he found 'em." He nodded at Doocy Meek. "And after what Mr. Meek and Commander Leedom saw on their scout up the Zambezi, I took the liberty of telling Jumbo to patch his ships on the double, but stay put for now. We may want 'em down here."

"What about Commodore Kek-Taal?" Keje asked. He'd never much liked the Sularan, but they'd known each other a long time.

"Went down with his ship," Spanky answered solemnly. "They say smoke probably got him and everybody else on the bridge." He shook his head.

"On the bright side—if you can find one after the licking we took—General Alden just transferred to *Sular*, which is nearing Mahe in company with *Tarakan Island*. He and General Lord Rolak both report that First and Third

Corps are virtually intact and can be combat ready as soon as they get ashore somewhere and get everybody sorted out. That won't be near as easy to manage as it was to say, but we're damn fortunate in that respect. We lost too many planes and pilots, fuel and ordnance, but most of our heavy combat equipment and the new squadron of MTBs made it through okay aboard the heavies that got away. And *Tarakan Island* and some of the fast transports had a fair number of crated Nancys and Fleashooters aboard. Not near what we hoped to get, but some. As you know, Colonel Mallory has pulled out all the stops to get Mahe's airfield fully operational, and in addition to the mixed wing of surviving planes he's patched together, he wants some of the carrier's pilots and support personnel dropped off with him as well. Says we need to put airfields all over the Seychelles, and even the Comoros Isles, eventually."

Matt considered that. "Very well. Mahe's as good a place as any to muster the survivors and see what we have left. And as for the additional airfields . . ." Matt took a long, frustrated breath. "I would've liked to have done that already, if we'd had the planes and personnel."

Tikker blinked frustration. "But we didn't have 'em."

"No, but Mahe was a start—and it's a good thing we had it." He rubbed his face. "Let Ben have at least a few crated planes, and he can shanghai half the support personnel he asks for. But make sure he gets whatever we can spare in the way of heavy equipment and engineers to get the airfields up and running. He's our new northern picket, after all, and we need those strips for forward recon and dispersal as much as for protection. Have him set up a *supportable* patrol schedule for his Nancys and one of the Clippers, far enough out to do some good, but close enough that he can scramble some help if they run into trouble. We'll need most of the planes and pilots here, though. At least until we get more replacements through. *Salissa* and *Arracca*, not to mention Grik City, are down to the bare bones. And I want Fisher and his Clipper down here. We're going to have to keep a very close eye on the Zambezi." He looked at Doocy Meek. "Which brings us to you, in a roundabout way." He nodded at the maps in front of the Republic liaison.

"So it does," Meek replied, pushing one of the maps across the table and turning it around. "Most of Captain Galay's photographs were quite good, actually, but their size made the details difficult to see. Your Lemurian cartographers are bloody talented artists, though. I'd say they enlarged the photos very faithfully."

Matt stood and stared down at the map, while others leaned in to see them as well. "That's Sofesshk?" Matt asked.

"Aye. The 'palace' looks a great deal like that mucking great mound on shore here, doesn't it?" He gestured vaguely in the direction of the Cowflop. "You'll note the striking difference between the part of the city surrounding it and the rest across the river. You'll also note it's a bloody *big* city!"

Matt looked up at him. "And you didn't take any ground fire at all when you flew over it? None of those damn rockets?"

"None. Though I doubt that means they weren't there." Meek snorted. "They seemed quite surprised to see us." He pushed another map across, with the east end of a large lake dominating the thirty-six-by-forty-two-inch sheet. "It was a different story here, of course. I'm sure they saw us coming. Heard us, perhaps. Or, being predominately military Grik, they may've just been more observant." He pointed at several places. "Concentrated rocket batteries here, here, here, and here. The . . . 'plain'—I suppose that's the best word—here to the south was an immense marshaling yard for zeppelins, as you can see, but they weren't bunched together or secured to one another as they are when they make their attacks here, so they presented a rather poor target. My assumption is that they gather and bind them to one another much closer to here and perhaps only build and disperse them from Sofesshk or the lake. In any event, with our aircraft already damaged, Commander Leedom chose to bomb one of the large warships anchored offshore of those interesting sheds." He peered closer and pointed. "That's the very one, in point of fact. It was heavily damaged, at least. You can see from the drawing that the ships are just as large, but different from others we've encountered. I have larger drawings of them, rendered as well as possible, that seem to imply fewer but bigger guns, in addition to some other modifications that weren't clear enough to accurately render."

Matt was staring hard at the map. "No aircraft carriers, like hit TF Alden?"

"None," Meek confirmed. "Granted, we didn't fly the length of the lake, and they may have other ships anchored farther inland . . . but certainly, if they had such ships or the planes they carry, they would've pursued us, don't you think? Even surprised, they could've gotten those up in time to catch us." He frowned. "I haven't had the displeasure of encountering him before, but I'm well aware of your suspicions that the force that attacked TF Alden, though allied with the Grik, is under the control of that devil Kurokawa. I suspect as you do that only he could—or would—produce aircraft so similar to your own and they and the ships that launched them were probably under his direct, exclusive control. I honestly don't know what to say about that, or have any idea what we should try to do about it. He remains a threat, despite the pranging Colonel Mallory gave him in return, and you're far better qualified than I to devise a strategy to deal with him. My focus remains on the Grik my own people must fight through to join you at Sofesshk, if that city remains your primary objective."

Matt looked at Meek for a long moment before nodding. "It does. For now. Like we've been discussing, though, we have to see what we have left to do it with—and how much Kurokawa's going to screw with that. I've always said, now we have this place, we can't just keep waiting for the Grik to push us off. We have to keep after them. Figuring out how, with what we have, is the trick."

Meek nodded. "Then it's my conclusion that the Grik are gathering an armada, as we suspected, but it doesn't look"—he shrugged—"well, 'complete,' I suppose. Many of the ships were still fitting out and undergoing the modifications that you see. Most important, though, there were huge numbers of tents across the plain around the lake . . . *tents*, gentlemen," he stressed significantly, then nodded graciously at Pam, Safir, Risa, and Tabby. "And, ladies," he added, "the tents certainly imply a number of things, but most particularly they indicate the presence of a truly enormous army gathering to invade. If that's the case, however, where are their transports? As you can see, there appears to be very little capacity for *moving* their army."

"What's under these long, low structures?" Russ Chappelle asked. "Could you see at all?"

Meek frowned. "We tried, and Commander Leedom spared a pair of bombs for them, but we were forced to fly off before we could go 'round for another look. We might assume they're keeping some new type of warship covered there, something with a low freeboard perhaps, that they must keep out of the rain?"

"Could be barges," Spanky said. "Troop barges the big steamers might tow across."

Meek looked at him. "I hadn't thought of that. Very good. You may be right. Very vulnerable to attack, if so, and liable to render the warships towing them quite vulnerable as well." He shook his head. "I'm no Mr. Herring or Inquisitor Choon, but I still think, though they're clearly getting ready to have at us again, that we have some time yet. No doubt they can come whenever they please, but I don't . . . *feel* as though they're quite ready."

"Okay, say you're right," Matt said slowly. "That may leave us—and the Republic—with an opportunity. Those Grik troops came from somewhere, and I doubt it was right across the strait from us. Probably down south, across the frontier from the Republic, where they don't expect an attack." He raised an eyebrow at Meek. "Bekiaa reports that your Republic 'Legions' have good equipment and 'dress pretty,' but they're basically a bunch of amateurs playing at soldiers," he said gently, but with a bite. "She also says they're finally straightening out, though, after a bunch of bureaucratic grab-ass," he allowed.

"Skipper," Spanky interrupted, holding up one of his message forms. "That's actually some of the only good news we've had. The latest from Bekiaa still says the Republic army is 'screwy,' but she, Choon, and General Kim have kicked their first Legions into place at their jump-off point near Fort Taak on the east coast. She also confirms your theory some by saying their scouts are seeing very few Grik across the frontier—fewer than ever. So despite the 'akka chase' getting the Republic troops ready, the Grik apparently still don't expect an attack."

"Really? Well," Matt murmured, looking back at Meek, "then *if* that's so, and remains the case based on Bekiaa's continuing assessments, and *if* we can get First and Third Corps sorted out quickly enough"—he looked at Safir Maraan—"and if you can finish incorporating the Maroons into your Second Corps to bring it back up to strength, I think we need to start planning right now to hit *the Grik* in conjunction with an attack from the south. . . ." Matt's face turned hard as he absorbed the flickering eyelids, swishing tails, and sudden, stunned silence in the wardroom. "We just got our asses kicked, and it hurts bad," he admitted. "And it could be months before we get significantly more troops and materials down here. But that leaves plenty of time for the Grik to launch their big show, or for Kurokawa to lick *his* wounds and possibly hit the *next* task force too, if we just sit on our butts. So the way I see it, in spite of the last few days, we have a narrow window of time—maybe weeks, maybe a month or two—while we're still stronger relative to the enemy than we can ever count on being again."

He stopped and looked at his coffee cup on the green linoleum-topped table, the one that had CAPTAIN USS *WALKER* DD-163 stenciled around it. Over time, it had formed dark spiderwebs in the white glaze, and there were a number of rough chips at the rim that would cut his lips if he wasn't careful, but he still cherished the stupid thing. In a way, it had become a kind of symbol in his mind for the old, battered destroyer that had served them all so well, but more significantly for him, it represented a constant reminder of the obligation he'd accepted when he first assumed command. His responsibilities had since morphed and expanded far beyond anything he felt remotely qualified for, but he still accepted them as his duty. And that ugly, worn-out cup, so often filled with the bitterest of brews, always reminded him of where it all began.

"Robert E. Lee is considered one of my country's greatest generals," he began, startling some with the apparent departure from the subject. "Maybe he was, maybe he wasn't, but he was one of the first 'modern' generals, in many ways." He looked up. "He was also one of the last of the 'old' generals, at least in my country, in the sense that even though he fully understood the concept of 'total war,' he was always desperately looking for an opportunity to end his war the old-fashioned way, with one big, decisive battle." Matt shook his head. "He tried it a couple of times, marching his army into places where his enemy—other countrymen of mine," he added ironically for the benefit of those who didn't have a clue what he was talking about, "*had* to fight him decisively, or maybe, just maybe, give up." He shrugged. "In the end, a lot went wrong. We all know *that* happens. He wound up accepting battle where he probably didn't have to, and honestly, I think he was just so sick of it all and wanted it to end so badly, he got anxious." Matt took a deep breath. "Maybe I'm with him there. Maybe I'm making the same mistake." He looked at Safir Maraan. "One mistake I won't make is to try to command the army myself. That's for Pete Alden, Lord Rolak—and *you* to do. I don't have any of General Lee's good qualities as a land force commander"—he managed a smile—"and I think you've gotten over any of the bad ones you might've once shared with him. And regardless how it turned out for General Lee, his scheme *almost* worked." He looked around at them all. "So . . . I say we go for it."

There was alarmed but positive, almost eager blinking all around the table from humans and Lemurians.

"It is true we are wounded," Keje agreed in his gruff tone, "but it is the wounded gri-kakka that destroys the chase boat of its hunters. And whether the Grik at Sofesshk were in concert with Kurokaawa or not, the last thing they will expect is a full attack by us while they prepare for their invasion here. Such an attack, as has been pointed out, will catch them in disarray and poorly deployed to stop it."

"Which gives us all the more reason to keep a close eye on them," Matt continued. "Leedom's Clipper is almost repaired, and we'll soon have another. For now, first thing, we'll shift them to the Comoros Islands. That'll cut their flight time, and they'll be safer there anyway. The Grik don't bomb the islands. Then, if we can get *Big Sal* or *Arracca* close enough without stirring up a hornet's nest, we can hammer those sheds—and zeppelins—with firebombs from our shorter-range planes. It won't matter as much how spread out they are. Even if that lake is just the source for the zeps they send someplace else to attack us here, that'll cut their numbers. Our planes can do the rest, and get them the hell off our backs."

Major Jindal grimaced. "Isn't it possible that the continued reconnaissance and air attacks will make them change their plans? Expect an attack?"

"It is possible," Safir agreed, "but I must doubt it." She patted the map before them. "Just look at this again. Even after we have taken their Celestial City from them, their arrogance cannot allow them to contemplate that we might do the same at Sofesshk! They have deployed some few air defenses, but there are no ground defensive works visible at all, beyond a few coastal guns at the mouth of the river. No," she continued. "They will expect air attacks, now that we have found them, but I suspect it will only cause them to disperse their forces more widely until they are ready to move, likely making that move more lengthy and difficult."

"And making them more vulnerable to our ground attack—if it comes swiftly enough," Jindal said, nodding.

Matt smiled at Safir, impressed by her evaluation. Then he looked around the table. "Can anybody think of a better short-term plan while we work out the bigger one? At least as far as it comes to dealing with Grik that *don't* have aircraft carriers?"

There were several suggestions, mostly involving logistics, but no objections.

"Has there been any word from Colonel Chack, Mr. Bradford . . . and Chief Silva?" Pam Cross asked suddenly, looking hopefully at Spanky's message forms. She was doing her very best to hide her concern when she said Silva's name, but her eyes revealed her desperation for news. Safir allowed a quick blink of searing concern for her mate Chack as well, but quickly controlled her emotions.

"Ah, no, Lieutenant Cross. Still nothing. Sorry," Spanky replied uncomfortably. Nat Hardee had finally returned with the Seven boat the day before after a long, very creepy wait in the Mangoro River in case the explorers decided to return to the boat, but they never had. There was no escaping the conclusion that either they were dead or they'd actually found what they were looking for. After Hardee's account of the creatures—and people—they'd encountered along the river, few would've been willing to lay odds on the latter.

Spanky cleared his throat and turned his gaze to Matt, raising the final sheet in his hand. "That, uh . . . I guess there's just one more thing to add before we all get busy." There was nervous blinking around the table, inspired by his tone. It implied that, no matter how bad things seemed just then, there was more to come. "Skipper?" he said. "Captain Reddy, I'm damn sorry to tell you"—his gaze swept around the room—"to tell you all that SMS *Amerika* is no longer considered 'overdue.' There's . . . absolute proof that she was . . . sunk by that damn League battleship *Savoie*. There were survivors," he hastened to add. "About three hundred. Yeah," he ground out, "only about ten percent of those aboard, but they were able to confirm what happened." Quickly, guiltily, not looking at his captain, Spanky related the details concerning the loss of the old liner, as well as why it took so long to find the survivors *after* the ship was officially overdue. The search began tentatively at first, with transmissions flying back and forth, once it was determined that *Amerika* had never been seen by anyone in the busy Jaava Sea. That left the vast region between the Sunda Strait and Diego Garcia to search, and nothing was found in the vicinity of either. Finally, a scout plane off the fast oiler *Pecos*, just back from the West and headed for Diego, spotted floating debris southwest of the Sunda Strait. *Pecos* pursued the strong current from there, the debris leading her straight to a collection of lifeboats, lashed together. The survivors, mostly already wounded before they'd been cast adrift, had been in pretty bad shape after twelve days in open boats. Only when Spanky returned to the survivors' accounts of what they thought had happened to Matt's wife did he meet his captain's eyes again.

Matt was . . . numbed by horror, he supposed, and consumed by a rushing, roaring inferno of fury. After everything else, now this. He couldn't think clearly, could barely focus on Spanky's next words: "The boat with Adar, Captain Lange, Gunny Horn, and the rest, including . . . Lady

Sandra"—Spanky probably didn't even realize it was the first time he'd used that mode of address—"were all taken aboard *Savoie*. There was no doubt whatsoever about that, by anybody in any shape to see it," he quickly added. "And that little Jap, Miyata, confirmed it as well." He hesitated. "It's damn small consolation, sure, but at least *Savoie* didn't fire on the lifeboats. And whatever they wanted Adar . . . and the others for, they didn't hurt them either."

"Okay," Matt said, his voice deceptively mild, while his mind whirled. What could he do? He had to *do* something! He wanted desperately to chase *Savoie*. But what with, and where? Tabby couldn't do anything for the number three boiler, but she'd patched number two back together—barely—so *Walker* had two relatively reliable boilers again. But how far would they take her before one—or both—crapped out? And what could *Walker* do, alone, against *Savoie*? Particularly in the shape she was in. He looked around the wardroom. And of course these people, his friends—his *family*—deserved better from him than to simply run out on them after he'd just declared what they all had to do. That's when he finally realized with a sick, bitter certainty that there was almost nothing he *could* do for Sandra, Adar, or any of the others except finish the job. There'd be a terrible reckoning for *Savoie* and the entire "League" she served, Matt swore, but first he must at least ensure the chore at hand had the greatest likelihood of success. So how best to do that? First, whatever else they did, Matt, Sandra, and the entire Alliance needed *Walker* as fully operational as they could make her, period.

"*Tarakan Island*'s at Mahe, or soon will be," he said softly. "She's got the parts and dry dock we need, and I don't want her unloading her cargo here under Grik bombing attacks anyway. She'll offload there, and that's where we'll stage First and Third Corps." He looked at Spanky. "*Walker* will get underway at first light. Make all preparations. We steam for Mahe, and a *two-week* refit, no longer—if conditions permit even that. Without it, we won't have a chance in hell of dealing with the Grik, Kurokawa, *or* the goddamn League. Maybe in a few days we'll have a better idea what we have to do to sort this mess out."

*   *   *

USS *Walker* had taken on fuel and supplies from *Santy Cat* and was preparing to steam away from Grik City the following dawn. There weren't many fires ashore, after the nightly raid. There wasn't much left that would burn, and the Grik firebombs usually burned themselves out fairly quickly. Matt was seated in his chair on the bridge, sipping Juan's vile "coffee" with a tired frown on his face. He hadn't slept at all, imagining all sorts of scenarios—most having to do with his wife. He simply couldn't help focusing on that.

"Skipper!" came a cry from aft. "Skipper!" It was Ed Palmer's voice, accompanied by the rumble of his feet on the stairs behind him. He sounded . . . excited, sort of, not like he carried news he dreaded to deliver.

"Yes, Mr. Palmer?" Matt answered as Ed rushed to his side.

"Cap-i-taan!" called Minnie, the bridge talker, pointing at *Santa Catalina* beyond the port bridgewing. Her Morse lamp was flashing in the brightening dawn.

"Yes, sir." Ed nodded, holding up a scrap of rough Baalkpan paper. "That's what *this* says, I mean. . . ."

"Well, what is it?" Matt demanded irritably. Usually, Ed's boyishness was rather charming, but there were times when the communications officer could try Matt's patience, particularly after the night he'd had.

"There's a Grik zeppelin creeping over the wall of trees to the south, Skipper. The morning air patrol spotted it and called it in."

"So?" Matt asked. There were often damaged stragglers from the night's raids, wandering around in the vicinity of the city. Part of the morning patrol's duty was to make sure they wouldn't crash on or near any troop concentrations or defensive positions and then shoot them down.

"Sir . . . they called it in because *this* zep's goofy markings are blotched over and it has . . . 'DD-163' painted on its side!"

"What?" Matt jumped up and bolted for the starboard bridgewing, reaching for his binoculars. Sure enough, a battered-looking enemy dirigible had just cleared the high wall to the south just beyond the Celestial Palace and was headed directly for the old Grik airship field that now served as one of the Allied airstrips. And there, very crudely daubed on the thing, was his own ship's number.

"Secure all stations from getting underway," he snapped. "Stand by the whaleboat!"

"Ay, ay, Cap-i-taan!" answered the talker.

"Ah, sir, there's something else that came in at the same time."

Matt shook his head and snatched the paper away from Ed. He scanned the young man's scrawl for a moment, and his eyebrows rose in surprise while his lips compressed in rage at the same time.

"What should I reply?" Ed asked, almost plaintively.

"Tell them to go ahead," Matt said, his voice sharp but even. "Have Commander McFarlane accompany me in the whaleboat . . . along with Lieutenant Cross. And inform General Maraan to have plenty of security meet us at the airstrip."

"Aye, aye, Captain."

———————

The zeppelin had already—basically—crashed by the time they arrived at the airfield. It wasn't burning, but it had landed hard and the rigid envelope had collapsed down on the twin gondolas underneath. What gas remained—there couldn't have been much, judging by the way it barely cleared the wall of trees—must've immediately gushed out and the thing then rolled onto its side. A large number of Chack and Risa's Raiders had gathered around it, and some were clumped together near the forward gondola as Matt, Spanky, and Pam Cross, joined as they arrived by Safir Maraan, walked briskly out to join them.

"Hey! Hiya, doll!" roared a big man bursting from the crowd, still holding Risa-Sab-At close to his side with one arm. Blood was streaming down his face from a gash on his forehead, matting the bushy blond beard on his cheek. His clothes were . . . destroyed by all he'd been through, and he looked like hell, but it was unmistakably Dennis Silva. Pam hesitated just an instant before breaking into a run and launching herself at him.

"Whoa, now! I knocked my noodle around when we lit, an' I'm kinda woozy! Both of you're liable to tump me over an' smush somebody!" Risa stepped back, grinning hugely, and for a moment Pam Cross had her man all to herself.

"I *will* be goddamned," Spanky grunted. "I figured we were rid of him once and for all this time, and here he comes, floatin' back to life in a giant flyin' turd."

Dennis heard him and snapped to attention, not quite dropping Pam. He saluted. "Chief Gunner's Mate Silva, here ta' ree-port, Cap'n Reddy! Commander Spanky!" He grinned. Both men returned the salute, then Matt just spread his arms, encompassing the wrecked zeppelin. "I guess this'll be a good one. And I see you've brought some . . . friends along," he added, catching his first glimpse of Silva's "aircrew" as they emerged from the group gathered around them and approached. They were obviously Lemurians of some kind, but they were certainly different in a number of ways. Or was it just that they looked slightly less . . . cultivated? The Maroons looked different from Imperials even though they had the same origin, Matt reminded himself. He realized one of the new 'Cats was a female youngling, and she was dragging Silva's monstrous rifle by the barrel. "Are they the same ones Mr. Hardee reported?" he asked. "And where are the rest of our people? How are they?"

"Nat's back with the Seven boat? Good," Silva said with a nod of relief. "I been worried about that kid. No, these 'Shee-Ree' 'Cats are way different from the ones we met on the river. They're swell fellas." He raised his voice in warning so others could hear. "But even if they *look* a lot like regular 'Cats, an' they're rare fightin' fiends, don't leave nothin' layin' around they're liable to take a fancy to. They'll piss on it, sure."

Matt couldn't wait to hear what that was about. "And our people?" he pressed.

"Fine. Just fine . . . mostly. Can't speak for Corp'ral Miles. He ee-lected to stay behind an' help in the fightin' there." Silva glanced meaningfully at Spanky. "Honest," he added, then looked back at Matt. "Ever'body else'll be along d'rectly, steamin' up the coast with more o' the new friends we made." He gestured behind him and shrugged. "Long story," he said, then puffed out his chest. "And it *is* a good 'un. Hell, I guess I'm like some kinda damn *magnet* for gatherin' up folks that want to fight the lizards! But back to Chackie an' Mr. Bradford: you might wanna send a ship 'er two down to meet 'em. Their vessels ain't exactly what I'd call fit for blue water in a rough sea." He waved back at the wreck. "An' besides, like I said, there's been some fightin' and likely to be more. The Griks is shuttlin' troops across—real troops," he added significantly, "with their very own soljer suits an' decent muskets. Only they mean to creep up from the south by land this time." He grinned again. "We might'a put a little kink in that."

"Shuttling?" Matt asked.

"Yes, sir. Barges behind paddle steamers, across the strait."

"Mr. Meek and Mr. Leedom saw no large numbers of tugs up the Zambezi," Matt said to Spanky.

"No, sir."

"But those sheds might cover barges after all, like you suggested. Still, they *must* be bringing troops across from farther south, which further confirms why Bekiaa reports so few of them in front of Republic forces."

Silva scratched his head. "Sirs? What the hell's been goin' on? Risa tried to tell me, an' I caught a little gibberish about us getting' licked at sea, but we're fixin' to *attack* the mainland? An' Lady Sandra's been swiped again?"

For several minutes, as best they could, they all caught each other up. The Shee-ree stood and watched for a while but let their attention wander to the dispersed planes, and particularly to the well-armed, uniformed people gathered around who looked so much like them and seemed so friendly.

"So that's it," Matt finished simply, his face grim.

Silva appeared deep in thought, which was very unusual for him. No one bought that he was as big an idiot as he pretended to be anymore, but he rarely spent much time thinking before he spoke—or acted. "I'm with you, Skipper," he said at last. "After what we seen, I'd bet the lizards have big plans. I doubt they will—it was a pretty big operation—but even if they put the brakes on their stunt down south after word o' what we did seeps back, their main attack had to be timed to when them troops could'a marched this far north. That'll take a spell through them jungles an' across them rivers." His growing, gap-toothed grin widened. "'Specially with all the folks livin' down there stirred up against 'em! We send a few crates o' rifles down—even muskets . . . add a couple comp'nys o' raiders, an' we can really give 'em hell an' slow 'em right down to a crawl." He nodded. "Right now strikes me fairly well as the very best time to jump right down their throats while they *think* they're puttin' the sneak on us."

"There's more," Matt began, but cocked his ear to the sound of airplane engines.

Safir heard it as well. "Major Risa, please do reconstitute your security detail," she said formally, but then favored Silva with a radiant smile. "And Colonel Chack *is* truly well?" she asked.

"Fine as frog hair," Dennis assured. "We set down once, along shore, an' he scraped up the paint to put *Walker*'s number on the gasbag from one o' the tugs we swiped. Even took hold o' Petey for me. You'd think that stupid little tree-hoppin' toad'd be used to heights, but he don't much like 'em at all." He heard the plane now too, through his gun-damaged hearing, and they joined the others as they walked past the wrecked airship to stand beside the line of troops Risa had deployed. They could see it now: a low-wing trimotor, sweeping down around the Cowflop to approach the field. Its dingy camouflage scheme of brown and tan was badly weathered and the colors were beginning to blend together. The markings were still fairly clear, however, recognizable as something similar to the device on the huge submarine they sank, embraced by a pair of fasces.

"Who the hell's that?" Silva asked in a loud whisper.

"Our newest enemy," Matt ground out.

The plane landed in a cloud of dust and taxied close before the pilot cut the engines. Two of them coughed white smoke in an unhealthy manner. The big plane had apparently been in the weather and been denied proper maintenance for some time. Several minutes later, a hatch opened in the side of the fuselage and two men stepped out. One was impeccably dressed in tall boots and a round-topped hat, his blue uniform catching some of the dust as it settled. His expression was inscrutable behind the thin mustache he wore. The other man wore dark khakis and an overseas cap, and looked extremely uncomfortable. The first man seemed to be waiting for them to approach him, but when no one moved, he actually sighed and stepped forward. A few yards away from Matt, he and his companion stopped and saluted.

"I am Capitaine de Fregate Victor Gravois, emissary of the Benevolent League of Tripoli! This, my pilot, is Oberleutnant Walbert Fiedler. We were the only persons aboard the plane," he added when a squad of Risa's Raiders charged through the door of the aircraft behind him, carbines at the ready. "I do hope one among you might be Captain Matthew Reddy of the United States Navy?"

"A goddamn real *Heinie* Nazi is with the French one!" Spanky hissed sharply.

"I'm Reddy," Matt said, his tone neutral. He didn't salute, and the two men lowered their hands.

"It is a distinct honor to meet you, Captain Reddy," Gravois said earnestly. "I have heard so much about you, from your enemies . . . and your friends. Thank you for allowing us to land and communicate directly with you at long last." He paused, and his eyes flicked about. Something about the way they moved reminded Matt of a snake's tongue. "Based on your reputed achievements against your enemies, and a physical description by a particular friend, shall we say, I was given to expect a man of your general height and countenance, but"—he frowned at the scene around them, the crashed dirigible and ubiquitous evidence of the nightly bombardments—"not necessarily the . . . disaster area, few little planes, and the paltry, exhausted, 'fleet' of ships we saw from the air that you seem to command." He held up a hand in the face of Matt's mounting rage. "Please! Absolutely no offense was meant! Quite the contrary. That you have accomplished so much with so little is utterly remarkable. My compliments."

Matt's rage was undiminished, but it had nothing to do with what Gravois said about his command. "I don't give a *shit* about your compliments, you slippery bastard," he seethed. "What has your damned League done with the prisoners *Savoie* took after it sank a *hospital ship*?"

Gravois was slightly taken aback, but assumed what

looked like a genuinely pained expression. "That, my dear Captain Reddy, is exactly why I am here: to reassure you of the good intent and continuing, scrupulous neutrality of my government in regard to the ongoing . . . martial disputes affecting this corner of the globe we all inhabit."

"Neu-traal-ity!" Safir Maraan practically gasped.

Gravois looked down at her appraisingly. "Indeed," he said. "A neutrality that has been abused by various of the belligerents in this dreadful conflict"—he looked back at Matt—"but most recently and egregiously by one in particular. I therefore considered it my duty to bring you word—and warning—that *Savoie* not only most assuredly does *not* represent the League, but is—and was during the terrible incident you described—in the hands of a demented maniac I understand you know of, by the name of Hisashi Kurokawa! He seized her from her rightful, peaceful crew, and it was he who ordered the destruction of your hospital ship and imprisoned your wife and friends. They were quite safe when I fled to bring you this dreadful news," he quickly assured, "but I could not secure their release, even with promises of forgiveness for the theft of our ship—and the atrocity she participated in, in our name." He paused and gestured modestly at himself. "I can only hope that my helpless presence here, entirely at your mercy, will convince you of my sincerity."

"Bullshit!" Silva barked.

The pilot named Fiedler blanched and looked even more uncomfortable, even . . . ashamed? It was hard to tell. And Gravois merely continued speaking. "A large Marine named Arnold Horn told me to expect you to react with almost exactly that particular phrase, and that you would require proof. Very well." He went on to briefly describe all the prisoners and finished with the revelation, new to most present, that Sandra was pregnant.

"All that proves is that you saw them," Matt said. "It doesn't mean you aren't the very bastard who took them yourself. You say you're here to 'reassure' us. So do it. What's the League going to do to get *Savoie* back from Kurokawa?"

Gravois spread his hands. "Sadly, there is nothing we can do. We have nothing nearly as powerful in this sea with which to confront her. And, of course, it remains our desire to remain neutral in your dispute."

Spanky snorted, but Matt just nodded. "So you 'warn' us. What's in it for you?"

"Just your goodwill—and safe passage. We have done all we can to prevent your war from expanding completely out of control. We have failed, and sadly see no choice but to leave you with it. We will be removing all our people and assets from this 'Indian Ocean' at once."

"Safe passage? In that?" Matt asked, nodding at the trimotor.

"I think not," Gravois answered reluctantly. "Oberleutnant Fiedler assures me that it will not make the trip—and cannot carry enough fuel to fly us all the way home in any event. Obviously, we cannot expect to be refueled at Zanzibar."

"Zanzibar?" Matt demanded.

Gravois blinked. "Oh? Did I not tell you? That is where the madman Kurokawa makes his base—and holds your wife and friends hostage, Captain Reddy." He watched the reactions on the various faces but made no comment. "Consider the plane and the intelligence I just revealed a token gift, as some meager recompense for whatever the League may have inadvertently done to . . . inflame your, ah, situation."

Matt's mind was working, but he put his personal thoughts aside. "So how will you get out of here? We're damn sure not taking you anywhere."

Gravois waved that aside. "One of our ships, an Exploratori Class destroyer named *Leopardo*, will call on this port in several days. We would take passage aboard her, if you will allow it. If you do not," he continued less amenably, "I cannot guarantee that our two powers will be able to maintain the . . . amicable relations they now enjoy."

"Threats, now," Matt said calmly, but his face hardened into stone. "Okay, then here's the deal. I don't believe a single damn word you said about what happened to *Amerika* or how Kurokawa got *Savoie*, and I consider the League of Tripoli our enemy. I may allow you to leave aboard your ship"—he sent a glance at Fiedler—"or I may hang you both as pirates. I'll take it under advisement. But if *Leopardo* tries anything we consider offensive in nature, we'll blow her apart. Do you understand? Furthermore, after she leaves here—with or without you—I'll issue standing orders throughout our entire alliance, in this ocean, around the cape of Africa, and clear across the Pacific, that if any unit of our Allied Fleet so much as lays eyes on anything flying your dopey flag, they're to sink it on sight. Do you understand *that*?" He turned to Safir. "Arrest these men and get them out of my sight."

When the two men had been escorted away, Gravois acting indignant and Fiedler more resigned, Matt finally exhaled. He was so furious he had the shakes, and he grasped his hands in front of him.

"Shit, Skipper!—pardon my Grik, but . . . damn! Sandra's gonna have your kid? We gotta get her back!"

"I *know*," Matt seethed through his teeth.

"But Kurokawa's got a goddamn *battleship*!" Spanky snapped at him. "And carriers, planes, *torpedoes*, and God knows what all else—and we have an avalanche of Grik about to fall on us, if we don't jump on them first!"

"We must do *something*," Safir said hotly.

Dennis Silva looked back and forth between the faces around him; then, suddenly, he pinched Pam's cheek and grinned. "We will, Gen'ral," he told Safir and looked at Matt. "Don't worry, Skipper. We got 'em right where we want 'em! Gen'ral Pete, Ol' Rolak, an' Gen'ral Maraan here can grind up the land lizards here an' across the strait. I told you these new ones are more like real soljers, but that might make it *easier* in a way. Just me an' Chackie, Larry an' Mr. Bradford licked a bunch of 'em with nothin' but guys shootin' arrows against their muskets. You just worry about the Navy war, Skipper. What's a battleship but a big-ass target for you an' *Walker*, anyway?" Finally, he nodded at Risa standing a short distance away, listening. "She an' me an' Chackie'll take the Raider Brigade an' get our people the hell off Zanzibar. Then you can burn the whole damn island down to the sea." He scratched the dried blood in his beard, remembering what he knew about Simon Herring's "project," and considered the ramifications. "Prob'ly have to, come to that," he said enigmatically.

Matt looked at him, immediately suspicious. "Did you ever happen to talk to Miles about anything Commander Herring might've been working on before he died? Any goofy plans he had?"

Silva arched the brow over his good eye as if surprised by the question. "Me an' Miles never talked a lot, Skipper," he hedged. "Sure, we had words on occasion, but they was mostly about how I was gonna . . . well, help him get squared away, in a manner o' speakin'. If Herring ever did come up durin' one o' them little chin-waggin's, I don't recall a single thing about any plan," he stated innocently. Matt studied the big man a moment, not completely convinced, but finally nodded. With Silva, you often had to ask very specific questions to get straight answers, and even if he had any, Matt didn't want to have that conversation there, right then. "Okay," he continued. "So. I guess that's the big plan in a nutshell. Pretty much what we'd already roughed out, with one new little angle. I just hope we can get everything ready, and have the time we need to pull it off." He sent Spanky a bitter frown. "Do you remember what I said, just a couple of weeks ago, about there being blood in the water?"

"Yes, sir, I do."

Matt sighed. "I wish I'd known then how much of it was going to be ours."

EPILOGUE

Kotopaxi

Captain Blas-Ma-Ar stood at the sound of warning cries and stepped out from under the awning in front of her tent in the center of what had been the quaint mountain village of Kotopaxi. It was a bright, damp morning, and the camp that now included nearly a thousand Christian rebels and *ocelomeh*, "Jaguar Warrieos," in addition to the company of Vengadores and her entire 2nd Battalion of the Second Marines that had moved up to join them shortly after their arrival, was stirring in preparation for the day. Nothing but charred timbers and blackened stone walls remained of the town, but at least all the bodies had been gathered and buried. The Vengadores had insisted on burial for "their" people, as opposed to cremation, and it made no difference to Blas's Marines. They were used to the weird notions of humans by now, and a few of them had even requested that they be buried as well, when the time came. Any lingering stench of death had been washed away by heavy, crisp rains, and the cookfires serving a force that had grown to over twenty-five hundred troops and native warriors produced a benign, pleasant smoke that bespoke normalcy—and breakfast. Blas had been eating breakfast herself, joined by Teniente Pacal, first Sergeant Spook, and the two acknowledged leaders of their new "regiment" of auxiliaries: "Captain" Ximen and "Captain" Ixtli. They stepped out now as well, to join her as she watched the head of a column of Allied troops march into camp up the Chimborazo-Kotopaxi road. Two men, one woman, and a single grizzled Lemurian led the column, mounted on horses.

"There's Gener-aal Shinya! An' Sister Audry's got Col-nol Gaar-cia an' Sergent Koratin too!" Spook declared as Teniente Pacal moved past him to greet the newcomers. Captain Ximen hastily stroked his beard to tame it, then clutched his cross and hurried after Pacal.

"It's about time," Blas groused, staring down the line of troops. She recognized them as the rest of Audry's Vengadores by the small white crosses painted on their helmets. But nothing was behind the wagons and artillery that brought up the rear in the distance. Her tail swished behind her. "Let's go say hello, Captain Ixtli," she said to the younger local who'd remained with her and Spook. Together, they joined Pacal and Ximen and the growing crowd of uniformed men and 'Cats, backed by a large number of their new friends. The latter said nothing, nor did most of the 'Cat Marines, but Teniente Pacal's men called out to marching comrades. The leaders brought their horses to a standstill in front of Blas's group, and Shinya raised his hand.

"Vengadores! *Alto!*" Colonel Arano Garcia called behind him, echoed by junior officers and NCOs down the line, and the column ground to a stop. Blas, Pacal, and Spook all saluted, and Shinya, Garcia, and Koratin returned the gesture. Sister Audry, smiling happily, stepped down from her horse and embraced them all, much to Blas's discomfort. Then she beamed at Ximen and his followers—and all the crosses she saw.

"General Shinya," Blas said neutrally, wondering if he'd been ill again. He looked older than he had just a couple of weeks before. She nodded back the way he'd come. "I guess you an' Sister Audry's regiment outran the rest of the army."

Instead of answering, Shinya looked at Garcia. "Colonel, your men may fall out by companies and erect their tents." He looked questioningly at Blas.

"Teniente Pacal will show you where, Col-nol," Blas said. "We've already laid out plenty of space for you"—she looked back at Shinya—"and the *rest* of the army," she pressed again.

"Thank you, Capitan Blas," Garcia said, favoring her with a genuine smile. He dismounted and followed Pacal, leading his horse. Sister Audry blinked apologetically at Blas in the Lemurian way and stepped after Garcia, followed by a grumbling Koratin, Ximen—and a buzzing cloud of forest people. Blas expected Audry would address them as soon as her troops were quartered, and was actually anxious to discuss Ixtli's revelations with the human holy woman herself. But first things first. She looked back at Shinya as the former Japanese naval officer dismounted and stood before her, nearly alone at last.

"The rest of the army isn't coming here, *Major* Blas-Ma-Ar," he said simply.

Blas blinked, at the emphasis he'd placed on her apparent promotion, and with concerned confusion. "And why is that . . . Gener-aal?" she demanded, suspecting she wouldn't like the answer.

"Actually, because of the report you sent back when you arrived here, along with what little aerial reconnaissance we've managed," he replied. "As is obvious, Don Hernan has fled north through the forest in the direction of Popayan. As you also observed, we must attempt to prevent him from reaching there or he will have an open road back to the heart of the Dominion, not to mention uninhibited supply. We simply can't stop him by chasing after him, not in the jungle the emissaries you sent to me describe. The terrain is incredibly difficult, more like the interior of Borno than anywhere else we have been, complete with large numbers of similar . . . monsters, I understand. For those reasons and others it is wholly unsuited to launching any kind of decisive attack even if we caught him."

"Then . . . what will we do?"

"Right now, General Blair is racing to stop him by a more roundabout route," he explained. Blas noted absently that Blair had finally been promoted too. "He, Saan-Kakja, and the Governor-Empress are taking the army from Chimborazo to Quito, on the coast." He paused. "I will join them there. Together, we will strike east once more in hopes of reaching Popayan from that direction in time to block the enemy. It would seem impossible, given the distance involved," he confessed, holding her gaze with his, "but I am reliably assured that the relative ease of movement will more than make up for that."

Blas shook her head, even more confused. "So . . . what are we doing here? Why are *you* here with the Vengadores? Why didn't you just order us to march on down the Quito road to meet the main army days ago?"

Shinya took a deep breath. "I came here on my way to Quito specifically to talk to you. Regardless of the terrain, someone must still pursue Don Hernan. Make contact and maintain it, harass him, slow him however possible—even hurt him, if the opportunity arises. We have to convince him that we are doing exactly what he wants, following directly after him, and he has all the time he needs to reach Popayan. Is that clear?"

"Me," Blas said glumly. "This is what you want *me* to do."

Shinya nodded, his lips pursed. "In more ways than you imagine. Though Sister Audry will be in nominal command, everyone understands that she will not exert . . . tactical control. And despite your difference in rank, even after your well-earned promotion, Colonel Garcia will defer to your—and Sergeant Koratin's—judgment. His and Sister Audry's apparent supremacy is more"—he frowned—"political than anything else. The primary reason for that lies in the fact that you will likely receive more assistance from the Christian rebels than from the 'Jaguaristas.' Yet, even they should be satisfied to know that it is you who holds final authority."

"As for all that . . ." Blas shook her head, mind reeling. Apparently, Shinya already knew a great deal more about the two primary rebel factions than she did. She'd definitely have to sort that out. It wouldn't do for her to say something stupid that might put them at each other's throats.

"Please understand," Shinya continued earnestly, "despite any . . . displeasure you may harbor toward me, it is my regard for you as a soldier and a leader that compels me to entrust you with this assignment. Your race is a factor, of course, as it pertains to influencing the Jaguar Warriors," he confessed, "but Saan-Kakja and Admiral Lelaa-Tal-Cleraan are probably the only Lemurians in this theater who command greater respect, and even if they had your experience I'm sure you'll agree that they cannot be *allowed* to go."

Blas gestured around. "So . . . it's just what we've got here, plus the rest you an' Sister Audry brought in? That'll take us up to about thirty-five hundreds or so. You do realize Don Hernan's prob'ly still got fifty or sixty *thousands*, right?"

"Actually, I'm taking most of your dragoons with me. I'm informed that horses will not serve you well where you are going. But essentially, yes, if that's your current force. On the other hand, I've been assured that you'll also have large numbers of . . . additions along the way, as the local resistance moves to join you." He gestured at the long line of wagons where the tail end of his column had been. "And we brought five thousand muskets with which to arm them. They're Imperial muskets, not recovered Dom weapons. Better in every respect—particularly when it comes to ammunition supply—and the socket bayonets, I'm sure you'll agree. They suddenly became available when they were replaced by shipments of more modern weapons that were already en route before the Battle of Malpelo. Sergeant Koratin will be in charge of training your new recruits on the march." He smiled, and a predatory gleam appeared in his eyes. "When you do finally prod Don Hernan into contact with us at Popayan, the rest of the 'Army of the Sisters' will be almost entirely armed with Allin-Silva breechloaders at last, and I promise you we will greet him most warmly." In an uncharacteristic display of emotion, he suddenly drove his right fist into his left hand. "We *must* destroy Don Hernan and the evil Dominion he represents as soon as possible! Things . . . haven't gone as well as we may like in the West, of late. Sister Audry and Sergeant Koratin will give you more details regarding that, but suffice to say that Captain Reddy and the rest of our friends need us there rather badly, Major, and I mean to join them as soon as we possibly can!"

"I'll sure agree with you on that," Blas murmured, concerned about what might have happened, but her mind was already racing, planning. "When do you want us to start the chase?"

"Almost at once," Shinya replied apologetically. "The sooner the better. Don Hernan may already wonder why we have not yet pursued him beyond Kotopaxi."

Blas nodded. "Ay, ay, sir. I'll get with Sister Audry and Col-nol Garcia as soon as they're settled, and the local leaders as well. We'll get things sorted out and on the move."

Shinya started to leave her, recognizing the concentration blinking he'd seen so often that meant her mind was already somewhere else. "Oh!" he said. "I almost forget to tell you."

Blas focused back on his face. "Sir?"

"You'll be glad to know we finally received a wireless transmission from Lieutenant Fred Reynolds and Ensign Kari-Faask. They actually made it, it would seem, and after various adventures they managed to contact representatives of the people their Captain Anson was associated with. There are few details at present, but it's possible we'll soon have even more assistance in this war after all. Saan-Kakja has conferred full diplomatic status on Fred and Kari." His smile turned lopsided. "I certainly hope they don't 'blow it,' as certain of our American destroyermen friends often say."

"That's very good news, Gener-aal Shinya," Blas said with sincere, surprised relief. "Any word from Cap-i-taan Gaar-ett and *Donaghey*?"

Shinya shook his head. "Nothing yet." With that, he finally turned completely to climb back on his horse. "You may keep a squad of dragoons. You may need messengers. Please have the rest join me by the wagons in one hour. We will leave immediately after that." He sat very straight in his saddle. "Good luck, Major. I will see you in Popayan."

Baalkpan Advanced Training Center

"Good afternoon, Mr. Chairman," said Lieutenant Abel Cook as he, Stuart Brassey, and Major I'joorka raised their hands in salute.

Alan Letts hesitated and frowned when he stepped on the dock from the MTB that had carried him and a number of his staff out to the Baalkpan ATC. "That's going to take some getting used to," he said self-consciously, returning the salutes and glancing past the Khonashi and two young men at the regiment of human and Grik-like troops arrayed to receive him. "Good morning to you all," he added belatedly before introducing his companions. All but two were middle-aged Lemurians with various-colored pelts, dressed in styles roughly identifying them as delegates from Baalkpan, Maa-ni-la, and Sular. Commodore Sor-Lomaak, of *Woor-Na*, had been acclaimed the representative for the seagoing Homes. The humans were Henry Stokes, now director of the Office of Strategic Intelligence, and Lord Bolton Forester, ambassador from the Empire of the New Britain Isles. Stokes had been on HMAS *Perth*, arriving on this world with the prison ship *Mizuki Maru*. He'd been elevated to his current post upon the death of Simon Herring. Ambassador Forester had been scheduled to return to New London for some time but continually postponed his departure while his country's closest allies created a new union. Now, Alan reflected, faced with the current crisis, it was a good thing he'd stayed.

There remained a sense in Baalkpan that the war against the Doms was going poorly, despite recent victories. That was probably due largely to the fact that those victories had been so costly, and the Grik threat was understandably perceived as closer and more urgent. But along with the chaos surrounding the finalization of the framework for a new, mostly Lemurian nation came news of the disaster that had befallen TF Alden, rumors of vast Grik armies poised to throw the Allies off Mada-gaas-gar, and perhaps most devastating of all, the loss of *Amerika* and the confirmation that both Chairman Adar and the much-beloved "Lady" Sandra were prisoners of the hated "Kuro-kaa-waa." It had, in fact, been Bolton Forester who strongly advised that his nation's allies must immediately acclaim a new chairman to prevent the chaos from becoming catastrophic, as well as any perception by their enemies that the Alliance would be paralyzed by the loss of its leader.

Alan Letts presided over a whirlwind meeting of the new legislature—the very first official assembly—and a number of measures were proposed and adopted. The first was a name for their country. That had been delayed until Adar's return, out of respect, but now everyone recognized how important it was to have that seemingly inconsequential but highly symbolic issue settled at last. The name, "United Homes," had been accepted and acclaimed unanimously, though most continued to call it the "Union." A committee had been established to create a flag emblematic of all the members in some way. Resolutions of support for the armies in the field and fleets at sea were made, along with appropriations (mainly contributions from the various Homes, at this point) for the continued expansion of the armaments and shipbuilding industries in Baalkpan and Maa-ni-la, as well as assistance in creating or expanding those facilities in Austraal and Indiaa. That caused the first real grumbling, particularly when it was argued that some resources must continue to flow to the East and the war against the Doms. But the New Britain Isles didn't need money, material, or even troops anymore; they just needed more examples of the latest weapons, technology, and machines so they could build them for themselves. Ultimately, that was passed as well.

There remained only the final momentous decision of who would be the very first "official" chairman, essentially prime minister, of the new nation. It had been a given that Adar would take that post upon his return, but now he wasn't coming back. At least until they could rescue him. And, like Forester said, they couldn't leave it with him, even in name, as long as he was in captivity. Someone else had to do it. And so it was that Alan Letts, to his stunned amazement, was unanimously acclaimed chairman of the United Homes. He couldn't believe it. Not only was he clearly associated with Captain Reddy's "American Navy" Clan, he wasn't even a 'Cat, for Chrissakes! His clan apparently didn't matter then—or yet. Any chairman would always be a member of *some* clan, after all. And they were at war. Who better than a representative of the most intrinsically martial clan to lead them? Even the Sularaans voted for him, probably in a rare fit of practicality, considering the critical state of the war. Despite agreeing completely with Forester's reasoning, Alan desperately recommended that he just continue to "keep Adar's seat warm." His proposal was not accepted.

Well, he thought now, rather hopefully, looking at the delegation of officers he'd come to see, *they can always boot me out. Probably will.* He cleared his throat. "If you know I'm chairman, I guess you got the rest of the word. About TF Alden—and that roach nest on Zanzibar."

Cook, Brassey, and I'joorka all nodded. "Then it may not come as a surprise that you won't be going east after all." Cook didn't react, but I'joorka leaned forward. "That's right. In light of the current situation, the First North Borno will immediately be issued Allin-Silva rifles from the Baalkpan Arsenal and prepare to embark for the West. Once there, you'll report to Captain Reddy for operations against the Grik." He nodded at Cook and Brassey. "You've already been acting like it to this point, helping Major I'joorka, but I'm making it official. You're both breveted to the rank of Marine captain." He smiled slightly. "That'll keep you in the skipper's 'Navy' Clan, and make it easier to assign you to the First North Borno for the duration of its deployment, since King Scott has, not surprisingly, aligned his Home with the Navy." He closed his eyes and shook his head. "I'm sure this'll all be second nature to us someday, but right now it's still confusing as hell. And I helped write the damn 'Articles of Union' myself!"

"Lord Forester?" Brassey asked with an undertone of excitement. "Is this acceptable?"

Bolton nodded, rubbing his gray mustache. "Of course, dear boy. You have seen more action than most men twice your age. And any number of our people have been assigned to Union forces and hold Union rank." Brassey grinned happily, looking at his friend Abel. Both had been excited to return to the Empire, Cook in particular, due to his affection for the Governor-Empress. But this would certainly do as an alternative. Captains! At their age!

Letts looked at I'joorka. "Of course, these appointments are all subject to Major I'joorka's okay."

I'joorka was displaying what amounted to a Khonashi grin, despite the terrifying array of teeth it revealed. "Glad to ha' they," he said. "Glad to ha' the Allin-Sil'as too." He gestured back at the ranks of troops behind him. "Us are . . . delighted to ser' King Scott, Ca'tain Reddy, and our country against our greatest ene'ies. Do you know how Ca'tain Reddy is going to use us?"

Alan shrugged. "I might as well tell you. For security reasons, none of your troops will be allowed in Baalkpan before you sail anyway, and that could be a few days. We're having hell scaring up enough transports. You'll need the time, in any event, to familiarize yourselves with your new weapons when they arrive." He raised his chin. "My guess is that the First North Borno will join the First Raider Brigade when it hits Zanzibar, while the rest of the army goes for Sofesshk. You'll root out that bed of Jap-Grik snakes once and for all."

I'joorka seemed immensely pleased. "Good. Us got a lot to . . . show," he admitted. "To show all the country that not all Grik-like . . ." He searched for a word for "people" that he could say and gave up, waving. "Us are *not* Grik. This is our chance." He paused. "There is one other thing I'd ask o' you though, 'ister Chair'an."

"Oh?"

I'joorka glanced at Cook and Brassey, then swung his gaze back to the chairman of the United Homes. "Us go to Zanzi'ar and land on shore against real Jaaphs . . . I'd like to ha' the 'tanks' you showed us."

Alan actually grinned, then cocked his head to one side, recalling that I'joorka and his people had fought Japanese before. "Okay," he said. "I'll see what I can do."

SPECIFICATIONS

American-Lemurian Ships and Equipment

USS *Walker* (DD-163)—Wickes (Little) Class four-stack, or flush-deck, destroyer. Twin screw, steam turbines, 1,200 tons, 314' x 30'. Top speed (as designed): 35 knots. 112 officers and enlisted (current) including Lemurians (L). Armament: (Main)—3 x 4"-50 + 1 x 4"-50 dual purpose. (Secondary)—4 x 25 mm Type-96 AA, 4 x .50-cal MG, 2 x .30-cal MG. 40–60 Mk-6 (or "equivalent") depth charges for 2 stern racks and 2 Y guns (with adapters). 2 x 21" triple-tube torpedo mounts. Impulse-activated catapult for PB-1B Nancy seaplane.

USS *Mahan* (DD-102)—(Under repair at Madras.) Wickes Class four-stack, or flush-deck, destroyer. Twin screw, steam turbines, 960 tons, 264' x 30' (as rebuilt). Top speed estimated at 25 knots. Rebuild has resulted in shortening, and removal of 2 funnels and 2 boilers. Otherwise, her armament and upgrades are the same as those of USS *Walker*.

USS *James Ellis*—*Walker* Class four-stack, or flush-deck, destroyer. Twin screw, steam turbines, 1,300 tons, 314' x 30'. Top speed (in trials): 37 knots. 115 officers and enlisted. Armament: (Main)—4 x 4"-50 dual purpose. 4 x .50-cal MG, 6 x .30-cal MG. 40–60 Mk-6 (or "equivalent") depth charges for 2 stern racks and 2 Y guns (with adapters). 2 x 21" quadruple-tube torpedo mounts. Impulse-activated catapult for PB-1B Nancy seaplane.

USS *Andamaan*—Protected troopship converted from Grik BB—800' x 100', 18,000 tons. Twin screw, triple-expansion Baalkpan Navy Yard steam engine, max speed

16 knots. Crew: 400. 100 stacked motor dories mounted on sliding davits. Armament: 4 x 4"-50 dual purpose.

USS *Tarakaan Island* (SPD—Self-Propelled Dry Dock)—Twin screw, triple-expansion steam, 15,990 tons, 800' x 100'. Armament: 3 x 4"-50 dual purpose, 6 x .30-cal MGs.

USS *Santa Catalina* (CA-P-1)—"Protected Cruiser." Formerly general cargo. 8,000 tons, 420' x 53', triple-expansion steam, oil-fired, 10 knots (as reconstructed). Retains significant cargo/troop capacity, and has a seaplane catapult with recovery booms aft. 240 officers and enlisted. Armament: 4 x 5.5" mounted in armored casemate. 2 x 4.7" DP in armored tubs. 1 x 10" breech-loading rifle (20' length) mounted on spring-assisted pneumatic recoil pivot.

Carriers

USNRS (US Navy Reserve Ship) *Salissa*, "Big Sal" (CV-1)—Aircraft carrier/tender, converted from seagoing Lemurian Home. Single screw, triple-expansion steam, 13,000 tons, 1,009' x 200'. Armament: 2 x 5.5", 2 x 4.7" DP, 4 x twin mount 25-mm AA, 20 x 50 pdrs (as reduced), 50 aircraft.

USNRS *Arracca* (CV-3)—Aircraft carrier/tender converted from seagoing Lemurian Home. Single screw, triple-expansion steam, 14,670 tons, 1,009' x 210'. Armament: 2 x 4.7" DP, 50 x 50 pdrs. 50 aircraft.

USS *Maaka-Kakja* (CV-4)—(Purpose-built aircraft carrier/tender.) Specifications are similar to *Arracca*, but it is capable of carrying upward of 80 aircraft—with some stowed in crates.

USS *Baalkpan Bay* (CV-5)—(Purpose-built aircraft carrier/tender.) First of a new class of smaller (850' x 150', 9,000 tons), faster (up to 15 knots), lightly armed (4 x Baalkpan Arsenal 4"-50 DP guns—2 amidships, 1 each forward and aft) fleet carriers that can carry as many aircraft as *Maaka-Kakja*.

Frigates (DDs)

USS *Donaghey* (DD-2)—Square rig sail only, 1,200 tons, 168′ x 33′, 200 officers and enlisted. Sole survivor of first new construction. Armament: 24 x 18 pdrs, Y gun and depth charges.

Dowden Class—(Square rig steamer, 1,500 tons, 12–15 knots, 185′ x 34′, 20 x 32 pdrs, Y gun and depth charges, 218 officers and enlisted.)

**Haakar-Faask* Class—(Square rig steamer, 15 knots, 1,600 tons, 200′ x 36′, 20 x 32 pdrs, Y gun and depth charges, 226 officers and enlisted.)

***Scott* Class—(Square rig steamer, 17 knots, 1,800 tons, 210′ x 40′, 20 x 50 pdrs, Y gun and depth charges, 260 officers and enlisted.)

Corvettes (DEs)—Captured Grik "Indiamen," primarily of the earlier (lighter) design. "Razeed" to the gun deck, these are swift, agile, dedicated sailors with three masts and a square rig. 120–160′ x 30–36′, about 900 tons (tonnage varies depending largely on armament, which also varies from 10 to 24 guns that range in weight and bore diameter from 12 to 18 pdrs). Y gun and depth charges.

Auxiliaries—Still largely composed of purpose-altered Grik "Indiamen," small and large, and used as transports, oilers, tenders, and general cargo. A growing number of steam auxiliaries have joined the fleet, with dimensions and appearance similar to Dowden and *Haakar-Faask* Class DDs, but with lighter armament. Some fast Clipper-shaped vessels are employed as long-range oilers. Fore-and-aft-rigged feluccas remain in service as fast transports and scouts. *Respite Island* Class SPDs (self-propelled dry dock) are designed along similar lines to the new purpose-built carriers—inspired by the massive seagoing Lemurian Homes. They are intended as rapid deployment, as heavy-lift dry docks, and for bulky transport.

USNRS *Salaama-Na* Home—(Unaltered—other than by emplacement of 50 x 50 pdrs.) 1,014′ x 150′, 8,600 tons. 3 tripod masts support semirigid "junklike" sails or "wings." Top speed about 6 knots, but capable of short sprints up to 10 knots using 100 long sweeps. In addition to living space in the hull, there are three tall pagoda-like structures within the tripods that cumulatively accommodate up to 6,000 people.

***Woor-Na* Home**—Lightly armed (ten 32 pdrs) heavy transport, specifications as above.

Aircraft

P-40-E Warhawk—Allison V1710, V12, 1,150 hp. Max speed 360 mph, ceiling 29,000 ft. Crew: 1. Armament: 6 x .50-cal Browning MGs, and up to 1,000-lb. bomb.

PB-1B "Nancy"—"W/G" type, in-line 4 cyl 150 hp. Max speed 110 mph, max weight 1,900 lbs. Crew: 2. Armament: 400-lb. bombs.

PB-2 "Buzzard"—3 x "W/G" type, in-line 4 cyl 150 hp. Max speed 80 mph, max weight 3,000 lbs. Crew: 2, and up to 6 passengers. Armament: 600-lb. bombs.

PB-5 "Clipper"—4 x "W/G" type, in-line 4 cyl 150 hp. Max speed 90 mph, max weight 4,800 lbs. Crew: 3, and up to 8 passengers. Armament: 1,500-lb. bombs.

PB-5B—As above, but powered by 4 x MB 5 cyl, 254 hp radials. Max speed 125 mph, max weight 6,200 lbs. Crew: 3, and up to 10 passengers. Armament: 2,000-lb. bombs.

PB-5D "Clipper"—4 x 10 cyl, 410 hp radials. Max speed 145 mph, max weight 7,800 lbs. Crew: 5–6, and up to 8 passengers. Armament: 5 x .30-cal, 2,500-lb. bombs/torpedoes.

P-1 Mosquito Hawk or "Fleashooter"—MB 5 cyl 254 hp radial. Max speed 220 mph, max weight 1,220 lbs. Crew: 1. Armament: 2 x .45-cal Blitzerbug machine guns in wheel pants.

P-1B—As above, but fitted for carrier ops.

P-1C—10 cyl, 410 hp radial. Max speed 265 mph, max weight 1,740 lbs. Crew: 1. Armament: 2 x .30-cal Browning MGs in wings.

Field Artillery

6 pdr on stock trail carriage—effective to about 1,500 yds, or 300 yds with canister.

12 pdr on stock-trail carriage—effective to about 1,800 yds, or 300 yds with canister.

3″ mortar—effective to about 800 yds.

4″ mortar—effective to about 1,500 yds.

Primary Small Arms—Allin-Silva breech-loading rifle conversion (.50-80 cal), Allin-Silva breech-loading smoothbore conversion (20 gauge), 1911 Colt and copies (.45 ACP), Blitzerbug SMG (.45 ACP).

Secondary Small Arms—Rifled musket (.50), 1903 Springfield (.30-06), 1898 Krag-Jorgensen (.30 US), 1918 BAR (.30-06), Thompson SMG (.45 ACP). A small number of other firearms are available.

MGs—1919 water-cooled Browning and copies (.30-06). 41 lbs without mount, 400–600 rpm, 1,500 yds.

Imperial Ships and Equipment

These fall in a number of categories, and though few share enough specifics to be described as classes, they can be grouped by basic size and capability. Most do share the fundamental similarity of being powered by steam-driven paddle wheels and a complete suit of sails, though all new construction is being equipped with a double expansion engine and screw propeller.

Ships of the Line—About 180′–200′ x 52′–58′, 1,900–2,200 tons—50–80 x 30, 20 pdrs, 10 pdrs, 8 pdrs. (8 pdrs are more commonly used as field guns by the Empire.) Speed, about 8–10 knots, 400–475 officers and enlisted.

Frigates—About 160'–180' x 38'–44', 1,200–1,400 tons. 24–40 x 20–30 pdrs. Speed, about 13–15 knots, 275–350 officers and enlisted. Example: HIMS *Achilles* 160' x 38', 1,300 tons, 26 x 20 pdrs. New construction follows the design of the *Scott* Class DD.

Field Artillery—The Empire of the New Britain Isles has adopted the Allied 12 pdr, but still retains numerous 8 pdrs on split-trail carriages—effective to about 1,500 yds, or 600 yds with grapeshot.

Primary Small Arms—Sword, rifled musket (.50 cal), bayonet, pistol. (Imperial service pistols are of two varieties: cheaply made but robust Field and Sea Service weapons in .62 cal, and privately purchased officers' pistols that may be any caliber from about .40 to the service standard. The Empire is issuing more and more domestically manufactured weapons comparable to those of its allies to its troops.)

Republic Ships and Equipment

SMS *Amerika*—German ocean liner converted to a commerce raider in WWI. 669' x 74', 22,000 tons. Twin screw, 18 knots, 215 officers and enlisted, with space for 2,500 passengers or troops. Armament: 2 x 10.5 cm (4.1') SK L/40, 6 x MG08 8 x 57-mm (Maxim) MGs.

Coastal and Harbor Defense Vessels

Princeps Class "Monitors"—235' x 50', 2,150 tons. Single screw, 11 knots, 190 officers and enlisted. Armament: 4 x 210-mm guns in two turrets, 8 x MG08 8 x 57-mm (Maxim) MGs on flying bridge and deckhouse. 110 officers and crew.

Field Artillery—75-mm quick-firing breechloader loosely based on the "French 75." Range: 3,000 yds with black powder propellant and contact fuse exploding shell.

Primary Small Arms: Sword, revolver, breech-loading bolt action, single-shot rifle 11.15 x 60R (.43 Mauser) cal.

Secondary Small Arms: M-1898 Mauser (8 x 57 mm), Mauser and Luger pistols, mostly in 7.65 cal.

Enemy Warships and Equipment

Grik

ArataAmagi **Class BBs (ironclad battleships)**—800′ x 100′, 26,000 tons. Twin screw, double-expansion steam, max speed 10 knots. Crew: 1,300. Armament: 32 x 100 pdrs, 30 x 3″ AA mortars.

Akagi **Class CVs (Aircraft Carriers)**—800′ x 100′, 12,000 tons. Twin screw, double-expansion steam, max speed 14 knots. Crew: 1,100. Armament: 10 x 3″ AA mortars, 10 x Type 89 MG (copies) 7.7 x 58 mm SR cal.* 40–60 aircraft.

Azuma **Class CAs (ironclad cruisers)**—300′ x 37′, about 3,800 tons. Twin screw, double-expansion steam, sail auxiliary, max speed 12 knots. Crew: 320 Armament: 20 x 40 or 14 x 100 pdrs. 4 x firebomb catapults.

Heavy "Indiaman" Class—multipurpose transport/warships. Three masts, square rig, sail only. 180′ x 38′, about 1,100 tons (tonnage varies depending largely on armament, which also varies from 0 to 40 guns of various weights and bore diameters). The somewhat crude standard for Grik artillery is 2, 4, 9, 16, 40, 60, and now up to 100 pdrs, although the largest "Indiaman" guns are 40s. These ships have been seen to achieve about 14 knots in favorable winds. Light "Indiamen" (about 900 tons) are apparently no longer made.

Tatsuta—Kurokawa's double-ended paddle/steam yacht. It is also the pattern for all Grik tugs and light transports.

Aircraft—Hydrogen-filled rigid dirigibles or zeppelins. 300′ x 48′, 5 x 2 cyl 80-hp engines, max speed 60 mph. Useful lift 3,600 lbs. Crew: 16. Armament: 6 x 2 pdr swivel guns, bombs.

    AJ1M1c ("M" for "Muriname") Fighter—9 cyl 380-hp radial. Max speed 260 mph, max weight 1,980 lbs. Crew: 1. Armament: 2 x Type 89 MG (copies) 7.7 x 58 mm SR cal.*

DP1M1 Torpedo Bomber—2 x 9 cyl 380-hp radials. Max speed 180 mph, max weight 3,600 lbs. Crew: 3. Armament: 1 x Type 89 MG (copy) 7.7 x 58 mm SR cal.* I torpedo or 1,000-lb. bombs.

> *Note: No MG of any type is available to any Grik other than those under the command of Hisashi Kurokawa on his ships, or the island of Zanzibar.

Field Artillery—The standard Grik field piece is a 9 pdr, but 4s and 16s are also used, with effective ranges of 1,200, 800, and 1,600 yds, respectively. Powder is satisfactory, but windage is often excessive, resulting in poor accuracy. Grik "field" firebomb throwers fling 10- and 25-lb. bombs, depending on the size, for a range of 200 and 325 yds, respectively.

Primary Small Arms—Teeth, claws, swords, spears, Japanese-style matchlock (*tanegashima*) muskets (roughly .80 cal).

League of Tripoli

Savoie—548' x 88', 26,000 tons. 4 screws, 20 knots. 1,050 officers and enlisted. Armament: 8 x 340 mm, 14 x 138.6 mm, 8 x 75 mm.

Leopardo—*Leone* (Exploratori) Class destroyer. 372' x 34', 2,600 tons. Twin screw, 30 knots. Armament: 8 x 120 mm, 6 x 20 mm, 4 x 21" torpedo tubes. 210 officers and enlisted.

Holy Dominion

Like Imperial vessels, Dominion warships fall in a number of categories that are difficult to describe as classes, but, again, can be grouped by size and capability. Despite their generally more primitive design, Dom warships run larger and are more heavily armed than their Imperial counterparts.

Ships of the Line—About 200' x 60', 3,400–3,800 tons. 64–98 x 24 pdrs, 16 pdrs, 9 pdrs. Speed, about 7–10 knots, 470–525 officers and enlisted.

Heavy Frigates (Cruisers)—About 170' x 50', 1,400–1,600 tons. 34–50 x 24 pdrs, 9 pdrs. Speed, about 14 knots, 290–370 officers and enlisted.

Aircraft—The Doms have no aircraft yet, but employ "dragons," or "Grikbirds," for aerial attack.

Field Artillery—9 pdrs on split-trail carriages—effective to about 1,500 yds, or 600 yds with grapeshot.

Primary Small Arms—Sword, pike, plug bayonet, flintlock (patilla-style) musket (.69 cal). Only officers and cavalry use pistols, which are often quite ornate and of various calibers.

THE
DESTROYERMEN
SERIES

by Taylor Anderson

The crew of the WWII destroyer USS *Walker* is mysteriously transported to an alternate version of Earth, where their technology and knowledge could shape the face of an interspecies war.

Find more books by Taylor Anderson
by visiting prh.com/nextread

"Gripping and riveting."
—S. M. Stirling, *New York Times* bestselling author

"Pick up the Destroyermen series and kick back and enjoy."—**SFRevu**